# THE SEER

## BOOK 3

## THE SECRET TALES

## SANNA BRAND

**Afterworld Publishing**

 Formatted with Vellum

# CONTENTS

# EPIGRAPH

"I will not follow where the path may lead, but I will go where there
is no path, and I will leave a trail."
—Muriel Strode

# DEDICATION

*To Aria Jones*
*My superb editor, whose acumen, patience, and rigor consistently elevate*
*my novels. Aria is the GOAT!*

CHAPTER

# ONE

**1**819

Claire Cassandra Pheland wished to discard her skin, her nerves were *that* prickly.

Rain beat against the windows on this gloomy March day. What was she doing here, about to present a paper to London's Society of Antiquaries? She must be mad or foxed. Sadly, she was neither, as she surveyed the audience of Fellows and attendees from her seat—all male.

She had wrangled her presentation with the help of the Marquess of Ravenscroft, her brother-in-law, along with aid from Viscount Hawthorne, another brother-in-law. She sat between them in the audience, their expressions stolid.

No fool, Claire had made her request to the society using the initials CC Pheland, avoiding any hint of gender.

As she listened to a clever paper on Roman coins, sweat greased her palms beneath her gloves. Her foot jiggled, too, an altogether inappropriate activity. Yet Claire could not seem to stop.

As a small child, she had worried about anything and everything and would plunge into a disturbed state of anxiety. As time passed, she realized her flusters upset her sister and Mama, so she had learned to conceal them, hiding her upsets behind a mask of serenity. As years passed, her worry subsided to no more than an itch.

Now her anxiety reappeared in full force.

A trustee called her name. *God help her.* As she rose, then moved stiffly between legs and chair backs to reach the aisle, she pictured her pup Cullen begging for a treat. He was just outside being tended to by a footman. That imagining—for sweet Cullen was her protector—enabled her to push her fear down to a manageable level.

Murmurs began, then voices rose, while several men pointed fingers as Claire approached the dais.

Eyes forward, spine stiff, Claire endured. Naturally, a woman's presence was a surprise. She tried to encase herself in iron, but as she reached the podium, she almost tripped on her cursed skirt. Women's clothes were so very inconvenient.

The murmurs rose, as did her vexation at their disrespect. Nonetheless, she laid her notes on the podium, staring at her written words as if they might leap off the page and attack. To her right, a worker carried a small veiled bust onto the dais and set it on the table beside the podium. With a deep breath, Claire raised her head and perused the crowd. She reminded herself to project her voice and smiled.

"My paper will illuminate and substantiate my hypothesis about the ancient Greek statues, busts, and other marbles we so admire. A hypothesis also noted by the esteemed artist and antiquarian, Jean-Baptiste de Saint-Non."

The room quieted momentarily, much like the sea receding from the shore in preparation for a tumultuous wave. Discordant ripples arose from the audience.

She raised her large monocle, a gift from her sister Charlotte. Unlike Lottie, who was outgoing and effusive, Claire was perceived as shy, a fine disguise for her introspective nature, Claire having little interest in the chatter of others. Chatter just like this, voiced by thick-headed, uninformed men.

The crowd's whispers rose, and a council member hushed the audience. Claire proceeded. "From my examination of numerous statues, stelai, and plinths during my time in Greece, along with my studies in England, I have come to the conclusion that the Greeks, rather than being admirers of austere white sculptures, favored bright colors and painted patterns, which adorned the majority of their figurative works. I would even go so far as—"

Exclamations and murmurs bounced off the walls, and Claire didn't know whether it was due to her hypothesis or her gender. Perhaps both. It mattered little, as the commotion drowned out her words.

"Let her speak," hollered a man in the audience.

"What is this woman talking about?" yelled another. "I cannot hear her."

"She is deranged!"

Claire tightened her grip on the podium and spoke, digging deep for patience. She would *continue*, and damn them all.


Lord Theseus Ashworth was disgusted with the behavior of his esteemed colleagues. No matter that a woman expounded at the podium, members of the Society had read her paper and deemed it worthy of discussion.

He could barely hear her above the chatter and mutters. Unconscionable.

No dialogue was to be found here, all due to her gender, which was absurd. Though he admitted Lady Claire's premise was implausible. He recalled Quatremère de Quincy's work that had made such a stir, claiming the marbles were brightly colored. Most antiquarians concluded Quatremère's polychrome concept actually addressed the "natural" coloration brought about by the Greeks' use of the many varied materials used, rather than paints. Not Theseus' area of interest, so he had paid it little mind.

Ravenscroft and Hawthorne, both acquaintances, and his good friend, the Duke of Devonshire, all appeared as furious as he. But there sat the offensive Lord Elgin, arms crossed, wearing a smile, and lobbing jeers with the rest of them.

He was acquainted with the beautiful Claire Pheland, daughter of famed artist Reginald Pheland, Baron Halafair. He didn't particularly like her, for her tongue was sharp. Nonetheless, she was Devonshire's friend, thus she must have some redeemable qualities. That was neither here nor there. The Fellows' behavior was inexcusable.

Theseus rose, and given his height, bulk, and respect as an antiquarian, the audience took notice. "Hush, you cretins! Let the woman speak!"

His booming baritone succeeded in silencing the room...for a moment. Yet after he retook his seat, the mumbles, laughter, and raucous commentary soon recommenced.

Ravenscroft ascended the dais and whispered in Lady Claire's ear. She nodded, then faced the crowd.

Theseus leaned forward to hear her words.

"Gentlemen, my work stands on its own! If you are too blind to see it, then I am too mute to speak. You should be ashamed of your unwillingness to listen to a perspective that differs from your own. Ashamed!" Her ladyship gave the audience a viperous stare.

*Devil it*, the woman was impressive.

With that, she hefted the small bust to her chest, fisted her notes, and stepped from the dais.

With her free hand, Claire took Rhys' arm, and he led her to a side door.

"It could have been worse," he said.

Claire didn't see how, but she nodded in what she hoped was a sage response as they stepped outside.

"How can you say that?" Patrick said, awaiting them outside in his wheeled chair, his handsome face wearing a grim expression. A footman handed off Cullen's lead for him to hold, and he wheeled alongside them down the wide alley, her pup beside him.

Rhys gave him teeth. "Not with ease, which should be obvious."

Dim gray light pooled onto the alley, shaded by the building and overhanging trees, as they walked toward the street.

Striding toward them was a brawny man wearing a black tailcoat and waistcoat, buff pantaloons, and Hessians.

Now what?

As he moved closer, she recognized Lord Ashworth, the man who had been kind enough to silence the crowd, if only momentarily. A taciturn fellow she knew from several family events as well.

When he stood before them, he tipped his hat to the two men and offered Claire a bow. "Again, I apologize for the Fellows' poor behavior."

Another kindness, one she would not forget. "Thank you, but it was no worse than I expected, and…"

"But you hoped?" Ashworth said.

"I did." She smiled with chagrin.

"Might I carry the bust for you?" Ashworth didn't look at either Patrick or Rhys, but it was obvious he wondered why she was still clutching the heavy bust.

"Thank you, my lord, but no," Claire said. "Aspasia was a gift from my father and has been a friend for many years. Silly, I know, but I must carry her myself."

"Lady Claire clings to the thing as if it were gold," Patrick said, wheeling beside them as they walked.

"Aspasia means much to you," Ashworth said. "That is obvious."

"She does indeed."

"Might I see her up close?" Ashworth said.

"Oh! Why, of course." Claire lifted the veil covering the bust as Ashworth removed a monocle from his pocket.

He bent close and examined Aspasia with his famed antiquarian eye. "She is quite lovely. A fine reproduction."

Claire tilted her head. "You caught that."

"You did not assume she was Greek?" Ashworth said.

Claire shook her head. "My father bought her in Greece, and I have had her since I was small. Aspasia has always been a part of my life. But..." She thrust the marble into Ashworth's hands and lifted her own monocle. "Note the smile lines beside Aspasia's eyes, the arrangement of hair, and the facial features. Though they are finely rendered, they signify a Roman reproduction."

Claire straightened to stare into Ashworth's bright green eyes, then retrieved her sculpture, tucking it again beneath her arm.

"You are correct," Lord Ashworth said, surprised. "Whether Roman or Greek, she is a beautiful piece. I would suggest from the Imperial era."

"I agree about the era. Aspasia remains my treasure." Claire gazed at the bust, seeing instead her father and his warm, smiling face.

Rhys lightly squeezed her arm. "I am afraid we must depart, Ashworth. Thank you again for your consideration of Lady Claire."

Claire would have liked to speak further with Ashworth and to request entry to study the famed marbles at his estate. But the men bowed, she curtsied, and they were off.


The second week in April, a month after Lady Claire's fiasco at the Society of Antiquaries, Theseus received a note from the woman herself tucked within a missive from Devonshire, a clever way to avoid society's censure. He peered out his study window at the dismal rain, wishing winter's last sigh would abate. On the day of her ladyship's debacle, he'd observed an appalling demonstration of men's prejudice. Fools. Their meeting afterward had been pleasant enough. Though she seemed simultaneously curt and shy, given her courage at the podium, he found her admirable.

Lady Claire's brief note thanked him again, then she requested to study his father's extensive collection of Greek sculptures.

*Damnation.* While he favored her desire to view the works, Lady Claire would want time, more time than he could afford, given his nearing departure for the Greek Isles.

Theseus intended to repatriate his father's collection to Greece.

Appropriated with the blessing of the cursed Turks, they belonged in their homeland, not arrayed in some English manor. His idea was perceived as eccentric and fraught with dissenters. The Crown wished him to keep them, as did the British Museum and that cursed Lord Elgin, the mawworm who took the Parthenon sculptures from their homeland.

Though an outlier for his point of view, the antiquarian community esteemed him for his own antiquarian work, and none could deny his credibility. His own small collection of antiquities came as gifts from his Greek friends and other ethical sources.

He cared not one whit for the dissenters. His father's marbles should reside in Greece.

Throngs wished to examine the sculptures, and he had accepted many of those requests, often from members of the Society. But as the pressures of time, distance, and weather grew short, he could offer them little access to the statuary. And still the pleas poured in.

The blasted Ottomans, occupiers of Greece, gleefully tossed away Greece's heritage, his father's haul merely one of many dispersed throughout the world. The concept infuriated Theseus. Not the discoveries themselves, of course, but the draining of Greece's birthright. Few shared his viewpoint.

He would soon set sail, accompanying the collection, to return the thirty sculptures to their home, where they *belonged.*

His father's rapacious need for acquisition made his blood boil.

He set Lady Claire's letter beneath the marble shard on his desk, then leaned back, tenting his hands. Physically, Claire Pheland was exquisite—blonde, amber-eyed, with a fine figure and proud carriage. Yet the few times he'd met the woman, she seemed oblivious to her own beauty. An act? He wondered.

How much *did* the woman know about the ancients? Where had she studied? Private tutors, he assumed, as women had no access to British universities. Another absurdity. Women had graduated universities in Italy, Germany, Sweden, and other countries. Outliers all. No woman could attain a university degree in England.

Shortsighted, for men persisted in seeing women as less intelligent, which astounded him. He knew numerous bright-minded women equal to or surpassing men's acuity.

Outside, the rain had ceased, and he rose and headed for the mews, eager to fly Ares, his favorite goshawk.

Given Lady Claire's history as a titled and entitled daughter of a baron, she pursued her unique subject with uncommon fervor. She may have failed to finish her presentation, but what little he had heard gave him pause. Yet his incredulity remained. He recalled the French antiquarian who posited a similar idea. Yet colored statues? He could not fathom it.

Lady Claire was on some wild goose chase. Nonetheless, given her bravery at the gathering, he would think on admitting her to the marbles' room.

He headed to the stable yard when Captain Russell hailed him. The man captaining the war frigate he'd purchased for the journey was a good sort, but why, each time he ventured to fly his birds, did someone interfere? With resignation, Theseus walked to meet him.

CLAIRE HAD YET to hear from Lord Ashworth, yet she must get inside his sculpture room. Time was growing short, for Rhys had explained Ashworth intended to sail soon for Greece. The Ashworth pieces could further her premise, her aim to collect enough evidence that no one, not the Society of Antiquaries, not the Royal Society, not any damnable society, could refute her proof that ancient Greece had boasted brightly painted statues, stelai, and friezes. They were not, and never had been, starkly white.

Lauded antiquarian Johann Joachim Winckelmann had made matters worse by claiming white stone figures equaled purity of form, à la Plato. She recalled his famed quote. "The whiter the body is, the more beautiful it is as well."

*Balderdash!* What a challenge to convince those old fogies that their concept of ancient Greece and their admiration of whiteness were based on false information.

No, they embraced the idea that the absence of colored statues showed the Greeks' creative restraint, highlighting form over decoration, decoration being considered in bad taste.

*Absurd.*

Converting them to her way of thinking was a challenge Claire willingly embraced.

What if she showed up at Wolf Court? The carriage ride from Halafair to Woolacombe was but six or seven hours. Doable in a day. Ashworth was reserved, with a gruff demeanor, but Claire recalled how he had come to Lottie's aid after a tumble from her horse and his kindness during her presentation.

If she appeared, would he turn her away? Perhaps.

The idea was scandalous, she was well aware. Yet impossible to ignore.

Claire sat at her secretary, dipped her quill, and wrote a letter to her aunt Agnes, just returned from her adventures in America.


On another chilly late April day, Theseus stood agog in his foyer, staring at the beautiful face of Lady Claire Pheland, who had arrived, unbidden, on his doorstep. For such a reticent soul, the bold move near made him smile. What nerve.

Her immense Irish wolfhound, Cullen, stood beside her, the other side occupied by a vibrant older woman wearing a purple turban, her yellow gown embellished with purple accents. He was near blinded.

"Lady Claire. This is a surprise."


CLAIRE TOOK one look at Lord Ashworth's grim face, knowing he might be unreceptive to her idea. *Bollocks!* Though her face remained pleasant and optimistic, her hope died.

And yet... As he crouched to pet Cullen, her massive wolfhound with very large teeth, the man's severe face relaxed. How endearing.

She peered down at Ashworth. A contradictory, yet compelling man. From their first meeting on horseback to their conversation in the alley after her presentation, Theseus Ashworth had defied setting him alongside other gentlemen of his stature. She'd seen him both casual and stern, amenable and prickly, commanding and kind.

A confusing man.

If she were honest, Ashworth had intrigued her from the first, though she would audibly deny it. Most men she met either had no interesting conversation or their personas failed to attract her. Yet the earl's discourse compelled her in the extreme. Their previous brief chats may have been fractious, but his mind, his perceptions on ancient societies, fascinated her. Curse it. Worse, much to her surprise, his rough looks drew her far too much, for she found his unfashionable bronzed skin and muscled form appealing. For a moment she stared at his tumbled auburn hair—dragon's blood hair, the color discovered on the Canary Islands.

Claire snapped her mind to attention to find Aunt Agnes peering at her with a small smile.

Ashworth rose to stare between her, Cullen, and Agnes.

Auntie, Mama's sister, had gleefully agreed to accompany her to Wolf Court as chaperone, Mama reminding her that Agnes was a bit...eccentric. Claire and Lottie both enjoyed her aunt's foibles, and her mother had laughed, saying she felt pity for poor Lord Ashworth.

Oh, those fabulous sculptures. She knew they were exceptional, though she had never seen them. But rumor was rife. Her mouth practically watered at the possibility of examining them. She smiled up at the man who would say yea or nay to their entry.

# TWO

Theseus took a moment to compose himself. He could turn her...them away, though the tiny woman in the demonstrative outfit gave him pause. Small she might be, but also rather terrifying. Yet he could do it, and Lady Claire and her minions would stomp off, not to darken his door again.

He stared at her ladyship with incredulity, her expectant amber eyes sincere rather than disingenuous. Like him, she was friends with Devonshire. Yet what a bother.

Those eyes... He saw hope fade, a feeling she valiantly tried to conceal. It pained him, that sensation. Quite a bit, a fact he found damned odd.

*Why the hell not allow her in?*

Because she would be a pain in his arse.

Theseus cleared his throat. "How lovely to see you, my lady, as well as your pet and your companion," he said, putting off the inevitable.

The lady grinned, and it was audacious. "May I introduce my aunt, Miss Agnes, and Cú Chulainn, my pup? As you have met before, you know I call him Cullen."

Surprised yet again, Theseus gestured to the hound. "You named him after the warrior who *killed* a wolfhound?"

"Well, yes, but he greatly regretted it and was always associated with wolfhounds. He himself became Chulainn's guard dog."

The woman looked utterly pleased as she reached into her large reticule and produced a tin, presenting it to him.

"I recalled a dinner you attended at Woodbine where you enthused over the *boudoir* biscuits. I brought these for you."

"A bribe?" He gave her a smile, the one he knew frightened a man...or ten.

"Indeed!" she said with enthusiasm.

She brought to mind Calypso, the nymph who detained Odysseus for seven years. He took the tin with caution, as if it might bite him, yet widened the door. "Thank you. Will you not come inside?"

Her smile was warm and wide and beguiling. "Thank you, but let me explain my purpose—I am determined to prove the Greek sculptures were commonly painted." She clasped her hands tight enough her glove fabric gloves might burst. Cullen huffed.

Words stuck in his throat, his jaw clamped like steel.

She stood straight as a ruler, shoulders thrown back in a proud stance. Yet those amber eyes, damn them, shined with hope.

"I see," he finally said. "Until I sail for Greece, you are most welcome to study my father's sculptures."

"My aunt will accompany me, my lord, as well as Cullen, if you approve."

He sighed, knowing his sweet spot for Canidae... Though the aunt was oddly more intimidating. "Of course. Cullen is welcome, as is your aunt."

Ashworth did not walk, no, he strode with intense purpose through the foyer. Her trio followed, Claire lugging her heavy case that included her microscope. A footman had offered to carry it, but no one touched her precious equipment but herself.

They proceeded down a long hall parallel to the staircase lined with niches highlighting a variety of sculptures, though none of the pieces were Greek. Auntie oohed and aahed.

"Your hall includes many artifacts," Claire said. "Do you intend to return them to their countries of origin as well?"

He shook his head. "Some are governmental offerings given to my father or grandfather, others sourced on my Grand Tour or received as gifts."

"I see." She spotted a Byzantine bust and a miniature pharaoh and his queen from Egypt's Old Kingdom until coming upon a statue that gave her pause.

The artist had rendered a man in marble, maybe six inches high or perhaps seven, and quite abstract. He was seated, and his hand held a harp or lyre that rested on his stool. His form was only suggested, his arms broken off below the elbow, as was often the case. Nonetheless, the small sculpture was a masterpiece—suggestive, pure, perfect.

"What is this?" Claire said. "I have never seen its like before. It is exquisite." ttt

"A knickknack," Ashworth said. "One I admire as well. My father brought it back from Greece many years ago. He purchased it in Athens, though the seller did not know its origin."

"I find it stunning." Claire leaned closer, hoping to spot a dab of paint. She raised her monocle and took care examining the statue. None. Ah, well.

Theseus nodded and proceeded until they reached a pair of open doors and entered a sitting room. Not what she'd expected.

He waved to a settee. "Ladies, do take a seat."

She did as requested, though he'd barked the words. Cullen sat beside her feet, while Auntie took a wing chair near the fireplace, her face piqued with interest.

Ashworth sat opposite Claire, a delicate table between them.

"I wish you to explain your hypothesis again."

Claire almost sighed. Almost. "Most of the Grecian statuary, even the bronzes, were painted. This is not a new supposition. Are you familiar with Jean-Baptiste de Saint-Non's work, *Voyage picturesque de Naples et de Sicile?*"

He became quite still, and she could almost see the cogs and wheels turning in that powerful brain. "Vaguely."

"In that work, Saint-Non often depicted the ancient statues with vivid colors. My thesis is not original." She continued to expound as he sat back, tenting his hands.

"You are not shy in the least, are you?" he said.

Claire startled. "Pardon?"

"Many comment upon your reticence and retiring demeanor."

His insight made her deuced uncomfortable. Shrugging to avoid the topic, she examined the elegant room with its lavish paintings, furniture, and bibelots. "What an exquisite salon, my lord."

Ashworth puffed out a breath in obvious frustration. "Let me show you the marbles room."

He approached walnut double doors embellished in gold, a reflection of the previous generation's devotion to elaborate trimmings.

Ashworth swung the doors wide, and the view stole Claire's breath. Dozens of busts rested on plinths, with several statues standing in various locations, along with several stelai and friezes. The walls were hung with gorgeous woven tapestries, scenes of ancient Greece, while a large table contained pottery and marble fragments. Excepting the tapestries, all was a wonderland of white.

But Claire hoped that within the creases of chins and elbows, draped clothing, and pursed lips, hidden color remained.

She paused, doubts slithering into her brain. Each time she confronted a sculpture, she worried she would find no residue of paint. That the experts were right. That she was a fool. Claire hated such insecurities about her hypothesis. But it was part of who she was. She must accept that and simply get on with it. She mentally shook herself.

Her eyes were drawn to the tapestries, for they were a riot of color. One was of a female in men's clothing assisting a pregnant woman. Agnodice, she'd bet. The other depicted a woman racing a chariot. That must be Cynisca, the first woman to compete and win in the Olympic Games. Claire walked closer. The bright colors showed no sign of deterioration in the weave. They must be of fairly recent origin, then.

Alongside her, Cullen's behavior was impeccable, whilst his lordship directed Auntie to a wing chair before the fire, the chill in the air palpable. He led Claire to a large worktable, its wooden surface scarred with dents and scratches.

"Will this suit?" he said.

"Very much so." Perfect for her microscope and chemicals.

"You truly think you will find colors amongst these?" Ashworth waved an arm across the thirty or so sculptures.

"I am sure of it." A boldfaced lie.

He chuckled. "You are awfully certain of yourself, my lady."

"Thank you. I shall take the compliment."

Her eyes shifted from the earl to survey the room. There, amongst the stelai and friezes, was a familiar bust.

"You have an Aspasia," she said in breathless tones.

The bust's earthy quality made her eager for a closer look, for it could be a copy of hers, yet instinct said it was different.

He gave her an assessing look. "She does not travel with us to Greece."

Claire held her breath, for there was much he wasn't saying.

"You may use the room in the morning between ten and noon and in the afternoon between two and four. You move nothing without my approval. And you will be silent."

"No singing if I am alone?"

"Harrumph."

She chuckled. "In truth, how very generous of you to welcome us, my lord. I shall follow your edicts to the letter."

Ashworth did not roll his eyes, but she'd swear he wanted to.

Instead, he reached down to scratch beneath Cullen's chin. He paused as he rose. "Where are you staying?"

"At the inn in town."

"Bah! That is no place for gently bred ladies." He lowered his head and sighed. "I presume your maid accompanies you along with Miss Agnes and Cullen?"

"She awaits us in the carriage."

"The dower house," he mumbled in obvious discomfort.

"Pardon?"

"At present, the dower house is empty, and it is far more suitable for your sojourn here than the inn, particularly with Cullen, for he can stretch his legs at Wolf Court." His heavy brow bunched. "The Prancing Rabbit's element is often unsavory."

A reluctant gift, but one she would accept. "Thank you, Lord Ashworth. I and my companions much appreciate the offer. I shall send my maid and the carriage to collect our baggage from the inn." She peered down at her pup. "Cullen will appreciate your offer most especially."

Ashworth cleared his throat. "I expect so. He is a handsome fellow."

She grinned. "And a fierce one! A gift from my mother."

"The dower house is yours." He snapped her a nod and fled as if pursued by banshees.

Having settled their things in the dower house, Claire went to work, and though she was bristling to examine the marbles, first she settled Agnes by the fireplace, then set out Cullen's water dish and his cozy blanket. Fingers atingle, she forced herself to lay out her instruments, chemicals, and other paraphernalia before she perused the stone.

Her anticipation increased as she walked to Aspasia. First she circled the piece, considering the different angles the sculptor had created. The stone itself, of a finer quality than her Roman Aspasia, included a tall marble stand, or herm. Upon closer inspection, the bust differed slightly from hers, but those variations were significant. This Aspasia was a touch more idealized and refined than her copy, a touch more beautiful and more ethereal as well.

Claire ran a hand over her head. Greek. No doubt about it. Her first look had revealed no hidden color, but she would save a more thorough examination of Aspasia for later. A treat for the very end.

Her hands shook with excitement as she approached a plinth holding a bust from Piraeus. Hope rose as she raised her loop, followed by disappointment. She moved to a statue of a Hellenic warrior. Nothing.

It was happening, her doubts flourishing like weeds. Too often, when marbles were excavated, they were scrubbed clean of dirt, detritus…and any remaining paint. She looked across the sea of Greek antiquities, dozens of them, chiding herself for her qualms, not an attractive trait.

Claire rested her hand on the bust of Socrates, picturing the room filled with color. The *kore,* or maiden, standing near the wall in bright yellow and white, her cheeks pink, her lips flushed with red. She moved to the bronze of Perseus, who would have been painted a golden hue, with white leather wrappings around his wrists and forearms, his eyes colored green, blue, or brown. She wished she knew. She pivoted, imagining a kaleidoscope of polychromy adorning the marbles.

"They are all so beautiful, Auntie, are they not?"

Her aunt swiveled, setting aside her embroidery. Claire was a bit terrified of Auntie's needlework—her last piece said, "You are tight as Dick's hatband." After having it framed, Auntie gave it to her solicitor. Claire could only imagine why.

"They are, indeed," Auntie said.

A knock distracted her musings, Cullen rising to an attentive stance.

"Come in." Claire placed a hand on her dog's brow to reassure him all was well.

A footman entered and began dousing the lamps around the

room. Beyond the floor-to-ceiling windows, the sky had darkened, though it felt she'd been working for mere minutes. Claire realized it was more like hours. She checked the watch pinned to her bodice. Ten minutes after four o'clock.

Her first hours with the marbles, and she had not found a single dab of color.

Claire left most of her paraphernalia on the table but repacked her precious microscope in its case. Charlotte and Patrick had gifted her the instrument for Christmas, and she treasured its refinement and accuracy. She smiled, recalling her first microscope, one she had built herself.

A footman stood by the double doors, closing them as they left for the day. Though they had settled into the dower house, she turned to ask the footman how to exit the manor, an immense pile of stone with numerous winding corridors.

The man was gone, perhaps nervous around Cullen, whose jaw was open, tongue lolling? More likely Auntie scared him. Much more likely.

"I go to the kitchens," Auntie said, her ostrich feathers waving as she tilted her head.

"How will you find your way?"

Auntie tapped her nose. "Scent."

"What do you seek?"

"A maid mentioned marzipan." Her grin was diabolical.

"Happy eating."

# THREE

Claire had not toured the manor, though the butler had offered. Now, Cullen followed her down the main hall toward the great room with many doors, massive fireplaces, and several sofa groupings. She paused. One branched corridor went left, the other right, and she stood in shadow, unsure of which way to go.

The knocker pounded, then the sound of the butler swinging the door wide. She peeked around a corner toward the foyer. The visitor was dressed to the nines, from his beaver top hat to his walking stick.

"I have an appointment with Lord Ashworth," the gentleman said in a terribly plummy voice.

The butler took his hat and cane just as Ashworth strode into the foyer, face tight, eyes sharp, and lips thin. She doubted this a welcome meeting.

"Greetings, Mr. Planta." Ashworth bowed, as did Mr. Planta.

*God above!* That was the British Museum's Principal Librarian, the man in charge of it *all*. Claire slid deeper into the shadows.

A member of the Society of Antiquaries, Planta likely had

attended her aborted presentation. He had also probably heckled her, as many had done.

He must be here about the Ashworth sculptures.

His lordship led Planta from the foyer, requesting the butler deliver refreshments.

On light feet, Claire followed the men until they disappeared into a room and closed the door.

Which hadn't snicked tight.

She shouldn't. She really should *not*.

Claire peered over her shoulder for the refreshment's arrival. All clear. She whispered for Cullen to shush, pressed close to the door, and listened.

At first, the voices were too muffled to reach her ears, but they soon rose.

"What are you offering this time, Mr. Planta?" Lord Ashworth said in what sounded like exasperation.

A throat cleared. "How would you like to be a marquess? An interested party, an authority, has promised an elevation in the peerage should you choose to donate the previous earl's marbles collection to the museum. An elevation that would include funds added to your coffers."

"And who might this 'interested party' be?" he said.

A pained smile. "I am not at liberty to disclose the gentleman's name."

Another pause and what sounded like a shuffling of papers, though Claire couldn't be certain.

"Are not Elgin's marbles enough?" Ashworth said with disgust. "Raising my station holds little appeal."

"Is that so?" Planta tapped his walking stick. "How very... unique."

A chuckle. "I am comfortably set up, funds-wise, and see no advantage to gaining another title."

"Then what can I offer, man?" Planta's voice barked with frustration.

"Nothing, I am afraid." Ashworth chuckled. "Neither you nor the Crown, no matter the inducements, can alter my path."

Low murmurs, then sounds of clinking. Drinks, she presumed.

Claire turned to leave as the butler, followed by a footman, rounded a corner, the footman carrying a large tray filled with sweets and savories.

"Oh, hello!" She offered a smile. Cullen smiled, too, which made the phlegmatic butler grin.

"I understand," the butler said, "your party now occupies the dower house."

Claire felt much as a bug beneath a microscope. The men knew she had been eavesdropping, curse it. "That is so."

"I shall have you escorted to the house." He smiled, eyes twinkling.

Her mouth opened, and nothing came out. She cleared her throat. "That would be lovely. Shall I wait in the…"

He signaled the footman to hand him the tray. "Ferguson will guide you."

She nodded and followed, back straight, head held high, making good her escape.

The dower house, though small, was a distinctive Tudor jewel, complete with exquisite tapestries and comfortable furniture, reminding her of Woodbine and then her family. She missed them already and vowed to write letters after dinner.

"Aunt, are you here?"

No answer. Off gadding about, Claire assumed.

While changing, Claire again mulled over the conversation between Ashworth and Mr. Planta. What an inducement Planta had offered. Yet the earl rejected it. Shocking. What determination on Ashworth's part!

Talking to Planta, Ashworth was the perfect earl, albeit a stiff one. But his refusal implied he was more—a man so fixed on his purpose, he could not be swayed. Both admirable and unusual.

Claire couldn't help but wonder what "more" there was to Ashworth.

She sat at the vanity while her maid arranged her hair, Cullen observing as always. For some reason, her coifs fascinated the pup.

Ashworth had invited her and Agnes to join him for dinner, surprising her near as much as the return of the marbles. He even said Cullen was welcome, equally unexpected.

The earl fascinated her, excitement prickling her skin. What was his elusive quality that affected her so? She buried her anticipation deep, yet it felt much like a pebble wedged in a shoe, a vexatious one.

"I shall not attend the meal." Agnes stood in the doorway, *en deshabille.*

Claire rose. "Are you well?"

"I fear the marzipan did not settle."

"How can I make you more comfortable, Auntie?"

Her aunt sniffed. "I fear you cannot. I shall have a tray sent over, though I cannot guarantee it will be eaten."

"All right." Scandalous to dine alone with Ashworth. Yet who would know? "I shall say you have a megrim."

Her aunt frowned. "So banal." Auntie grinned. "Perhaps the pox!"

"Definitely the pox!" With a laugh, Claire kissed her aunt's cheek, retrieved one of her throwing knives, and slipped it into the holster strapped to her thigh, reachable through her pocket. Upon Rose's recommendation, all her gowns had pockets. A wise suggestion, especially after the tumult of the past few years. She always wore at least one knife on her person. Often more. Why pockets were not ubiquitous in ladies' gowns, she did not know.

Dinner was quite delicious, the conversation odd, for Ashworth had little use for such topics as the weather, a new play, or the food, offering monosyllabic replies. But once she attempted a discussion of Cullen's antecedents, Ashworth transformed into an enthusiastic participant, even comparing the Irish wolfhound to the Scottish deerhound.

Also notable, Cullen oft drifted from her side of the table to Ashworth's, and she suspected the earl was offering him tidbits. An indulgent man, though few could refuse Cullen's pleading eyes.

Ashworth reached for a sip of wine, his deep-set eyes boring into her. "Tell me, Lady Claire, is eavesdropping part of your research?"

Her mouth dried, her thoughts scattered. Yet...yes, his eyes warmed with laughter. "Is it not obvious?"

"I fear it is not," he replied, his tone clipped.

"Mr. Planta is the Principal Librarian of the British Museum. The..." She'd almost uttered "damned." "The museum will not permit me to examine the marbles on exhibit, nor even the ones in storage. I am curious about Planta, and I was even more intrigued by what you and he had to discuss."

He tilted his head as if her answer were inconceivable. "Are you not ashamed for sneaking about and spying?"

She pondered for a minute, refusing to lower her eyes at his penetrating stare. "In truth, I should be. I admit to being hesitant, yet I found the conversation irresistible, my curiosity piqued. The latter, a sad trait I acquired from Lottie."

He barked a laugh, leaned back, and crossed his arms. "Placing the blame at your sister's feet, I see. And what did you glean from our discussion?"

"I find it a conundrum as to why you are returning the marbles. Though I cannot say I am fond of Mr. Planta or his policies, I am surprised you resisted the man's estimable offer."

"Bribes do not interest me."

She stared at that brutal, tanned face, noting the lines fanning from his eyes. Smile lines. Yet in the brief times she had met him, his smiles were few and far between. She *liked* his smiles.

"You are examining me," he said, "as if I were one of the specimens beneath your microscope."

She laid her serviette on the table. "Forgive me, my lord. I shall retire for the evening. Thank you again for the delicious meal."

He reared back, his face both curious and surprised, and he waved her back to her seat as she began to rise.

"I have been to Greece many times and for long periods," he said. "I like her people, and I admire their pride in their heritage. Much has changed since the sculptures were carved, and now Hellas is under Ottoman rule, which her citizens abhor. The Turks easily part with Greek history, an attempt to eradicate it. The marbles deserve to be in Greece, not here nor in some British museum, which only the privileged can view. Do you not see the irony of that? The absurdity? The average Englishman cannot view the museum unless they have some upper-class connection.

"Should not a museum be for *all* those interested, not just some? That is neither here nor there, for I would still return them to Hellas."

Claire must think. She vaguely knew not all were admitted to the museum but had not thought much on it. Yet it felt similar to her being denied access to study the museum's sculptures.

Should not all be welcomed at the museum? She rose. "You have given me much food for thought, my lord. Now, if you will excuse me."

"I shall accompany you to the dower house." Ashworth approached to loom over her, for she came but to his shoulder. The man probably didn't realize how intimidating his presence could be. At times, Rhys had that same habit. Thoughts of her brother-in-law and her family made her go wistful.

"Thank you, my lord. That is kind."

"I do hope your aunt is feeling more the thing," he said as they walked.

Outside, the air was crisp this late April day, yet today spring was bursting. Claire loved winter, its sleigh rides and snowball fights a treat, but now she welcomed spring's fragrant blooms and unfurling leaves.

Ashworth said nothing as they crossed the drive, and when they arrived at the house, warm and welcoming, lit with beeswax candles, she turned to thank him. The man bowed and fled.

·  ·  ·

THE PROMISE of the new day awakened Claire, helped along by her pup's icy nose nudging her neck. Soon, she and Cullen stood at the table surrounded by statuary, and she began setting up her equipment. Auntie was again ensconced by the fire, plying her needle.

As Claire dusted off her microscope, she eyed the forest of sculptures for a likely candidate.

She passed a bust of Hera, another of Achilles, and one of Homer, stopping briefly to check for paint. Nothing. Nothing. Nothing. Cursory checks only, but she wished she'd found *some* color by now. She came upon a stele of a sleeping child, two adults hovering over him, the design in relief. A commemorative inscription marked the base of the capstone. Claire sucked in a breath. Had she seen a dab of green, or was she again chasing rainbows?

Claire withdrew her loupe. *There.* In a crevice, where the child's head rested on his hand. She whooshed out a breath, savoring the moment. *Thank the heavens.* With each find, the world became bright and new again.

Her find confirmed, she retrieved her tweezers, a sharp knife, and a dish to hold her specimen, then returned to the stele.

She stepped back and examined the block of marble as a whole, circling around it. The facial expressions of those on the grave marker were profound.

The young child was *loved.* Deeply, from the looks of it.

Blinking away tears, Claire scraped a tiny bit of pigment from the marble into the small ceramic dish. Peering at it through her microscope, a thrill suffused her. She opened her journal and described the stele in detail, noting from where she had taken the pigment. She then made a quick sketch of the stele.

Finally, she slid the pigment into a tiny box, one of the many she carried in her case, then labeled and sealed it.

Claire held her breath. The first of many more, she hoped. Over her years of study, she had found many colors—Egyptian blue was ubiquitous, as was madder red. Cinnabar, ochre, azurite, malachite —she had found them all at one time or another. But never Tyrian purple. Perhaps here she would discover that elusive color.

Just as she was choosing what next to examine, Ashworth breezed in, his large form tight, as action was but a breath away, his face wreathed in determination.

*He is so alive!* She dismissed the thought as she rose from the chair and curtsied. "My lord?"

He rested his fisted hands on his hips. "I wish to see evidence of what you are about."

"About?" Claire said, notching her chin to challenge his fierce demeanor. Until she remembered she was at Wolf Court on his sufferance.

Ashworth waved a hand. "What have you found?"

His formidable stance resembled a stalking lion. She didn't much like being prey.

Claire led him to the grave stele, showing the spot where she had found paint, with more of the green remaining. "This."

"I see a muddy color that might or might not be green."

"Of course it is green!"

"Not dirt of some sort?"

"Do not be ridiculous, sir. I have examined it beneath my microscope!"

"Who is to say the color was not added millennia after the creation of the stele?"

She huffed. "Why in all creation would someone paint a stele years after it was carved?"

"Why not?" He spread his hands, palms up. "Have you found any others? Ones better than this sorry specimen?"

"That question is offensive, my lord, as is your tone."

He drew back and paused, squeezing the bridge of his nose. "I do apologize, for I am out of sorts and, yes, out of line. Yet this is but one small exemplar of... What did you call it?"

"Polychromy." Claire sounded stiff, as if she were in a snit. Well, she guessed she was. "Is not that the point of my being here? Finding more examples of polychromy to substantiate my hypothesis?" Claire drew in a deep breath, nostrils flaring. That man had said he was out of sorts. Given his upset, she evened her voice to soothing. "I would be delighted to discuss my research in more detail."

Agnes snickered. Ashworth didn't react, yet he must have heard. He dragged over two hardback chairs and gestured for her to sit. Once she did, he followed suit.

He stared at her, stoic-faced. "Well?"

"As I have noted before, I believe the ancient Greeks painted most of their work, the statues and busts, even the bronzes."

His brows ascended nearly to his hairline. "Continue."

She described her research in Greece, how she had examined a wide range of marbles, all of which advanced her belief.

"Most think your premise outlandish."

"Most are wrong." Claire sniffed. "I am neither the first to propose this, nor will I be the last."

"I know," he said, nodding. "I reviewed Quatremère de Quincy's treatise, 'Olympian Zeus.' He opposed Winckelmann's ideas in certain areas."

Claire leaned back and laughed. "Winckelmann! The bane of my existence." She flipped pages in her journal until she came to a particular passage. "I quote, 'The whiter the body is, the more beautiful it is as well.' Do you believe this? Winckelmann opined, 'Color contributes to beauty, but it is not beauty. Color should have a minor part in the consideration of beauty because it is not but structure that constitutes its essence.'"

Ashworth said nothing, his eyes distant.

"*Well?*" Claire said. "Does the whiteness of the statues imply Platonic purity? Is it that whiteness that raises them to lofty artistic heights?"

He frowned. "I cannot say I agree with those statements."

"Have you heard of the Temple of Aphaia?" Claire said, bright-eyed.

"I have seen it myself."

"Many of its sculptural adornments were brought to Munich by an antiquarian traveling in Greece."

His face darkened. "I know this."

"The excavators found traces of pigments, primarily blue and red, on the sculptures. Yet the art establishment ignores this."

Ashworth smirked. "So there is some monstrous conspiracy at work?"

"No," she said. "And stop sneering. It does you no favors. Those on high—the art community, the museums, even antiquarians—are seemingly incapable of understanding the truth. All because it goes against their entrenched beliefs. So they ignore any verification. What of that statue of Artemis, the one found in Pompeii? The piece is visibly colored!"

Ashworth crossed his arms. "I understand Winckelmann declared it Etruscan, not Greek. I have not seen it myself."

"Ha! Etruscan?" Claire flung her arms wide. "It is *Greek*. That smile Winckelmann talked about exactly matches the Greeks' Archaic period depictions. Most interesting, at least to me, is that late in life, his point of view shifted to believing paint existed on Greek and Roman sculptures. Clear evidence was found in his notes written just before his death. No one talks about that! Antiquarians ignore his reversal whilst revering his earlier pronouncements."

"Your reasoning is sound, Lady Claire," Ashworth said. "Show me, then. Give me more examples than a dab of muddy green. I do wish to accept your thesis."

# FOUR

Theseus did want Lady Claire to succeed. "If esteemed antiquarians such as de Quincy and Winklemann go unheeded, how shall you turn the antiquarian community to your way of thinking?"

Claire crossed her arms as well, mirroring him. "You imply my gender will make it more difficult."

"Well...yes. Sadly, that is a large part of it." He held up his hands as if to appease. "I do not feel that way, having known clever, capable, and intelligent women, but the world certainly does."

Lady Claire had done her due diligence, and Theseus admired that. Yet he oft lost her words whilst he marveled at her sparkling eyes, the way all of her came alive with enthusiasm. Compelling. Society said ladies should not exhibit excessive emotion. He delighted in Lady Claire's. A reaction most unlike him, his focus usually honed to a razor point.

"I admire de Quincy," Lady Claire said. "I often esteem Winckelmann as well, though he frustrates me. You see, I have faith in myself, in my research, and in my conclusions. If it takes a thousand daubs of paint to convince the hierarchy of my thesis, then I shall do exactly that." She graced him with a dangerous gleam that presaged terrors to come. "Now, it is my turn, your lordship."

"Your...turn?" he said.

"Yes." Lady Claire nodded. "I have thought much about your repatriating these marbles to Greece. I see your point, to a certain extent."

She sang the song many others had. "'A certain extent?'"

Claire laughed. "Well, yes."

"Just as you believe in your...cause, so do I believe in mine, whether you see my reasoning or no."

Lady Claire tilted her head. "I know all about causes."

He shrugged. "It is simple. These marbles belong in Greece."

"A land now ruled by the Ottomans."

"That is neither here nor there," he said. "They belong home. The last place they need to be is decorating some stuffy English manor house like bonbons, scattered about to impress."

"I agree with Lord Ashworth," her aunt boomed.

"Thank you, Miss Agnes."

"What of the Greek artifacts you are keeping?" Claire said. "Should not they be repatriated as well?"

"An excellent question, my lady." He nodded. "Eleven in my personal collection were snuck out of Greece by Hellenes wishing them safe from the Turks. Two were gifted to me by Greek families who held them for millennia, unlike the marbles of my father, which were sold to him by the Ottomans. That is how Elgin acquired the Parthenon marbles, which equates to bribery."

Lady Claire clasped her hands, her attentive look and that nibble of her bottom lip alluring. She confused him utterly.

He checked his timepiece. "I must go." He scratched Cullen's chin, bowed to the ladies, and offered Claire a mischievous smile over his shoulder.

What was that smile about—like the glee a pirate felt as he slashed his saber? Did sabers slash?

What a confusing, mercurial, and engaging fellow, with an intelligence to easily battle hers. Ashworth was both invigorating and frustrating.

She gathered her dignity, sadly lacking during their conversation, and returned to work.

A week later, as they walked the hall to the sculpture room, her aunt's disgruntlement reached her ears.

"I miss Arthur," Agnes said.

"I am sorry."

Agnes waved a hand. "Oh, it is to be expected, but I hate for us to be apart."

True, for Auntie dearly loved the capuchin monkey her aunt had rescued from a brutal organ grinder. She must concede Arthur was unique. On a visit to Hawthorne, Arthur had seen Lottie painting and become fascinated. Once home, Auntie had set up paints and an easel for the monkey. His strange, swirly paintings often surprised Claire, evoking feelings of joy or excitement.

"Perhaps we could—" Auntie shook her head.

"We cannot, Auntie." Agnes had wished to bring Arthur to Wolf Court. "Whilst he can be wonderfully behaved, he—"

Agnes waved her fan. "Can be wonderfully *mis*behaved. Ah, well. How does your work progress? I so admire your pursuit."

"Slow as usual." Claire always found her aunt's support heartening. "I must be meticulous, or they will find me at fault." "They" being the men who judged such things.

"What do you think of Ashworth?" Agnes winked.

She usually found Agnes' perpetual quest to find Claire a husband diverting, for they both knew Claire believed she would never marry. Her knee-jerk reaction was to say she liked him very well. A bad idea to voice those thoughts. "He is an interesting man." There, that was quite unexceptional.

Agnes halted. "I have never heard you say such about any gentleman other than a family member, and they do not count."

*Bollocks.* "I am sure I have found other—"

She pressed her closed fan to Claire's chest. "Never."

A footman swung wide the doors, and Agnes took her chair by the fire, while Claire set up her equipment.

Agnes bent to her needlework, though she would not reveal the piece until its completion. Auntie loved her surprises, to the horror of many, particularly double entendres. Her last creation blared, "Time wounds all heels." Quite hilarious, actually.

Hadn't Claire found other men interesting? She was certain she had. Traveling the world as she did, Auntie was often absent. *Of course* Claire had met interesting men. The trouble was, she could not think of a one.

Except for Ashworth, though of late he'd become a ghost. He had refrained from joining them at meals or checking her progress on the sculptures or even sharing tea. She suspected preparations for his departure had inundated him. In truth, Claire wished he pestered her more about her findings.

Perhaps all for the good. He might be pleasing to look upon, very pleasing if she were honest, but he was a prickly fellow. Mayhap it was his prickliness she found interesting? That could not be right.

Claire shrugged as she scraped what she hoped was a small dab of Naples yellow off Eros' elbow fold.

To her, these marbles were a rich field of exploration. So far, Eros was the second marble to offer anything up. Not enough to impress Ashworth. Nor anyone, indeed.

Ashworth Senior must have had these pieces fiercely scrubbed, as did so many antiquarians. Claire sighed and got back to work, dozens remaining unexamined, for her study was slow and painstaking. Inspecting them all would take months, time she did not have.

Ashworth appeared before the gallery doors, but she paid him no mind as she placed the speck of yellow on the plate, then carried it to her worktable. She noted in her journal the sculpture's title and Ashworth Senior's description of the piece and its original location while footsteps strode across the gallery to where she sat.

It bothered her that she could feel the man, though she had not looked up.

Finished, Claire stood and curtsied.

"Lady Claire, I have news."

"Why, Lord Ashworth, I thought you may have passed to the great beyond, as I have not seen you for days."

"Still here." His eyes narrowed. "Regrettably, I have moved the date up for our departure to Greece. We sail in seven days."

A *week*. Her heart went triple time now that the hours had become the greater enemy. "Thank you for informing me."

He turned to leave.

"Why?" she asked in a soft voice. "I believed I would have many more days to study them."

He stared at her, impassive, though his eyes hinted at a myriad of emotions—regret, anger, frustration.

"I have no right to ask," she said. "I know that. But it is a terrible disappointment that you will sail so soon. Might I extend my four hours a day in the room to five? Or perhaps six?"

"Forgive me, but I cannot grant you more time, as we must pack the ship, a lengthy task." He stood yards away.

"I see," she said, approaching him slowly. "I apologize for making things worse."

"In truth, you were but the feather that broke the camel's back." He scraped a hand through his too-long hair and chuckled. "Not really. Only but one small voice in the endless harangue."

Being constantly pecked at could drive one to madness, and she could not blame the man.

Claire was so frustrated she wished to scream. Not at him. No, but rather the situation.

If only...

What if she could accompany him to Greece? Claire glanced at Agnes. If her aunt joined her, the trip would be proper. *If* Auntie agreed. Given her adventurous spirit, she would.

"Your expression says you are plotting mischief," he said.

"Never!" Claire winked, returning to the worktable. She slipped onto the stool and slid the sample of what she hoped was Naples yellow beneath the microscope.

"What do you see?" He strolled to where she was perched above her microscope.

"Do look." Claire pointed.

He bent over her microscope. "Yellow."

Claire gestured to Eros. "From our friend over there."

"Our *friend?*" Ashworth laughed, raising a brow. "He is no friend of mine. It seems you now have a muddy green and a yellow specimen." He gave her a long look. "Antiquarian studies oft take much time and patience. I shall hope you find at least one more color. Three is always a good sign, do you not think?"

The man was trying to put a positive spin on her paltry discoveries. More than a dozen samples rested at home, though that was not near enough to convince anyone.

Recalling her sojourn in Greece, the palpable excitement of it all. She would relish another visit. Perhaps she could continue her research onboard, and once in Greece, she would venture to examine marbles *in situ,* ones unavailable on her earlier trip.

All she had to do was get Ashworth to take her along.

"I understand, my lord. Seven days, it is."


The following day, Agnes was resting while Claire took her constitutional on the sandy walk overlooking the Celtic Sea. Cullen loved this walk for his many opportunities to chase seabirds. On her way, she'd spotted Ashworth exiting the mews, leather jesses in hand, while some hawk or falcon bobbed on his forearm. She'd never flown a bird, and the prospect was rather enticing. Perhaps they might... No, Ashworth had little time before he sailed.

The wind was wild today, billowing her clothes, the air bracing. She'd rather be in the sculpture room, but exercise was essential to her health, as she would not allow herself to grow sick or weak in body.

So she walked. The gunmetal clouds darkened near the horizon, the air thick with impending rain. A fierce gust plucked her bonnet from her head, saved by the ribbons, to thump against her back.

She slapped the hat back on her head and tied the ribbons tighter. Agnes might be gleeful about a trip to Greece, but she doubted her maid would react so positively. Not today's worry.

Claire sank into her imaginings, picturing the Acropolis' *kores* painted blue, yellow, and red. A grave stele in a rainbow of colors. The Parthenon friezes with a riot of color and glittering decoration. Egyptian blue, azurite, conichalcite—the pigments bound with beeswax in the ancient encaustic tradition. Claire could see it all.

The great Phidias had sculpted the *Athena Parthenos*, a thirty-eight-foot-tall chryselephantine structure covered in gold and ivory. Long destroyed or stolen, some said, small copies remained. Claire pictured the grandeur of the original epic creation.

With her hand shielding her forehead, Claire watched several dunlins hunt amidst the rocks for food. Her mama loved birds, particularly shorebirds, and would delight in the sight. She missed her.

Claire checked her watch. "Come, Cullen!"

As she turned back, a flurry of dust rose along the drive, a carriage or horsemen headed toward Wolf Court. At first, she found the estate's name pretentious until she learned the nearby town of Woolacombe literally meant Wolves Valley. Sadly, wolves no longer roamed England. She would like to see a wolf someday.

That was due to a fervent curiosity, a fault both she and Lottie shared. It also compelled her to see who was descending upon them at such speed.

# CHAPTER
# FIVE

Theseus, already in a sour mood, given that the precious oranges for the trip had failed to arrive, peered out the entry sidelight. He now must contend with the carriage nearing the manor, which bore Ravenscroft's crest. Annoying. He had planned, *finally*, to fly his goshawk, Ares. *Damn.* He could have Sims inform them he was not at home. Yet he and Ravenscroft were friendly, and in good conscience, he could not. Aggravation awaited, for he had much to accomplish before they sailed.

As Sims opened the door, Theseus saw not only Ravenscroft descending from the carriage but also Sir Joseph Banks, the famed botanist and a trustee of the British Museum.

The old man stood before him, each hand resting on a cane, cloak billowing, face eager. Ravenscroft, conversely, bore the look of one who had suffered much.

"Come in, gentlemen!" Theseus said. "Do come in."

Behind him, Sims sniffed at Theseus' disregard for the proper order of things, since he had spoken before Sims announced the gentlemen. Having been with the family for more than twenty years, one would think Sims had grown used to Theseus' ramshackle ways. It seemed not.

The butler collected their cloaks and hats, noting he would bring a tray, and the men followed Theseus to the small receiving room, Ravenscroft helping Banks to his seat on the sofa.

Once the marquess took the wing chair across from both men, they discussed the weather as Theseus poured them each a fine glass of single-malt scotch, shipped to him by his friend at the Hosh Distillery.

They all sipped.

"This is awfully good," Banks said.

Sad to see the baronet so frail, for he was a famed explorer, one who'd had countless adventures and made unprecedented discoveries. Banks was an empire builder, like Theseus' father and many others. Take, take, take for the greatness of England. Albion was plenty great without the rapacious greed for more land and power.

"How may I be of service, gentlemen?" Theseus said.

"I wish to see your sculpture gallery, Lord Ashworth," Banks said.

"I would be delighted to show you, Sir Joseph."

When Theseus opened the double doors, Sir Joseph gasped. Theseus' eyes arrowed to the workbench where Lady Claire scribbled away.

Ravenscroft's eyes narrowed, and he leaned toward Theseus. "I see Lady Claire is here. I received her letter regarding her unorthodox visit."

Miss Agnes faced the hearth, embroidering in a wing chair. She turned, a smile beaming, and leapt to her feet, hands outstretched. "Joseph!"

Sir Joseph grinned as he hobbled toward Agnes and kissed her cheeks. "Of all things."

"So good to see you, my dear. It has been a year, has it not? I remain so very sorry."

"Thank you, Agnes," he said, eyes bleak. "Sarah Sophia was not young, but…"

"Your sister was always young at heart."

He nodded with solemnity. "Are you here as Lady Claire's chaperone?" He glanced at Claire, who was watching their exchange.

"Indeed, I am," Auntie said.

"Lady Claire has some unconventional ideas," Sir Joseph said.

"Her ladyship." Theseus nodded toward Claire, addressing both Sir Joseph and Ravenscroft. "Means to prove the polychromy of Greek marbles. Ravenscroft supported her at the Royal Society lecture."

"I would do so again," Ravenscroft said. "I read her paper and found many cogent points that confirm her thesis."

"As did I," Theseus said.

"Harrumph!" Sir Joseph said, scoffing. "How can either of you give any credence to a *woman's* rantings?"

Theseus caught Sir Joseph's wink, though he doubted Claire had.

She moved toward them, graceful as always, but paused at Sir Joseph's barked comment. Her amber eyes sparked as she stepped closer, offering all three men a curtsy.

Sir Joseph thrust out one of his canes for Ravenscroft to hold and took her hand, wobbling a bit, but his eyes twinkled. "My Lady Claire. I observed you approach and was teasing. My beloved sister Sarah Sophia had as keen a mind as any man's."

Her eyes warmed to caramel. "What a trickster you are, Sir Joseph. I should not be surprised, given you are obviously a friend of my aunt."

He nodded solemnly. "My predilection to tease is one of my great failings, of which I have many."

Agnes tittered, whilst Claire's trill of laughter filled the room. Gods above, she was mesmerizing.

Rhys took Claire's hands in his and kissed her cheek, her ladyship offering him a warm smile.

"I doubt that you have many failings, Sir Joseph," Lady Claire said. "I am quite aware of Lady Sarah Sophia's renowned assemblage."

"She was enraptured with ephemera," Sir Joseph said. "More than thirty thousand objects fill her collection, if you can imagine! All now reside in the British Museum." Sir Joseph cast a gimlet eye at Ashworth, then cleared his throat.

"Would you like to peruse the room, Sir Joseph?" Theseus said.

He offered a sweet smile. "I fear my legs cannot afford the walk at present."

"Do come and sit," Lady Claire said, helping him to the settee beside Agnes.

Once they were all seated, Theseus notched his head, a silent message for the ladies to retreat.

Claire returned an equally subtle shake of her head, Miss Agnes ignoring them both.

Two mischief-makers.

Yet another Battle of the Sculptures was about to commence, the humor fodder for a book he would never write.

"I have learned," Sir Joseph said, "that war is imminent in Greece."

"Imminent?" Theseus said. "No. The Greeks have been preparing for war against the Turks these past four hundred years."

"The War Office claims this is different," Ravenscroft said. "It appears the Greeks are whipping themselves into a frenzy against Greece's Turkish Muslim citizens. The Ottoman Empire remains strong, too strong, but I fear the Greeks will attempt to force the Turks out of Greece."

"This is correct," Theseus said. "As far as it goes. But Hellas is a good two to three years from true conflict. Skirmishes, yes. But that is all, and they are minor."

Sir Joseph raised pale eyes. "You may not survive, my lord."

"This, from a man who explored the world with Cook." Theseus chuckled. "Danger certainly never deterred you, Sir Joseph. But, in truth, little threat awaits, and I shall be long gone when true war commences in Greece."

"Lord Ashcroft is correct," Agnes said. "My sources agree war is years away." She turned to Sir Joseph. "And you know how reliable my sources are."

Sir Joseph leaned toward Theseus, a hand resting on a cane. "Do not let these exquisite pieces fall into the Turks' hands."

"They never shall," Theseus said.

Claire listened, impressed by Ashworth's ability to hold his own with Sir Joseph, a most formidable presence.

As they volleyed back and forth, she pondered Ashworth's belief the marbles belonged in their home country.

Claire had visited the British Museum many times, touring its halls filled with artifacts from Greece, Italy, Egypt, and other exotic lands. Should all foreign items in the museum be returned?

There would be no museum.

Yet her reaction had been spontaneous, a rejection, rather than giving the idea of repatriation true thought.

Wonders abounded within the museum, ones never seen in England. Did they not symbolize the great empire Britain was building? The thought troubled her, much as a small splinter would beneath the skin of one's thumb. Did England *need* an empire?

No, but... "Would not having such artifacts to examine be of value?"

"A fine point, my lady," Sir Joseph said.

"I do not disagree, Lady Claire," Ashworth said. "I have studied many of the British Museum's artifacts, some on cultural exchange and temporary loan. A more fitting way of acquiring artifacts from afar."

Claire saw Ashworth's point, albeit reluctantly. She owned many items from the trade networks established by Britain. The clothing on her back likely came from France or Belgium, whilst her tea came from India or China. Ashworth's complex issue oft tied her in knots.

"My Greek friends eagerly anticipate their repatriation." Ashworth rose, pacing. "Headmen, architects, villagers, engineers, antiquarians, others know of their impending return. I would not disappoint them."

"What of the marbles' protection?" she blurted.

Ashworth's brow wrinkled. "They will be safe."

Claire wasn't so sure. Now, as the men continued to disagree in utterly civilized tones, she pondered their words, both pro and con. Each position was strong. She'd heard Ashworth's viewpoint echoed in Mary Wollstonecraft's writings, though her treatise on women's rights was better known, a work Claire heartily applauded. Adam Smith, Wordsworth, even the poet Coleridge thought the same.

Interesting that Rhys refrained from the verbal fisticuffs.

"Lord Ravenscroft," Claire said. "Do you, too, intend to convince Lord Ashworth to donate the marbles?"

Rhys cast her a baleful glare. "My presence served to introduce Sir Joseph to Lord Ashworth. Nothing more."

"Ah," she said. "So you have no point of view on this matter?"

Ashworth's lips twitched, whereas Sir Joseph's eyes glimmered with humor.

"I suspect Ravenscroft agrees with Ashworth here," Sir Joseph said, chuckling. "His silence is due to his reluctance to offend me."

"I see," she said.

"Do you, Lady Claire?" Sir Joseph said. "Wish the Ashcroft sculptures to remain in England?"

Three pairs of eyes focused on her, Ashworth's hooded.

"My thoughts remain in flux," she said. "Though it would be wonderful to bring this collection to the eyes of the British public."

Ashworth snorted. "The public, meaning the upper echelon."

"Yes, well," Sir Joseph said. "While only the elite can view the museum's treasures, that is up for debate amongst the trustees. Many push to allow the rabble access."

"A day I hope to see soon," Ashworth said. "So few can view the treasures within."

The exclusions were at her mind's forefront, having recently discussed this with Ashworth. The rabble? A rather poor term for those of the middle and lower classes—merchants, physicians, and solicitors amongst them. Should not all people be included? What of night-soil men? Linen drapers? Farmers or pin makers? All meant all.

Claire recalled a maid at Halafair Hall, one who adored Renaissance art. Claire had noted more than once her studying the manor's paintings or reading a book on just that, a surprising skill for a housemaid. She should be admitted, should she not?

Claire had much to think on.

Rhys assisted Sir Joseph to rise as the men concluded their discussion, and they all walked to the foyer to say their farewells.

As she chatted up Sir Joseph and Auntie, Rhys drew Ashworth aside.

Claire couldn't help wonder what that was all about.

Later that afternoon, Ashworth paid another visit to the sculpture room, his determined look boding ill.

"My lord?" she said.

"With much regret, I have moved my departure forward. I leave in four days rather than seven."

"But—"

"There is no 'but,' my lady."

"May I ask why?"

His smile, that pirate one, made her frown.

"My next visitor, five days hence, according to Ravenscroft—Lord Liverpool."

"The prime minister?"

"Indeed." He grinned. "Going toe-to-toe with Liverpool might be entertaining, but I am beyond weary of these discussions."

"Turn him away!" Agnes chimed in. "Say you are not at home."

Theseus' lips pressed together, his look telling her that would not do, which Agnes knew very well.

"I see." Claire's heart thudded, her window now shrunk to pinhole size.

He moved closer, a towering man with an inflexible intention, yet she saw a plea in those piercing eyes, a plea for understanding.

"Lady Claire," he said. "I again sincerely regret the shortened timeline."

His apology surprised her, making her somewhat uncomfortable, though she was unsure why. She fiddled with her hair, replacing a loose pin. When she looked up, he was gone.

The man had a habit of doing that, and Claire found it most annoying.

Claire, deep in thought, walked the manor halls headed for the small salon. Agnes had gone for her afternoon nap. Unfortunate, as her sense of direction was far better than Claire's.

She had misplaced her second journal—her notes on her previous Greek trip. She'd been reviewing it earlier, when she'd sat to repair a rip in her gown.

In total, three of Ashworth's sculptures had given up their secrets, affirmed by her microscope. Not enough.

If only she could accompany Ashworth to Greece. Perhaps she might uncrate one at a time on the voyage, plus upon their arrival, numerous opportunities existed, for it would take his lordship time to disperse the collection.

Might she stow away?

An absurdity she could not consider.

Claire looked up, only to realize she had no idea where she was in this immense pile of stone.

Down a hall, yet another lined with art-filled niches, coughing alerted her to someone's presence.

She followed the sound, intending to ask for directions. When Claire rounded the corner, she stared at a resplendent solar, rays of light pouring onto the greenery. She opened the door and entered, the scents of oranges and lemons delicious. Smaller foliage, ferns, and flowers covered the room, and she followed the stone path until she came upon a charming seating group and a table set for tea. On a divan reclined a young woman with hair black as Charlotte's, her face porcelain, her lips bowed, who was raising a handkerchief. A beauty, a wan one.

Dear heavens, could this be Ashworth's mistress, tucked away in the far reaches of the manor? She dressed as a woman of station, and yet... The thought pinched. How awful.

But, no, more likely she was Ashworth's sister, the one Lottie said was bedridden. The woman seemed of an age with Claire, though she lacked a certain robustness. Mistress or sister, Claire needed directions.

"Pray excuse me for interrupting your solitude," Claire said. "I am a visitor at Wolf Court, and I seem to have lost the way. Might you help me?"

CHAPTER
# SIX

The woman sat up, only to cough into her handkerchief. "Why, hello there! I am Penelope, Ashworth's sister." Cullen sat beside Claire, and Penelope scratched beneath his jaw. "What a fine fellow!"

"He is Cullen and a love."

"I suspect you are one of my brother's mysterious female visitors?" Lady Penelope's smile was warm and welcoming. "I confess I questioned whether you were more than his—"

"Friend? Acquaintance?" Claire smiled, stepped closer, and introduced herself. "Prior to my visit here, I met Lord Ashworth on several occasions. Yet though I have heard of you, I have never met you, my lady."

Lady Penelope patted the seat beside her. "Do sit, Lady Claire. I neither go out much nor have many visitors, for Ashworth tends to treat his little sister as a fragile egg about to crack."

"Oh, my, that sounds rather dreadful!"

"It is! Would you care for some tea?" Lady Penelope gestured to the pot, steam rising.

"I would. Thank you, my lady."

"Good God, call me, Penelope!"

"But we just—"

"Yes, yes, we have only just met." Lady Penelope flapped a hand. "But we are two young ladies, alone, in the wilds of Devon. I loathe formality."

"Indeed," Claire said, in wont of an intelligent response. She accepted the teacup from Lady Penelope. "Then you must call me Claire."

"I shall," Penelope said. "Claire is lovely, but someone had a predilection for the Greek myths to choose your middle name."

"Cassandra?" Claire did not recall the myth. "I believe I was named for a great-aunt."

"Yes," Penelope said. "But Cassandra was the famed lover of Agamemnon, a great seer, one who was perpetually disbelieved. Her curse. We at Wolf Court are quite attuned to the Hellas peoples and myths."

"You are named after Odysseus' wife." As he had named Theseus after the famed mythological hero...or villain, depending on perspective.

"I am, indeed."

"Penelope has always been a favorite of mine," Claire said with enthusiasm. "A stalwart soul who managed to keep a legion of suitors at bay whilst weaving a tapestry until her husband's return."

A small cough, a sniffle. Claire said nothing, but it was worrisome.

"I have neither consumption nor any other illness we have been able to discern," Penelope said. "Yet my cough and sniffles continue, my breath shortening, particularly in summer. Ashworth wraps me in cotton batting."

"That must be tiring."

"Very much so." She winked. "When he is away on one of his digs, I ride, fish, and even—pray God do not tell my brother—have learned firearms from our armaments-crazed steward. The latter is quite enjoyable, and I have become a crack shot with both pistol and rifle!" Her grin was wicked.

Claire grinned, too. "Quite impressive!" The woman was pale and slim but with a bright, effusive spirit. Agnes would like her. Claire certainly did.

"Regarding the more womanly pursuits." Penelope gave Claire a long look. "Those which males deem acceptable, I weave, an irony given my name."

"Do you?" Claire said. "I tried to weave once, at a demonstration my mother took my sisters and me to. Rosamund had a knack, and Lottie wasn't too terrible." Claire grinned. "I, on the other hand, somehow got the threads all confused! Are those tapestries in the sculpture room yours?"

Penelope nodded, peach pinkening her cheeks. "And you are here because..."

Claire laughed. "I should have explained when I introduced myself. Do forgive me. I am studying the sculptures your father collected."

"Are you indeed?" Penelope said. "To what purpose?"

Claire explained her thesis, as well as the opposition to it, whilst Cullen became particularly attentive to the sweets tray.

"What an odd thing," Penelope said. "I can only imagine the marbles as white. I have always held the idea they are an unattainable aesthetic ideal."

Claire slipped Cullen a chunk of dried meat from her skirt pocket. "You and the rest of the world. Though several respected scholars have noted the coloration on Greek statues and such, the artistic and historic communities at large refuse to consider the idea. The Greeks *painted* their marbles, the bronzes, too. I suspect Lord Elgin's marbles from the Parthenon were colored as well, if I ever get close enough to examine them."

"Those ideas are truly compelling, Claire," Lady Penelope said.

"Perhaps I can check some marbles when I am in Greece, as I am going with Theseus, for I am a *philhellene* and could not be more excited."

"I am unfamiliar with that word."

"It means a friend of Greece and one who admires the country and her people."

"You sail in four days," Claire said. "I am envious."

Lady Penelope tilted her head, much as an owl would. "I was sure Theo said a week hence."

Claire sipped her tea and took a bite of her biscuit with the creamy filling she savored. "He did. Sadly, that changed when his lordship learned the prime minister planned to visit Wolf Court."

"Liverpool? Is he really?" Lady Penelope said in an angry voice. "I do not understand their continued pestering of my brother. Father paid for the digs and brought the marbles here. If Theseus wishes to return them, it is his right and privilege to do so."

Whether Claire accepted Lord Ashworth's reasoning or not, she agreed with his sister. He was well within his rights to do whatever he wished with them. "Is there a particular locale you hope to visit?"

Penelope fiddled with her cup, circling the rim with her index finger, but her eyes gleamed. "You might find me rather eccentric should I reveal the truth." Eccentric? Penelope had yet to meet Auntie.

"I enjoy eccentric."

"I have been in correspondence with a woman from Kastri, another weaver, one said to be Greece's finest."

"Kastri. Is that not the village that sits atop Delphi's former site?"

"It is," Penelope said.

"Surely there is more."

"Well, yes." Penelope stiffened her spine. "The weaver is also the current Pythia of Delphi. The famed Oracle."

Agnes would love this, though Claire failed to imagine what Ashworth would think. Had Penelope told her brother about this woman?

Claire walked beside Penelope to her suite as they discussed the Greek woman's correspondence.

"I had understood the Pythia and her maidens had vanished with Delphi's destruction. Or so it was assumed."

"The Roman emperor Theodosius destroyed the temple, its buildings, and works of art in AD 390," Penelope said. "All of which allegedly ended the Delphic Oracle."

"I have read that," Claire said. "An earthquake added to the devastation, did it not?"

"Yes, yet according to Xanthe, the position of Oracle, along with her attendants, survived down through the centuries. An interesting thought, would you not say? My friend has sent sketches of her weavings, and I am eager to view them in person."

"Has Xanthe spoken of her prophecies?"

"You can see for yourself, if you like." Penelope's eyes shone with eagerness. "Shall I show you her letters?"

The Pythia—she who prophesied the future. Impossible. Yet captivating, too.

They soon stood in Penelope's expansive suite of rooms done up in lovely peaches and greens as Claire read several of the missives.

"My, her written command of English is excellent," Claire said. "The woman seems both educated and knowledgeable, with a spark of humor thrown in."

"She is all that," Penelope said, smoothing the stack of letters beneath her hand.

"And a fine storyteller," Claire said, stirred by the immense stack.

"We have corresponded for years." Penelope pulled a sheaf of paper from a desk drawer. "These represent some of her weavings."

The first was an abstract using the traditional Greek key motif, the second had Athena surrounded by the Fates, but the third was most striking. Arachne, depicted as a spider, hovered in one corner weaving a scene of mother and child below, the mother's expression recalling Rose's whilst holding little Gareth.

"I see why you are drawn to these," Claire said. "How did you meet the Pythia?"

"Shall we sit?" Penelope carried her stack of letters, coughing as she led Claire into her sitting room, arrayed with comfortable furnishings and a welcoming balcony shielded by diaphanous drapes. Once seated, she continued. "Spyros, an old friend of Theseus, has long known my passion for weaving. It was he who introduced me to Xanthe, Greece's premier weaver. Only later in our correspondence, much later, did she reveal herself as the Pythia."

"Like a myth come alive," Claire said. "I had not the opportunity to visit Delphi on my previous trip."

Penelope's eyes widened. "You have been to Greece?"

"I had the privilege of doing so, yes, with the esteemed antiquarian, Louis-François-Sébastien Fauvel," Claire said. "For six weeks last winter."

"You must tell all!"

Claire checked her watch. She must soon go to hunt down that pesky journal, yet the letters' contents captivated her with their detailed descriptions of life in Kastri and her stories with their amusing take on human folly.

Penelope rifled through the envelopes, then drew out a well-worn piece of foolscap. "This, '*Sing, daughter, of the journey to your birthplace, your true homeland.*'" She clutched the missive to her chest. "You see?"

Claire nodded.

"Perhaps I am being gullible." Penelope sighed.

"Perhaps. But what if you are not?"

"You must come with us!"

Her ladyship had read her thoughts. "I would very much like to, but..." She shook her head. "I doubt your brother would agree. Why have I never met you prior to this, not even at dinner?"

Penelope's snort was both indelicate and amusing.

"I did not know you nor your aunt," Penelope said. "Hence my reticence. My coughing and sniffling can irritate guests, so I mostly eat in my room when we have visitors. Now that I have met you, I shall gladly join the meal." Penelope wandered to the French doors that opened on the balcony and pushed wide the curtains. "I suspect I shall like your aunt as well."

"I am glad," Claire said. "Auntie will be a surprise, for she is great fun." Excepting when she veered into outrageous territory. Though she suspected, Penelope would not be bothered...much.

Claire rose. "I am afraid I must find my journal and return to work."

Penelope gave her directions to the small salon.

"I will see you at dinner," Claire said. "It has been a great pleasure meeting you!"

"And you, as well, Claire!"

Using Penelope's directions, Claire soon found the small salon and her elusive journal.

How likable was Ashworth's sister, with her bright intelligence, great enthusiasm, and kind nature. Not to mention the Pythia. Claire would be lying if she were not intrigued by the possibility that the Delphic Oracle still prophesied.

Perhaps she *could* find a way to return to Greece.

THE FOLLOWING DAY, with but three days remaining, she and Agnes slipped from the manor house to head for Lord Ashworth's large ship.

When she'd told her aunt of her flight of fancy—stowing aboard ship—Agnes charged ahead with glee, saying they must scope out the ship for hidden access points.

Oh, my, Auntie was quite serious.

Cullen, sensing her aunt's excitement, cast bright eyes at Claire, and she raked a hand through his wiry fur. "Yes, you can come, too."

Gulls wheeled overhead as they climbed the ramp to the dock, accompanied by the staccato of Cullen's nails. Claire was struck by how much larger the ship appeared up close. The vessel looked like a warship, a small one, admittedly, with several guns mounted on deck and additional gun ports poking from its sides, though she did not know its type. As they neared, a man appeared by the rail.

"Hello," she said, waving. "Might we come aboard?"

The man gave Cullen a long glance. "I am afraid not, ladies. No one may come aboard the *Nemesis* other than the crew and Lord Ashworth."

Agnes leaned close to Claire and whispered. "We must see the layout to determine how to sneak aboard."

This had been a poor idea, but Claire plowed ahead. "We are guests of his lordship. Would he not approve our visit? I am Lady Claire Pheland."

The sailor's eyes widened. Shame on her for using her courtesy title, but in a good cause, she supposed.

"This is my aunt, Miss Agnes Pemberton, and my canine companion is Cullen."

"A moment, m'lady, miss." He spared Cullen another glance, then disappeared.

Minutes later, a second man stood in the same spot wearing what appeared to be an officer's jacket. "Greetings, Lady Claire, Miss Pemberton." He waved them up the ramp.

They hiked their skirts and soon stood on the gently moving deck beside Captain Russell, short and round with an authoritative air.

Russell's gray eyes warmed with pride. "My lady is a sixth-rate frigate, who once carried twenty guns on deck."

"A sixth-rate," Agnes said, nodding.

Whatever that signified. "What does that mean, exactly, Captain?"

"For a warship, she's a small gel, but nimble. Fast and maneuverable."

A good thing, Claire supposed, but small? She peered over the side to the water far, far below.

They toured the ship, Cullen's nails click-clicking, and Claire spotted another smaller ramp near the stern.

"Do you see it?" Agnes said in a low voice, cocking her head toward the ramp as Captain Russell walked on. "I suspect there is an entry point onto the ship from that second ramp, probably used for freight and supplies. A less observable entry point. Do you not think?"

Claire agreed, though the idea of sneaking aboard held less and less appeal, imagining themselves, Cullen, her equipment, their clothing, and their maid. In fact, it was patently absurd.

Yet she enjoyed the tour of the impressive ship with its large captain's cabin, Ashworth's even more expansive. The captain chattered away as they viewed the sailors' bunks, the kitchens, and various other rooms aboard ship, including oars should they be becalmed.

"Do you have enough sailors to use the oars?" Auntie asked.

"Not on this journey, no," the captain said. "But were we to be becalmed and pirates appeared, we have six mounted guns, two on either side of the bow, with one mounted on the forecastle and quarterdeck."

"Impressive," Claire said, knowing little about mounted guns and even less, thankfully, about pirates.

"Under another name," the captain said, "*Nemesis* captured many prizes during the wars. His lordship was fortunate to acquire her. She is a noble lady and well guarded."

Now back on terra firma, Claire said, "Auntie, we cannot stow away."

Agnes made a moue, then sighed. "No, I suppose not. But viewing the ship was enjoyable, was it not? I liked that Captain Russell."

Agnes' eyes were bright as stars, for she liked men of all sorts. Men liked Agnes, too, for even at her age, she was a beauty, one with exceptional wealth. Men also liked that. "He seems a solid fellow."

With a smile and a spark in her eyes, she said, "I do hope so."

. . .

THAT EVENING, dinner was a lively affair with all in attendance, including Lady Penelope. It was obvious Ashworth was pleased his sister had joined them and, for once, discarded his taciturn air for an amiable demeanor, one more lighthearted and humorous.

"I have a joke," Penelope said.

Ashworth rolled his eyes. "Penny has discovered our grandfather's joke book."

Penelope sat up straighter, frowning at her brother. "This is a good one!"

Ashworth rolled his eyes as Penny began to expound.

"*A butcher in Smithfield, lying at the point of death, said to his wife, 'my dear, I am not long for this world, therefore advise you to marry our man John; he's a lusty strong fellow, fit for your business.'*

'*O dear, husband,' said she, 'never let that trouble you, for John and I have agreed upon that matter already.'*"

Ashworth barked a laugh, shaking his head. Agnes found it hilarious, as did Claire, who thrust the linen to her mouth so her guffaw was not audible. Penny grinned, looking immensely pleased.

"Naughty puss," Ashworth said, lips twitching.

Penelope's eyes sparkled, spearing her brother with a warm glance, their affection obvious.

"Our predecessors were a wild bunch," Agnes said.

"What say you to a game of charades?" Penelope said.

Claire had trouble picturing Ashworth enjoying them, but he surprised her by rising, "If you play the piano as well, Pen."

Penelope lowered her eyes as she rose, a smile on her lips. "Of course, brother."

They entered the family salon and took seats, Ashworth beside Claire, whilst he went first. He flashed a grin and began.


"*MY FIRST DOTH AFFLICTION DENOTE, Which my second is destin'd to feel And my whole is the best antidote That affliction to soften and heal.*"

· · ·

Ashworth's sly look gave Claire pause. He was awfully self-satisfied. But she knew the answer. And where the question originated. She was well and truly shocked.

"The first word is 'Woe,'" Claire said.

His teeth gleamed as he leaned forward. "Correct."

"Very good, Claire!" Penny said. "I have not any idea."

Ashworth studied her, and Claire drew it out. "The second..."

"Yes?" he said. "Stumped?"

She offered him a serene expression, then lifted her chin. "The second word is 'Man.' So the word is 'Woman.'"

"Yes!" he said, chuckling.

"I saw the charade in *Emma*." His intense eye contact gave Claire chills. "You have read it, my lord?"

"Indeed I have," he said. "Along with Austen's other works."

Knock her down with a feather.

"*Northanger Abbey* was a particular favorite," he said.

"I introduced Theseus to Austen," Penelope said.

"I am a devotee, as well," Claire said, though still surprised Theseus enjoyed the novels.

He joked. He laughed. And he lured Claire with those flashing green eyes and that devastating smile, complete with a dimple! Who knew? This Ashworth was vexingly appealing.

How absurd. The man was as indifferent to Claire as a woman as he was to her research.

She must convince him to take her to Greece.

Penny had completed a Mozart piece and now sipped a glass of port. Claire leaned a bit closer to Ashworth.

"My lord, I wish to accompany you and Lady Penelope to Greece." There, she'd said it. "How much trouble could I be? Aunt Agnes would come, also, so I would be well chaperoned. I am a quiet lady and will keep to myself as well as being companion to Lady Penelope. Plus, you would have two others to keep watch on the marbles." She smiled.

"I am afraid not, Lady Claire," he said.

Claire wanted to continue, to express how very useful she might be. Yet the pleas stuck in her throat. She had some pride, after all. "I see. As you will."

She would speak with Penelope on the morrow. Perhaps she might convince her brother.

# CHAPTER
# SEVEN

As Theseus prepared for bed, he was in a conundrum. He liked Lady Claire, admired her, in fact, even if she was adept at ruffling his feathers. His involuntary reaction to her request had been a resounding no. Yet he mulled over her offer of companionship to Penny, one he could not provide. His sister's semi-reclusive life included few friends near her age, ones she saw but on rare occasions. She and Claire seemed to get on well, enjoying each other's company.

He scrubbed his face, tired yet eager to be at sea. He moved to his secretary, lifted a quill, and dipped it into the inkpot. For Penny, he would send a messenger to Ravenscroft and Lady Fielding, Claire's mother, asking permission for Claire to join their journey. If they acceded, then the gods help him, so would he.

THE DAY BEFORE THEIR DEPARTURE, Penelope found Theseus in his study poring over lists yet again. The voyage for the sculptures' return had been a massive undertaking, but her brother was up to the challenge.

She stood before his desk. "Theseus."

"One minute, Penelope."

He scribbled a note beside a column of figures, then looked up, his eyes narrowing. "Sit. Sit." He flapped a hand. "You want something."

Penny slipped into the seat opposite his desk. "You can always tell."

He raised a brow. "Out with it."

She coughed and coughed again, then dabbed her lips with her handkerchief. "According to you, the voyage will take ten to thirty days for us to arrive in Piraeus. Then we travel to Delphi, more days passing, not to mention the time it will take arranging the marbles for distribution. I should like a companion. To be specific, I should like Lady Claire to accompany me...us."

Theseus huffed. He had received replies from both Ravenscroft and Lady Fielding, assenting to Claire accompanying them to Greece. Nonetheless, he didn't wish to make this too easy for Penelope. "Let us not forget Miss Agnes. The women will be a bother."

"Lady Claire understands Greek and speaks it passably. She is quiet and reserved."

*Quiet? Reserved?* Not in his estimation. "How could you possibly know that? You have just met her."

"Yes, and I like her quite well." More coughing and a sniffle.

His sister was a beautiful woman, yet her health greatly disturbed him. His secret hope was that the dry air of Greece might be a sort of tonic. He should stop teasing her. Yet seeing her so impassioned and lively made him hesitate. Crossing swords with his sister was fun. "I shall think on this."

PENNY LEANED FORWARD. "We depart tomorrow. Lady Claire and Miss Agnes must have time to pack and apprise her maid of the trip."

"The maid." He threw up his hands. "Yet another woman to account for. Really, Pens, Lady Claire and her retinue will be a bother."

Theo's vehemence surprised Penny, was even somewhat over the top. Yet she had caught a momentary spark in his eye that hinted of pleasure. He was *relishing* their banter, as was she. They hadn't engaged in a verbal duel for years, though once they'd enjoyed them a great deal.

Fascinating. All, she suspected, because of Lady Claire. She discomfited and intrigued Theo, a first for any woman. "What do you fear regarding her ladyship, brother?"

"Fear?" he said in an incredulous voice.

"Well, yes. Lady Claire would be a boon companion for me, and yet you refuse."

"I..." He sat back in his chair and glared.

Her brother was putting her on. He must be. Well, she could dissemble, too. Penny sighed, casting down her eyes. "So very sad if my health took a turn, and I, with no friend to assist me."

When she peered up at him through her lashes, he tried to mask his amusement. He failed.

"If your health took a turn," he said in a sonorous voice. "We would sail home immediately. What are you about?"

A laugh tumbled out. "Other than including Lady Claire and Miss Agnes on our trip? Give over, Theo. You will be off with your men. Is Spyros coming?"

"He is, as is Pantelis," he said.

Spyros was a vivid character, Theo's dear friend from their university days. He'd visited Wolf Court often over the years, and Penny liked him very much, though she had never met Pantelis.

"You did not need a companion before Lady Claire's arrival," Theseus grumbled.

"True," she said. "Yet would she not be a marvelous comrade on our journey? For both of us."

His eyes flashed. "You are relentless."

"One of my finer qualities." Penny winked. "I believe I learned persistence from you."

Theseus was acting out of character, almost...teasing, much like the Theo of their youth before their father ground them both down.

Her brother shuffled some papers, and she gave them a glance. "Why have you a note from Lord Ravenscroft? I see his crest on the stationery."

Of all things, Theseus flushed.

She plucked the foolscap from the desk before he could stop her and read, then stared at him with narrowed eyes, flapping the paper. "This letter gives Lady Claire permission to accompany me to Greece."

He nodded.

"Well?"

His eyes warmed. "You are not the only one who thought her ladyship would make you a good companion for the voyage."

"Why, you beast!" She tossed the letter at him and laughed. "You did all this just to tease me!"

He leaned back in his chair, tented his hands, and grinned.

CLAIRE WAS bent over her microscope. Twenty-four hours. She stared at the remaining marbles, particularly the bust of Herodotus, the man Cicero called the father of history, Thalia, a small frieze of an old man, and the Greek herm of Aspasia.

She tilted her head. For some reason, Aspasia looked...different. Claire approached the herm, which stood about five feet tall, its pillar-like form topped with Aspasia's bust, her name inscribed on its base.

Close up, this piece was not the same as the one she had first seen, this one an obvious Roman copy. Damn. She'd been saving Aspasia for last, the Greek Aspasia.

Where had the original gone? Hadn't Ashworth said it was remaining here? Or had she fantasized those words?

How very odd and irrelevant. She had a single day to convince

Ashworth to take them along, which meant leaving the marbles room to peck him yet again.

He had been battered by demands, suggesting that was a poor way to go about obtaining his agreement. She hadn't enough money to bribe him, which mattered little. The man had plenty of pounds sterling himself. Nor could she offer to translate. Well, she could offer, but Ashworth spoke Greek far better than she. She could sketch but failed to see any worth in that.

A sexual lure, perhaps? Claire had never done so.

A shiver tingled her spine. Not even for her research would she so debase herself or him.

Tears would accomplish nothing. They never did. In truth, she could not call them on command.

A tap on her shoulder, and she whirled to see a grinning Penelope. "I did not hear you enter."

"You were deep in thought," Penelope said with a broad smile. "I spoke with Theseus, and he has agreed you and your aunt may accompany us to Greece. Cullen, of course, too."

"Truly?" Agnes rose from her chair.

Claire blinked, dumbfounded.

"My brother is a mystery," Penelope said. "I suspect he was at war with himself about your joining us. Yet he wrote to Lord Ravenscroft and your mother, who gave their permission."

How peculiar. Then, reality set in. She was going to Greece! Oh, my! Though Mama and Rhys knew of her departure, she must write the family immediately, as they must wish for word directly from her. She hoped they would understand. Of course they would. They applauded her determination to prove her thesis, though she suspected they would natter on about her journey, especially Rose, who could be quite mother-hennish.

Penelope's laugh pealed. "Oh, my dear Claire! You look utterly baffled."

"Well, I..." Claire smiled. "In truth, I am over the moon."

"As am I!" Agnes said with a jaunty wave of her hand, then

resumed her seat, lifted her embroidery, and returned to her stitching.

Later, Claire continued to work when a draft brushed her neck. She shivered. The room looked sad and empty, most of the marbles packed and taken aboard the ship. Thalia remained. Next, she would examine Thalia, the Muse of Comedy, though she would question Ashworth about the Roman Aspasia.

She walked to the bust. Ashworth's father had discovered in Epidaurus, apparently broken off from what must have been a full statue, the remainder never found.

The earl flung open the doors when Claire was deep in thought, several men bustling inside to pack more marbles.

She slipped off her stool, approached him, and opened her mouth.

He held up a hand. "The answer is no."

"But Aunt Agnes and I are coming," she said, a pinch of panic in her voice. "Penelope said so."

"You are, indeed, but if you are about to ask for anything else, you cannot have it!"

"Good heavens, you are in a tizzy."

"A...*tizzy*? Men do not have tizzies!"

She bit her cheek so as not to laugh at his expression. "A conniption, then?"

"Harrumph!"

"You are foxed! You must be!"

He tried. Claire would give him that as his face tightened, but his lips soon wobbled into a smile, and then...his laugh boomed. "I find you an amusing woman."

It was Claire's turn to harrumph. "And I find you disrespectful. You do not value my work at all!"

"You are wrong," he bit out. "I do, indeed, but I cannot take precious time out to fiddle with someone's hobby."

*Fiddle! Hobby!* "Why you—"

Ashworth held up his hands, then took a deep breath, his chest billowing. "I *do* apologize, Lady Claire. In truth, I do not deem your serious work a hobby. In fact, I find your pursuit quite profound. I just..." He sighed.

His complimentary words flushed her with pleasure—he found her work *profound.* As she returned to her worktable, a chip beneath the microscope, she remained shocked by his apology as well.

"Do you wish to see?" The chip was an especially pleasing yellow, a color she had found in Greece as well. The ancients must have liked it a great deal.

"Not now." Lord Ashworth towered over her. "Are we settled?"

"Do not loom, good sir, for you are blocking my light."

He chuffed. "Are we *settled*?"

She smiled pleasantly. "It seems we are."


Theseus was on a tear as he assisted with loading the marbles. After that discomforting conversation with Lady Claire, he'd sought physical activity to keep his swirling emotions at bay.

*Fanciful woman!*

A workman wobbled a crated marble, and he barked, "Careful!" Each piece might be well-packed with straw and rags, but dropping a crate would prove disastrous.

Today, the marbles' room would be cleared out, but for a few small busts for Lady Claire's study until they were transported to the ship this evening.

Were she to acquire numerous samples of paint, she imagined the Society of Antiquaries would accept her thesis.

Not in his lifetime. Those hidebound men saw only what they wished, a stagnant viewpoint. Nonetheless, they were fixed on the marbles' purity of form and would be immovable.

Lady Claire stood not a prayer, no matter which respected authority she cited. Nonetheless, he admired her hope and determination.

He glanced at a crate being heaved onto the deck. Oh, how Theseus wanted these pieces gone. Once done, he could resume his antiquarian studies without the burden of Hellas' heritage languishing at Wolf Court.

He tried picturing the ladies aboard ship and could not. Would they all become seasick? Or bored? Would they complain at the harsh conditions, so different from the comfortable manor? And Penelope —he worried for her health. She'd always been a plucky thing, her spirit far more robust than her flesh. Though he did not know the particulars, he was aware of her various pursuits when he was off on digs.

Over the years, he should have spent more time with Penny. Guilt rode him hard.

Penelope would be fine. She would take to the sea and its bracing air well.

Yet his concern persisted. *Bah!* He was overthinking things.

He must forget the women, for he had much to do.


CLAIRE PACKED for Greece like a madwoman. Her maid had refused to accompany them, as did Penny's. In truth, all three could all act as each other's maids without issue.

Cullen always sensed her emotions, and her huge dog bounced around like a six-month-old pup.

A knock at the door made Claire tremble. Perhaps it was Ashworth, giving them the heave-ho. Had he changed his mind?

He would not do that. Would he?

Oh, why did he tie her in knots? No man had prompted her anxiety or anticipation as Lord Theseus Ashworth had done. Nor had any other induced tingles or sighs as that damned earl managed to do.

Except for James Strathmore. Claire was eight, and James was a stable boy at Fielding, where they had recently arrived after Mama's remarriage. James found Claire ridiculous, which now made her smile, for he was but ten. At the time, she had been crushed.

James had been tall and dark and brooding as well...for a ten-year-old. But he'd also been bright and wonderful with animals, at least to her eight-year-old perception.

Other than James, not a single man had attracted her, which was rather sad if she thought on it. Since her come out, several had attempted to court her. Though at the time, their little family in dire straits, both Mama and Lottie had approved when Claire denied them all. They were bland men with acceptable address, dull minds, and no curiosity for any subject other than hunting, horses, or their clubs.

One was a marquess, another a duke's younger son, and the third an unofficial scion of the prince himself, a foolish young man with little to address.

And yet Theseus Ashworth compelled her. She admired his commitment to his undertaking and the great care he'd taken with Lottie after her tumble from a horse. He was easy to look upon, too, Claire finding her occasional desire to touch him unnerving. Her fingers often itched with the urge to brush an unruly lock from his forehead or to straighten a collar.

In her heart of hearts, she wished Ashworth would show some sign that he found her appealing or interesting. And yet he never did with word nor action.

A rap on her bedroom door, and Claire took a deep breath, smoothed her hair, and swung it wide.

Lady Penelope stood frothing with excitement.

"Penelope? What is it?"

"Theseus is hauling crates with the men." Penelope clutched her hands tight. "We are almost ready to depart!"

Agnes joined them, and they found Ashworth carrying boxes onto the frigate along with the other men, his loose linen shirt flapping in the breeze above his belt. Beneath, he wore pantaloons and top boots. No waistcoat or jacket. Not even a cravat.

*Oh, my!* God's bones, why did she react this way? Yes, he looked dashing, much as a pirate would, but his dress was improper. Not that she cared one whit.

Claire smiled inwardly, the devil urging her on. "Lord Ashworth, are you aware that you are improperly dressed for mixed company?"

He jerked, almost tumbling the massive crate he held, then set it down with care.

"Does it disturb you?" he asked in all seriousness.

"As a lady," she replied in a plummy voice when she wished to giggle. She straightened, hands clasped. "I felt it imperative to remind you of your station."

"Ha! My station." He caught she was bamming him and tossed her a toothy grin. "My estate, my rules."

If that wasn't piratical, she didn't know what was. She raised a brow. "As you will." Claire nodded, trying for a sage look, but a giggle slipped out.

He burst out laughing, as did Penny and Agnes.

She waited until their laughter eased to speak. "I again wish to thank you for your concession and your kindness, my lord. Penny and I shall rub along well."

"I see you are on a first-name basis with my darling Penny. As you may have gleaned, she is quite clever and can be a rascal."

Claire dipped her head so he'd not see her smile. Penelope was a rascal, and Claire adored it.

Agnes waved a hand, her bright-eyed look engaging all of them. "Our quest is an exciting one, and I must finish my packing! Bye-the-bye, I have a monkey, Arthur. He is simply adorable and a well-behaved fellow. I thought I might..." She peered up at Ashworth, whose eyes widened with horror.

Agnes laughed. "Just a tease, my lord. Arthur abides at home and is in good hands."

"Might I assist you, Miss Agnes?"

"Delighted!"

The two waltzed off arm in arm. They did that on purpose, leaving Claire alone with Ashworth, who removed a kerchief from his back pocket and wiped the sweat from his face.

CHAPTER

# EIGHT

Claire's nerves tingled. For no reason whatsoever. So frustrating.

"I confess I am rather sick of all this 'yes, my lord' and 'no, my lord.'" Ashworth said, wearing a dour expression. "In consideration of our sea voyage ahead, do call me Theseus or Ashworth, and I shall call you Claire or Pheland, if that is acceptable."

She started, then mulled over his suggestion. "All right... Ashworth." She snapped him a nod.

His chuckle was deep and long. "As you will."

A much-welcomed ray of sun peeked through the clouds.

"We shall soon have full-on sunshine, which I shall welcome," he said. "Shall we sit, my la...Claire?"

He led her on deck to a spot set with couches and a table, shaded by a canvas awning. They took opposite seats.

"In Greece, the air is dry," Theseus said. "The sun, pervasive. Quite different from England, as I suspect you know. This shade will prove useful on our voyage."

"I remember the heat well," Claire said. "I hope, as the air is dry and the climate so different, Penelope's cough and sniffles will ease."

"That is my hope, too."

"How long to reach Greece?" Claire said. "My previous journey took us more than a month, though we made stops. I was also told our ship was not particularly fast."

"My *Nemesis* is," Ashworth said. "She has the best canvas and the finest rigging to be found. I expect we shall take between ten and thirty days to reach Piraeus."

"Ten days!" Claire said. "That does not seem possible."

"It is, though I doubt we shall achieve that. Her top speed is fourteen knots, but not sustainable for long. Much depends on the wind, the weather, and the seas. We have a forty-man crew, which includes many former Navy sailors. Is there anything you wish to discuss?"

Claire's mind went blank. "I..." He stared at her with an intensity that felt like a mighty weight, which somehow added a corresponding prickle to her flesh. A perplexing response.

"No?" he said, cocking his head much as Penelope did.

She fussed with her skirt. "The sun seems to have addled my brain."

"The sun, is it?" His smile was laced with neither irony nor satire but was genuine, his eyes warm. Claire was spellbound.

A gull landed nearby and began pecking at the deck, lifting Claire from her musings. She rose. "I shall leave you to it, for I have much to prepare for tomorrow's departure."

He stood as well, shook his head as if he was about to ask her something, but held his words. He winged out an arm and escorted her down the ramp.

"Another time, perhaps?" he said.

"Another time?" Claire said, wishing she could peer into his mind, his thoughts.

"Yes," Ashworth said. "We shall have days at sea and much time on our hands for discussion."

Bewildered and... all right, she was a bit befuddled. But just a bit.

Ashworth accompanied her to dry land, then returned to hauling crates onto the ship.

Two busts remained in the marbles room—Aspasia's reproduction and Herodotus—yet Claire forced herself to walk the ocean path for exercise. A plume of dust wafted skyward, someone hurrying down the manor's drive. She hastened toward the courtyard, her slippers sliding a bit on the sand.

A magnificent black gelding cantered into view, a colorful man in a bronze topcoat and green hat on his back. Beside him rode a woman in a stylish blue habit atop a stunning gray, followed by a woman in black bouncing atop a raw-boned bay as if she'd never been on a horse before. The lady's maid, she presumed.

Claire wished Rose could see the horses, for the first two were beauties. The black might be a Friesian or something similar, not nearly as good as her sister on breeds. The gray looked to be a thoroughbred, a dainty mare, while the bay was an angular mystery.

Claire reached the courtyard as the man leapt from his steed in a theatrical move, flinging the reins to a stableboy, then proceeded to assist the woman in blue from the saddle. She slid into his arms with a saucy grin, while a footman assisted the dour woman in black. That they had not come in a carriage was unusual, especially given their maid's poor equestrian skills.

Cullen stepped in front of Claire, his stance one of alert protection.

"Hello, hello!" said the fellow as he approached wearing a jaunty smile, the woman on his arm. She was lovely, with cornflower-blue eyes and shiny brown curls wreathing her head beneath her smart bonnet. The maid trailed them, her striking features and mocha skin hinting at some eastern or possibly Italian heritage.

Cullen growled.

As the trio drew close, she found the man's features terribly English, with a long aristocratic nose, brown eyes much darker than Claire's, and blond curly hair that bounced beneath his top hat. Attractive in a rather jaunty way,

"Good day, sir, ma'am," Claire said with a curtsy.

They stopped six feet away, perhaps because Cullen's teeth were in evidence.

"Good day to you, Lady Claire." He executed an elaborate bow while the lady curtsied.

"I am afraid, good sir, ma'am, I do not recall our introduction."

He chuckled, his smile widening. "We were not formally introduced, but I observed your speech at the Society of Antiquarians."

Claire damned the blush tinting her cheeks, unable to help wonder if he had jeered or laughed. Or perhaps he'd thrown that rotted apple at her.

"May I introduce us? I am Lord Alfred Garland, Viscount Garland, an old friend of Lord Ashworth's, and my wife, Lady Frances Garland. Had Ashworth not spoken up, I surely would have, for your treatment by the antiquarians was unconscionable."

Claire nodded before resting a hand on Cullen's head. "This is Cullen, my friend." She whispered in her pup's ear, "Steady."

The change was instantaneous, for Cullen became a friendly, happy fellow. Nonetheless, he could rip out a throat in fewer than six seconds. His tail thumped, his mouth open, tongue lolling.

"Might I pet him?" Lady Garland said.

"You may."

Her ladyship leaned down and proceeded to lavish attention on Cullen, the pup lapping up the adulation.

"We must be off to Ashworth," he said as her ladyship rose. "A pleasure to meet you in person, Lady Claire."

"Yes, a very great pleasure," Lady Garland echoed with enthusiasm.

Claire's curious thoughts escaped. "By the by, are you here about the sculptures?"

"Indeed, we are," Garland said.

"We cannot wait to see them!" Lady Garland clasped her hands, her eyes animated. "Particularly the herm of Aspasia, sculpted by the great Phidias! She was the most famous woman in Greece and Pericles' partner and advisor, you know."

"I did, in fact," Claire said, pleased with the woman's enthusiasm. She did not mention few of the sculptures remained or that the remaining Aspasia was Roman. Ashworth would explain. "The bust is splendid, though I am afraid a lower portion of the herm is damaged."

Lady Garland waved a hand. "That matters little, for it is her face I wish to see."

Garland chuckled. "I do not doubt that we are two of a throng to see the famed Ashworth sculptures."

"Indeed, sir, that is true." Claire found them overly keen. "Are you an antiquarian, Lord Garland?"

He gave her a self-deprecating smile. "I dabble." Garland laughed, tipped his hat, and proceeded toward the manor, the maid following.

Hard picturing Ashworth with such a jocular friend.


Theseus had dozens of tasks to accomplish when Lord Garland and, he presumed, his lady wife appeared at the front door, along with a stoic-faced woman, dark-haired and strong-boned. Most likely the maid, though she vaguely reminded him of someone. Garland, an old acquaintance, tossed his hat to Sims, Lady Garland blushing. Interesting. The man's dramatics hadn't changed since Harrow.

Introductions were made, and Garland approached Theseus. "How goes it, old man?" He slapped a hand on Theseus' shoulder.

Garland acted as if they were chums, which was untrue, for Theseus found the man suffocating.

"Sorry to intrude," Garland said. "We are salivating to see your collection before you sail it away over the sea."

Theseus nodded, leaving unsaid an appointment would have been the proper course of action. He wished Penny or Claire were around to buffer Garland's annoying fervor.

"Of course," Theseus said, not offering tea or refreshments, which would have been proper. He wanted them gone. "Do understand that most are packed for shipment. My father's remaining two will soon be aboard ship."

"You must have some of your own, do you not?" Lady Garland said. "Did you not acquire those as your father did his?"

"You mean buying from the Ottomans?" he said. "I did not." These people did not need to know more.

A footman opened the doors to the sculpture room, and they preceded him inside amidst the Garland's oohs and aahs.

Her ladyship's maid arrowed to the herm of Aspasia, and he led Lady Garland to the bust. Both stared at it with grave intensity, oohing and ahhing.

They might exclaim over Aspasia but failed to truly see her, as he had instructed the original returned to his suite, replacing it with the Roman copy, which would also remain at Wolf Court. He had wished Claire to examine the Greek original but had no intention of showing the Garlands. It soon became obvious the Garlands were unable to discern a Greek from a Roman sculpture. Every serious Hellas antiquarian would spot the difference.

He glanced at Garland, who was focused on Herodotus, exclaiming as he examined the artifact.

"What is the purpose of this?" Garland asked, waving his hand across Herodotus' large rectangle of stone. "What is it called?"

Theseus ambled over. Garland had been a boy who skimmed the surface of many things rather than delving deep with a few. Given his lack of knowledge about the object, his nature appeared unchanged.

"This is a stele," Theseus said. "Most often made of stone, though occasionally of wood, they are crafted for many reasons—a funerary memorial, government notices, property lines, and memorials to battle. Funerary stelai are the most common."

Garland's languid eyes and unfocused air evidenced the man's boredom, making it apparent he knew little about ancient sculpture and cared even less. Theseus continued. Perhaps Garland would fall asleep standing.

"The stele's surface often contains text, though this one does not, and frequently exhibits ornamentation such as these laurel leaves. Stele can be inscribed or carved in relief."

The man's eyes drooped, and he leaned heavily on the marble. Garland really did look as if he might drop off.

"Garland!" his wife said.

He started, then blinked rapidly. "Yes, love?"

"Do come see Aspasia!"

Garland trotted off, and Theseus was tempted to toss them out. But, damn, how could he? The man was an old school acquaintance. It was not the done thing. Theseus prayed they would soon depart.

Naturally, his prayers went unanswered.

Theseus' planned departure the following day was aborted through no fault of the crew, nor the women's, either. First, Cullen had gone missing and, blessed be, was found uninjured, though he'd tangled himself in a poacher's snare. Theseus had grown damnably fond of the beast, not that he'd inform Cullen's owner of that fact.

Once the pup was sorted, the second issue reared its head. When the footman had moved the Greek Aspasia, he had failed to place her in Theseus' suite, interrupted by the need to accompany Miss Agnes to the village. Nor could the man recall where he'd left the sculpture.

Though Aspasia would remain at home, they would not sail until she was found. All searched, with Penny finding her in the orangery, of all places.

Once discovered and settled, they sailed for Greece a day after intended. A minor change.

Now, Theseus stood by the ship's rail, enjoying the sea's rhythm beneath his feet. The gulls were ubiquitous, while Atlantic gannets and bonxies would give way to grebes and herons once they passed through the Strait of Gibraltar. It felt good. Better than good.

His dream would soon be realized, his heart lightened. The

endless months of preparation had wearied him, as had the annoying attempts at bribery by various parties.

Money, prestige, position, even land—all had been on the table —were he to give the sculptures to the British Museum.

Those lures mattered little, for his years in Greece had built and strengthened his connection to her people and their country. Having lived beneath oppressors for centuries, they nonetheless retained great pride in their identities and heritage. These pieces were sculpted by Hellas' hands millennia ago. Each deserved to return home, even if he must do so in secret, for the Ottomans fiercely opposed their repatriation.

His Greek friend, Dionysus, had assured him they could moor in Piraeus, near Athens, with little issue, as he'd labeled the sculptures as spirits, cloth, and other sundries, the key on a list in his cabin.

Sighing, he leaned against the deck rail. He would never again see Hera, nor his namesake, nor any of the dozens of carvings, ever-present during his childhood and youth. All old friends—a startling thought, for he'd never imagined them as such. He shook his head. How absurdly maudlin.

Claire climbed on deck, looking daisy fresh. Surprising, as she'd spent hours in the hold, opening, examining, and resealing a particular marble at a time. A tenacious woman, her ladyship.

Her pursuit was earnest, her mind agile and bright. Theseus recalled when she had "discovered" a Renaissance bust he had planted in the marbles room ages past, a joke for Spyros. It was a fine tease for her as well, and he smiled, recalling the incident.

The bust was allegedly from Hellas' Archaic era, the head of a *kouros* wearing a slight smile and braided hair, eyes closed, quite typical of that period. The jagged neck, a deliberate affectation by the sculptor, was crafted as if it had detached from a larger Greek monument.

In truth, it was an obvious Italian copy dating to the fifteenth century, apparent due to the refined carving techniques, though the smile and chin bore tentative strokes. No Greek sculptor would score the stone with such hesitation.

That morning, upon his return from riding, a footman said Lady Claire requested him in the marbles room. He entered with caution, Claire not wont to ask for his presence. Upon seeing him, Lady Claire strode over.

"Lord Ashworth," she said. "I am in transports. Come, you must see."

He stared at her with skepticism but followed until they stood before the bust of the *kouros*, the Renaissance one.

"I must say..." Claire rested a hand on the bust's head. "This is the most exquisite piece in all your collection of Greek statuary. The execution... The expression... The grace..." She had droned on about the Archaic period and where the *kouros* fit in its timeline. "It is beyond all I ever imagined."

That was when she had peeked up at him, her eyes filled with devilry. He was amused as well and had trouble hiding his smile.

"You are about to burst into laughter." She batted her lashes, all innocence. "Why, may I ask?"

He peered down at her, solemn-faced, though his lips twitched. "That was quite a performance, my lady."

"Performance?"

Oh, the artlessness in that gaze, those plush lips pursed in fake confusion.

"Quite." He chuckled. He couldn't help it. "You obviously recognized the bust as not being Greek but rather a Renaissance reproduction. It is a trifle I picked up in Epidaurus at a market stall. Your act was obvious payback for what you imagined as my perfidy in testing you."

Lady Claire's chin jutted out. "It was a poor attempt, my lord."

"I am unsurprised you saw through the deceit." His eyes blazed. "In truth, the bust here was an accident, a joke on my friend, Spyros, which I forgot to have removed. I shall see you at dinner, my lady."

He had waltzed out, the bust clutched beneath his arm. How he had enjoyed their exchange that day.

Now, he strode to her ladyship, her hands clasped about the railing.

"How goes your work?" he said.

She looked up, her eyes reddened, but she smiled. "Hello, Ashworth. I was absorbed."

"What is wrong?" he said. "Have you been weeping?"

She shook her head, eyes blinking rapidly, though aimed at the cresting waves. "I just finished examining a grave stele. Silly, I know, but they tend to get me emotional and contemplative as I imagine the person they represent."

"They *are* grave markers after all."

"I know. Yet they are so poignant. Those souls honored with stelai were loved, admired, and esteemed. The children are the worst."

A soft heart, his Lady Claire. And why in hell had he thought "his" when she was no more his than the moon was? Nor would he wish her to be.

He caught a glimpse of wings. "Look there," he said, pointing. "That is Eleonora's falcon, a mostly Mediterranean bird. This one is male."

"I have never heard of them. He is beautiful."

"They live like seabirds and are said to be messengers between the earthly and spiritual realms, as well as guardians who watch over the land and its inhabitants."

"A fine legend," Claire said. "Let us hope they guard us throughout our journey."

A lookout from the crow's nest hollered, "Ship ahoy off the port stern!"

Theseus raised his spyglass. A mail packet cut through the waves, headed their way.

. . .

THE MAIL PACKET had been the most exciting event in the first two weeks of their journey. That, and the two-day blow they'd just weathered. Theseus climbed to the deck to see Claire dozing in a chair beneath the awning, surprised to see her.

"How fare you, Claire?" He ducked beneath the awning to take a seat.

"Remarkably well after all that tossing and heaving," she said.

"Would you care to take a turn around the deck?"

"Very much so."

Claire rose, as did Cullen, and she took Theseus' extended arm. "Sadly, Penelope is not well, her stomach in a roil. Agnes is another wounded, though not from *mal de mer*."

"Miss Agnes? What has happened?"

A gentle gust sent a cooling breeze, the sun ablaze as they sped through the waves, the scents of the sea making her inhale deeply.

"I am afraid Auntie fell with the tossing of the ship," she said. "You and the captain were busy keeping us afloat, so I sent for the surgeon." She rubbed her forehead. "She had broken her forearm."

He paused in their perambulation. "Gods above!"

Claire patted his arm. "Your man set her arm to rights and put her in a sling. She is in pain, but we have Chuan Xiong for that."

"Never heard of it." He moved on, and they continued around the deck.

"A Chinese potion Auntie introduced me to ages ago. It is quite effective for alleviating pain and improving blood circulation. She is resting comfortably, so I thought to get some air."

He sighed. "I am sorry to hear about your aunt, an amusing woman, though I suspect she is not at the moment."

"In that you would be wrong, for her spirits, once the pain eased, are in fine form. It is Penny who is most low, angered at herself for being sick."

"Penelope should not be. Many a hardy man becomes bilious during a storm. Be sure she takes plenty of liquids."

"I knew this from Patrick and have done so."

"You most certainly have your sea legs."

She smiled, her eyes closed as if recalling a sweet memory. "I feel a bit guilty about that. It is all due to Patrick. He and Lottie purchased a yacht, small and swift, and our family takes much enjoyment from it." She shrugged. "I took to sailing and found I like being at sea."

"As do I."

CHAPTER

# NINE

They were silent for long moments, enjoying the breeze, the roll of the ship, and the caws of the seabirds accompanying them. Every so often, Cullen would dash after a landing seagull, much to Claire's amusement.

Aboard ship, Claire enjoyed this different Ashworth, one less driven and almost—dare she say it?—relaxed. Not easy-going, per se, but much of the tension enveloping him at Wolf Court had dissipated at sea.

A bird swooped across the ship's stern. "Beautiful hawk, is it not?"

"Beautiful, yes. A hawk? No. That is a short-toed snake eagle."

Claire raised a brow. "A what?"

"They are a medium-sized bird of prey from the family *Accipitridae*. Gmelin described them in his revision of Linnaeus's work. Handsome, are they not?"

"Indeed, yes. You know much about birds. Is that because you are a falconer?"

He nodded. "I am most knowledgeable about birds of prey,

though all winged creatures intrigue me. I do use falcons and hawks to hunt, but otherwise am not much into hunting as sport."

"Would you explain?"

"I am a fine shot, a decent bowman, and acceptable in hand-to-hand, though none of those pastimes intrigue me. Hunting large game does not, either, with the exception of flying my birds."

"What of fox hunts?"

"I do not care for them. The sport strikes me as patently unfair."

"I am of the same mind," Claire said with enthusiasm. "Nor do my brothers by marriage, though we all love a good gallop."

"That, I do love." He laughed. "I fly my birds for the sheer joy of observing them."

How lovely. Yes, she could imagine that joy. "Perhaps you picture yourself in flight, too."

Theseus looked at her, his glance quizzical. "Perhaps I do."

Claire could almost envision herself in flight, too. Almost. "I should like to hear more about the birds you fly."

"Both peregrines and goshawks have different attributes, the peregrine an amenable, high-flying bird, whilst goshawks are facile in wooded places, though they tend to fierce likes and dislikes and quirks." A smile tipped his lips. "Would you like to be a falconer, Claire?"

"I believe I would." She thought for a moment, for she had seen Theseus wearing his regalia for hawking. "I saw you carrying a bird on your forearm. What does that feel like?"

"The birds are light, incredibly so. My favorite bird, goshawks, are a challenge to train. Demanding creatures all, when they pursue prey, they fully commit." He curled a fist. "They are fearless."

Challenging. Demanding. Fearless. Much as Theseus himself, for he had fully committed to his "prey," returning the sculptures. He also appeared unstoppable. "I see the appeal. How do you raise them to fly for you?"

"My goshawks were bred and raised in captivity."

"They are no longer wild ones in England, as I understand," Claire said.

"That is true. I hand-feed the chicks, and at around five to eight weeks, as they begin to fly, they see me as a source of food. Gradually, they grow in confidence, and soon we introduce a creance, a long cord attached to the bird's leash, which prevents escape whilst training. I do not tend to hood my hawks."

"Why not? At the manor, I saw you with a hooded hawk on your arm."

The breeze sharpened, and they returned to the lounge area and sat, Theseus leaning forward. "Might I offer you some refreshment?"

"Please do!"

He poured them glasses of wine from the carafe and continued. "You must have seen my hooded kestrel. We found her injured in the wild, so she was not imprinted. She became a fine bird, but I prefer the calmer visual bond I have with those I have raised by my hand."

"It sounds terribly complicated." A pause. "I like that, the complexity."

"Do you? I suspect, given your attention to detail and patience, you may become a fine falconer."

Claire imagined raising her arm and releasing the bird. A thrill. "What is most key in flying your birds?"

"Weight." He added more wine to her glass. "As they grow, we learn each bird's proper flying weight. If too heavy, their hunger is assuaged and they have no motive to return to the falconer. If they are too light, having not fed enough, they can become unwell or aggressive. We weigh them daily and chart their weight for optimum flight. What set your curiosity afire?"

Claire scritched Cullen behind one ear. "I have seen birds flown once or twice, and it always stirs me, makes my heart beat faster."

His crow's feet tightened with his smile. "It is all that and more."

"You mentioned Ares," she said. "He is your favorite, yes?"

He bellowed a laugh. "He was the most ornery, contrary chick. Yet as he settled, we have become fast friends."

"Indeed?"

"He is smart. So smart. And loyal near to a fault, much like Cullen." Cullen's tongue lolled, as if pleased by Ashworth's compliment.

She observed man and dog with fondness. "I often prefer Cullen to people, I confess. My mare, the dogs at Woodbine, even Percy the parrot delight me. I prefer them, too. Oh, not over my family, of course! I adore them all."

Theseus shook his head, then cocked it. "I must agree about animals and people—the creatures are straightforward, loving, and true. They do not exhibit humans' duplicitous nature."

He leaned his forearms on his thighs, hands clasped.

Claire agreed. "People would be wise to heed their more forthright animal companions."

"I suspect not many hold our view. We all see the world a bit differently, do we not?"

"I think so," she said. "Though there is commonality, of course. Shared feelings and experiences."

The sun's low rays warmed Claire's face.

Theseus paused, a slow smile lifting his lips. "You have turned golden, m'lady."

Claire dropped her eyes, embarrassed by the heat in her cheeks.

"You are a curious person," he said. "Oft surprising me."

"Curious strange?" she said. "Or curious nosy?"

His soft chuckle was warm. "Dare I say...both?"

She bit her lip so as not to bark a laugh, a very unladylike response. But his quip begged a smile. "How so?"

"Now you are simply fomenting trouble."

*How could she resist?* She *was* an odd woman. Claire knew it, as did everyone else, for her perspective and passions were unlike most ladies of the *ton* or, in truth, any other ladies she could imagine. Her pastime of knife throwing was another oddity. Did Theseus know of it? She peeked up, her grin widening.

He leaned forward. "When you arrived, you noted Aspasia's herm."

Claire went still, as if any movement would break the moment. "I did."

"You examined her?"

"A cursory one."

"Did you find paint?"

She frowned. Where was he going with this? "I did not. I was saving her for last. A hopeful treat."

"I had her placed in the room for you, but she was never intended for our journey."

"You knew the Garlands would come?"

He shrugged. "No. But when I learned of Sir Joseph's visit, I thought it prudent to switch the two."

"A wise move, indeed," Claire said. "Where did your father find the Greek Aspasia?"

"He did not. She was loaned to me years ago by Athenians of the *Philikí Etaireía.*"

"The friendly brotherhood?"

As he leaned forward, he clenched his fists before him, his face tightening. "A group who intends to wrest control of Greece from the Ottomans."

"Why did they give you the herm?"

"For its protection until Greece is free. Aspasia is unique. No one other than myself, the Greeks, and you knows of her existence. Several Roman copies abound, as does at least one Renaissance one. The Athenians claim the herm sacred to Athens." His eyes flashed. "Tell no one."

"I shan't."

"I confess, I cursed the day the Garlands arrived."

"No worries there," Claire said. "Lord Garland was quite uninformed, though her ladyship fixated on that particular bust, albeit the Roman one."

Theseus rolled his eyes, which made her chuckle.

"She intimated," he said. "I do not make this up—she implied she was Aspasia reborn."

"Oh, come now."

"Perhaps I misheard, but she is infatuated with the woman and imagined it the true Greek Aspasia carved by Phidias. Lady Garland is no antiquarian. Unlike yourself."

All of which made Claire warm in the vicinity of her heart.

A SECOND MAIL ship came and went, having delivered a single letter to Ashworth, the ship waiting for his swift reply before its departure. Claire could not help but be curious about the letter but kept her silence. Excepting for that one bad storm—the most excitement they'd had on the voyage—all had gone as planned, with balmy days and pleasant nights upon reaching the Mediterranean Sea. Penny's sickness had abated, and even with her injured arm, Agnes' stomach was well. In a few days, they would make land.

That was until they were becalmed, a frustrating, boring experience, to say the least, as all were frothing to reach Greece.

Penny appeared on deck with enthusiasm, her eyes bright. Auntie followed, and the only sign of Agnes' pain was her complexion, paler than usual. But she was old. Well, older than Mama, Claire worried.

Agnes smiled as she approached the rail to look out to sea, her peach-turbaned head and green walking dress accented in a military style complete with epaulets.

"Flat as a pancake," Agnes said. "And stifling."

"That it is, Auntie."

Penny was simply bursting with excitement. "Might we give throwing a try today? We have not done so since we were last becalmed. Theseus is taking a rest in his cabin below. What say you?"

Claire loved teaching Penny to throw knives, though she questioned how Theseus would react to his sister's latest enthusiasm, not to mention Claire's instruction. "Let me retrieve my knife roll."

In minutes Claire returned. "Shall we head to the stern? Our target awaits. Will you join us, Auntie?"

Agnes shook her head and walked to a lounge chair beneath the canopy. "Much as that would delight me, I fear I must rest up for our arrival in Piraeus."

She kissed her aunt's cheek, and they trekked toward the stern. "You seem to be grasping the process well."

"I hope so," Penny said. "We shall see how I do today."

Once up the ladder to the stern deck, Claire set her knife roll on one of the stairs. The precious leather was a gift from Mama on her fifteenth birthday, with its clever handle and slots for her dozen knives. The gift had been a secret, for Lord Fielding would have found her pastime horrifying. The man himself had been horror personified.

After these many years, the roll was well worn, smooth and supple, and Claire took pride in its aged appearance. She unrolled the case, took a knife for herself, handing another to Penelope.

"I have tacked a paper square with my bullseye sketch to that cushion. See? It is again set at ten feet, so remember you only want one rotation in your throw."

Penny nodded. "When I throw farther, I shall need more rotations, correct?"

"Yes. Let us wait to be on land before we attempt further. Your hammer grip works well, so use that. Remember your balance."

Penelope nodded and squared her shoulders to the target. Good. She locked her wrist, and Claire hoped she wouldn't flick it as she released the knife, something Penelope tended to do, as did Lottie.

Penny raised the knife.

"Elbow to ear, remember?" Claire said.

"Got it!"

The deck was steady, almost like being on land, an odd feeling after weeks of the rolling deck.

Penny threw, pointing her hand at the target after release, as she'd been taught.

The knife landed well, embedded near the target's center.

"Good momentum!" Claire said. "Remember, the more contact on the knife, the slower the rotation. The less contact, the faster the rotation. Well done!"

"What is well done?" came a baritone both knew as Theseus climbed onto the stern deck.

*Damn.* Ah, well, their secret was out.

She and Penny froze. Perhaps aiming for invisibility?

Theseus said nothing but approached her knife roll and removed a knife. He nodded. "Nice balance. I am pleased you did not choose lightweight ones."

In a blinding move, Theseus threw. The knife landed dead-center on the target, vibrating like a tuning fork. "These are small for my hand, but they are ideal for you and Penelope."

The man grinned, winked, and trotted down the steps to the deck.

Penny stared at Claire, wide-eyed. "That was...different."

"I was sure he would be furious."

Withdrawing another knife, Penny nodded. "As was I. My brother is full of surprises."


Claire leaned against the rail beneath a star-spangled canopy. Captain Russell said they neared Greece, and she was both eager and sad for their journey's end. Claire had enjoyed her time with Ashworth, their conversations absorbing. She noted how he did not talk down to her and had never done so. Well, not much and not lately.

Claire had learned the focus of Ashworth's research involved the Bronze Age Mycenaean civilization in the Peloponnese. The ruins had been visible for centuries, but the builders of its massive walls had been lost to time. Theseus theorized Mycenae had been a major center of Greek civilization and a military power, her legendary founder, Perseus. It was the alleged home of King Agamemnon, the Greek commander of the Trojan War. Theseus had talked of the magnificent Lion Gate, revealed by a Venetian engineer in 1700 who had used Pausanias' description of the Lion Gate to identify the ruins as Mycenae. Theseus agreed with the Venetian, but though he'd spent much time excavating, he had found little to validate that thesis.

Russell, a retired Royal Navy captain, seemed more than competent, but Ashworth had surprised her when he took the helm. His body language, expressive face, and vivid eyes said how much being at sea pleased him. He always seemed busy, whether helping with the rigging or other physical tasks, moving with authority yet without the arrogance she had seen in many peers. The earl was a natural onboard ship, and Claire found pleasure in his delight.

Claire soaked in the cerulean skies with hints of purple and orange, a whisper of twilight to come. They'd had another hot, sunny day, and she was thankful for her Leghorn bonnet. Ashworth took no such precautions, yet to Claire's discomfort, she found his bronzed visage echoed her imaginings of Odysseus, a foolish thought that nonetheless stuck.

With night nearing, the wind had softened, men scurrying to adjust the sails.

The hours she had spent below opening, examining, and sealing crates had been both exhausting and exhilarating when she found color. She had grown quite skilled with a puller, hammer, and nails. Claire was eager to land, yet all she viewed were endless waves in every direction.

Ashworth neared, for she did not have to look to know it was he.

"We shall reach safe harbor in two days or fewer," he said, glancing at the crewmen passing behind them.

"I confess, I crave solid earth beneath my feet," Claire said. "We landed in Piraeus on my first visit as well. It seemed a town evolving. Greece is marvelously colorful, do you not think? Its skies, the sea, the homes, even the people. I am most eager to arrive and can near taste the *taramasalata*, *dolmades*, and *keftedes*. And the fish. Oh, how I love the Greek fish!"

He grinned. "Have you tasted *baklava*?"

"Yes! Divine! I had forgotten. Will you be dispersing the marbles yourself?"

Ashworth chuckled. "I have neither the time nor the resources for that task. Once we arrive, my friend Dionysus Alexopoulos, a Greek antiquarian, will assume that task."

"No Ottoman panoply?" Claire said. "No pomp or circumstance, and all of that upon our arrival?"

His lips thinned. "That is exactly what our government wants, and what I wish to avoid. Just before we sailed, I received a missive from Liverpool giving his approval for our mission, which I did not need. He directed me to contact the British ambassador and alert the powers that be."

Claire almost snorted at the irony. "So our government has deigned to put a positive spin on you returning the marbles."

"So it seems," he said.

"I cannot say I find that unexpected."

"Nor do I." His voice held no bitterness about the workings of the government. "I did not inform those people of our impending arrival."

"Because...?"

He tilted his head closer. "Only I and the captain know where we shall dock."

"Not Piraeus?"

# TEN

His eyes turned feral, his grin wide. "Itea. The village lies fewer than eleven miles from Kastri, our destination. We shall moor at sea, her cove hiding us from curious eyes."

Kastri sat atop Delphi. Rather than taking more than a week's time, they would arrive in a day, perhaps two. Penny would be in transports. "I am unfamiliar with Itea."

"Itea is a fishing village with a tiny population where we must moor rather than dock. I am certain word has reached the Ottomans of our impending arrival. As their goal is to erase Greece's heritage, I distrust our safety in Piraeus. Revolution is coming, and the more stealth we use, the more protected we shall be. I prefer the Turks remain unaware of our true destination."

The word "revolution" made Claire apprehensive. Revolution implied guns, swords, and death. She was barely competent with a pistol, though she had her knives. *Those* she knew. She must tell Penny about Delphi. "If you will excuse me, I shall—"

He placed a hand over hers. "I have been mulling over a question, Claire."

Claire remained silent, curious for him to continue, the heat from his hand intense.

He leaned close. "Has no one asked why you believe the statues were painted?"

"Well, yes, which is when I show them the paint chips and my wealth of documentary evidence."

Theseus shook his head. "Not what I mean. What set you on your course? Why did you begin looking for paint on statues?"

"Oh. You are correct. No one has ever asked me this, at least not since I was small."

"And now I have." He peered down at her, eyes dark with curiosity.

"As a child, our father had many books on all sorts of mythology—Greek, Norse, African, Asian, others. He said they helped with his painting. I fell in love with the myths, and as a consequence, my attention turned to history, anthropology, and ultimately to my antiquarian studies."

He offered his piratical grin. "Might I ask how old you were at the time?"

That took a moment's thought. "I must have been six or seven, for Charlotte was already enraptured with my father's paints, whilst I would sit on his studio floor reading his books. I would spread them about me, and he never objected to my sprawl. That was a wondrous time in our lives, both Charlotte's and Mama's and mine."

Embarrassed at her ramblings, she ducked her head. "Does that answer your question?"

"It does not, I am afraid. Continue."

"With time, I homed in on the Greeks—their histories, their plays, their wars, and, of course, their mythology. I read about their pastimes, foods, and entertainments. What they drank. How they danced. I saw many depictions of Greek statues and busts sketched in the texts, which expounded on how the statues' whiteness imbued a purity of form.

"Yet the more I studied, the more perplexed I became about the real Greek people. Not the concept of "Greekness" that is so esteemed, but rather the human beings. They were a lively people, full of laughter and celebration. I grew confused by the whiteness, for it seemed so...bland for such a vibrant people. Then, Father received a bust in trade for one of his paintings. A real Greek marble! I was in heaven! The bust was of Aspasia, I soon learned, and as you have noted, it is a Roman copy."

"Your copy is a good one, ancient, and though it is Roman, it mirrors the Greek one."

"You have kept your Greek Aspasia because she is not yours?"

"Yes. She will return home when Greece is under her own rule."

A seagull landed, and Cullen dashed toward it, the gull flying off in ample time.

"So your father received Aspasia, and then...?"

"I believed her Greek, and I remember running for my father's magnifier to view Aspasia more closely. Her hair was in tight sausage curls, above which were the folds of her headpiece. When I held up my magnifier, I saw colors—red and green—in crevices. Yellow, in the drape across her chest, and umber, most startling, inside her ear. I believe that may have been her skin color."

"And you were how old when you discovered this?"

"That I remember with great clarity. I was eight. Papa had died, and Mama was being courted by Lord Fielding. They married soon thereafter, and we went to live at Fielding Manor."

His lips twitched. "I suspect the bust came with you."

"Of course she did." Claire remembered their flight, a shiver roiling through her at the years spent with that awful, predatory man. "When we escaped that fiend's home, I took her then, too. She sat on my lap all the way to Auntie's house. Now, Aspasia rests at Halafair."

"In your bedroom, I suspect."

She smiled, for he was right.

"A marvelous tale of a child's wonder and delight."

His warmth seemed so solid, so right. "Roman copy or no, I love Aspasia dearly."

His arm shot out, pointing. "Look there!"

A dolphin pod frolicked near the stern, as was their wont, coming closer, almost touching the hull, then swimming away again. As if it were a game.

"They always seem to be enjoying themselves," Claire said.

"Ha! In truth, they are fishing for dinner!"

They laughed, which was when she realized his large hand still rested atop hers, and it was...a comfort. Those persnickety prickles skated up her arm. "Ashworth, do you not see how much sense my thesis makes, given the Greek peoples' joy and exuberance? Plain white statues would not be for them. Why, they even bejeweled some of their marbles, though the stones are long gone."

His eyes narrowed. "While I question some of your reasoning, particularly about the Greek personality, I understand the source of your notions."

A spurt of anger stiffened Claire's spine. *Notions.* "If you will excuse me."

His hand squeezed hers. "I have done it again, have I not? My abrupt speech, too precipitous to be appropriate, oft squeezes me into a bind. Your thesis is no notion, and I apologize."

That she could understand, and her ire subsided. He looked so very remorseful. But she could not let it lie.

"You still see my pursuit as frivolous, a daft idea rather than one obtained by serious study."

"No! I find your thesis both significant and worthy."

She inhaled, nostrils flaring. "Are you or are you not convinced?"

"I am somewhat—"

"Somewhat!" She could not resist teasing, for her anger had subsided, and she found his contrite demeanor sweet. After all, he no longer *disbelieved* her. Yet he was so very serious. She wagged a finger. "You shall see, my lord."

"So we are back to my lording again." He sighed.

In the waning afternoon light, they moored near Itea, a few lights already shining from cottages surrounding the coved harbor. The sea and gunpowder scented the air, the latter wrinkling Claire's nose.

Though they'd arrived late in May, the air nipped, the lack of humidity making temperatures sink steeply at night. Claire tightened her shawl. Whilst the nights were chilly, Theseus assured her they would reach a comfortable warmth on the morrow.

Penny rushed up. "Is this not thrilling!"

"Very much so!" Claire said.

"See there?" She pointed to the mountain rearing high beneath the waning light. "That is Parnassus. Delphi sits in a valley on its southern slopes. Parnassus was home to Pegasus, Bellerophon's winged horse, you know."

Claire was impressed with Penelope's erudition. "You are so knowledgeable and enthused! You sound as if you have been here before, yet I know you have not."

Penny clenched her hands to her heart. "In my dreams and books, I have!"

"I shall inform Agnes." Claire disappeared, reappearing in short order, her lips pinched tight.

"What is it?" Penny said.

"Even with her injured arm, Agnes wishes to come along. She is not well enough to go tramping around Greece. She must remain aboard, safe with the captain and some twenty men. I shall stay as well."

"Bollocks on that!" Penny said.

Claire laughed inwardly at the expletive.

"I have heard Theo swear a time or two," Penny said with a shrug. "I thought I might try it out."

"You did well," Claire said with admiration. "I am rather fond of swearing but leash my tongue. Mostly."

Ashworth stepped on deck, and Penny rushed over, their heads bent close, talking rapidly.

Theseus strolled over. "Penelope tells me Miss Agnes must stay aboard, with you as her caregiver."

"Well, yes." Claire was crushed, but she would don a bright face and do what was necessary.

"What of an alternative solution?"

"I can see no other, Ashworth," Claire said.

"We shall bring her into town, where she will have ample food and entertainment."

"A fine idea," Claire said. "Nonetheless, I must stay with her."

"Kostas and Elina are old friends," Theseus said. "He is the headman, and she is the headwoman and his wife. Elina also acts as the town's midwife and surgeon. If Miss Agnes is willing to stay with them, she will have excellent care and be entertained."

Claire closed her eyes. "Might that be all right?"

"Of course it will!" Auntie bellowed. "I do not wish you as nursemaid, dear Claire. Heaven forfend."

"But, Auntie."

"No buts," Agnes joined the group. "I understand my foolishness at expecting to accompany you. Why, I can barely lift my arm."

"I will stay—"

"No, you will not." Agnes straightened to her full height. "My visit to Itea shall count as yet another adventure, whilst you, dearie, will go to Kastri."

Auntie could be so dictatorial. And sweet. Claire harrumphed. "We shall see."

They conferred with the captain about transporting Agnes to shore without further injury. Russell peered at her aunt, who glanced up...and offered him a devilish grin.

What did *that* mean?

Claire fervently hoped Auntie did not stand Itea on its head.

A fleet of colorful small sailing and rowboats sped toward them, distracting Claire. They would ferry marbles and people to shore, making a colorful rainbow display as they zipped through the gentle waves.

Agnes was taken ashore with great care, and as Claire descended the perilous rope ladder, she thanked her sturdy boots for their support. She dared to look down at the bobbing sailboat awaiting her. How should she maneuver onto it without tipping?

Firm hands banded her waist, lifting her from the ladder to the boat. Theseus. That man.

Though it was not full dark, torches lined the quay as they disembarked. She and Penny walked beside Ashworth toward a small group of waiting women while men continued to row and sail from the ship to the quay carrying the marbles. Once ashore, more villagers hauled the crates onto wagons, while others ferried numerous *Nemesis* sailors ashore, men who would accompany them to Kastri. Many of the Itean men wore their *Foustanela* dress, the pleated skirt above billowy pantaloons that ended just below the knee.

After Ashworth introduced them to the crowd of village women, he joined the captain to oversee the loading. Too many crates in a wagon spelled disaster, while too few wasted space.

She and Penny stood about four feet from the crowd of women, dressed in skirts and blouses, some in embroidered aprons, many with shawls, and all wearing headdresses or scarves.

Claire hooked her arm through Penny's, the place strange to her senses.

"I cannot believe I am here." Penny seemed to look everywhere at once. "That I am actually standing on Hellas soil."

Claire felt it too, the difference in the air, the voices of the people, even the waves pounding the shore were far different than England's.

An older woman approached with a wide smile and warm hands as she reached out to clasp Claire's first and then Penelope's.

"*καλωσορίστε ταξιδιώτες. Είμαι η Τζαλίνα. Είμαι η γυναίκα του επικεφαλής.*"

Words of welcome. Her name was Elina, though Claire missed the latter sentence.

About to thank the woman, Claire refrained when Penelope erupted with a string of excited Greek.

The woman startled.

"What did you say?" Claire said. "You spoke so swiftly, I barely caught a word."

"Forgive me," Penny said. "I was so excited I became rather effusive. I fear I surprised these lovely ladies. Elina is the headman's wife. It is she and other women who will care for Agnes, now settled in her own cottage. I also said we were thrilled to be here and thanked them for their hospitality. My Greek is quite good, which surprised her."

Elina's hand waved them forward, and as they moved, the village women followed. They walked across the beach and up the slight hill to the village proper, where the path led them to rows of homes. They stopped at a white, stuccoed cottage overlooking the sea, where Elina knocked, then led them inside.

The largish cottage included a chair, a small table, several lamps, and a good-sized bed where Agnes now rested with, of all things, a teacup-sized floofy pup on her lap.

Claire sighed. Auntie attracted animals of all sorts, including Arthur the monkey and, apparently, this pup, now licking Agnes' chin.

The woman, who had oohed and aahed over Cullen as he'd trotted alongside them, entered the room, sniffing everywhere, everyone, and everything. Elina eyed him askance. "I have never seen such a large beast."

"Cullen *is* very large," Claire said. "He is called a wolfhound, as his forebears hunted wolves."

Elina's eyes widened.

Penny ruffled Cullen's fur. "He is a very sweet boy who will do you no harm."

"Our protector," Claire said with a smile.

Elina snapped her a nod. "A good companion, then."

The pup cuddling with Agnes stood and yipped.

Cullen's head shot up.

*Oh dear.*

The little one had a Napoleonic attitude, for he leapt from the bed and pranced over to Cullen, who leaned down, way down, and sniffed.

"You could swallow him in one gulp," Claire said in English. "Behave."

Cullen's tongue lolled, and he woofed.

The small pup yipped, too, and proceeded to lick her wolfhound's nose. Cullen had made a friend.

Which was when gunfire erupted, sparks flashing from the window in the now-fallen night.

Penny and Claire dropped to a crouch, yet the women laughed, as did Auntie. One waved her hands amidst a string of rapid-fire Greek, spoken too fast for Claire to comprehend.

"Could you talk slower, please?" Claire said as she stood.

More laughter, accompanied by the women's nods.

Elina repeated the woman's words. "Our men are celebrating our victory."

"Victory?" Penny said as she stood and brushed off her skirts.

"They ambushed some Turks in the pass and were victorious." Elina's eyes gleamed. "A minor skirmish, nothing unusual. But I sense we will soon be free of the oppressors. We are rising to reclaim our homeland."

"Is that not exciting!" Agnes said.

The word that came to Claire's mind was "alarming." She reminded herself she had been through worse, the recent conflict with St. Michaels quite indelible.

Ashworth had spoken of the brewing revolution, but Claire hoped to be far from Greece when war broke out.

The women ushered them from Agnes' room, both she and the pup drowsy, and they proceeded up the dirt path to their own cottage.

When Elina swung open the bright blue door, a woman bearing a torch entered and began lighting candles and lamps as Penelope and Claire followed. The small, neat living area held a table and two wood chairs with a door that led to a room with two single beds and a nightstand holding a crock of blooming flowers.

Elina again spoke in Greek. "This is where you shall stay while you are here."

Claire replied in Greek, understanding the words. "The cottage is lovely."

The door opened to a procession of trunks and food, men carrying the trunks and women carrying platters of exotic Greek dishes they placed on the table.

"We thought you might be hungry after your long journey," Elina said.

Claire recognized most dishes. Boiled wild greens served in oil, *tzatziki*, and *dolmades* with their vine leaf parcel holding minced meat, and other fish and meats. The heavenly scents made Claire's mouth water until she spied the marinated octopus. Sadly, not a taste she enjoyed.

A platter of *baklava* for dessert and jugs of retsina wine and anise-flavored ouzo accompanied the meal, all favorites.

Claire pointed to a platter, asking Penny in a whisper, "Do you know what this is?"

"I have only seen colored plates in books," she said. "But I believe it to be *souvlaki*, small pieces of meat grilled on a skewer. This is all so beyond my imaginings!" Penny clasped her hands tight.

Claire winked. "It seems we are on a culinary escapade as well!"

The earth trembled.

Claire's hand flew to her chest, the other gripping the wall, the sensation alien.

"The earth shakes," Elina said, grinning wide.

All the women nodded, except for Claire and Penny's anxiety-filled ones.

"Just a little tremble," Elina continued. "A welcome for you from Poseidon, the Earth-Shaker."

Claire leaned toward Penny. "That was something."

"Indeed! I hope Poseidon stays in charity with us."

Claire swallowed. "As do I!"

CHAPTER

# ELEVEN

The following day, Claire and Penny's new Itean maid helped them pack away some of their hardy travel clothes, exchanging them for lighter ones intended for the hotter Greek clime.

Claire opened the door. A sweet breeze played across the warm air, the temperature moderate even this late in May. Penny was gone, so Claire visited Agnes to find the woman entertaining Captain Russell, of all people, along with three of the village women and the teacup pup. She squeezed into the room, all faces turning her way.

At the bed, Claire bent down. "How do you fare today, Auntie?"

"Well!" she said with a bright smile. "Did you know the beaches here are perfect for ocean bathing?"

"I...did not."

"Elina has a bathing costume for me," Agnes said. "Once I feel more the thing, I shall go for a swim!"

Agnes' obvious excitement was tempered by her pale complexion, though from the dishes on the table, she had eaten well. "Not too soon, Auntie. Please do not overdo."

Agnes closed her eyes and sighed, though she continued to stroke the pup. "I shall be as good as gold."

Captain Russell rolled his eyes. "I'll make sure Miss Agnes rests until she is well enough."

"You shall do no such thing, Oliver!" her aunt said with a smile.

"I shall, Miss Agnes, whether you like it or no. Hrumph!"

Her aunt laughed.

THE DAY WAS ABOUT LOGISTICS, and after they'd rearranged their trunks, they observed the sailors and townsmen organizing the marbles on the wagons for their transport to Delphi. All the village prepared for their departure, including the women cooking portable meals. The trek would be a challenging one, considering they must climb Parnassus to reach the site, the six wagons carrying the marbles pulled by mules. The animals had been purchased by Theseus and roamed a large corral beneath several olive trees.

Men strapped the marbles to the wagons using thick ropes, while Claire and Penny tried to assist the village women with their meal preparation. Though they were allowed to chop vegetables, that was the sum of their contribution.

But the villagers' excitement was infectious. Kostas knew the purpose of Theseus' group, and his joy infused the air with revelry and anticipation. The preparations took many hours, and that afternoon, Claire and Penny explored the village of about three dozen cottages set above the beach, with more climbing the hillside. Red, blue, and yellow fishing boats bobbed in the water or were beached ashore, their bellies to the sky.

Cullen gamboled with several dogs while the children played some type of stickball. A few shops dotted a small square—a store with cloth and sundries, one devoted to boat and fishing supplies, and a third selling fish and meats. On market day, according to Elina, many stall vendors would fill the area.

Her time for examining the packed marbles was passed, so she and Penny carried their sketchbooks and pastel cases and climbed a small hill to sit beneath a tree's shade, Cullen flopping down beside them. They began renderings of the village, the boats, and the mountain on paper.

"How long do you think it will take to get to Delphi?" Claire said.

Penny looked up from her sketch. "Two days? Three? More? It is hard to say because of the terrain. You understand there remains nothing of Delphi's sacred temples and buildings."

"So I have read." Claire spotted a man atop one of their few horses, and she put her pastels to work. She hesitated to ask, the subject being extremely strange, yet she must. "Did the Pythia say anything about your arrival in Greece?"

"She expects me by the thirtieth," Penny said. "We seem to be on track for that."

"Was she not expecting us to arrive in Piraeus?"

"Our small change in route will not discourage Xanthe. Our correspondence indicates she is a singularly determined person."

"Then all will be well." Even if the idea of the Oracle sounded rather fantastical. "See that man on the prancing horse?" Claire pointed, then began to sketch him.

"He is quite good-looking, is he not?" Penny said. "That is Spyros. He and Theseus went to Trinity together."

"Really?"

"Indeed. I have always enjoyed his visits to Wolf Court. You will like him." Penny pointed. "See that other man, the one in the bright white shirt wearing a *fustanella*?"

"I do," Claire said, intrigued.

"I believe that is Pantelis, another friend of Theseus," Penny said.

"He wears the pleated skirt I saw on my trip last year, though I learned little about the garment."

"My brother pointed him out when we arrived. His *fustanella* is made of spun wool, the belt above it of leather. I love those billowy pantaloons, but some wear tight breeches beneath, whilst others prefer their legs bare."

"Unusual," Claire said. "Skirts for men, I mean."

"It is said the *fustanella* consists of four hundred pleats," Penny said. "They represent the four hundred years of Ottoman oppression and rule over Hellas."

"You are a wealth of clothing information, Penelope!"

"I have had much time to study Greece. As Father and Theseus repeatedly voyaged to Hellas, the Greeks' preferred term for their homeland, my interest grew."

"Our group's leader said the costume's origin was originally that of an Albanian warrior."

"That is so." Penny lifted a pastel, turned a page in her sketchbook, and began a new sketch. "Though I have no idea how the *fustanella* arrived in Greece, the revolutionaries have adopted it as their dress."

They were amongst revolutionaries. Claire's disquiet bloomed, and she tamped it down, knowing full well there were risks to any exotic journey. Not that it helped.

"Your face has gone unusually pale, Claire," Penny said. "Please do not worry. We are watched by guards and at all times are protected." Penny pointed to another man, an older one. "I believe the man wearing the *fustanella* is Kostas, the headman. Oh!"

"What?"

"I must get that child down on the page." Penny's pastel stroked across the paper in rapid movements, depicting a child leading a donkey.

"That is very good!" Claire said.

Spyros trotted up the hillside toward them. He wore clothes much like Theseus but also carried a rifle and bristled with knives. Cullen sat at attention as he dismounted.

The man smiled as he spoke in rapid-fire Greek.

Claire missed most other than "stele."

"What is happening?" she asked Penny while giving Spyros a reassuring smile, though Cullen growled softly beside her. She whispered, "Steady," in Cullen's ear.

Penny laughed. "Theo asked Spyros to speak in Greek so I could practice mine. Is that not sweet? Of course, he is conversant in English as well. Trinity, remember? He wishes to show you a stele known to the village. For you to examine."

"Does he?" The idea of studying a sculpture *in situ* fizzed her with excitement.

"Theseus' idea," Penny said, sliding her a sideways look. "It was he who asked if the village had any marbles. For *you*."

"*Ευχαριστώ*," Claire said, thanking him.

"*Παρακαλώ*." Theseus' dark-haired friend was tall and well-built, with an olive complexion and an abundance of muscle, much like Ashworth himself.

"My lady," Spyros said in perfect English, complete with a fine accent. "Many years ago, the Iteans found the stele. It is the pride of the village. Theseus said you might like to view it."

*That man.* Claire would not forget Ashworth's thoughtful gesture. He might not be yet convinced of her premise...but had arranged for this.

They folded their sketchpads and replaced their pastels and pencils in their case, returning them to their knapsacks.

"*Κυρία Κλαίρη, να σας συστήσω τον Σπύρο*," Penny said.

Claire held out her hand, and Spyros bowed over it with a smile.

"Follow me," he said.

They traveled down the hill toward the base of Parnassus.

"I met your aunt, Lady Claire," Spyros said. "She is a most interesting woman."

"That she is, Spyros."

The bones of Mother Earth dotted the landscape, from immense boulders to small stones resting in the sandy soil alongside the ubiquitous gorse.

Some people believed stone sentient, according to Claire's readings. Amidst a landscape far more raw than England's, she could not deny the possibility.

They ambled away from the village until a wide rock opening appeared at the base of the mountain. A cave, perhaps?

To their surprise, Ashworth stood by the entrance, wearing a sweat-soaked shirt that stuck to his chest in the most interesting places. Built on mighty proportions, his chest echoed a warrior's, all curves and planes and power. But it was the keen intelligence flashing from those eyes that so compelled her.

Cullen trotted up to him, and Theseus…Ashworth…ruffled his fur.

"I thought you would enjoy inspecting the stele," he said to Claire. "You have your monocle with you, do you not?"

Claire wagged it. "Always."

"You, dear sister," he said, "have prosed on about the Greek caves. This shall be your first."

Penny's eyes sparked. "Caves were often used by the ancient Greeks for spiritual purposes. The Dictaean Cave on Crete is the fabled birthplace of Zeus."

Ashworth appeared solemn as he nodded, but his sister punched his arm.

"You want to laugh, do you not?"

"Perhaps smile?" he said. "I doubt you will find Zeus or any other god in residence here."

Penny wagged a finger. "Or perhaps I will!"

"Do be wary of the bats and rock doves, as well as snakes, dear sister."

"I shall do as bid, dear brother," she said, feigning solemnity.

Theseus snorted, then they moved inside the cave, dark and chill encompassing them, though two hanging lanterns offered a faint light. Theseus handed one to Penny, taking one himself. "Come."

Down a dark passage, then around a bend, where a wall was carved with a large, smooth niche created by man rather than nature. Ashworth raised the lantern to reveal a large stele, perhaps four feet high, resting on a three-foot platform of rock.

"My heavens," Penny said. "It is beautiful." She brushed a hand down the statue's arm. "I am off."

She left, Spyros following, and Claire signaled Cullen to attend the pair venturing deeper into the cave. Her good boy did as asked.

Ashworth held the lantern high as Claire began to study the memorial, for it was a funerary stele, pausing to remove her journal and a pencil from her knapsack.

"This reminds me of a stele you are taking to Delphi."

He nodded, and she caught a hint of sadness in his eyes. "Much like. It is...was a favorite of mine."

The memorial depicted a seated older woman who held a swaddled infant, her head bent, her gaze locked on the infant, the child peering up into her eyes. Claire's hand clenched reflexively. Funerary stelai were carved with love, longing, and sorrow. The one before her was no exception.

Both long gone. Claire stepped back to take in the whole piece. She lifted her journal from the platform, first making sketches, then notes. The woman's robes appeared as if Zephyr's breeze moved them, a strong indicator that it was carved between the fourth and fifth centuries BC.

"From the Classical era," she said.

"Indeed," Theseus commented. "The village treasures this marble. They do not worship it, per se, but they certainly revere it. Pregnant women of the village leave offerings in hopes of a live and healthy birth."

"The carving is a thing of great beauty."

After more scribbles and another sketch, she bent to the inscription.

*MY DAUGHTER's beloved child is the one I hold here, the one that I held on my lap while we looked at the light of the sun when we were alive and that I still hold, now that we are both dead.*

. . .

CLAIRE WAS vaulted to the Greece of centuries ago, where she held an infant, mere days old. Her granddaughter was a warm and lively child as she smiled up at her.

Fingers brushed her face, returning her to the present.

"Do not cry, little bird," Theseus said in a soft voice.

Claire startled. A tender nickname. Her pleasure warred with her anxiety, so confusing, humor the perfect distraction. "I am the least little bird you ever met."

Ashworth boomed a laugh. "True."

Oh, when he laughed, his eyes turned to green fire. "You have most certainly lifted me out of the glooms, and I thank you. When I examine stelai, I often become terribly sad. Silly, I know. But the grandmother and babe are so poignant. At least they are remembered."

Theseus nodded. "They are, indeed."


As THESEUS and Claire clustered around the stele, Penny held her lantern high and ventured deeper into the cave, her imagination soaring. The Earth Shaker had created many throughout Hellas. The sandy floor felt cool beneath her feet, or so she imagined. Rather than forbidding, the cave felt...welcoming. The walls were relatively smooth, the sea having sanded them over the millennia. As they went deeper, more and more stalactites pointed downward—an upside-down forest creating an unearthly ambiance.

Penny inhaled the chill air redolent of the sea and strode on, looking for...an indefinable something that eluded her normal senses. The place was wondrous, filled with mystery and spirituality.

A flurry of wings whizzed near her head, making her jiggle the lantern. She clutched the handle tighter.

"Are you well?" Spyros said.

"It was just a rock dove."

She steeped her senses into this place, a holy one, though her rational mind said that was absurd.

A glimmer of light, and Penny raised the lantern. "Oh!"

A clear crystal sat embedded in the rock face, glinting back at her. A beautiful thing, a good two feet tall, that sparked in her lantern's light.

Behind her, Spyros cleared his throat, while Cullen leaned against her leg.

Onward.

"Do not go too far, Penelope," Theseus hollered. "Or Spyros will haul you back here."

"I shan't!" Her brother was such a hand-wringer.

A day after reaching Greece, Penny noted how the clime seemed to ease her cough and sneezes. Her thick head cleared, too, and she felt energized. An unfamiliar sensation.

Inhaling deep, she moved forward.

The cave bent back on itself, and Penny took care placing her feet, not wishing to trip or surprise snakes, and thankful she wore her sturdy boots.

The cool air was surprisingly fresh and most welcome. Penny took a moment to lean against a wall and close her eyes, her hand pressed to the rock. *Σπίτι.* Yes, *home,* her mind winding back in time through the ages of Hellas—the Ottoman occupation, Roman Greece, the Hellenistic period, the Classical, then the Archaic, the Minoan, and Mycenaean, all the way to the Bronze Age—in search of a source. The beginning.

Up ahead, a whooshing sound. She looked at Spyros, then proceeded around a bend to discover a small cavern. A warm mist rose from its floor, enveloping her, whirling and twirling as she inhaled the delicate scents of hyacinth and myrtle, heady and sweet. Penny breathed deep, flushed with a sense of wellness that had eluded her for years, a lightness that made her dizzy.

Cullen yipped, the moment broke, and she reached for her kerchief to wipe her face, then froze. She stepped back with a jerk, fear urging her to hide within Spyros' arms. But she stood her ground.

A form coalesced. A woman's. She wore a white chiton, or tunic, that fell to the ground, a sapphire brooch fastened at the shoulder, while a linked gold belt girdled her hips. The woman raised her arms to the front, either in supplication or calling Penelope forward.

She was translucent, yet Penny could see every detail of clothing as well as her dark hair, warm smile, and beckoning arms.

The woman's call hummed through her bones, and Penny stepped forward.

CHAPTER

# TWELVE

"Ah!" Claire leaned closer, trying her best not to touch the stele. "Look. Look here." She slipped her leashed eyepiece from her neck and handed it to Ashworth. "Here is yet more evidence."

The man schooled his features. Perhaps he wished to frown or raise a brow?

"Do look through the lens, Mr. Skeptic," she said.

Ashworth braced a hand on the rock wall and leaned over the stele.

Claire held her breath.

Theseus stared at a dot of pinkish-yellow...something. Hard to tell what in the lamplight. He wished to believe, for Claire. But it looked much like a bird's dropping to him.

Still, he was loath to make a jest. Perhaps it was her eyes, liquid amber filled with hope. Or the way her hands clenched tight, her body leaning toward him.

He took a deep breath. "I see a dot of yellow."

"With pink undertones? Do you see those?"

"I do."

Yes! She ran a light finger just above the inner bend. "See here? I think the color represented the woman's skin tone. Note where her robe drapes her shoulders. Look there. Do you see the green? That must have been the color of her dress or drapery."

"Most compelling."

"Ha!" She stepped back, as did he, returning her monocle to her. The man was trying to be kind, but his healthy skepticism remained. Disappointment near overwhelmed her, for she had come to respect Ashworth. She wanted him to believe so very much. More than the antiquarians or the museum directors. More than anyone.

"I do see green," he continued. "And...peach. I want to see what you do, Claire."

Truth. And caring. Though his voice remained skeptical, it was obvious he *wished* to believe.

Just as she wished to understand his repatriating the sculptures. Upon reflection, she realized she was beginning to do just that.

Ashworth was giving her theories a chance. He was trying.

To convince him, she must do more. Much more.


"Penny!" Theseus called. "We must go. Need I come fetch you?"

Noise...annoying, for Penny's entire focus was on the woman in the mist. She reached out a hand to touch her. The woman shook her head and made a brushing-away movement.

"Penny!"

Spyros laid a hand on her shoulder.

"Coming!" she said.

But how could she leave the woman?

A whisper in her ear. Penny blinked. Spyros.

"We must go," he said.

One more look at the woman with the beatific smile. Then Penny raced down the cave, Spyros and Cullen at her heels.


Penny reappeared so swiftly she startled Claire.

"Are you well?" Claire said.

"Yes!" Her eyes glittered with excitement and an elusive distance, as if part of her was still deep in the cave. Penny gripped her hand tight. "Oh yes, very well."

Spyros and Cullen appeared, the hair on Cullen's spine standing on end.

Theseus pointed to Cullen's fur. "What happened?"

Penny widened her eyes. "I have not the faintest."

He harrumphed. "Sister mine, you should take more care."

Penny stepped beside her far taller brother and poked a finger to his chest. "Just as you do, brother?"

"Christ, Pens, I am experienced in these environs. You are not. Caves are dangerous places with asps, bats, and other foul creatures that could injure you."

Bright sunlight splashed them as they exited the cave. "They could. But I was neither bitten nor pounced upon. Though a monstrous big rock dove flew by my head." She chuckled, then turned to Claire, her smile mischievous.

Theseus stared at the two of them as if they were a puzzle he could not assemble. "I am needed at the wagons. Do not forget we leave in two days."

"We shan't." Penny turned to Spyros and whispered. "Did you see the woman?"

Spyros wore a smile. "I did not, Lady Penelope. I suspect whatever you saw was meant for you alone. That is how these visions often work."

"Thank you."

Pantelis waved from the crest of a hill and trotted toward them. After introductions, he said, "We have a problem with one of the mules."

Pantelis and Theseus strode off at a rapid pace, leaving Spyros to accompany them to the village.

Once back in their room, Penny whirled on Claire. "I must tell you!"

"What did you see?" Claire said. "I have been dying to ask once I saw Cullen's raised hackles and you bouncing with excitement."

Penny recounted a tale of the crystals and mist and a woman dressed in ancient garments. She waggled her hands. "I know what I saw. She was like an apparition and yet not. She moved but did not speak. I cannot help but wonder who or what she was."

Claire was flummoxed by Penny's recitation. Her friend was eminently practical in many ways, yet she was fanciful too. She would not discount Penny's tale. "I do not know what it all means. Or what you actually saw."

Penny huffed. "I know *exactly* what I saw."

"I believe that. I do, and yet... No! Let us take it for what it was. We shall store it away and see if anything else unusual occurs. We must tell Aunt Agnes. She will be all agog."

"I shall!" Penny's lips thinned. "But do not tell Theseus."

"I have no intention of doing so. He would say I had downed an overabundance of ouzo."

That chilly evening, they sat on cushions in the town square around the large bonfire to celebrate the villagers' recent triumph over the hated Ottomans. Cullen sprawled in front of her, basking in the warmth. Theseus sat to her left, alongside Pantelis, while Auntie sat to her right, the wee pup in her lap. Beside them, Penny was talking with Spyros.

Spyros looked like a typical Greek, swarthy with dark hair. Pantelis' looks drew a comparison to the ancients, with his light complexion, blond hair curls, and piercing chocolate eyes. His compelling beauty could be that of Apollo come to life, but Claire had yet to take the man's measure. He was a far more solemn soul than the cheerful Spyros.

She was excited for the party and even more so for their nearing departure, though she remained loath to leave Agnes. A group of men played instruments as the townspeople began a circle dance around the fire. From her previous trip, Claire recognized the Greek instruments as a flute, a *kithara*, and the *lyra*. She leaned to her left. "What are the drum and tambourine called?"

"Marvelous, are they not?" he said. "The drum is a *toubeleki*, whilst the *rhoptron* mimics a tambourine." Theseus gave her a toothy grin.

When had she begun thinking of him as Theseus, rather than Ashworth?

As the villagers circled the bonfire holding hands, they kicked up their heels.

"Do you dance?" she asked. Claire ached to join the circle.

Theseus gave her a rueful smile. "When I have drunk an excess of ouzo."

She was tempted. Oh, why not? "Shall we?"

He chuffed a laugh and raised his glass. "Not enough yet."

Her grin was saucy. "Your choice. You will be all right, Auntie?"

"Little Milo will keep me company." She brushed a hand across the pup's coat, and he licked it. "As will Cullen."

Claire approached the circle, and it parted for her, hands extended so she might join the dance. Claire had watched with care, and though the steps were unfamiliar, she was soon laughing and moving her feet, mimicking the other dancers. The blaze warmed her, and she moved faster and faster as the tempo increased. The sensations thrilled her. The wild music. The flickering light. The grins and shouts of the other dancers. Claire threw back her head and laughed.

A new hand replaced the one to her right, one much larger and rougher. She looked up to see Theseus' grin down at her. Pantelis took her other hand, straight-faced but with eyes alight. No words were necessary as they went round and round the bonfire in celebration.

The dance ended, and Claire gasped. "That was glorious!"

"And exhausting!" Pantelis said, laughing. "I need more ouzo!"

Theseus grinned, and it sizzled her bones, his face burnished in firelight, his eyes sparking. God above, he intrigued her so.

Claire wanted him for herself. Oh, my. Did she?

"Not quite the minuet," he said as he escorted her back to their cushions.

"I have never experienced its like." She was still breathing hard, though not entirely from the dance.

"The joy is infectious," he said.

"It is!"

The players began a new tune, the villagers assembling, and she watched them kicking and jumping and twirling. Claire sighed. "I confess I am worn out, and yet somehow they keep dancing."

"There are strong folk, and they dance often and hard."

"How shall Penny and I travel to Delphi?"

"On donkeys."

"Can the wee creatures carry us with our heavy clothes and cloaks?"

"That and more, for they are strong little beasties."

"I have not seen Penny ride. Will she be all right?"

"She is a fine rider."

"I did not realize..."

He raised a brow. "We ride out often when I am home. As we travel, Spyros will assist Penny on and off her mount, as well as guard her. You need not fret."

"He is a dear friend, yes?"

Theseus grinned, but his eyes were far distant. "We had many adventures together while in school and here in Greece. He joins us at his insistence, for he is most keen for the repatriation."

*Oh, that devil on her shoulder.* Claire dropped her eyes. "As Spyros will assist Penny, how shall I mount and dismount my donkey?"

"You will do fine on your own. You are far stronger than Penelope."

She steeled her features not to react, though she was a bit hurt. Why had she bothered flirting with him anyway?

Theseus leaned close, his breath warm on her ear. "I am teasing, Claire. I will help you on and off your brave steed."

Claire flushed, foolishly pleased. She peered across the square and beyond to the small hill, where in the distance, a pen held several donkeys. Their steeds, small and furry with profoundly large ears, were quite adorable, though she suspected riding them would be anything but.

"I am glad." In the flickering firelight, the planes and angles of his face molded into something...dear. The man promised surety and strength, his powerful will and resolve complemented by the gentleness that oft took her by surprise, given his imposing figure.

He caught her eyes, and his warmed. Perhaps an echo of her feelings, a slight smile gracing his lips. Time dissolved, moments stretched. Theseus leaned forward, and she mirrored the movement, wishing to be closer still.

A paw on her thigh broke Claire's trance. Cullen, of course, grinning up at her, tongue lolling, and demanding attention. She ruffled his fur and scratched behind his ears, slipping him a tidbit from her meal.

Captain Russell had stolen Theseus' attention, but the moment lingered, at least for her.

What had it meant? Or had she imagined his desirous intention? She must have done, for Theseus had never implied more.

No matter. She savored the connection until it dissolved like a fairy light in the mist.

Undressing that night, Claire longed for sleep. "I am so tired I cannot wait to climb into bed."

Penny peeled off her clothes down to her chemise. "I feel the same."

Claire retrieved her journal, pencil, and eraser from her knapsack and climbed beneath the covers. She began to review that day's notes, making corrections and additions.

Her eyes grew heavy, Penny already burrowed beneath the covers, asleep. Claire added notes to their day's adventures, and she realized Penny had barely coughed all day. In truth, she seemed live-lier, too.

Claire tapped the pencil against her lips. The Greek clime was having a positive effect on her friend, pleasing her enormously. She jotted a few more lines about the bonfire and dancing, then laid her journal on the floor, then reached to scratch Cullen. He usually slept in bed with her, but this pallet, comfortable though it might be, was far too small for both of them. So his piled blankets on the floor must serve. "How are you liking our adventure so far, dear boy?"

Her pup failed to answer as she drifted off.


Cullen's growl awakened her.

Claire's eyes flew open, but she remained absolutely still and regulated her breathing to resemble sleep. All of which was moot when Cullen's happy yip sounded.

"Hush," the voice said, and Cullen obeyed. Theseus.

Claire pushed herself to a sitting position, tendrils of moonlight splashing across the floor. "What is wrong?"

Theseus pressed a finger to his lips.

She glanced at Penny, who remained fast asleep as he moved close to her bed, crouching beside it. Cullen promptly leaned against him.

"We depart for Delphi," Theseus said.

She rubbed her eyes and reached for her glass of water, taking a sip. "Why?"

"Explanations must wait. I will fetch you and Penelope in a few minutes. Dress and be ready."

"But my aunt... I must say farewell and make sure all is well for her comfort."

His lips thinned, his eyes full of regret. "We cannot, Claire. We must leave."

She did not wish to leave Auntie without at least a farewell. "I shall follow."

He shook his head. "Your aunt will understand. Please."

"At least allow me to write her a note," she whispered.

A breath, then, "A short one."

Theseus whispered outside, and Cullen must have sensed the tension, for he remained silent yet alert. She roused Penelope, and they quickly donned their traveling clothes, then wrote Auntie's note. Though she was heartsore, she scribbled as best she could, saying how she loved her, that she would miss her, and to stay safe. She underlined that last bit.

Once sealed, Claire took her knife roll from her knapsack and slid a knife into her bodice lining, another into her pocket, and the third into its sleeve in her stocking. She removed her special hairpin from the roll and wove it into her coif.

"That is an impressive array," Penny whispered.

"One can never wear too many knives." From her trunk, she removed a thin leather belt with its sheath and knife, then wound it around her waist, then locked her trunk.

Most of her knives were for throwing, but the one at her waist was intended for up close and personal. She prayed it would never come to that. When she had tutored Rose's former governess on throwing knives, in turn, Lucy had taught her several Kalari moves, a martial art of which she was a master. That might come in handy, too. Claire shivered.

As Penny slid her pistol into its holster, an impressive-looking thing, a knock, then the door eased open. Pantelis and another man took their trunks, Cullen smelling each as they hefted their burdens. They followed the pair on silent feet, and Claire slipped her note beneath Agnes' door, then walked the path behind the cottage toward the empty corral where the mules had been housed. A line of wagons and two saddled donkeys awaited them.

The near-full moon pearled the landscape, accompanied by the stomping of feet, the jangling of tack, and the animals' musky scent. An owl hooted, and the wind trembled. Claire trembled, too. What were they doing? Would Auntie be well?

Once their trunks were settled on a wagon bed, Spyros lifted Penny onto her saddle.

"Is all well, Lady Penelope?" he said.

Penny smiled down at him. "It is about time you called me Penny or Penelope."

"I think not, my lady," Spyros said.

"You have known me forever, Spyros. Please?"

Spyros' smile blazed. "Yes."

Something was up between those two, their conversation lost when Theseus appeared. "Ready, my lady?"

"I am."

His hands banded her waist in a firm—admittedly pleasant—grip. In a swift movement, she was atop the little beastie and a bit breathless, the latter her reaction to Theseus' hands hugging her waist.

"You wear a knife."

"I do. And I fervently hope I need not use it!" She fisted her hand so as not to brush it across his auburn hair. "Cullen, heel!"

The pup took up his position beside her donkey, and he was near as tall as the equine. A laugh bubbled up. Perhaps she should ride *him*!

Theseus remained beside her. "Where are your throwing knives?"

Her face flushed. "On my person, where you shall not find them, sir."

He clamped his teeth, and in the moonlight his eyes lit with humor. He winked and strolled away. "One never knows," he tossed over his shoulder.

He was *flirting*. Theseus never flirted. He was the most confounding man, unlike any other gentleman she'd encountered. He neither dismissed her intelligence nor focused his eyes on her breasts, addressing her as if she had a brain, all of which was lovely. She hadn't believed he noticed she was female, not in the way she hoped. Yet just now...

So confusing.

CHAPTER

# THIRTEEN

The carved leather saddle did not accommodate riding like a proper Englishwoman, so Claire swung her right leg over the donkey's back, thankful for her many adventures at Woodbine riding astride. Her split skirts had been sewn on Rose's suggestion for her first trek to Greece and allowed her to sit astride. She had given two of the precious skirts to Penny, who accepted with great enthusiasm. Her friend looked as comfortable riding astride as Claire felt.

Theseus led the group atop a sturdy mount that stood much taller than her donkey, pony though it was. All took up their reins, and at Theseus' signal, they moved forward in silence, their group consisting of *Nemesis'* sailors and village men, trained fighters all. Soon, they began to climb a path that led up Mount Parnassus to Delphi.

They ascended for hours—the quiet, her donkey's sway, and her conflicted feelings about leaving Agnes—made her eyes heavy. Claire pinched herself to stay awake, but her lids persisted in creeping downward.

A hand shook her, a voice hissing, "Claire!"

Her eyes flew open, and she reeled, the hand steadying her. "Apologies."

"Not necessary," Theseus said, his mount striding alongside hers.

She looked to Cullen, reassuring herself of his presence. "Why did we leave in the dead of night?"

He spoke in a whisper. "At last night's celebration, an old Itean friend suggested I think twice about leaving the marbles at Delphi. He recommended we wait a few more days and mull it over, suggesting instead we sail them to Patras in the Peloponnese."

"Why?" she said.

Theseus shook his head. "A good question. My alarm bells sounded when he strongly hinted at some problem or other with our party, yet he would say no more. Something is wrong. I do not know if someone is colluding with the Ottomans or not, but my instincts said we should leave."

"Do you always follow your instincts?" Her donkey moved on, Theseus on her left, Cullen on her right.

"Not always, but often." He shrugged. "The man avoided my eyes, furtively looked around, and lowered his voice to a whisper. His demeanor was both unusual and worrisome. I discussed our route many times with the villagers, as many have joined us. Now, we take a different one."

"Perhaps the man was wrong." She touched his arm.

"Perhaps he was bamming me, but I was unwilling to take the chance." He laid a hand over hers and squeezed. "I must speak with Penelope. Stay awake."

Theseus' words disturbed her. True, their troop bristled with rifles and sabers, yet her anxiety increased, knowing that Ottomans on swift horses might attack before they reached Delphi.

On and on they went, climbing a narrow track up Parnassus, men guiding them with lanterns.

When strong arms lifted her from the saddle, Claire startled. Damn, she'd again fallen asleep. Pantelis set her on the ground.

"You were tilting out of the saddle, my lady," Pantelis said. "I feared you would topple."

"I appreciate your assistance, Pantelis." Claire leaned against her sweet donkey as dawn broke.

The view of the mountains and sea truly stole her breath, the turquoise waves tinted red with the rising sun. A petulant wind whipped her skirts, her bonnet near flying off. Not that she cared. Every bone ached. Claire was exhausted.

They rested for an hour amidst the olive trees and gorse and a few Kermes oaks, feeding and watering the animals, then breaking their fast with bread, dried fruits, and bowls of yogurt prepared by the villagers. Penny looked as poorly as Claire felt, her straw bonnet askew, her face coated with dust. She must appear equally wan and disheveled, the watch pinned to her bodice coated in dust, which she wiped away.

Cullen smelled everything, marking numerous spots as if he now ruled this land. The funny boy was such a good friend and companion.

Once they ate, they moved out once again.

A dozen or so men flanked the wagons that carried their precious cargo. Theseus hadn't said the alternate route they took was more dangerous. He didn't have to.

The trail looked more goat path than road, though wide enough for the wagons and mules. Claire reached for the map inside her knapsack tied to the saddle. Hard to tell, but they appeared to be on an old trade route that would take them to Kastri and Delphi, albeit in a more circuitous and bumpy way.

Parnassus' towering rock flanked the track, its sharp edges, some like bleak cowls overhanging the trail, ominous and fearsome. On occasion, the path widened, the rock falling away to reveal the sea, as well as the terrible plummet downward if any of the animals, wagons, or humans slipped. Cullen's sharp claws made him the safest amongst them.

But the glistening sun, the crystalline air, and the magnificent vistas—all of which Claire found invigorating—made up for the dangerous climb and her anxious mood.

Up ahead, Theseus rode tall and proud on a rugged pony with a thick neck and large hooves that appeared to easily scale the mountain path. They climbed and climbed until Theseus raised an arm for them to halt.

Claire checked her watch. He'd said they would travel until past noon, yet it was only ten. Something was wrong, and she leaned forward and squeezed her donkey's sides to pick up the pace until she reached Theseus.

An immense boulder blocked the trail.

Theseus had dismounted and was surveying the huge stone. She slipped onto the ground, leaning for a few moments against her donkey until her legs' pins and needles subsided, then climbed to meet him.

"Go away," he said.

"Do *not* growl at me."

He cast her a scathing look but then sighed. "Apologies. I am sure you understand my foul mood."

She pointed to a niche in the mountainside. "It must have come from there. Can you roll it back?"

His hands rested on his waist, sweat glistening on his face and neck. He whooshed out a breath. "Perhaps. The danger is the boulder crashing downward into the wagons."

"Then it makes sense to turn around and take another trail."

"We cannot." He went to scrape his hands through his hair, realized he was wearing a hat, and cursed. "There is no place to turn about, nor can we back the mules down, as it is far too perilous."

Her skin prickled. "We are trapped between Scylla and Charybdis."

"Quoting Homer does not help," he said.

"But really, what is more apt?" She flicked a hand, though she was deeply disconcerted.

"Remain here and try to stay safe." He shook his head as he walked away.

*Damn the man*, of course she would stay safe. She hoped. Claire waited, remaining silent, as he called several men to his side.

Penny joined her, and they peeled off to sit on a flat rock beside the path, discomposing a squirrel who dashed away. Cullen stretched out in the sun beside them.

"Theseus said I was to stay safe." Claire ran her hand across the bone handle of her knife. "So here I sit."

"This is disastrous," Penny said.

"Rather terrifying, in truth," Claire said. "And I believe quite deliberate."

"Deliberate?" Penny said, glancing at the niche and the rock. "Yes, I see."

"If the Ottomans have got wind of us…"

"That makes sense, actually. They do not wish the marbles repatriated."

"A fine point." The breeze picked up and almost stole Penny's bonnet. She slammed her hand atop it, and Claire retied the loose ribbons for her. As the wind increased, their skirts billowed about them, and though the day was warm, the shadows' chill seeped into her bones.

"Could our own countrymen have done this?" Claire said.

Penny shook her head. "Though few in Britain wished the marbles returned to Greece, I cannot see it. Too much trouble."

"We are marooned," Claire said. "We cannot go down, nor can we proceed."

A shout in the distance.

Cullen leapt to attention and sniffed the air.

Theseus reappeared while half a dozen men climbed upward, two carrying a large oaken tree trunk. Theseus walked toward the men and examined the trunk. "This will break. Find another."

An older Greek spoke. "Our lookout spotted men and ponies at the base of the trail."

"Bollocks!" Theseus said. "Where are Spyros and Pantelis?"

Cracking and popping burst around them. *Shots!*

She and Penny dropped to the trail floor, Theseus crouching above them in a protective move.

"This is over and above all," Claire said, fear making her voice curt.

"Oh!" Penny said.

"Stay down!" Theseus said, then ran up the hill to the boulder and men.

Shots continued to pepper their party, whilst shouts were barked and orders hollered. Had anyone been hit?

Claire simply could not remain motionless one minute more. "Come on." She began to crawl toward Theseus.

Reaching him, they huddled against the side of the trail.

"The Ottomans?" Claire said.

"No," Theseus said. "Brigands, bandits for profit. They have much to gain were they to acquire the statuary. Yet taking on a well-armed caravan is not their usual style. They prey on the weak and unprepared, though they must have placed the boulder on the trail."

"Well, this is outside of enough, really," Penny said, face tight. "Bandits!"

Wide-eyed, Claire watched Penny drop to a crouch and head downward toward the wagons. Of all the odd things. Spyros appeared out of nowhere and followed, keeping Penny in his sights.

"Penelope, dammit," Theseus barked. "What the hell are you about?"

"I have had enough of this folderol," she hollered back, continuing down the slope toward the nearest wagon.

"What is she doing?" he said.

"I have not the faintest," Claire said.

He growled, then yelled at the sailor holding a musket. "Change the angle of your shot, man!"

By now, Penny had reached the second wagon. She unlocked her trunk and retrieved a long parcel, though Claire couldn't imagine what was inside.

Surrounded by bandits, Claire kept Cullen close. She pressed against the rock, raising a hand to block the sun, and eyed the surroundings.

Their attackers had scattered amongst the rocks above and around them, stationed on precipices and in crevices. Two men, bent like old women, trod upward, hauling a remnant from what looked like a pillar.

Penny, now beneath a rocky overhang, spread out a cloth, her hands moving like a symphony conductor. Claire wished she could see what Penny was doing.

"What is Penelope about?" Theseus headed toward his sister, who rose to a crouch position holding a long musket or rifle.

"Penelope?" Theseus said as he reached her.

A glint from an outcrop well above Claire's head. "Theo, down!" she yelled.

He responded, a bullet missing him by inches.

*Sod it*, that was close. Claire's hands shook, her heart beating triple time, sweat coiling down her back like an adder. She pressed against the rock and gritted her teeth.

Anxiety would not control her.

She had mastered it before, and she would now. Claire side-stepped downward to find her friend and Theseus arguing, Penny clutching the enormous weapon in both hands.

"Do not be ridiculous!" Penny said as Claire reached them.

"What in hell's bells are you doing with a Ferguson?" Theseus said.

"As you know, our old steward is quite fond of me. Do not be angry with him." Penny raised her chin. "He is an armaments enthusiast, and it was in his collection. When I became proficient in its use, he insisted I take it on our journey, saying it would keep me safe."

"Safe! They constantly break."

"They do," Penny said. "I have learned how to repair them."

Theseus' nostrils flared. He seemed about to explode but scrubbed his face, muttering to himself while shots peppered the air.

The two men hefting the marble fragment had reached the boulder uninjured, thank the stars.

"Stay there," he said to the two men. "I am coming up." Theseus stared at the two women, eyes narrowed. "If either of you gets injured..." He paused, clearly overset. "I will never speak to you again!"

He bent low and ran, pistol in hand, toward the boulder.

Penny's face reddened with fury. "This is absurd. The Pythia awaits me, the sculptures must be returned, and you must find your colored statues. Simply intolerable!"

A burst of gunfire, then a pause...stillness.

Claire retrieved her opera glasses and raised them, surveying the scene, as Spyros moved close, popping up occasionally to fire a shot.

Odd how with shots whizzing, rocks cracking, and seabirds' caws, it felt as if a giant muffler wound around their perch.

"I am terrified," Claire said.

Penny nodded. "The weapon's familiarity gives me comfort. I shall pretend I am merely out practicing at Wolf Court." She offered a wan smile. "I shall try, at least."

Penny checked her rifle, then in a flurry of skirts, she bounced up, blew off a shot, and rebounded down beside Claire. Penny counted, her body shaking, face masked with fear, eyes wide. Then seconds later, she repeated the action six times in total.

Above, to their right, a man plummeted to earth. One bandit down.

"Impressive," Spyros said with a smile, admiration in his eyes.

"Six shots before reloading?" Claire said. "I have never heard of such."

"The beauty of the Ferguson." Penny still trembled. She bit down on her lip as she burrowed into her knapsack.

"What are you doing now?" A cool breeze brushed Claire's neck, producing prickles.

"I must lubricate the breech screw before I reload, or the rifle will foul. She is a tricky beast."

None of which made sense to Claire, but she nodded.

"You were well trained, Penelope," Spyros said.

Was that a blush on Penny's cheek?

Claire wished her throwing knives might reach a bandit, but the villains were far too distant.

As Penny reloaded, Claire raised her opera glass once more.

Theseus was appalled. His frail, fragile sister, who could barely catch her breath in England, was wielding a breech-load Ferguson, a gun rarer than hen's teeth. She used it well, had already downed one villain. There she went, hitting another who slumped over a crevice, his weapon tumbling to the sea far below.

Theseus did not know his beloved sister at all. Not at all.

Amidst the chaos, this thought near paralyzed him. All these years, how had he been so obtuse? What else had his steward not told him? And why did she feel the need to keep her abilities secret from him?"

Perhaps she feared he would forbid her participation in them.

*Christ.*

Stranger still, as the first shot rang, his one thought had been to protect Claire. Not his men, not Penelope, but *Claire.* That alarmed him more than...

"Down, Theo!" Spyros shouted.

He landed with a thump, a rock chip from the striking bullet cutting his cheek. He had no time for this shite.

Lunging up, he reached the boulder where the men had rested the pillar shard, bullets whistling as the man beside him returned fire.

"Will this do, Theseus?" the older man queried.

The shard was long, relatively thick, and pointed at the end. "An excellent find that should be the lever we need to move the rock."

Except they could not simply lever the boulder and release it, for it would barrel down to decimate their caravan. He needed at least half-a-dozen men to guide the boulder so it rested back in its niche off the trail.

He stooped as he ran down the line, pulling drivers off wagons, the mules having nowhere to go. The men raced upward as he continued, collecting more men.

Bullets flew, a man hit, a sailor from the *Nemesis*. Theseus raced toward him. But his left arm had been winged, relief coursing through Theseus as he ripped his own shirt to tie off the wound.

"Stay here," he said to the burly man with a shock of red hair.

"Not a chance, my lord."

*Stubborn*. Theseus watched as the sailor ran toward the boulder.

Now to deal with Claire and Penelope.

CHAPTER

# FOURTEEN

Claire observed Theseus crawl to them beneath the rock overhang, shirt ripped, face dusty, expression stolid.

"All well here?" he said through gritted teeth, giving Penny a sideward glance.

"Indeed!" Penny said with enthusiasm, though her muscles were rigid, her eyes glistening with unshed tears. "These are my first live targets."

"For which I am thankful," Theseus said, running a hand across her shoulder.

"I have learned I do not care to kill people. Yet..." She frowned. "Whilst under attack, I find doing so both distasteful and... satisfying."

Claire's eyes darted from one to the other, Theseus' expression best described as one of horror.

Sweat shined his face as he spoke. "Once we have moved the rock to its niche, the men will return to the wagons, and we shall proceed. Untie your donkeys from the sapling and be prepared to move out."

Claire began to dab his face with her kerchief.

He took it from her, swiped, and then stared at the filthy thing, tucking it into a pocket. "I shall purchase you a new one."

"No need," Claire said.

"It could have been worse," Spyros said. "Given the attack's poor execution, these are not Turks."

"They were not. Bandits, I imagine, thinking us easy marks." He glanced at Spyros and grinned. "They were wrong."

"True." Spyros shook his head. "Yet I detect another hand behind this. These hill bandits always prefer tamer targets."

"Not their style, I agree," Theseus said. "After our business in Kastri is done, I shall pursue this."

"Alongside me," Spyros said with a growl.

More pops from gunfire, but the bandits had become more cautious. The wind had picked up, too, which wasn't helping matters.

"So the brigands as perpetrators are a good thing," Penny said in a curious voice.

"I would not describe it that way, sister."

Claire surveyed the chaos. "*Touché.*"

"I will give the signal to move out. Try not to get shot before then."

"Oh, my," Claire said, her voice dripping with sarcasm. "But we were planning on it."

He cast her a dour look and turned to his sister. "Keep your barrage up without risking yourselves. You and the others will hold their attention whilst we move the boulder."

"May I have one of your pistols?" Claire said. "You have an extra, do you not?"

"I do."

"I am not a terribly good shot with a gun, I admit," Claire said in a neutral tone. "But I know how to fire them. Whether any of my shots reach the brigands or not, I can help keep them occupied."

He hesitated.

"It is only common sense, Theseus." Claire held out a hand. "The gun, please."

She could be hurt or killed. Aware his fear far outpaced her simple request, he handed her a pistol, a gun more than a foot long with two barrels, one atop the other. "This is almost a rifle!"

"You will have to fire using both hands."

Claire agreed, as the pistol was too heavy to keep level one-handed. "I shall."

"The gun is loaded. You can get two shots off before you must reload due to the double barrel." He handed her a pouch. "Here are two dozen paper cartridges. Do you know how to load the thing?"

"I believe so."

"See how its lower barrel revolves? Note that the pistol has but one hammer, so you must prime the pan again before firing."

"Understood."

He gave Claire a long look and another for Penelope, who had resumed firing on the bandits.

"Keep them safe," he said to Spyros, then moved off bent in a crouch.

Claire watched Theseus ascend, stomach clenched, easing when he reached the marginal safety of the boulder, the men huddled around it so as not to be targets. They went to work, and Claire peered above the overhang, snaking the pistol up to rest on the rock. She spotted a shooter raising his rifle. Claire braced and fired, its kick jerking her backwards. She grabbed the stone, stopping her descent as chips of rock startled the bandit.

Which was when Penelope shot him with her rifle.

Claire primed the pan for her second round, hands greasy beneath her gloves. It took a moment, but she regained control and continued.

Was it her imagination, or had the bandits' shots become less frequent?

The pan primed, she rested the pistol again on the rock, noting the strange silence blanketing them. A hush, with no flicker of movement, no flashes of white or red, nor glints off gun barrels from the enemy.

Penny sighed. "I am exhausted."

"Shush."

"Oh, the bandits are gone."

"What if the quiet is a ruse?" Claire said.

"It is not." Spyros approached, his expression dour. "They took us on and lost. I shall see what is happening with the boulder."

"But what if…"

"Let me check once more." Penny lifted her spyglass, whilst Claire raised her opera glasses.

"Clear!" Someone shouted from down the slope.

"Clear here!" Another just above them barked.

"Here too!" Penny chimed in.

Gone. They were gone. Claire's muscles trembled, her terror a constant hum since the shooting began.

Her bum flopped onto the rock, her stomach lurching. Oh, no. Not here. Not now. But her gorge rose, unstoppable, and she vomited, clutching the rock wall as a lifeline. *Oh, God, she had been so scared.*

But she hadn't panicked, at least.

A soothing hand rubbed her back in circles.

"Better?" Penny said.

"This may help." A water flask appeared in Spyros' hand.

Claire felt like an utter fool. No one else had gotten sick or shaken like a leaf. "Thank you both."

She swigged water, spat, then drank. "My apologies."

"No need," Penny said. "You were stalwart during the attack. One never knows how one will react to danger until one faces it. The aftermath is unimportant."

Claire supposed so.

"I am pleased that I did not faint," Penny said.

"Faint?" Claire's chuckle was thready. "You were the antithesis of fainting."

"I was, was I not?" Penny said with surprise. "Who knew? I believe we both did quite well." Penny reached across her lap and squeezed Claire's hand.

Claire returned the gesture, every muscle aching. "Unfortunately, I am rather atremble now. In fact, I wish to cry."

"Then do so, dear Claire," Penny said in a whisper.

Claire stared at Penny's sweet smile while a tear or two dripped to her cheeks. "I cannot go full-bore. Good heavens, that would panic everyone. It will be all right." She raised a hand to her bonnet, straightening it, retying the ribbons, and brushing out her skirts—mundane actions that eased her trembles and made her feel more normal. Though after a gun battle, how did one ever feel normal again?

"Come," Penny said. "Let us see what progress Theseus and the men have made."

Atop the rise, she and Penny stood near the men and the immense rock but far enough away for safety. Men clustered around the stone as Theseus shouldered the pillar shard, its tip resting between the boulder and the ground. God above, she'd never seen such strength.

Theseus' shirt flapped, torn to pieces and spotted with blood and dirt. The sun was unseasonably warm, all the men glistening with sweat, though Claire suspected the intensity of the assault contributed.

"Now!" Theseus shouted. He pushed the pillar shard downward, muscles bunched as he strained.

The sight made Claire's mouth dry, a totally inappropriate response.

The boulder did not budge.

"Spyros and Pantelis!" he shouted. "Get the hell up here!"

The men sprinted to Theseus.

Spyros grunted and affixed his hands high on the lever, Pantelis clasping his hands above Spyros'.

Theseus shouted again. "Again!"

The men pushed while Theseus, Spyros, and Pantelis shoved the lever downward.

Penny watched with rapt intent, her gaze on Spyros. It was obvious he fascinated her. Humm.

The boulder moved. The men rocked it. It moved again, then began to roll in a downward trajectory.

The men dropped the lever to help those guiding the boulder to its niche.

Faster and faster, and a man tripped, fell away, fortunately clear of the boulder.

Shouts, then, "Release!"

The boulder sped downward, bounced once in its niche, sending up a plume of dust before it settled.

Men flung up their hands, shouts and cheers filling the air, hers and Penny's included, as Theseus whirled. His arms reached out to give her a huge hug.

"We did it, Claire!"

She grinned up at him. "Most definitely!"

They looked at each other, at their embrace. Both startled, Theseus the first to step back. He turned to the men, grinning, and raised a fist. The company's huzzahs filled the air.


A FEW OF their men were injured, though none badly, for which Claire was thankful. Her nerves might be frayed, her clothing askew and filthy, but she was alive. Penny was alive. Theseus was gloriously alive and in command. Not a soul in their party had died, yet she strained to bury her anxiety. Claire wiped her brow with a kerchief, trying to dismiss the shakes that felt as if the ground beneath her trembled.

The ground *was* trembling, and she clung to the wall of rock like a limpet.

"Poseidon is welcoming us yet again," Penny said with enthusiasm, also pressed to the cliffside.

"Yes," she said, breathless. "It does seem so. I pray the earth does not open up and swallow us whole. I am all for Poseidon's hellos, but after the bandits, this is a bit much."

"Hellas offers many surprises, does it not?" Penny said.

"I am full up with surprises, I fear." Claire's nervous laugh made Penny frown.

Penny ran a hand down Claire's shoulder. "I understand, yet I suspect more wonders await, too."

"As well as just a touch of calm?" Claire said.

"That, too," Penny said softly, nodding.

The tremble ceased, and Claire eased out a breath she had been holding forever, unwilling to release the rock until she was sure the trembles had ceased.

On the rise above, Theseus signaled the wagons to prepare. Their donkeys, good boys both, stood patiently nearby, seemingly unaffected by Mother Earth's rumpus.

Once all were mounted, Theseus, astride his pony, signaled the caravan to move out.

The next stretch of trail was at a gentle downward slope, which led to a small valley of gorse and olive groves, where they made camp. Soon, the animals were enclosed in a makeshift corral, fed, and watered, and the men set out their thick sleeping blankets and started a cook fire, whilst others patrolled the camp.

Penny's eyes glowed. "Tomorrow we make Kastri."

"The village is quite small," Claire said.

"Certainly smaller than Itea, perhaps two hundred souls."

Claire's blood fizzed with their impending arrival, and while she knew the temples, statues, and amphitheater were buried deep beneath the earth, she pictured its former splendor. The "Omphalos," or center of the world to the ancient Hellenes. Perhaps some of the stone monuments, also known as the Omphalos, survived. Claire had viewed many renderings of the ancient temples, and in the taste of the crisp air, the scents of olive and juniper, her imagination took flight.

A pilgrim would tread the sacred way, which ran up Parnassus and through the sanctuary. Their eyes would widen in wonder as they came first upon the Sanctuary of Athena Pronaia. Above stood the immense pillared Sanctuary of Apollo, and beyond it, the expansive amphitheater set into a hill. An epic sight she wished she could see.

Cullen nudged her leg, and she ruffled his fur. She believed a few marble remnants may have worked their way to the light, ones that contained pigment. Finding a Delphic shard was a moment she dreamed about.

Penny and Spyros were talking by the campfire, whilst Theseus checked the crated sculptures. His Greek friend from Athens would take charge of them, distributing them to their proper locations. Theseus would be relieved. Overjoyed, in all likelihood. Yet she suspected he would be saddened, too, for he treasured all things ancient and had lived with these artifacts for decades.

Penny's insouciance awed her. Claire sat on the blankets, removed her journal, and began to detail the day's events. When her hand began to shake, she repeated that all was well, that they were safe. No more guns or knives. She closed her eyes, wishing to will away her fear.

"What are you writing?"

Her eyes sprang open as Theseus sat beside her. He looked weary, fresh lines scoring his forehead. But his eyes danced with excitement.

"My journal. I am jotting down the day's events."

"Do you use this for your field notes as well?"

"In this case, yes. I usually carry two notebooks, one for daily musings and the other for research, but there was no point in carrying a second book on our adventure."

"Adventure. It has been that. How do you fare?" He skimmed a finger across her jawline, eyes intense, and for a moment, safety and reassurance blanketed her. "Today was like nothing you have experienced."

She nodded. "I would judge that a great understatement."

He chuckled. "You were remarkable in the face of a terrible assault."

"I would say Penny was the remarkable one."

He sobered. "Indeed."

"Had you any idea she could shoot like that?" Claire tucked away her pencil and journal.

"Not really. Our steward mentioned lessons, but the extent of her mastery? No. I believed it a trifling amusement. Nothing more."

"Your sister takes her pastimes quite seriously. Much like yourself."

His forearms rested on bent knees, his hands clasped, the campfire flickering shadows across his face.

"What is it?" Claire said.

"I fear I do not know my sister at all. I always saw her as...fragile."

"Perhaps you interpreted the coughing and shortness of breath as fragility, wholly understandable. Have you noticed how her coughs and sniffles have receded?"

"I have." Theseus appeared to struggle with his words. "*Christ!* She is my *sister*. I should *know* my own sister."

Claire rested a hand on his arm. "We all of us think we know someone, but we usually only perceive a portion of the person's inner workings, do you not think? At Wolf Court, Penelope has taken life into her own hands. But she is still the sister you know and love. That has not changed."

"Perhaps."

"Talk to her," Claire said. "Tell her your feelings. She loves you very much."

His jaw tightened, and he closed his eyes for a moment. "Are you prepared for the morrow?"

A resounding slam on the topic. Men and their feelings. But Theseus was hurting, and she loathed it. She would speak to Penny about his concerns. "Indeed, I am all set for Delphi!"

"Good." He rose abruptly. "I will see you later."

# FIFTEEN

oth Claire and Penny had shocked him with their competent demeanor under fire. He recalled the first time he had experienced an assault on the Peninsula. He had cast up his accounts in front of officers, much to his embarrassment, but had forgotten the incident. He would tell Claire so. All emotions roiled after battle.

He crossed the camp to check on the animals when Spyros hailed him, drawing him aside.

"What is it?" Theseus said.

Spyros stared him in the eye, chin thrust, jaw clenched.

"What, Spyros?" Theseus said, hands on hips.

"Pantelis is nowhere to be found."

A spurt of unease. "He helped with the lever. Perhaps he was wounded and we did not realize?"

"No." Spyros' jaw clenched. "Earlier, he joined a sailor and me to scour the site. Yet, minutes ago I realized he was missing."

Theseus surveyed the scene of people, animals, and wagons. *Where had Pantelis gone?* He slapped his thigh with his hat. "You are positive he did not fall, perhaps get his foot stuck in a crevice or some such?"

"I searched again. He has vanished."

"I see." Pantelis' disappearance disturbed him greatly, for it hinted at dubious undertakings. "Dispatch a man to check the way down and in Itea. This is most disturbing."

The excitement was palpable the following day as they prepared to leave the grove for Delphi. Sad to say, they went nowhere—a wagon wheel had loosened and cracked, and Theseus, Spyros, and others worked for hours righting the problem.

Everyone ached to reach their destination, and Claire dug for patience at the delay. After writing in her journal, she gathered her knives and walked to a stand of trees to practice. She was good, better than good, in truth, but continued training was essential. She withdrew the knives from their roll and began to throw, again and again and again.

As the sun headed toward the far horizon and night approached, Claire was sweaty, her arm aching when she sensed a nearby presence. Theseus, for she always knew when he was near.

"Do you wish to throw?" she asked him.

"I do."

Claire retrieved the embedded knives and handed them to him.

He took a solid stance, drew back his right arm, and threw. The first knife landed with a thunk in a tree a good five yards beyond her own targets. "You have been keeping your light under a bushel."

Theseus lifted the next knife and threw. Another solid hit. "Oftentimes, when my father and I finished our day's work on a dig, we would pass the time throwing knives. He was abysmal, which really stuck in his craw." Theseus shrugged. "I found it fun."

She lifted a blade and aimed for Theseus' more distant tree, hers landing beside his. "It is fun. Also quite useful when needs be." The hullabaloo at Hawthorne House had proved *that* when the awful St. Michaels had tried a second time to kidnap Lottie.

Theseus growled. "Having waded through the political muck back in England, I imagined Greece a bit more hospitable, skirmishes or no. It appears I was wrong."

They stood side by side and threw, the rhythm familiar and pleasing, yet his very presence alongside her was a distraction both appealing and disturbing.

Claire wished she knew how to cast lures, the urge to do so rather ridiculous, in truth. Theseus' eyes told endless tales, yet she had never glimpsed desire in them. At least, desire for her. She would recognize his interest, would she not? Claire felt at sea.

For the first time, she had feelings for a man. They did not appear to be returned.

Theseus could throw for hours. These were well-balanced knives, and yet the discomfort he felt standing beside Claire made him itch. He wished for her to look at him, not as an antiquarian or as an earl, but as a man. One she craved as he craved her.

The longing had come upon him slowly, snuck up on him, really. This urge to touch her, to kiss her, to entice her into his arms—an alien sensation, like the discovery of a new star. His star. His *to asteri mu.*

Few women intrigued him, for he disliked airs and affectations in both women and men. Even fewer were intellectually adept at discussing anything other than the weather or the day's fashions, none of which held his interest. Whereas Lady Claire held her own in all matters with her inquiring mind, fierce passion for her work, and shocking courage. And those gorgeous bright eyes and bold lips.

The woman had snuck inside him...somehow. He had seldom experienced these sensations, and never with such power. He was both confounded and spellbound.

Theseus threw another blade, relishing the physicality coupled with the delicacy. He lifted another.

Claire and Penny had shocked him during the attack with their stalwart determination to fight off the bandits. How many other women hid that sort of light beneath the costume of fragility? No matter, for it was this woman he wanted, one who both drove him to distraction and delighted him.

He stared down at her, willing her to look up at him, to see the longing in his eyes, and to feel the same desire.

Claire raised her face to his, a slight smile trembling her lips.

Which was when he stepped forward, slipped an arm around her waist, and kissed her.

STARTLED, Claire froze. Theseus had paralyzed her by his shocking action, the feel of his lips on hers, a gentle exploration, and the way his tongue slid across its seam. Claire gasped, and he slipped inside.

The knife she held dropped as his passion, woven with his sandalwood and musk scent, made her dizzy, like the champagne she'd once tried. No, the sensations were far more delicious than any potable. Claire stood on tiptoe, wrapped her arms around his neck, and leaned into their kiss.

He cupped her face as he eased away, staring down at her with wonder, eyes blinking, while she gazed up at him, her emotions running riot.

Would he apologize? She hoped not, for that kiss was one of the loveliest, most exciting moments she had ever experienced. She offered him a tentative smile.

Theseus' brow furrowed, and he swooped in again, this time fierce and hungry. She met his hunger with her own, becoming lost in the touch of his hands moving across her back, down her waist, pulling her tighter into his embrace.

"Claire!" Penny called out. "Claire, where are you?"

They drew apart, reluctant to abandon this fever dream of pleasure. Claire knew not what to say, and it appeared Theseus was equally silenced.

They stepped back, eyes glued to one another, to stand side-by-side, his hand lingering on hers.

For the first time in years, when she threw her knife, it landed in the dirt.

Penny arrived in a flurry of skirts and anticipation. "When do we leave?"

Theseus cleaned off her poorly aimed knife and returned it to Claire, stiffening as he stepped to his sister.

"The night is near upon us," he said in calm tones. "We leave on the morrow."

"But we are so close," Penny said. "We can make Delphi before dark sets in."

"You overestimate the speed with which our mules can pull the wagons."

"I do not think I do," she said.

"Penelope," he said. "The men are weary. *I* am weary. A good night's rest will serve us better than racing to Delphi at twilight, where we could lumber over a rock and break another wheel or injure an animal."

"You are right. I concur." Penelope began to pace. "Yet the Pythia awaits me, expects me today."

Claire observed the siblings' escalating frustration. Theseus had stiffened, and Penny stood stock-still.

"Dear Penny, I do not doubt the Pythia awaits you," Claire said. "I am sure she will not mind a slightly extended wait in light of the safety issues."

"That does make sense." Penny huffed a breath.

"I suspect Xanthe knows our trek is a dangerous one," Claire said. "She may have even heard of the bandit attack, for gossip flies on swift wings."

"I understand." Penny looked between Claire and Theseus, tossed them a smile, and walked away.

Claire and Theseus returned to the camp in silence. Penny's remarks were not discussed, nor were their kisses.

*Oh, those kisses.*

Like herself, Claire suspected Theseus was cogitating on both. Impossible not to relive those luxurious moments when he pulled her close, her whole body effervescent with sensation. She wanted more, to touch his arm, his back, his glorious chest. She wished to cup his cheek, to rake her fingers through his auburn hair. To *feel* him.

But what if he was not thinking about that at all? More likely, he was orchestrating their departure on the morrow. Theseus must have kissed many women. Dozens, even. He was a handsome, alluring peer of the realm. Ladies must fling themselves at him. How could he resist? Perhaps he had held them in his arms, placed his lips on theirs, and nuzzled their necks just as he had hers. She stuttered in a breath.

Had it meant something to him? Or nothing?

Spyros raced up to them, agitated, spewing a mouthful of Greek so fast Claire caught but two words, Penelope and pony.

Theseus' jaw clenched. He snapped a nod, returning a barrage of Greek, and Spyros stomped off, talking to himself and shaking his head.

"What is wrong? Claire said. "The Greek was too fast for me to catch."

Theseus crossed his arms, his face stoic. "Penelope has taken the pony. Spyros blames himself, as he was to keep watch over her. I, in fact, do not blame him in the least, for my sister has become a termagant!"

"We must go after her," Claire said. "Oh. We cannot, can we?"

He answered through gritted teeth. "No, we cannot, as she purloined my pony. A donkey would never catch her, and the mules must stay with the wagons." He drew in a deep breath. "Christ."

Theseus strode toward the men, Claire wishing Penny had not done such. She prayed for Penelope's safe arrival in Kastri and ached for Theseus, the incident underscoring his misconceptions about his sister. He loved her so.

Yet her thoughts veered back to their kiss and how it had shot her to the stars.

Off went Spyros on Penny's donkey, following her. Since he would not catch her before she arrived in Kastri, he appeared determined to be close behind.

As night descended, they ate around the campfire, its warmth stealing some of the night's chill. Afterward, Theseus showed her the makeshift tent they had rigged for her, which she found lovely but rather too privileged. Yet she could not help but appreciate his and the others' chivalric efforts.

Restless, Claire checked on the injured men clustered beneath an olive tree, pleased they were in good spirits. She then perambulated around the outskirts of their heavily guarded camp. She had hoped Theseus would join her, but he had many tasks, as always.

She clasped her hands. That passion... reason said it resulted from the heightened emotions of the attack's aftermath. A small shiver, a remembrance of that kiss, made her smile. Perhaps it had been more.

The night was quiet, the breeze gentle, rustling the leaves, the distant stream a comforting burble.

A shout rang out.

More shouts, the camp going on high alert, as she rushed to return.

"What is happening?" she asked a sailor, her voice calm, her feelings running riot.

"Riders. Coming our way. Four of them."

In seconds, Theseus was before her, handing her that same pistol she'd used during the bandit attack. Claire turned to enter her tent, but he stopped her.

"I would prefer you stay behind that large rock." He pointed to a massive boulder.

"If you wish." She dipped into the tent and again strapped a knife to her waist and reaffixed several throwing knives to her person. Then she raced across camp to slip behind the boulder to peer around the side.

Theseus directed the shooters to their posts, stomped out their fire, then stood in the center of the camp.

What was that crazy man doing? "You are making yourself a target!"

He ignored her. Of course. She checked if her pistol was ready to fire and then waited, anxious about the riders, nervous with Theseus standing for all to see. She pressed her head to the boulder. Calm, she must be calm.

The darkness was near complete but for the rising moon, stars emerging to festoon the sky. Damn Theseus for not taking cover.

Silence descended but for the clip-clop of horses' hooves, the jangle of their tack, and the chuffing of breath.

Light haloed the group as four riders approached, accompanied by five of Theseus' men on foot, one holding a blazing torch.

"What ho, the camp," shouted a rider in a plummy British accent.

"Hallo there, Ashworth!" hollered another British voice, one with a particularly pleasant timbre.

The group halted, and Theseus swiped another torch and approached, holding the flame high enough for Claire to see his face change from one of stoic determination to merriment.

"Claire!" he said with enthusiasm. "Do come! I wish to introduce a gentleman to you."

As she emerged, the quartet dismounted, and backslaps amongst the men and bows for two female riders ensued.

Theseus obviously knew them, and he relit the campfire while others set more torches ablaze, enabling her to see their visitors' faces.

Claire gasped, disbelieving. She recognized Lord Garland, his lady wife, and her maid, having met them at Wolf Court. Strange and surprising, but not shocking. No, it was their companion, dressed in full *fustanella* regalia of the pleated skirt, leggings, and embroidered vest, though tall Hessian riding boots somewhat ruined the effect.

It truly was *he*—the famous and infamous Lord Byron.

As she neared the fire, Cullen hugging her hip, Theseus drew Byron to her, her pistol lowered. Byron said something to Theseus, which made him smile. *Damnation.* The poet was an Adonis when smiling. Byron seemed Theseus' old...friend or acquaintance? Hard to tell. Theseus winged out an arm, and she took it as he drew her forward.

The presentations were made, and she did not remark at having met the Garlands at Wolf Court, for she was tongue-tied in Byron's presence. Adoring the poet's incandescent verse, Claire wished to say something profound or even interesting. Yet she remained silent.

They took seats around the campfire, and the men continued to talk while Lady Garland leaned near.

"This is my maid, Helene," her ladyship said.

"You were at Wolf Court," Claire said. "I am pleased to meet you."

Helene nodded, her face a mask of indifference. That Lady Garland introduced her maid using her first name implied a close connection. Even presenting Helene was unusual. Most likely the situation's casual nature, not to mention the abundant ouzo and retsina, was the cause. Cullen sat on the ground between herself and her ladyship, ever alert. Occasionally, he would peer at Lord Garland and emit a throaty growl.

Her mind blinked...and blinked again—she was sitting beside Byron, author of "Prometheus," "The Prisoner of Chillon," and "Childe Harold's Pilgrimage." *The* Lord Byron.

His lordship had been one of the few denouncing the "theft" of the Parthenon friezes by Lord Elgin, doing so in "The Curse of Minerva." The man and Theseus were of a singular point of view, though she was unsure of the Garlands. How odd they seemed—less substantial than Theseus or Byron.

"I could never believe it when Lord and Lady Garland appeared on my doorstep in Ravenna," Byron said. "They urged me to leave Italy and come to Greece, explaining that you were returning the sculptures your father unearthed to Delphi."

Theseus had kept their destination secret until they arrived in Itea. How did the Garlands know of their journey's end? How did they even know Lord Byron?

"I could not resist, of course," Byron continued, and his smile was breathtaking. "Hellas will soon rise against the Ottoman oppressor and take back their land, country, and heritage."

Theseus said nothing, but Garland chimed in. "Indeed. Any day now."

"You get ahead of yourself, Garland," Theseus said. "Whilst skirmishes have broken out and though the time is close, it is not now."

"I applaud your returning pieces of Greece's heritage," Byron said.

"As do we both," Garland said with much enthusiasm, taking his wife's hand. She smiled sweetly.

The lovely woman looked neat as a pin, as if she'd just left a garden party, which made Claire too aware of her own dirt and dishevelment.

Funny how she had not warmed to the couple upon their first meeting. Even now, in such a convivial group, she found the man's overly mirthful manner off-putting. Too enthusiastic? Too agreeable? Theseus was not nearly as companionable with Garland as he was toward Byron.

Why had the Garlands lured Byron to visit Greece? An oddity.

"We met your sister on our way here!" Garland said with great joviality.

*Oh, dear.* That would fan the flames of Theseus' discontent. Claire doubted the others noted Theseus' low-throated growl.

"Lady Penelope was nearing Kastri," Byron said. "I dispatched one of my attendants to accompany her the remainder of the way."

Theseus nodded, his face remaining stoic, but the firelight bared the relief in his eyes.

"That was well done, my lord," Claire said. "I was worried for Lady Penelope's safety, and you have eased my mind."

"Reward enough, my lady." Byron grinned. "Is that not a wolfhound?"

Lord Garland looked askance at Cullen, whose tongue lolled.

"Yes. His name is Cullen. He is my companion."

"He is quite wonderful!" Byron said.

"Take good care, Byron," Garland said. "For he is not the most amenable fellow."

Claire bristled. "I beg to differ, my lord." She gestured for Cullen to greet Byron, whereupon he trotted over, lay down, and rested his head in the man's lap, of all things. Byron began to pet him.

"You plan to accompany us to Delphi?" Claire said.

"Most definitely," Byron said.

The men launched into a discussion of what they called the "impending revolution," and Claire recalled the Iteans' victorious skirmish over the Turks, celebrated on their arrival in the village. Yet the idea of a cobbled-together band of Greeks overcoming the Ottoman Empire made her blood run cold.

Though she agreed mightily in principle, she prayed their revolution did not become a Greek bloodbath.

Garland moved closer to Theseus and Byron. While he was voluble and outspoken, Lady Garland remained quiet, hands clasped, though she would occasionally reach over and scratch behind Cullen's ears. Each time she did so, Helene made a moue.

"I prefer the Alopekis," Helene said, her voice low and pleasant. "Better guard dogs."

"We shall agree," Claire said, surprised at the woman's knowledge of Greek canids. "To disagree."

Helene nodded. Her ladyship's eyes continued to dart around the campfire in obvious apprehension. In truth, she looked as out of keeping as a rose amidst scrub.

"Are you well, my lady?" Claire said.

Lady Garland's eyes rose to hers. "I am. Thank you for your concern, Lady Claire."

"Here, we are three women amongst a horde of men. Do call me Claire."

The woman's soft smile appeared. "You may call me Frances."

Though her ladyship appeared to relax somewhat, Helene's expression remained dour.

CHAPTER

# SIXTEEN

In the firelight, Byron's visage was both alluring and strange, near otherworldly, his beauty stealing her breath whilst his genius seared her soul. Yet imagining that brilliance contained in that too-exquisite flesh challenged her, almost as if there were two distinct Byrons.

He continued fussing over Cullen, the dog immediately taking to him. Unsurprising, for he was a renowned animal lover and owned an assemblage of domestic and exotic animals in Italy. She hoped they were well cared for while he was away.

"Do join me in the tent, Lady Garland, Helene," Claire said. "It is quite comfortable and private."

Her ladyship sighed. "Thank you, Lady Claire, but Helene and I shall stay with my husband. We are accustomed to sleeping outdoors."

"Of course." That was a surprise, unable to picture the two very proper Englishwomen enjoying their slumber on the hard ground. Claire said her goodnights, Cullen rising with her. Theseus took up a lantern and walked to her tent, a fine construct of canvas that normally covered the wagons.

"Sleep well." He gave her the lantern, brushing fingers across her hand.

Claire warmed, an absurdity, yet he had touched her, his eyes warm in the lantern light. Setting the lantern on the crate beside her pallet, she donned her nightrail, then placed her precious monocle beside the lantern. Claire slid beneath the thin blanket, fine for this warm night. All the comforts of home.

*Home.*

Claire snuggled deeper beneath the covers. Charlotte and Patrick would have progressed on their improvements to Hawthorne House. Mama must have returned to Halafair as well. She smiled, imagining Rose and Rhys with their new baby, Gareth.

Cullen heard her sigh and raised his head. She ruffled his fur. "All is well."

Claire lifted her knapsack and removed a small painting, setting it on her stomach. Charlotte's Christmas gift. When packing, she had discarded jewelry and her second journal, but this she could not leave—the miniature of her family home. Her eyes burned, for she missed them all.

Had a bandit's bullet ended her life, she would have never again seen her beloveds. Eyes damp, Claire replaced the painting in its padded pouch inside her knapsack.

Tomorrow they would reach Kastri and Delphi. A thrill coursed through her at their impending arrival and at what she might discover. Yet that sensation recalled another of the day's events. The kiss. *Theseus.*

The low murmur of his baritone filtered through the thin canvas wall. She missed him, how absurd, for he was right beyond the tent.

Her admiration for the man had grown, as had her affection. Oh, my. Affection, in truth, though Claire was loath to admit it. Theseus was gruff, oft taciturn, yet those qualities concealed a nonpareil. She admired his sterling ethics, the way he gave respect to others of any station—Spyros, Kostas, and others she had witnessed. His kindness, though often subtle, was in evidence—when he had silenced the crowd or written to Mama and Rhys, permitting her to join their journey. His teasing delighted her, too, and she recalled how he'd seeded that Renaissance bust and they'd laughed at the outcome. None of which hinted at his remarkable intelligence, grouchy old sod or not.

Theseus' ardor, and hers—simply inflamed passions caused by the bandit attack. That must be it. Such fire diminished in time, did it not? These were heightened circumstances, after all. Or was she experiencing a more permanent ailment?

Claire hoped not, for it set her all a-dither.

Her eyes grew heavy waiting for Theseus. Since their arrival in Greece, he had bid her "sweet dreams" each night through the door. Though she bit her cheek to stay awake, he did not come, which bothered her far more than it should. Theseus mattered…a great deal.

There, someone outside the canvas?

No. She sighed, and sleep stole all thought.

The following day, the excitement palpable, Theseus relaxed when they finally left the small valley. Though later than planned, it was but two hours after dawn. A wagon wheel had come loose, again delaying their departure. A common and annoying occurrence.

Not only Claire, but Lady Garland and the maid had also helped break down the camp, while a sailor, Garland, Byron, and he repaired the wagon wheel. It took twice as long as it should, and he wished Spyros was there to help.

A good man, Spyros, and Theseus was glad he had followed Penelope, Byron's servant accompanying her or no.

A scion of a wealthy family from Kifisia who prized education and accomplishment, Spyros was in the same year at Trinity as Theseus, as was Devonshire. Their trio became boon companions until Spyros transferred after their third year to École Polytechnique to study engineering, one of his many passions. Yet they had remained close, Spyros visiting Theseus and his father's Greek digs and traveling to Wolf Court over the years.

The land dipped briefly before they began their final push to Kastri. Theseus sat atop the lead wagon, refusing to ride a donkey into Kastri. He was a large man and awkward atop such a small equine, his feet near dragging the ground. Not a state in which he wished to meet the village's headman and headwoman, though he acknowledged much was due to his damnable pride.

Garland was gesticulating wildly, Byron in whoops. The poet was quixotic, a narcissist, and, perhaps, slightly mad. Nonetheless, he was intoxicating, his appearance drawing accolades, his energy unflagging, his fitness inciting legions of admirers.

Over his shoulder, he spied Claire upon her donkey. Unable to resist her lure, Theseus drew his wagon beside her much shorter donkey. As he peered down at her welcoming smile, thoughts of marriage intruded, a first. Not that he would say such anytime soon, for he suspected she would find the idea ridiculous. Perhaps it was. Yet the thought of wooing her appealed, though he was unsure of how to go about it.

As Theseus had grown, he had so focused on his antiquarian pursuits—his studies, digging in Greece, and his evolving mission to return the sculptures—little time was had for engaging women in flirtation, let alone courtship. Nor had he felt the urge to do so.

Then he had met Lady Claire.

He flicked the reins, urging the mules to put one foot in front of another. The trail rose in a gentle slope until they reached a pass between two towering peaks, the ascent precipitous. The mules and donkeys were fine, but Byron's party on horseback would struggle as their mounts were more suited to green fields and sturdy roads.

*Why had they come?* As a subterfuge, perhaps, or was this but foolish paranoia, seeing villains amongst the olive trees? Yet he could not shake his discomfort with the party's arrival.

Claire noted the air thinning to a cool crispness on this first day of June, though at a little over two thousand feet, the elevation wasn't exceptional. Clouds flitted across the blue sky, ghostly wisps that hovered between Parnassus' peaks.

They climbed yet another rise to reveal a rocky plain abutting the mountain where a ramble of cottages clustered. Claire stared at the tiny village, a slight wind buffeting her, but pictured the pillars of Delphi beneath.

With enthusiasm, Claire looked to Theseus. His eyes warmed with equal delight, for before them was the most sacred space in all of Hellas—Delphi—once perceived as the world's navel.

Destroyed in 398 AD, the mists of time obscured Delphi's location for centuries until Cyriacus of Ancona rediscovered it in 1436.

Claire could not wait to see it all.

For millennia, no Delphic excavation had occurred, in part because Kastri sat atop the site. To dig, the village would have to be moved, a costly undertaking that the Ottomans dismissed.

Their arrival felt epic, and yet where once the great sanctuary sat, now sheep and goats grazed the plain and hillside.

As a serious student of ancient Greece, Claire had brushed up on the voyage. The land was now sparse and severe, but lush greenery would have greeted the supplicant in ancient times. The amphitheater would have seen plays and celebrations for the gods, particularly Apollo and Athena. Statues to the gods would have adorned buildings and stairways, all abounding with flowering plants.

As they crossed the plain, two men from Kastri on sturdy ponies approached. Theseus raised a hand, halting their caravan, and walked with Byron and Garland to meet them. After greetings were exchanged, all moved toward the small town. Claire wished to dig for shards, slide her fingers into the soil, and *feel*.

Patience. She must find patience, but her blood fizzed, her mind peripatetic with excitement.

Soon, she promised herself. Soon.

. . .

PENNY SAT outside a cozy cottage sipping tea on a bench alongside the Pythia, Spyros leaning against the cottage wall slipping a string of *komboloi,* or worry beads, through one hand. Since he had arrived in Kastri ahead of the others, he had become her shadow. Not a bad name for him, in truth.

The Pythia, a woman of indeterminate age, bore an aristocratic nose, high cheekbones, and black gimlet eyes that saw everything. Her complexion was nut brown, and her clothes simple but elegant, harking back to ancient styles. They had greeted each other as old friends, Penny feeling the weight of the Pythia's profound knowledge, though her demeanor was wry, much as her letters had been. The woman had offered Penny the use of her name, Xanthe.

Xanthe's weavings had sent Penny into transports, and these were but a few of her many textiles. One bore Perseus holding aloft Medusa's head, another of swallows swooping about a laurel tree, and a third of stylized horses galloping across a rocky plain.

Penny walked to the tapestry on a loom. "That is a lily, is it not? I am not familiar with the work's stylization."

"Ah!" Xanthe said. "Yes, a lily with crocuses surrounding it, taken from a cup found on the island of Thera. The cup is very ancient."

"I have never seen such a design. The delicacy is captivating."

Xanthe smiled.

Definitely not the woman Penny had seen in the Itean cave, and she had asked Xanthe about the vision.

"Did you not say a mist rose about you?" Xanthe said.

"Yes. When the mist surrounded me, I saw the woman."

The Pythia sent her a pleasant smile. "That is explicable, as I believe the mists rising from Gaea *create* the visions."

Penny sat up at that startling idea. "In truth?"

"Mine come in a similar fashion. Though Delphi has disappeared, our hills contain many caves, including one where the mist rises. A sacred one we use for our rituals."

Penny would not disrespect the Pythia by asking the location.

A young woman appeared carrying a tray of sweets, the small owl perched on her shoulder swaying as she walked.

"Do join us, my dear," the Pythia said. "This is Nomiki. She carries her *Athene noctua* she named Glauca."

"Hello, Nomiki." Penny stepped closer. "Your owl of Athena is beautiful."

Nomiki's eyes were lowered. "Hello, my lady."

"Nomiki found Glauca as an owlet on the ground," Xanthe said. "No other chicks remained in the nest, and a predator would have gotten her, so she brought her home."

"Do you fly her, Nomiki?" Penny said.

The girl's bright green eyes opened wide. "Sometimes."

"At home, my brother flies hawks and falcons."

Nomiki nodded, her eyes again lowered.

"All right then," Xanthe said. "Go about your tasks. But one of these days, my dear Nomiki, you must learn to engage more fully."

The young woman bobbed her head, eyes still on the ground. Glauca let out a squawk, and Nomiki departed as if Cerberus himself were chasing her.

"Nomiki will be the next Pythia," Xanthe said. "But she is horribly shy. Not the finest attribute in a forecaster, as she must interact with many, from lowborn to high. We are working on that."

"Why choose Nomiki?" Penny said. "I confess I am curious."

The Pythia's smile widened. "I did not choose her, Apollo himself did."

"How do you mean?"

"Of the young women who accompany me to the cave, only Nomiki sees the visions."

Which, of course, made Penny wonder why she had seen one.

"You could be the Pythia as well, were you so inclined."

Though the idea enchanted Penny, such a weighty responsibility terrified her. She searched the plain for the caravan, eager to see them, yet knowing Theo would thrash her hide, at least verbally. The tea helped, marginally.

"You are troubled," Xanthe said.

Penny fussed with her skirts. "My brother must be furious that I left rather...precipitously."

Spyros chimed in. "I would call that an understatement, my lady."

"You did steal his pony," Xanthe said in wry tones.

"I confess, I regret my actions." Penny didn't know what had gotten into her, and she was ashamed, but ever since they'd arrived in Greece, she felt wild and free and a little mad.

In the distance, two men on horseback crested the rise, flanked by two villagers on ponies. And there was Claire on her donkey and the wagons, with Theseus driving the first. Penny's stomach dropped.

"I shall go meet them," she said, intending to walk very slowly.

"Good!" Xanthe nodded. "Meet the fury head-on. You will survive."

She would, but it would hurt.


FOR SUCH A SMALL VILLAGE, the hullabaloo on their arrival was immense. They met the headman, a wiry soul with a beaming smile named Andreas, his cotton shirt and pleated-skirt fustanella billowing beneath a knee-length coat edged with fur.

Adults, children, and animals swarmed, cheering and raising their arms, seemingly euphoric over their appearance, particularly that of Theseus and Byron. Penny walked toward them looking composed. How Theseus would react was anyone's guess.

"He must be furious with me," Penny said when she reached Claire.

"I presume so," Claire said. "But he also loves you dearly."

"I do not know what came over me," Penny said. "Nor shall I blame his anger, though I am loath to receive it."

Theseus neared and pointed to a white cottage with a blue door flanking Kastri's single street. "Your trunks will be delivered. I expect you will find the accommodations suitable." He strode off, having only addressed Claire while pointedly ignoring his sister.

"Theseus, talk to me," Penny said, running after him.

Claire caught up. "Stop. He will settle and forgive."

"Theo always does, but I have hurt his feelings. My brother has a soft heart."

Claire took her hand. "Come. Shall we settle in our cottage?"

"Yes, let's. Last night, I stayed with the Pythia."

Penny was upset by Theseus' indifference, though it hid what she called his soft heart, which he did everything to disguise. A proud man, he would nonetheless forgive. Yet imagining him unhappy made her ache.

Of a sudden, a crowd of villagers swamped them with effusive greetings, dissolving all thought.

# SEVENTEEN

The two days after their arrival, the temperature rose amidst thunder and pounding rain. The third morning, a thud onto Claire's chest awakened her, a too-familiar occurrence.

She peeked out the window to see blazing sunshine. A relief. Muddy though it might be, she would dig today.

She stared into her eager pup's face, his nose a mere inch from hers. "You need out, yes?"

Cullen licked her cheek.

"All right." She groaned as she blinked away sleep, propping herself up to stare into those adoring eyes. "Just a moment."

Penelope's bed was made up. She must have risen at first light. On the small table between their beds stood a ceramic vase sporting a fresh spray of wildflowers. Today's blooms were yellow and pink and quite lovely. Penelope had been busy.

Claire flung off the covers, dressed, and gathered her knapsack and tool bag, then left their cottage so Cullen could take care of business while she went to find food for both of them.

The previous days' rain had raged like angry demons. Now, the sun seared the landscape, the sky cloudless, the air smelling fresh and new. Perhaps today she would find a marble shard in support of her hypothesis.

When Claire entered the small *taverna,* she spotted Lord Byron sampling a variety of breakfast dishes. He waved her over.

The day was heating up, but a pleasant breeze blew through the dining room, stirring the red curtains. Coffee. Claire needed coffee. Never a morning person, Claire was still groggy, while Byron fairly crackled with energy. She sat across from him, eyeing his spread— rich Greek coffee, cheeses, olives, and yogurt topped with pine honey. *Siglino,* or cured pork, sat beside eggs and *Lallagia,* a fried dough. Her mouth watered.

The *taverna,* like the other village buildings, bore stone walls and a floor mortared with clay, while a hearth, soon to be banked as the day's heat rose, warmed the room.

A young woman appeared with a platter of savory and sweet dishes for Claire, and she dug in. Byron took small bites of the various offerings but ate little, she assumed his battle with weight the cause.

"You dine alone," she said.

He nodded, sipping his coffee, his keen eyes taking her in. "Garland left at dawn for I know not where. The wife?" Byron shrugged.

Garland's singular jaunt seemed out of character. She wondered why...

"You plan to dig, m'lady?" Byron said.

She nodded, smiling around a spoonful of yogurt.

"I am off to find Ashworth."

Left alone, she savored the tasty dishes, and once replete, made up Cullen's bowl with a heap of pork and unsweetened yogurt. The breeze outside continued to soothe as she retied her bonnet. Exploring, Claire admired the pools of rainwater glittering between rocks, soon to disappear, and mused on nature's ephemeral beauty.

She double-checked her bag for the permits Andreas had generously offered. Confirmed, she walked the village's single thoroughfare, imagining the buried Temple of Apollo beneath her sturdy boots. If only... On the downward path flanked by hardy grasses, scrub, and rock, she aimed for the small stone shepherd's hut.

The mountain air was thinner here, the early summer breeze cool, the sun powerful. Her skin would burn to a crisp did she not take care, thankful for her wide-brimmed bonnet. She carried a flask for herself and Cullen and *must* remember to drink often.

On her first trip to Greece, her foolish mistakes had made her grow dizzy from poor hydration, her exposed flesh turning a scorched red from her improper dress. Those errors had stolen two precious days from her research. Claire would not make those same mistakes again.

She peered across the land in search of Theseus, spotting him seated beneath an olive tree, the urge to join him, to be near him, an irritation.

On her right, a boulder sat in a field of smaller rocks. She'd eyed the spot before, and today she would begin her dig there. Claire set down her tool bag, removed what she needed, and went to work.


Resting beneath the shade of an olive tree, Theseus tried not to worry. Dionysus was late by two days. His nerves, already frayed, felt they might snap if his friend did not soon appear.

The years he had spent planning this mission were an increasingly heavy weight. Life before his vow now seemed a dream, one he missed. He'd barely flown his raptors, paused his Mycenaean research, and failed to complete half a dozen papers, his vow, his *obsession*, all that mattered. Obsession it was—the full focus of his attention. Until Claire.

An Apollo butterfly, its brilliant red spots aflame in the sun, lit on a nearby rock. How sublime. The buzzing of bees soothed him, and Theseus stilled, observing a female rock partridge but two feet away leading her brood of new-hatched chicks. With luck, he would spot a golden eagle today.

Nature's lures delighted him, but with anxious eyes, he looked to the road. No dust plumes unfurled from a rider speeding toward Kastri.

If Dionysus failed to appear, Theseus must craft an alternate plan.

Traveling with the marbles to Athens or Thessaloniki was near impossible, arrangements taking too much time.

What to do? He gazed across the plain and its town, a clever mask for the treasures beneath. Delphi awaited some intrepid antiquarian, of that he was certain. How he would love to search. Claire was well prepared to "dig around," as she called it, having inspected her trowel, dibber, and soil knife. She stood in the distance, surveying the plain. A magical woman he wished to taste again...and again.

*Christ!* He was becoming poetic. Byron's influence, obviously.

As a child, when in Greece with his father, he'd found the people and the land rich in art and culture. Beauty was everywhere, yet it always surprised him to come upon a glorious statue beside a disused road or the remnants of a temple in an overgrown valley, each one an enchanting surprise.

Only later, perhaps when he was thirteen or so, did he see the rot of oppression that choked the country. At his father's insistence, he met the Turks who would sell them the marbles they had unearthed. Then, he understood the exchange as merely transactional. But by his sixteenth year, he perceived the Turks' reasoning behind the practice, for each artifact sold stole their history and diminished the Hellas people. A keen move on the Ottomans' part, but disastrous from the Hellenes' point of view.

Years later, the marbles room resplendent at Wolf Court, he had cemented his mission to return them with his father's passing.

"Ho there, friend!"

Byron strode toward him, all cheer and energy. Theseus was a fan of his exquisite poetry but found the man's affectations and eccentricities off-putting at times. Yet Byron had overcome much, from his unstable childhood to his poorly developed foot, and become a unique and exceptional human being. He liked Byron. But should he trust him?

He'd read "Childe Harold's Pilgrimage" many times. Therein, Byron had ridiculed the idea that the Greeks should "be grateful to the Turks for their fetters and to the Franks for their broken promises and lying counsels...to the artist who engraves their ruins and to the antiquary who carries them away." That last flogged Lord Elgin for plundering the Parthenon friezes, in the process destroying parts of the building. Unconscionable, yet all England praised him.

Byron flopped down beside him. "I had to get away from Garland, for he has been a tick on my back since landing on my doorstep in Italy."

"I believed you good friends," Theseus said.

"More like friendly acquaintances, and I have come to find him off-putting in the extreme. He assured me of his passion for Greece and her art, yet he knows nothing. We traveled first to Florence, and the Uffizi Gallery opened at my request. Garland was in transports observing the ancient Greek sculptures. Yet the Uffizi houses only Roman copies. He had no comprehension of the Archaic, Classical, and Hellenistic periods. Never heard of Mycenae and knows few myths. Good God, I observed him get a statue's sex wrong!"

"I am aware," Theseus said. "Garland accepts the superficial rather than delve into the soul beneath. Lady Claire's dog does not care for him, either. Another black mark. *Christ*, why did you join him, given the Turks consider you an enemy and you wish to conceal your presence?"

"The man prosed on about your mission, which I found enormously seductive."

Garland was a damned chatty fellow. Too chatty.

"The prospect of joining you was irresistible," Byron said. "Particularly as the Greeks will soon discard their Ottoman oppressors, when I shall return to fight alongside my brothers."

Fight alongside? Byron had shocked Theseus. Yet he'd noted the villagers acting as if he were one of their own. "Returning when war is declared sounds perilous."

Byron threw up his hands. "What is not? In a life fraught with drama, freeing Hellas seems but another adventure with a singular purpose. Aiding the revolution will fuel my writing and my soul."

Theseus worried. Byron's romantic admiration for military heroism was oft reflected in his poetry. Not the same as facing the barrel of an enemy's rifle or the steel of his saber. The black cloud of remembrance enveloped him. Not at all the same.

Dust in the distance revealed a man riding a sturdy Greek pony toward the village.

"I must go." He stood, and Byron rose with him.

"I shall accompany you." Byron pointed. "Might that be the man you are expecting?"

"Let us hope so."

They walked at a swift pace toward the village.

"I must relate further unease regarding Garland," Byron said.

"Unease?" Theseus said.

"I would not trust the man anywhere near your statuary. He has repeatedly asked my thoughts on their worth, which I found uncomfortable and inappropriate."

"I am unsurprised," Theseus said. "When he and his wife visited Wolf Court, he needled me about returning the sculptures, simultaneously professing his excitement for my repatriation. I sensed a hidden agenda, though his wife and the maid are stranger still."

"In what way? From what I have seen, her ladyship is a timid soul. Though that maid of hers is an oddity."

"Do continue," Theseus said.

Byron shrugged. "She feels like the ancient crow, an omen or harbinger of doom."

"She does, doesn't she? On their visit, one sculpture captured both females' attention, the bust of Aspasia, neither aware it was a Roman copy of the original Greek. I did not disabuse them of the notion due to her ladyship's surprising animation. Hadn't the heart to burst her bubble, as it were."

Byron nodded. "Pray, be certain Garland is far distant when discussing their disbursement."

They neared the village, and Theseus whooshed out a breath. It *was* Dionysus. "Rest assured, I shall not."

Garland and Andreas approached. "I would ask you to keep our friend occupied," Theseus said. "Whilst I speak with Dionysus."

Byron grinned. "Have no fear. It shall be done." He peeled off to approach Garland.

As he neared his old friend, he caught the dour expression in the man's blue eyes beneath his wealth of blonde curls. Theseus' apprehension grew, but he smiled as he held out his hand.

They had met when Theseus was thirteen, on his second dig with his father. Of an age, when time allowed, they would race ponies, climb trees, play leapfrog, or play a skill game using walnuts. They'd also talked for hours, as they were like-minded souls. On all subsequent digs, Dion accompanied them to whichever location his father chose—Crete, Aegina, Thermopylae, and others.

In later life, Dion had become an art dealer of contemporary Hellas and world art at his shop in Athens. Now he stood before him, of medium height and fit, but not wearing a smile. Concerning, as Dion was a cheerful sort.

They hugged and exchanged back slaps, for it was good to be in his old friend's presence again.

"It has been too long," Dion said.

"Very much so." Theseus stepped back, noting the tightness around Dion's eyes. "What is wrong, old friend?"

"Too much. Skirmishes have broken out across Greece, including the islands, a distraction from our ultimate purpose. But that is no matter. I have a situation with Koios, the man I contracted to disperse the sculptures."

"Situation?" Theseus said, leading Dion to a cottage where he would spend the night.

"The Ottomans have begun watching Koios closely, as it is he who acquires guns for our military. The Turks are nervous, and he must wait a month, perhaps six weeks, before he can safely collect the marbles. I may be able to find another recipient before then." He scraped a hand across his chin. "But that is doubtful."

*God rot it!* Theseus hid his shock and disappointment. "I shall find an alternate solution until the marbles can be transported by Koios or another. Will the wagons be a problem?"

"I don't expect so."

Theseus nodded, hands on hips. "We shall make it work. We must."

Dionysus' eyes shone with anticipation. "Once collected, they shall be meted out to their original locals, though they will be hidden until after the revolution. They will be home."

Theseus slung an arm around Dion's shoulder. "Come, you must be tired and hungry. The villagers intend a fine feast for your welcome. You shall meet my companions, an interesting group that includes Lord Byron."

"I am eager to meet more Englishmen, particularly your sister and Byron, for he is a celebrity in Greece, as I am sure you are aware."

"Know that he wishes not to expose his presence to the Turks."

"Duly noted," Dion said.

Theseus spied Claire down the hill, on her knees probing the soil. "You will find Lady Claire particularly interesting."

His friend gave him a sly look. "A woman has caught your interest?"

Theseus snorted. "An understatement for many reasons. She is as much an antiquarian as we are, though this is but her second dig in Hellas. She is very knowledgeable and has a premise you may find compelling."

"Does she?" Dionysus waggled his brows.

"You are incorrigible," Theseus said with a shake of his head. "You always were, and yes, she is quite lovely. Her ladyship believes the ancient Greeks painted their sculptures. In vivid colors, no less. She is quite ardent about her hypothesis."

Dionysus' eyes widened. "Ardent, is she?"

"Fervently."

"Smart woman." Dion grinned. For she is correct, my friend."

Theseus startled. "Pardon?"

They arrived at Dionysus' cottage, a replica of his own, and sat on the bench beneath a window.

"She is not singular in studying the marbles in such a way." Dion pulled out a small *chibouk* and lit it, inhaling. "I have made a passing study of them myself and have found enough paint remnants to agree with her. Antiquarian authorities are disinclined to pay attention. They believe my forebears valued excellence of form above all, which is merely part of the truth."

Struck dumb, Theseus slapped his hat against his knee, wearing a smile.

"This disturbs you?" Dion said.

"Not disturbed exactly. Rather, I am stunned by the enormity of your words and my ignorance for all these years." Claire had been right all along. That gorgeous woman was brilliant. Absolutely brilliant.

Dionysus shrugged. "It makes little difference what your Lady Claire or I believe. No authority—not museum directors, nor antiquarians, nor antiquities dealers—openly accepts the premise. I doubt they ever will."

Theseus had much to think on. "Come, let us enjoy the celebration while we determine what to do with the damned marbles until Koios arrives."

CHAPTER

# EIGHTEEN

Dion departed the following day, Theseus unsure of his next move. He lay in bed staring at the ceiling, a thundering headache muddling his thoughts, perhaps from an excess of ouzo? More likely from spending time with the garrulous Garland.

He glanced at Dodwell's recent book, *A Classical and Topographical Tour Through Greece*, sitting on the nightstand, the ribbon marking where he'd left off. *Damn*, but he'd wished to get a few more pages under his belt. Not with this damnable anvil in his head.

Remaining in Greece for another month or two awaiting Koios was out of the question. He refused to return the marbles to England. Where to put the wagonloads of sculptures out of sight?

*God rot it!*

He reached for the water glass. Claire must be off digging, his sister with the Pythia, or the woman who called herself by that honorific. Since their arrival, Penelope had been like a child in an ice cream parlor, and his sister's overly zealous feelings for Xanthe worried him. He prayed the relationship was harmless, given there was little he could do about it.

A booming knock lurched him upward, a spike piercing his noggin.

"Come." He didn't give a rat's arse who it was or that he was half-naked in bed. He took the water glass and doused it over his head, hoping that would help. *Bollocks!*

CLAIRE BREEZED through the cottage door and froze. Theseus sat up in bed, his chest rising and falling as water dripped across a wide expanse of bronze muscle and skin. Her heart fluttered. He was glorious. Beautiful. Like a sculpture, but better. Oh, much better. Her mouth dried, her lips parting. She had viewed many statues. Of course she had, but this... So *alive*.

Theseus leaned down, plucked his shirt from the floor, and donned it. A shame.

"At breakfast, Penny said you had the headache," Claire said. "I came to see if I might help."

His eyes narrowed as he scraped the hair back from his face. "As you can see," he said in clipped tones. "I am perfectly fine."

"It is obvious you are not!" Claire laughed. "Look at that growly face."

Given the situation's impropriety, Claire left the door open as she stepped inside, not that it mattered much, her eyes fixated on the shirt clinging to him.

Shocked at her fixation, she rummaged through her knapsack to extract a small box. "I thought you might find this of use."

"I would rather you left," he growled.

"You are in a foul mood. The powder is Chuan Xiong. We used it when my aunt broke her forearm, remember?"

"Indeed," he said, his voice desert dry.

"Given the quantity of drink you and your friend consumed last night, I suspect it will give you some relief."

He sighed and offered a weak smile. "Forgive me, Claire. This spike in my head has put me out of sorts."

She opened the wooden box and reached for the tiny spoon atop a pile of white powder. "I occasionally get headaches and thought…" She disliked him suffering. "It is what I use to soothe. Two spoonfuls in water should do it." She refilled his glass from the pitcher.

"*Fine.*"

"What are you staring at?" she said.

A smile twitched his lips. "I find you intensely fetching in your *loulaki* work apron. I do so love the ubiquitous indigo color."

She swallowed hard. "Thank you." Dropping two spoonfuls of the medicinal into the glass and stirring, she then handed it to Theseus. He downed it in one long gulp.

"Good." She replaced the medicinal in her knapsack. "Now I must be off."

He reached for her hand and squeezed, holding her eyes in that way he had, filled with intensity and…promise?

"Thank you, Claire."

She bobbed a curtsy, hefted her knapsack, and fled.

Penny had spent many hours with Xanthe, her handmaidens, and Nomiki, weaving. They sat at twin looms and wove, Penny having designed a new tapestry with Xanthe's assistance. She savored the old stories anew, for she would not call them myths. The Pythia existed. Why not Apollo himself?

Which was foolish, but a lady could wish.

She might belong to the Church of England but saw no disharmony in believing in the Greek gods as well. Yes, it went against Christian teachings, but reason said they might occupy different firmaments. Xanthe was a Christian, too, as were her handmaidens.

The four looms sat in a large space, the building separate from the rest of Xanthe's home. Across the room, the ever-present Spyros leaned against the wall, one leg crossed over the other, arms crossed as well, his eyes sleepy as he appeared to almost doze.

Appearances deceived, she knew only too well.

As the women told the old tales, they would examine them for signs and symbols, whilst both she and Xanthe listened keenly as they wove.

Penny admired the Pythia excessively, for she was a woman on a continuous quest for knowledge and understanding. All was not high-flown philosophy, for they talked of mundane subjects too. The villagers. The nearing revolution. Nomiki's owl. Breakfast teas. Even their admiration for Byron and his poetry.

His lordship had visited Xanthe's home, spending hours with her in conversation. The renowned animal lover made quite a fuss over Glauca and Nomiki as well. Byron revered all things Greek, though she suspected his adoration sprang from Hellas' ancient history rather than contemporary Greece. He planned to embroil himself in the revolution, and Penny feared for his life, for he was a unique, albeit eccentric, soul.

The following morning, the Pythia attended to personal business, pleasing Claire. She would have Penny all to herself, and they would practice with knives, after which they would dig.

Theseus had explained the problem of the sculptures' dispersal. Worrisome. Claire wished she had the faintest idea of how to help.

They would throw by the large boulder, well away from others, and then dig. Where? Perhaps under the large olive tree? Its roots may have loosened a shard or two beneath the earth. A good plan.

She had found a few unpainted marble shards, which would remain in Kastri. But once Xanthe and Andreas understood her mission, they would consider whether Claire might keep any painted piece she discovered.

As she and Penny dressed in their sturdy work clothes and aprons, Cullen scratched at the door, back from his morning ablutions.

Penny opened it for him. "Shall we ask Lady Garland to join us?"

"Certainly." Unenthused, Claire fussed with the monocle hanging around her neck.

"What is it?" Penny said.

Claire tied her large bonnet. "I confess I have not warmed to her."

"Nor I," Penny slipped her apron over her head. "Though lovely to look at, she is a mousy thing."

"Penny!"

"Well, it is true. I asked if she wished to join me one day to meet the Pythia." Penny strode outside, her own set of tools slung in a bag over her shoulder. She might be here to learn from Xanthe, but Penny loved digging in the dirt too.

After Claire and Cullen followed, Penny closed it with a bang. "She had no interest in meeting Xanthe! If you can imagine. Nor has she mingled with the villagers."

"I fail to imagine why she joined her husband on this trek," Claire said.

"A mystery," Penny said. "One I suspect we shall not solve."

The warm day's sky arched above, a bold cerulean dotted with wispy clouds. The electric atmosphere was due to market day, colorful vendors setting up stalls in the square and along the street, the air rich with floral and other appealing scents.

"Greece smells wonderful, does it not?" Penny said.

"You stole my thoughts." Claire inhaled deeply. "The air has a purity I have felt nowhere else."

Spyros materialized, and Penny rolled her eyes, leaning close to Claire.

"My watchdog," Penny said with sarcasm, ruffling Cullen's fur. "Much like your pup."

"A handsome one, if you ask me."

Spyros followed a few steps behind, though they invited him to walk beside them. He always refused.

As they proceeded, they waved to villagers setting up their stalls and sidestepped a wagon to arrive at the Garlands' cottage. In minutes, the door opened on Lady Garland in her dressing gown.

"We are off to breakfast," Penny said. "We then plan to practice throwing knives, followed by digging for Claire's shards. Would you care to join us?"

"Oh, my," Lady Garland said in a soft voice. "Knife throwing! Why, I never. Sadly, I have much correspondence to complete. If I finish early, I shall."

"Do join us," Claire said. "We will be at it for several hours."

"Thank you both," Frances said. "Are you headed to breakfast? If so, I shall accompany you."

"Excellent," Penny said. "We are happy to wait."

Frances bobbed a curtsy. "I shall be ready in a tick."

After her ladyship closed the door, Spyros grunted. "This is no place for a delicate flower like Lady Garland."

Claire kept silent, but she could not help but agree.


Theseus lifted a bar of soap, pumped water over his body, scrubbed, and rinsed while his frustration bubbled—he must leave the marbles as is until Byron and Garland left Kastri.

That morning, he'd helped a group of villagers build a new house, the physical labor enabling his mind to rest. He was now both sweaty and irritated, the bright side his spotting of a male red-footed falcon and a lovely Eurasian sparrowhawk, both exquisite birds of prey. Even that hadn't lifted his spirits, for interacting with Garland was a tiring experience, the man an endless bag of wind.

He dunked his head into the full bucket, rose, and whipped his soaking hair back with both hands. He pulled a leather cord from his pocket and bound his too-long locks.

Minutes later, Theseus entered the *taverna*, expecting to see others in their party. Garland and Byron were there, but the ladies had yet to arrive. Byron must speed the Garlands' departure, or he might punch the fatuous lordling.

Garland waved him over in his effusive way, and Theseus had to stop himself from grinding his teeth. The man was subtle as a hammer, yet what lay beneath? Did he truly have fewer brains than Cullen?

. . .

THIS SECOND WEEK IN JUNE, Theseus found the increasing summer warmth pleasant. Unpleasant was the swelling tension between his party and the Garlands', excepting Byron. Yes, Garland was annoying, but that wasn't the cause. A black cloud of dissatisfaction swirled around them, and Theseus' shoulder blades itched, as if eyes followed him, malevolent ones.

His instincts, always on alert, ratcheted up. He'd swear he smelled danger in the air.

Were anything to happen to Claire or Penny...

Theseus entered the *taverna* and breathed deep, his stomach rumbling at the appealing scents.

"Well met!" Garland said as Theseus approached the table.

Byron nodded, sliding a glass of retsina to Theseus and pulling out a chair.

"What have you been up to, Ashworth?" Garland said. "Byron and I have been trekking the mountain, imagining all that lies beneath."

"I worked with Lady Claire for a bit," Theseus said. "Then I helped some villagers shore up a wall."

Garland startled. "You are an *earl*, Ashworth. What of your dignity?"

Byron snorted. "He has none. Have you not yet realized this?"

Theseus raised his glass to Byron and nodded. "Very true."

A village woman appeared carrying a large pan of what looked like *yiouvetsi*, lamb served with orzo in a spiced tomato sauce, while another carried plates and cutlery. Once laid before them, the woman doled out heaps of the delicious dish, one of Theseus' favorites.

The ladies entered, followed by Lady Garland's maid and Cullen. Penny and Claire wore serviceable work clothes, while Garland's wife had donned a frothy confection more suitable for Hyde Park.

The men rose as the women joined them, Garland taking his lady's hand then glancing at the maid. Soon, plates were filled, drinks were poured, and cutlery was distributed. It seemed the women were as famished as the men, for they dug in like ravening beasts.

"Where is Spyros?" Theseus asked Penny. "I believed he would join us for lunch."

"He told me he had business to attend," Penny said. "And that he would see me in an hour. Theo, he is like a limpet!"

"A limpet?" Theseus boomed a laugh. "His purpose is your protection, dear sister, as well you know."

She harrumphed, but he'd caught a wee smile in his sister's eyes. What did *that* mean?

"Your man, Dionysus, left," Garland said. "I assumed he would take the marbles."

"Did you?" Theseus said. "He will collect them several days hence."

"Mr. Alexopoulos seems like a fine fellow," Claire said.

Theseus recalled those free and easy days in Hellas before he understood his father's sole purpose was to acquire any Greek antiquities he could lay his hands on. Those early days had been bliss, and Dionysus was a part of that.

"He is a great friend," he said.

"He seemed pleasant," Lady Garland said.

The maid harrumphed. Wearing all black and a permanent frown, she looked much like a bad-tempered crow.

"And very attractive," Penny whispered in Lady Garland's ear.

As Lady Garland scooped up a forkful of moussaka, she said in a neutral voice, "Indeed, he is."

Garland's face mottled. "Frances!"

Her eyes rose to her husband's, and Theseus would swear he saw fear. *Christ*, he hoped he was wrong. Abusing women or dousing their light was despicable.

Throats cleared around the table as Garland stared daggers at his wife.

"I found him quite attractive, as well," Byron said, waggling his brows.

"My lord!" Garland said.

Byron laughed, the tension broken. But Theseus would not forget the exchange between Lord Garland and his lady wife.

CHAPTER

# NINETEEN

That evening after dinner, Claire enjoyed the cool breeze—the moon fat and the air soft on the *taverna's* porch—the sky robed in starry velvet.

Theseus strode outside. "Would you care for a walk, my lady?"

Alone. With Theseus. How lovely. But she should not. Yet somehow her mouth failed to attend to her brain. "I would enjoy that."

He clasped her hand. "May I?"

Better still, their clasped hands felt...right. She nodded. Holding hands as they walked, they ambled from the village, Cullen joining them.

"I witnessed an uncomfortable exchange between Garland and her ladyship," Theseus said.

"Uncomfortable how?" she said.

"Her ladyship commented on Dion's looks, and Garland took serious offense."

They came to a boulder, and he leaned his back against it, resting his hands on her waist. "Might I?"

179

Again, she nodded, and he pulled her a bit closer. In truth, she wished he would tug her closer still, to rest against him.

What were Theseus' intentions?

"Though I do not agree," she said. "I see why Lord Garland might take offense. I suspect he has not the confidence of you or Lord Byron."

"That is not my concern, but rather Lady Garland's fearful reaction."

That gave Claire pause. Could Garland's oppression be why Frances was so timid? He did not seem that sort. "Do you think he strikes her?"

Theseus squeezed her waist. "It is possible."

Claire didn't like that one bit. "I shall keep an eye out. Yet it seems out of character to me. Not that we could do much to aid her if he is brutalizing her."

"See what you can learn." He leaned down and nuzzled her neck.

"That tickles!"

"I find you most irresistible, Lady Claire." He dipped his head for a kiss, soft, warm, and joyful.

"Lovely. *You* are lovely." He took her hand, and they began to stroll again. "So tell me, *to asteri mu*, is this your best adventure yet?"

"*To asteri mu?*"

"Later, sweetheart." He ran warm butterfly kisses from her ear down her neck. Though her flesh warmed, her mind had latched onto those words. She could ask Penny or anyone in the village. But she would rather Theseus tell her. He had called her sweetheart. That must mean something. Though some of the men she had known tossed around endearments as if they were bonbons.

"*Is* this your greatest adventure?" he said.

She squeezed his hand. "Yes and no."

"What is this yes and no?" Theseus said.

Her smile was wistful. "Do you know much about my family?"

"A bit," he said. "Your father was the famed artist, Reginald

Pheland, Baron Halafair. I have met your mother, sister, and her husband, along with the Ravenscrofts. Typical English families."

Claire laughed. Hard not to, for they were anything but. "You assume wrong, my lord! We are a ramshackle bunch who have had our share of adventures and disasters, I might add."

"I recall your sister coming before the Royal Academy for forgery and triumphing. No disaster, that."

Claire was silent for long moments. "And do you know about Lord Fielding?"

"Cedric Pheland? He strikes me as a dandified ass."

"He may be all that, but I meant the previous earl."

They came to a pile of rock that looked much like a bench, and Theseus removed his handkerchief to dust off the "seat." "My lady."

"What a courtier you are," she said as she sat.

He joined her, wrapping an arm around her waist, and leaned close, flashing his pirate grin. "I have been practicing!"

"Oh, dear! Have I unleashed another dandy?"

He feigned horror. "Never! What of the previous Earl Fielding? Rumors said he was a rough man with little respect for any but his cronies."

"You would not be wrong. He was our family's most notable disaster. My papa was a wonderful man. Fielding was not, though he appeared so initially. Mama believed him to be a good person who would give us stability after Papa's passing. She liked him a great deal, and so they married." Claire picked a small stone from a nearby pile and tossed it, Cullen speeding away in chase.

Theo was a patient man, and she appreciated his silence. She breathed deep. "Fielding was the antithesis of a butterfly."

"How so?"

"His caterpillar was kind and thoughtful, for he presented as a gentle and considerate man. But once wed to Mama, he shucked his chrysalis to transform into a fiend who pressed us beneath his thumb for years, particularly Rosamund. He came near to killing our mother. Fortunately, he failed."

"*Christ*, I had no idea," Theseus said. "I am sorry. Thank the gods you and your family escaped."

"That we did! But then Rose was nearly taken by a viscount, and after Patrick became engaged to Lottie, he had that terrible accident, and then a madman kidnapped her!"

His brow rose. "I was there for Lady Hawthorne's rescue, if you recall."

"I had forgotten!"

Cullen returned, rock in mouth, looking as proud as could be. As always, he refused to drop the stone. Claire withdrew a treat from her pocket. "Drop!"

Once done, Cullen sucked the treat from her fingers, she threw another stone, and he sped off.

"Do go on," Theseus said.

"Do you know of the crazy baron's attack at Hawthorne?"

He frowned. "Indeed, your sister's blow-by-blow description was unforgettable. We got him in the end."

"We certainly did."

Claire flashed him a grin, proud of their achievement.

Theo squeezed the bridge of his nose. "I would suggest the bandit attack was a mere postscript to your adventures."

"Not in the least," she said. "An incident never to be repeated, I hope."

"Would that I could guarantee such."

"Not likely." In the dark, she grew bold, and she turned his face to hers. "I should like to kiss you."

He sighed. "Please do."

She moved her lips across his, then stared into his eyes for long moments. "Your face, Theo, is a map I love to explore."

"Dash it, Claire, you unman me."

"Oh, stop. You are beautiful, even your scars, especially that one on your temple. From the Peninsula?"

He nodded.

She ran a finger across it. "You were there with Rhys, Lord Ravenscroft?"

"At the same time, though we never crossed paths."

"I almost failed to recognize him on his return," Claire said. "Given his black hair had turned white."

He shook his head. "The Peninsula was the definition of carnage. Obviously, Ravenscroft was deeply affected."

"I am sure you were as well."

"Men may play at war, but it damages the soul as much as the flesh." He fingered the hilt of the knife strapped to her waist. "I see you wear your knife. Your others, as well?"

"Not tonight."

"I first recall seeing you throw at Woodbine. I was shocked but admiring, too. How did a delicate English flower come to throw knives?"

She almost giggled, instead lowering her eyes and fussing with her skirt. "The circus."

"The *circus*?"

"I was quite young, perhaps seven? The circus was in town, and I escaped Halafair to investigate. Oh, I met all sorts of marvelous folk, including the knife thrower."

"And you became fascinated."

"I did, visiting on several occasions. Once Papa discovered my interest, he invited the man to Halafair to teach me while the circus remained in town. Lottie had no interest, preferring her paints, but the man was a marvelous instructor, and my passion was born. He gifted me a set of training knives, and I practiced constantly. When I outgrew them, I acquired my current set."

"I find your father's encouragement surprising."

She jabbed his arm. "*That* is all you say?"

He grinned. "Naturally I am in awe of your talent, but I am struck by your father's permissiveness."

"Papa, well, he was a unique man, for he saw no reason not to encourage me. What of you? You lost your mother as a child, did you not?"

"I was away at Harrow when she died, a warm woman and much unlike my father, though compared to yours, my life has been banal."

"I think not. I suspect you had many adventures on your trips to Greece and other lands. Remaining silent is like ignoring a tiger lying on the sofa."

He threw his head back and roared a laugh, then brushed a hand across her hair. Claire closed her eyes, the sensations delicious. Even more delicious were his lips on hers, his tongue seeking and hers answering.

When they parted, she paused. Rather than cooling, sensation rose from the heat warming her heart. For that organ was rather fervently engaged. A wondrous feeling. "You are more than I could have ever imagined, Theo."

"As you are my *αστέριμου*. My star."


Ten days after their arrival in Kastri, Claire remained frustrated at her lack of finding a single shard dabbed with paint. She buttoned her spencer, grabbed her knapsack and tools, and left the cottage, Cullen in her wake.

Her mind should be on her dig. Rather, it was preoccupied with Theo and the walks they had taken, the dinners they'd enjoyed, and the many topics discussed. Not to mention the kisses exchanged.

What did it all mean? Where would it lead?

She had read about this feeling of uncertainty in the ladies' periodicals, where the woman must wait for the man to first express certain...possible outcomes. How frustrating.

Yet were she in Theseus' place, what would she say? Would she ask for a betrothal? A marriage?

A passing cart billowed dust, and Claire sneezed, her musings broken. She knocked on Lady Garland's door, trying one last time to draw her out. Long minutes passed, and she knocked again.

"Coming!"

Helene opened the door wearing her usual stolid face to reveal her ladyship, *en déshabillé.*

"So sorry to disturb you," Claire said. "I am about to visit the Pythia. Penelope is there as well. I thought you might like to join us."

Frances' eyes softened. "I would love to do so, but I am afraid I cannot." She glanced at Helene, the maid's lips thin. "Perhaps another time?"

"Of course. Will I see you at luncheon?"

Frances's face went blank. "Possibly."

"I hope so. Have a lovely day." Claire headed for Xanthe's cottage. Lady Garland was sweet but rather vapid. How could one visit Greece and yet espouse neither interest in its history nor its environs? Frances was a puzzle—one who rarely queried Claire or others on how *they* fared. Self-absorbed, true. Yet she seldom asserted or defended herself. She was easily discombobulated—a man's shout might terrify her, as had happened two days earlier. The more Claire thought...perhaps Frances was beaten down by Garland. Mayhap not physically, but constant reprimands could destroy the spirit as well.

And her maid... Somber in the extreme, Helene watched her ladyship as a raptor eyed prey. Then again, she wore that same expression when observing Theseus or Penny. Hunger? Jealousy? Perhaps anger, even.

As Claire raised her fist to knock on Xanthe's door, it swung open. Nomiki greeted her with a smile, Glauca with a whistle. Surprising her, the girl leaned close. "It is good you are here. Spyros and Penelope are having a tiff."

As they entered, Claire reached to remove her hatpins, then drew her straw *bergère* from her head. "What about?

"Penelope wishes to go to the cave with the Pythia. Spyros cannot go, and he objects."

Claire entered to see Penny staring daggers at Spyros, whilst Spyros ignored her as he lounged against the wall.

Claire curtsied before the Pythia, whose face pleated into a smile, and eased down onto a bright red cushion. Penny joined her, leaning close.

"Spyros is being an absolute ass." Penny stared daggers at the man.

"He objects to you visiting the cave?" Claire said.

The traitorous Cullen trotted to the man under discussion, who began to pet him.

Penny huffed. "I accept his following me about, but only virginal women may access the cave, and Spyros forbids me to enter without him. I shall be perfectly safe!"

Claire slipped a glance toward the Pythia, who was speaking with Nomiki. The Oracle looked straight at her and winked. *Winked*!

"I suspect Xanthe," Claire said. "Or perhaps the sanctuary itself has methods of dissuading the uninvited from entering."

"Why, I never thought of that." Penny snapped her fingers. "That makes perfect sense."

Claire grinned. "I am tempted to come just to see what happens."

Penny's eyes slid again to Spyros, a flush staining her cheeks.

As much as Claire wished to see what happened, she left to dig.

Penny journeyed with the Pythia and her handmaidens to the cave, glad she had worn her sturdy boots, for it was more hike than walk. Spyros trudged beside her, thankfully making no conversation.

Her nerves bristled at the cave's opening, narrow and so small she must bend in half to enter.

"It is safe, Penelope," Xanthe said.

"Of course it is." Penny shot her a wan smile and entered after Nomiki and the handmaidens. Once inside, she stood easily, the ceiling far above. Nomiki took her hand, and as they proceeded down the torchlit aisle, Penny looked over her shoulder. Spyros had not followed.

The floor was smooth, and they soon reached a vast cavern hung with immense stalactites. Braziers and torches blazed, lighting the space. Oddly, a breeze whispered through the cavernous space, whilst atop Nomiki's shoulder, Glauca cooed as if in greeting.

A tall, open-legged tripod chair sat in the cave's center, a mist rising from the fissure beneath to envelop it, tendrils floating upward. Flanking it were two torches and a pair of massive omphalos.

"Would you like to sit in the chair?" A voice close to her ear. The Pythia.

Though wary, Penny was tempted. What would she see, visions of the past? The future? A shiver wove through her. Yet she yearned to do so.

"Does it call to you?" Xanthe said.

"It does." Penny approached the tall chair, though how she would mount it she had no idea until Nomiki carried over a tall stool and placed it by Penny's feet. Penny stepped atop it, and with great care, used her foot for leverage and eased atop the bowl-shaped seat.

She peered around at the women staring up at her, a small smile on Xanthe's lips.

Nerves made her hands sweaty. "Is there anything I need to know or do?"

"Open your mind, your heart, your soul," Xanthe said. "That is all."

Penny's practicality asserted itself, unsure how to do any of those things. Nevertheless, she relaxed as the mist thickened. She closed her eyes, and as she did so, the handmaidens began a lilting chant.

Breathing deep, the world began to alter, shapes shifting, senses heightening. She smelled the spice of Mother Earth from oils and herbs tossed on the braziers. The thick air redolent of frankincense, myrrh, and sandalwood. Mystery brushed Penny's skin, her understanding deepening, her joy increasing. She saw... *Everything.*

Penny stepped into a dreamscape, surreal and eerie, as she walked through a dense, misty forest where the trees whispered secrets, their branches twisted into fantastical shapes. Moonlight filtered through the fog, casting an otherworldly glow, whilst shadows danced and shifted to reveal mythical creatures—a centaur, the Cretan bull, the sphinx—ghostly figures that vanished as quickly as they appeared.

She came to a field of surreal wildflowers, their colors unnaturally vibrant. They pulsed and shimmered, a river of liquid silver flowing through their midst. Notes of the *aulos, bouzouki,* and lyre began to play in concert with the river's burbles, a haunting melody, both enchanting and discomfiting.

Venturing onward, a marble temple rose from the ground, its Ionic columns sparkling in the sun as wonderment filled her.

*Beware the Minotaur's seal,* whispered a voice, neither male nor female, but…other.

The vision snapped.

Penny gasped, opening her eyes.

She saw only black.

A hand slipped into Penny's and eased her down from the chair, the blackness stygian. Why had they doused the torches?

"Xanthe? Nomiki?"

A bird chirped. Glauca.

"It is Nomiki. Come, we must walk."

Magical visions still swirled in Penny's head, dampening her fear.

"Bend down now, for we are leaving the cave." Nomiki placed her hand atop Penny's head. Soon, a breeze danced across Penny's face. They stood outside, in the open, but blackness still enveloped her.

# TWENTY

Fear inched closer, and she squeezed Nomiki's hand, refusing to allow it to envelop her.

"You cannot see," Nomiki said.

"I cannot," she said in an even voice, though her heart beat triple time.

"A frequent occurrence after the first vision. Your eyes have turned milky white, but in several hours or perhaps a day, they will clear, your vision returning in full. This is the beginning."

"The beginning of what?" Penny said.

"Of becoming a Pythia, of course."

Nomiki guided her as they walked the path. For all Penny was entranced by the Oracle, her handmaidens, and Kastri, imagining herself as the Pythia gave her chills.

"The blindness happened to me the first time," Nomiki said in a conspiratorial tone. "And then it was gone!"

They walked, accompanied by Glauca's periodic coos. Footsteps approached, ones she recognized. Spyros.

Dear heavens, he would have a fit about her eyes. She shut them tight.

"Why in blazes are your eyes closed, Penelope?" Spyros barked.

"The light is too much, Spyros," she said. "I must rest them for an hour or so."

He harrumphed, striding in step with them. Penny sensed when the others peeled off in silence. They came to level ground and walked further. Glauca whistled, and they stopped.

Nomiki whispered, "We are at your cottage."

"Thank you for walking me home, Nomiki."

Someone swung open the door, and Penny stepped inside, accompanied by light footsteps departing. Nomiki.

Penny was alone with Spyros, and she turned toward the heat of the man who insisted on protecting her. She wished she could see his expression. She could not, of course, though she'd swear she sensed his concern.

How she wished he would touch her, enfold her in his arms.

Ten years earlier, when she'd first met him at Wolf Court, she had first admired his intelligence. Soon, she delighted in their conversations, for he was a caring man, a warm one full of humor, which tickled her funny bone. She had always felt a thrill when he arrived at the manor, but as the years passed, new sensations touched her, his physicality giving her prickles at the oddest moments. Poor sod, he would be horrified at her thoughts. "Thank you, Spyros."

"Where did you go?" he said.

She pictured her bed's location and walked to it, bumping her shin on the footboard. *Ouch.* She unpinned her hat, dropping it on the bed. "I entered the cave with the others."

"I saw no cave," he said with a low-throated growl. "I turned away for a moment, and the women had vanished."

Penny shrugged. "As I told you, women alone may enter the cave. As you are not one of those..."

He chuffed a laugh, his hands resting on her shoulders. Such a pleasant sensation.

"Are you well, Penelope?"

The worry in his voice made her soften hers. "I am perfectly fine, Spyros. Truly. I would like to rest, though."

He whooshed out a breath. "Of course. Do you need anything before I go?"

"Nothing. Thank you."

She sensed warmth near her face as if he'd raised a hand to caress it. But then it disappeared, and footsteps padded across the stone floor. "If you need me, call. I shall be outside."

The door snicked closed.

Penny flopped onto the bed. She groped for the water pitcher and poured a glass, sipping greedily, her throat parched.

She refused to panic, though she hoped her vision would return soon, as Nomiki had said. Replacing the empty glass, Penny pulled up the covers to rest her head on the pillow. She tried to review what she'd seen in the cave so as to remember, but the heaviness of sleep called. Her breath eased, and she slept.

A thump awakened her, eyes flying open. All she saw was Stygian black. Penny pushed to a seated position as the sound of the door closing made her stiffen. "Claire?"

"Tis I." A thud on the floor, Claire's tool bag, then a thump on the bed. A wet tongue swiped from her chin to her temple. Cullen. Penny buried her nose in his fur, listening.

"Penny, you are acting strange." Claire said. "What is wrong?"

The rustle of skirts, and Penny looked at Claire, eyes open.

A gasp. "My God! Your eyes are milky white!"

"So I have been told." Penny plucked at the coverlet.

"You cannot see! I shall find Theseus."

"Do not!" Penny flung out an arm, connecting with some part of Claire, as her words rushed out. "My brother and Spyros will pitch fits. This blindness will pass. Xanthe and Nomiki both assured me it would, for it is a typical occurrence when seeing the cave's visions for the first time. Do *not* call the men."

Silence so loud she could almost hear Claire thinking.

Claire huffed. "I do not know—"

"Please let it be for now."

A sigh. "If I must." The bed jiggled.

Claire sat and took her hand. "My dear friend, how may I help?"

Penny held up a finger, spooling back to the events at the cave. She recalled much, describing the space, the Pythia's chair, the temple, and the forest, which she detailed to Claire. Yet there was more, an important "more," which remained inaccessible.

"I must say, you seem unnaturally calm," Claire said. "Given you cannot *see*."

Penny shrugged. "You know that is how I react. On the outside. In truth, I am shaking in my boots. But what is the point of a hissy fit when I can do nothing to change the circumstances?"

"You acted the same with the bandits," Claire said. "You appeared calm as a cucumber then, too."

Penny laughed. "My body knew exactly what to do. But inside, I was absolutely horrified!"

"Whilst I was terrified both outside and in."

"But not paralyzed," Penny said. "You acted. That is a large difference. Today I felt as I had then, as if...well, acting in a play I had previously performed. Surprising, but not unwelcome."

"We do not know ourselves as well as we imagine, do we?" Claire poured more water into the glass and slid it into Penny's hand.

Penny swallowed with greed. "That tastes so good. Not only am I blind, but also parched."

"It appears no knife-throwing practice today," Claire said with a chuckle.

"It might be interesting!" Penny grinned.

"I suspect it would be," Claire said. "You said you heard a prophecy. What was it?"

Penny bit her lip. "I cannot remember."

A day later, Penny's eyesight thankfully restored, her friend was off again to Xanthe's while Claire and Cullen walked to dig in the third quadrant she'd laid out. Claire peered around. For all she knew,

Theseus had put a secret watcher on her. *No*, she thought as she petted her beloved pup. Theseus knew she already had a formidable guardian.

The especially warm morning made her dig arduous, for it seemed as if all the rocks in Greece had gathered in this spot. She wiped her brow with a forearm. Not a single shard of marble, pottery, or bronze had appeared.

Hours later, she looked up to see a woman in black standing beside the wood, her skirts fluttering in the breeze. Claire blinked. Helene? She dug out her opera glass, her back telling her it was time to stretch. When she raised the glass to her eyes, no one was there. Heavens above, was she imagining things? It mattered little, her mood was that sour.

As the day waned, the breeze remained stifling, though the sun hung low on the horizon. Claire plucked at her sweat-soaked neckline, picturing the spring-fed pond beside the wood.

The impropriety of going for a swim deterred her, but she might dip her legs into the cool water. Twilight crept near, a few stars winking in the sky.

She rolled her shoulders, feeling greasy, to gather her gear. Soon, she and Cullen marched off to the pond girdled by Kermes oaks. Their leaves were small and sharp-edged, very different from their English cousins.' The villagers collected the insects that fed on their sap to create a beautiful red dye, much like cochineal.

When she reached a large oak that loomed above the pond, Claire dropped her bags beneath the tree's shade. In the dusk, the pond gleamed like a silver mirror. Cullen dived in, the silly boy. Claire wished she could.

Seated, she shucked boots, stockings, bonnet, and gloves, then scootched forward to slip her legs into the cool, refreshing water.

Ah, relief. She splashed her face and arms, contemplating a dip. After all, the tree's branches hid a patch of pond in shadow. Who would see?

Best not. Claire swished her legs like a child. It felt so good.

A noise, the cracking of a stick, alerted her to another's presence. She peered around but saw no one.

Cullen leapt from the water, giving himself a good shake that felt like a glorious spring shower. Claire flopped back on the earth, legs swishing back and forth in the water, and closed her eyes. She drifted as the day waned.

The now-cooling breeze ruffled the leaves as birdsong and the rasping scream of a red-tail sounded. In the distance, the spring burbled.

Calm. Quiet. Bliss.

A splash. Claire jerked up, her eyes flying open. *Oh!*

Yards away, Theseus' head broke the water, and he flicked his long hair back to emerge naked from the pond.

Claire gasped. She must turn away. This instant. But... Theseus was exposed from head to knee. *All* of him. Unclothed.

His splendor of form stole her breath.

She'd observed naked warriors, statesmen, and gods as statues. Hundreds of them. But *living* flesh? Never. And never on a man who turned her world topsy-turvy.

His beauty transcended any statue, his musculature glorious—all planes, angles, and curves—with broad shoulders, his massive chest lightly furred with dark hair that arrowed to his appendage that was shadowed from view.

He plucked a bar of soap from the bank and began lathering himself, and Claire's whole body warmed, most definitely not from the sun's heat. His muscles moved as a symphony, expanding and contracting, like a graceful dance or lines of poetry.

Claire shrugged her shoulders, crossed her legs, then uncrossed them, restless, for what she did not know. Her day dress, once loose and serviceable, now rubbed against her flesh, her lower regions in equal discomfort. Not pain, exactly, but more of an ache.

Claire lowered her eyes to don her stockings and boots.

Why was Theseus' flesh so compelling?

"You seem to be enjoying yourself," came the soft voice.

Claire started so violently one stocking near flew into the pond. She rolled the silk and pulled it on, eyes focused downward. Frances had spoken, yet she was certain Helene accompanied her, an uneasy presence.

"I was just leaving." Claire finished tying her second stocking, then slipped on her left boot, tying it. When she looked up, she found both women feasting on Theseus, Helene's look holding a hint of the predatory. How strange and unpleasant.

"You may return to the village, Helene," Frances murmured.

Helene cleared her throat. "Are you sure, m'lady?"

"Helene?" Frances said.

The maid coughed, brow raised.

"When I think on it," Frances said. "You had best stay to see us all safe."

What a strange exchange between the two. Nor had either mentioned the "elephant" in the pond.

Footwear donned, Claire rose, then tied on her bonnet. "I am off." She lifted her tool bag.

Frances peered up at her, pointing to Theseus. "His figure is rather brutish, is it not?"

That stopped her. "Brutish?"

"No elegance whatsoever." The woman made a moue. "Look how all that musculature defeats the artistic line of his flesh, bulging here and there. So different from Garland, who is elegance personified, his waist narrow, with sinuous musculature and long limbs."

"Bah," Helene said, flicking a hand toward the water. "That one looks much like Agamemnon, who hated me."

"Pardon?" Claire said.

Helene waved a hand, offering a tight smile. "I am being fanciful, m'lady."

Both women were behaving oddly, disparaging the earl, though she'd been particularly offended by Frances' comments regarding Theseus.

Theseus climbed from the water and flung his head back, wiping water from his face.

Claire turned swiftly so as not to stare.

"His limbs," Frances said. "Do you see their bulk? So unattractive."

Claire found him magnificent. "I am afraid I must disagree." She straightened her spine and began to walk away. "You are being most inappropriate."

"I find Lord Ashworth rather repellent." Frances said.

That stopped her. "Pardon?"

"He is off-putting in so many ways, never acting the gentleman."

She whirled on the women. "That is offensive in so many ways, not to mention you are here in Kastri at Lord Ashworth's sufferance. To denigrate your host is unseemly."

"How worked up you are, my lady." Frances tittered. "Ladies must keep their composure at all times, do you not think? I was simply teasing, you see."

"The man is rather high in the instep," Helene chimed in, hands folded before her. "Yet you speak about him with such confidence."

"Perhaps overconfidence?" A smile trembled on Frances' lips. "I find that charming, do you not, Helene?"

How dare they? "Confidence," Claire said with a smile. "Is merely the art of disguising a certainty, one others have yet to perceive!"

Claire strode off, uncaring whether the pair followed or not.



DAYS PASSED, and as June waned, the Garlands and Byron prepared to depart. That evening, they convened at the *taverna*, taking seats around the table in rapt anticipation. The headman had insisted upon a feast prior to their leave-taking the following day, and the aromas made Claire's mouth water. Cullen looked toward the kitchen, a dollop of drool stretching downward from his jaw. He hoped for a treat, too.

"Silly pup," Claire said. She slipped Cullen a chunk of the *hori-*

*atiko psomi*, the village bread, before dipping a piece for herself in olive oil.

Village women appeared carrying steaming platters, the scents making her mouth water like Cullen's. They laid the dishes down the center of the circular table—*souvlaki*, veal sausage or *soutzouki*, *feta bouyiourdi*, *spanakopita*, and more.

They dug in.

Divine. The food was divine, as was the camaraderie. Laughter and chatter circulated, ebbing and flowing. Claire laughed at a quip of Byron's, and she slipped Cullen a chunk of *souvlaki*, who instantly gobbled it up.

"You should not," Helene said.

"Pardon?" Claire said.

"Feeding that creature at the table is inappropriate."

Garland sniffed. "I could not agree more."

Taken aback at the rude comment, Claire's devilish imp took charge. She sliced a chunk of sausage and handed it to Cullen.

Garland's eyes widened, while Helene's narrowed.

"I believe it is up to me when and where I feed Cullen."

"I do apologize, Lady Claire." Helene turned away, forking a *dolmade* into her mouth. "Delicious. Greek food is a favorite of mine. Do try one, my lady."

Frances demurred. "I confess, this..." She waved a hand across the table. "It is not to my taste."

Helene cast her a doleful glance.

The serving women reappeared with ouzo, *baklava*, fried *loukoumades*, and Turkish delight, accompanied by Greek coffee. Claire had developed a particular fondness for the brew.

"Are you pleased to be headed home, Frances?" Claire said, in hopes of elevating her ladyship's mood,

"I am." The woman shrugged. "Our purpose was to see the sculptures. *All* the sculptures. Did you know Lord Ashworth showed us but five, not even including the bust of Aspasia, which I do so admire?"

"As they are about to be shipped off," Claire said. "Uncrating and re-crating them would be an onerous task and take much time." Claire did not mention Aspasia wasn't amongst them.

Helene leaned close to her mistress, whispering in her ear, her eyes flashing fury at Theseus.

Frances waved a hand. "Ashworth should have accommodated us." Then, as if remembering herself, she lowered her eyes and said, "But I do see your point."

Claire did not believe either Frances or Helene saw her point in the least.

CHAPTER

# TWENTY-ONE

The next day, Theseus observed Byron's group set off, the men from Itea driving five of the wagons and mules they would keep. A single mule and wagon, along with the pony and donkeys, would remain for their party's departure.

Byron had kept his word, giving no hint of the sculptures' true disposition, for they would bury them, scattering them across the plain until Koios and his wagons arrived to collect them.

Garland, believing the marbles would depart two days hence, insisted on seeing them off. With many apologies, Byron said his presence in Greece had grown too dangerous and they must leave immediately.

The two women waved farewell, the maid's smile, the first he'd seen, reminding him of Penelope. He blinked—a trick of the light. He shook his head, relieved to see their backs.

A day later, Theseus, the village men, and the three sailors from *Nemesis* began to dig. It should take at least two full days to inter all of them.

They dug and dug, and to each artifact Theseus covered with

earth, he said farewell, for they had been a powerful thread in the fabric of his life.

The sun at its zenith, Claire wiped her wrist across her forehead as she continued to search for remnants of Delphi. So far, nothing. Many days of nothing. But she must not be discouraged. She had at least another two days to discover an artifact before they left. As always, Cullen surveyed the area, roaming near and far, sniffing, marking, and sniffing some more.

On her knees, Claire raked her claw across the earth with care so as not to injure anything that might lie beneath. She knew she could never dig deep enough to reach Delphi's true antiquities. But it was possible some ancient piece or shard had wound its way upward for her to reveal.

Cullen barked, her reverie broken. She raised a hand to shield her eyes. He stood far off, in an area where Claire had yet to dig.

"Cullen, come!"

He failed to respond. Unusual.

"Cullen, *come!*"

He gave the area a final sniff, then loped over, wearing a happy grin, tongue lolling. She looked into those beautiful black eyes and ruffled his fur. "You are such a good boy. What interested you so?"

She pulled a dish from her knapsack, filled it with food scraps for Cullen, and laid it on the ground. Seconds later, the plate was clean. He peered up at her, yipped, then raced back to his "smelly" area. He recommenced barking.

"All right," she said.

Cullen had joined her on several small digs in Devon and York-shire. Each time something caught his attention—chicken bones, a dead rat, an ancient spoon—he barked.

Claire stood like an old woman, having knelt for many hours. Hands on hips, she stretched backward, then walked toward him. "What have you discovered, Cullen?"

The more she walked, the more her muscles loosened until she trod the uneven ground with ease. From what she could see, he circled a bit of nothing. As she neared a grove of olive trees, Cullen began to paw at the ground. Strange. The earth had been disturbed with random clumps of grass atop it. "What is it you have found, boy?"

Claire kneeled and brushed the packed dirt with her gloved hands. The earth moved easily, and she dug deep until she touched something hard. A rock? She sat back on her haunches. Most likely, and she dithered about getting her tools. Cullen did love rocks.

Impatience won the day, and she continued to scrape away dirt until a piece of white marble poked through.

With great care, Claire brushed aside the dirt surrounding the piece's edges. She delved deeper and deeper until curled hair appeared, then a forehead wearing a band. A bust.

Yet she'd seen the map the men were using to bury the sculptures. This grove was not on that map. The headband and curly hair pinged a memory, though she failed to catch it.

Frustrated at her inefficiency, she retrieved her tools. Cullen hadn't moved from the spot, as if he were guarding a precious thing.

She took the large brush from her case and began brushing away the soil, digging again, brushing more soil away until...

Claire stared down at the partially uncovered bust, now incomplete, for there was a break on the man's cheek, his lower lip missing, his chin gone, the broken shards scattered beside it. How odd the nose remained, typically the first piece to break off a sculpture.

None of which said why Cullen had smelled the thing.

As Claire revealed more of the piece, she noted scraps of wood amongst the dirt. Realization hit, and her heart sank.

She replaced all the dirt and went in search of a marker, finding a smooth rock banded with a white line, which Claire placed on the spot. She went in search of Theseus.

Claire and Theseus stood above the hole, having once again removed the dirt surrounding the bust.

"It is blind Homer, is it not?" Claire said. "From the Hellenistic period?"

Theseus crouched, his fists clenching and unclenching. "A Roman reproduction," he ground out. "A copy of an earlier Homeric bust by Phidias from about 200 AD."

"It is yours, is it not?" she said.

"Found on an expedition of my father's before I accompanied him. He was convinced it was Phidias' original. It is not."

"You did not bury this here," she said.

He scraped a finger across his lips, looked toward the road wending down the mountain, then back at the bust. Claire could not imagine what he was thinking, for someone had obviously stolen the sculpture and somehow broken and buried it, along with the damaged crate.

"Garland," he said.

"You think he stole it?"

"A suspicion. Nothing more."

"At least it was a copy," she said.

Theseus laughed. "I suspect he did not know that, as it was simply labeled Homer. *Damn!* Copy or not, I am livid."

"Duly noted."

"I wonder..." He scratched Cullen behind his ears. "I suspect this fellow caught Garland's scent, and he homed in on it."

She squeezed Theseus' forearm rather than give him the hug she would prefer. "Cullen has found objects before, including a hair bob I lost in Halafair's home wood."

"We have begun burying the marbles," he said, rising.

"Shall we re-cover this one?" she said.

"Let it be." He placed a hand on the small of her back. "We shall move it with the others on the morrow, and upon our return home, I shall have a quiet chat with Lord Garland."

Claire was glad she would not be present for that conversation.

Penny left the Pythia's home carrying a small sachet of herbs

Xanthe had given her, ones to burn in the small brazier in their room. The blend was meant to relax and soothe. As she walked the path toward the village road, a stone had found its way into her boot, poking into the toes of her left foot. She sighed. It was hot, the day waning. She'd let it be.

Over her shoulder, Spyros followed dutifully behind her, their tether intact. Her shadow. Imposing and handsome, he distracted her with that twinkle in his eye and his clever conversation. Truth be told, he fascinated her, he always had, his liveliness in contrast to her brother's more reserved nature. Penny doubted that he found her equally compelling.

The stone in her shoe had grown *huge*. A fat boulder sat beside the path, and she rested her hand on it to remove her boot and the now-immense stone.

"No!" Spyros shouted, racing toward her.

Penny had no idea...

"Oh!" Something had pinched her hand!

She turned just as a large snake reared to strike her again.

Penny was lifted into the air by strong arms, and Spyros ran.

An *ochia*. Her rapid heartbeat increased, her panted breath mingling with her fear. Sweat beaded her temples, her stomach aroil.

An *ochia* was deadly, and one had bitten her.

Spyros kicked open her cottage door to find Claire bent over her microscope, the boom jerking her friend to her feet. "What's wrong?"

He laid Penny on the bed, his face tight. "She was bitten by an *ochia*." Spyros removed her bracelet, then started on her ring, which refused to come off.

"Take it off, Penelope," he said. "You will swell up, and it will become impossibly painful."

As Spyros gave her orders, Claire appeared with soap, a ewer of water, and white cloths, setting them on the bedside table.

Penny looked at her hand, noting red dots where she had been bitten, at least three or four of them.

"Wait!" she said.

"There is no time to wait," Spyros said.

Claire began cleaning the site.

Penny ignored her to stare at Spyros, who dabbed her forehead with a cool, wet cloth, his eyes panicked. He, the calmest of men, seemed about to ignite.

Claire retrieved her knapsack and began to troll within.

"What are you doing, Claire?" she said.

"Looking for my theriac to counteract the poison."

"Please, everyone stop for a moment," Penny said.

Both froze.

Penny drew in a slow breath to calm herself. "An *ochia* did not bite me."

"I saw it," Spyros said through clamped teeth.

"Yes, you did," Penny said, wishing the Pythia's calming herbs were wafting through the room. "A snake *did* strike me, but it was not poisonous."

"How can you say that?" Sypros said. "I saw it."

"What you saw was not an *ochia*, but I believe a four-lined snake, *elaphe quatuorlineata*. They are non-venomous. You know this as well as I, Spyros. They do not have fangs but teeth. See the markings on my hand? There are at least four." She held up her hand, showing red dots.

Spyros took her hand and stared, his thumb making whorls on the back, as if he couldn't help himself. He whooshed out a breath. "Yes, I see."

He gently laid her hand on the coverlet, then marched outside.

"Found it!" Claire said.

Spyros' reaction was the oddest thing. "What was that all about?" Penny said. "He looked as if the harpies were after him."

Claire reappeared at her bedside with bandages and the salve, which she dabbed over the wound. "I believe Spyros was rather overset by your injury."

She pushed herself up to a sitting position. "Well, yes, I know that, but why leave so abruptly?"

"Have you considered that his affections are engaged?"

"Engaged in what?"

Claire rolled her eyes as she wrapped the wound loosely with a clean bandage.

"That is the most unappealing expression, Claire," Penny said.

Claire smiled. "Not what, but who. He likes you, Pens."

"Oh, do not be absurd. I am but a little sister to him. He does not view me as a woman grown."

"You are wearing blinders, my friend."

Penny rose, sliding her hand in her pocket and drawing out the herbs Xanthe had given her. She retrieved the small brazier, added wood, and sprinkled the herbs atop the pile. Once lit, the scents rose. Heavenly.

Claire raised a brow. "I know just what you need, Pens. Oh, do keep on with the herbs. They are lovely." She dug in her trunk to lift a bottle of Rémy Martin cognac high. "Ta-da! A gift from my sister, Charlotte."

She set the bottle on the bedside table, then fetched three glasses, pouring two fingers of scotch in each.

Spyros reappeared, his stoic expression firmly in place.

"Just in time." Claire held out a glass of scotch, and he took it with a nod.

"Is there more?" he said. "I need it."

Claire slid a glance to Penny and winked.


They neared July, yet Dionysus' man had yet to appear. The marbles had been dug deep into Greek soil, scattered across the village and plain, with Theseus and the others mapping each location. Dozens had helped with the task, and once complete, he would make a full map from all the disparate notations.

He'd finished digging his last hole beneath a pine, intended for the bust of Hygieia, when Claire approached. He grunted a hello as he settled the final crate into its temporary resting place, then covered the crate with dirt, piling stones atop to mimic a more natural setting.

Rising, Theseus wiped his hands with a kerchief, slow and steady. The sculptures were gone, all interred in the Greek soil.

Better if Koios had taken the pieces to safety, but this solution worked as a temporary resting place. Theseus set his hands on his hips, staring at the plot of earth where Hygieia rested.

Years of work had finally come to fruition. He should feel relieved.

Rather, a void expanded in his chest.

Had he not loved these pieces as well or more than his father? How strange that he could no longer gaze upon their beauty, for they had been part of his world since childhood.

A hand on his arm drew him from his reverie.

"You look a bit lost," Claire said.

He huffed. "Perhaps I am."

Her eyes shone with understanding. "That makes perfect sense to me."

"Does it?"

"You've lived with these artifacts for most of your life. I know you loved them."

He said nothing, for what was there to say?

"As much as you wished to repatriate the marbles," she continued, "they meant a great deal to you. They are a part of who you are, Theo. I am sure you discovered several yourself."

He crossed his arms, expression dour. "More than several."

"So does it not make sense you feel bereft now that your task is complete?"

All this talk of feelings made him uncomfortable. He shrugged, unsettled by how Claire saw inside him. Few did. Most thought him crazed for his obsession.

"Your arguments for returning the sculptures always compelled me," Claire said. "Now, having spent time amongst the Hellas people, something I had not managed on my first dig here, I see your point more clearly. These artifacts are the fabric of the Greeks' history, woven into their lives and purpose. The Hellenes are a proud people, and I sense their closeness with the ancients far more than we do in England. It is hard to express—as if time were compressed and their past flows alongside their present. The marbles *do* belong here, not gathering dust in some foreign museum or English home."

Theseus cupped her cheek. "Thank you." He leaned closer to that lovely face, which veiled her powerful intellect and brave heart. He saw all of her, in full.

He touched his lips to hers, lightly, and when her hands rose to rest on his waist, he deepened the kiss, wishing for Claire to know all the admiration and affection he felt for her.

His tongue sought hers, his arms pulling her tight, her lips sweeter than ambrosia. A kiss that thanked her for her understanding and empathy and for her soul's beauty.

They parted, slowly, reluctantly, and he still could not take his eyes from hers. "There will be a bonfire tonight in celebration and heralding our departure. Will you accompany me?"

Her cheeks pinkened. "I should be honored."

"I must take charge of loading the wagon for tomorrow's departure," he said.

"I am off to find Penny."

She wore a mysterious smile, and he hoped it was a result of their delicious kiss.

An hour later, Theseus wiped his forearm across his brow, finally content with the wagon's arrangement. Now he must map the sculptures' locations, the villagers' paper notes a mishmash on where they were interred.

They would soon sail for England, a familiar pang pinching his chest at leaving Greece.

Britain might be home, but this country was fixed in his heart as well.

"Theseus!" Andreas ran toward him at a clip.

He met the headman halfway, noting his rumpled shirt and a large stain on its shoulder. "What is it?"

"Georgios has been slaughtered, and seven of the marbles are missing!" The lean man's breath came in gasps.

*Dammit to hell!* "Show me." Theseus had half-expected an attempt at theft and thought his precautions well enough. It seemed not. But the murder of a Kastri villager appalled him.

Andreas led him into the woods, and they trekked until they came upon a boulder surrounded by villagers bearing guns.

Behind the rock lay Georgios, bloody and still. Though he knew the man little, Theseus was aware he had a wife and small child. His jaw tightened.

"One of the dogs found him," Andreas said. "He lay beneath a shallow covering of leaves and dirt."

"Hasty work," Theseus said.

"This was clenched in his fist." Andreas handed a scrap of paper to Theseus, with seven of the listed marbles circled. "Georgios' task was to bury these missing seven. From what we found, he appeared to be colluding with the thieves."

Sophocles, Hera, the bronze of Doryphoros, Athena, a Hellenistic horse head, the bust of Theseus, and that of Penelope. Of the thirty sculptures, these were a random assortment in terms of value, some worth hundreds of pounds while others far less.

Theseus combed his hands through his hair, clasping them behind his neck as he peered at the blinding sky.

The villagers' flurried activity of burying the sculptures... Many village men and women had aided in their dispersal. A perfect opportunity, with Georgios' aid, to steal them.

But how did the thieves transport them in secret? Easy enough to hide a wagon in the wood. Yet they had turned on Georgios. A despicable betrayal. Why? He saw no point in the murder.

*Who was behind this?*

"I will question my people." Andreas shook his head. "Georgios was not Kastri-born, but wed a villager. We believed him to be one of us, but... He spoke often of missing the excitement of his birthplace, Thessaloniki. I think he found Kastri confining."

Theseus nodded, Georgios' death rasping his nerves. "Outsiders organized this for financial gain, I assume."

"An ancient tale," Andreas said, puffing out a breath.

"One oft repeated."

"Georgios had several friends visiting from Thessaloniki," Andreas said. "Their arrival coincided with your party's."

"Interesting." Theseus turned back toward the village, Andreas accompanying him. "How many?"

"Four, I believe," Andreas said. "Though I knew of Georgios' disgruntlement, I am nonetheless stunned by his treachery."

"I would lay odds his 'friends' are gone," Theseus said.

"You would win that bet, my friend," Andreas said. "They are nowhere to be found."

Perhaps the thievery was perpetrated by Greeks—a stretch, as only Andreas and Xanthe knew of his purpose before he arrived, and Theseus trusted both implicitly. No Greek had organized the theft. Garland? Impossible not to imagine him the perpetrator. But the planning was deft, one that left no one to tell the tale. Had the viscount the brains for it? He didn't believe so. Then who?

# TWENTY-TWO

Penny had thought long and hard about their departure and was discussing it with Xanthe when someone knocked at the cottage door.

Nomiki answered it, Glauca bobbing on her shoulder emitting calls of apparent excitement. The girl was stunning with an ethereal air. More important, she was kindness itself. Penny could very much see her as the future Pythia.

"Hello, Nomiki, Glauca." Claire stroked the bird's head with a gloved finger and entered, a smile on her face and questions in her eyes, the ever-present Cullen beside her.

"Forgive me for disturbing you." Claire curtsied to the Pythia.

Cullen approached the Pythia, then began to smell her.

The Pythia chuckled, scratching her pup beneath his chin. "This one is an old soul."

"Glauca likes him as well," Nomiki said, biting her lower lip. "He usually does not like dogs!"

"I would not blame him for that," Claire said, turning to Penny. "We leave in the morning. When I returned to our room this afternoon, I saw you had not packed a thing, not even the vase where you set out our daily flowers. I might add, I found them quite cheering."

Penny tilted her head. "Did *you* not leave the flowers? Each morning, fresh ones were left. If not you, then who?"

"Not me." Claire's lips twitched. "But I have an idea."

Claire looked toward Spyros, who leaned against the wall, one foot crossed over the other.

*Spyros?* Penny's heart clenched. *Had he?*

Enough. For she wished to tell Theseus her decision. Her brother might pitch a fit, but she was determined. Penny stood and thanked Xanthe and Nomiki for the tea, petted Glauca, now clutching a chair back, and hooked an arm through Claire's. "Come."

Outside, Claire paused. "You are in a dither."

"I am." They left Xanthe's for the village, Spyros trailing behind them.

"Where are we off to?" Claire said. "There is your brother."

Theseus amidst a group of townsmen. "Oh, dear. Perhaps I should tell you first."

"Your tone is rather portentous, Pens," Claire said.

"I plan to remain in Kastri for a time. Perhaps several weeks or a month."

Claire halted again. "Are you serious?"

"Indeed," Penny said. "Xanthe is a font of knowledge, and she has promised to teach me several more weaving tricks and techniques. I must take advantage of her knowledge."


CLAIRE MIGHT BE STUNNED, yet a part of her was unsurprised. Penny had evolved into a different woman on their trek, one who was more confident and determined. Perhaps she had always been so, but in Greece those attributes had blossomed. As they neared Theseus, she braced for the conflagration.

It came, just not the one she had prepared for, as Theo told them of the stolen marbles and a villager's murder, both shocking and sad.

As they entered the cottage, they were deep in discussion until Theseus surveyed the room. "Where are your packed trunks, sister?"

Penelope drew in a breath and straightened her spine. "I wish to stay for several more weeks in Kastri."

Theseus opened his mouth to speak, but Penny held up a hand, something Claire doubted Penelope would have done before this journey.

"I have thought long on this, brother, and it is what I must do. I have much to learn about weaving from Xanthe. Spyros has agreed to stay with me as my protector, and Xanthe will chaperone me."

Claire observed how Theseus' muscles bunched, his jaw tightening. Unsurprising, unlike his affirmative nod.

"I see," he said, his voice measured. "And how shall you return to England once we have sailed?"

"Andreas informed me that traders arrive monthly. When the wagons come, after they distribute their goods, I would travel with them overland back to Piraeus. From there, I shall easily find a ship to sail home."

Theseus frowned. "Spyros escorting you is well and good, but without me, a male relative, you need a female chaperone on the journey."

"As I said, Xanthe will join us, and Andreas offered two guards as well. They will protect Xanthe on her return journey. You cannot object to her chaperonage."

If anything, Theseus' tension wound tighter. "And what about on the voyage?"

"Easy enough to hire a woman in Athens and pay for her return trip as well."

"This troubles me greatly, Penelope," he said.

"I know, Theo, and I am sorry about that. But I am quite resolved. I will have my Ferguson, ample ammunition, and several knives. With Spyros, guards, and Xanthe joining me, you simply cannot object."

Theseus remained silent, as did Claire, impressed with Penny's planning.

"You have seemingly thought of everything, Penelope," Theseus said. "And what of the approaching revolution?"

Penny flushed, but she held her brother's eyes. "I admit that is a risk, but from all you, Lord Byron, and even Andreas have said, the conflict is a year or two away."

"Skirmishes have already erupted," Theseus growled. "You celebrated one with the Iteans!"

"Yes, and you allowed Claire and me to come on this journey. In addition, Xanthe has said our journey to Athens and my travels home will be uneventful. You *know* I will be as safe as possible here in the village and traveling to Piraeus." Penny smiled, her eyes kind yet resolute. "I have thought long and hard on this, Theo. I feel extending my visit is worth the risk."

"As head of our household, I could command you to return."

"You could," Penny said.

Minutes passed, Theseus paced, and Claire felt for him, for he deeply loved his sister. If revolution burst forth, Penelope could be caught in the crossfire.

Theseus probably wished to strangle Spyros, but the man would protect Penelope with his life.

"As you wish, Penelope. I shall speak with Andreas and request additional guards for you as well." Theseus turned to Claire. "Your trunks are loaded for our departure in the morning." He hugged his sister, then strode off.

"I think you are a bit daft, my friend," Claire said. "But your passion I understand."

"The Pythia awaits me," Penny said, grinning. "She has gifts for you, ones that I am certain you will find meaningful."

Claire could not imagine what. Perhaps incense? "I shall visit after I see Theseus. Perhaps I can soothe some of his upset."

"If anyone could," Penny said with a knowing smile. "It would be you."

Early evening in the town center, Theseus was joined by Claire, who took his arm. A large bonfire had been lit both in memory of Georgios and to celebrate their departure. Though their discussion about Penelope's remaining had been circular, Claire's advocacy had soothed him. Now, a powerful sense of emptiness pushed that calm aside.

Theseus felt at sea, his quest complete, years of work and strife ended. Even with the theft, he should be elated. Yet the void within ached. Another sip of ouzo. Where was the euphoria at the completion of his years-long task?

The flames glimmered upward into the darkening sky, barn swallows and swifts chasing insects through the air.

"You are contemplative, Theseus," she said.

He nodded. He'd left a sizable sum with Georgios' wife, his generosity pleasing Claire, though he failed to see his gift that way. Georgios' death—the man culpable or not—was on his head. His family was now Theseus' responsibility.

"I am eager for the journey home," Claire said.

"As am I," he replied.

Claire frowned. "I am concerned."

"About...?" He laid a hand on her back.

"Will the villagers keep silent about the sculptures? Will you pay them?"

"No," he said. "They value their return. Andreas and many villagers say they foreshadow Greece's renewed independence."

"But what if they speak to someone? A friend, say? Think of the Egyptian tomb raiders. They were Egyptians themselves!"

"No one will say a word."

"I still worry."

"These are not stupid people, Claire."

"No, they are not. But they haven't much money."

He chuckled, shaking his head. "Georgios was not of Kastri, if you recall, but wed a villager. Delphi is sacred, perhaps *the* most sacred site in all of Greece. Christian or no, their past remains fixed in their souls, and they obey Xanthe."

"Obey…"

His pirate's grin flashed. "Whether you deem her the Oracle or not, the villagers do. She has great power here, and no one would counter her order to conceal the sculptures."

"I hope you are right."

"Come," he said, holding out his hand. "Walk with me?"

CLAIRE TOOK HIS HAND, and a warmth wove through her as they strolled beneath the ascending moon past the village. A few lights twinkled far below in Itea and on *Nemesis,* bobbing in the waves. Though eager for home, Claire was reluctant to leave this land of blazing skies, olive groves, and welcoming people.

A breeze ruffled her cape as they walked, Theseus striding farther from the village. He paused, withdrawing something from his pocket. "I discovered this when I interred one of the marbles. I thought you would find it interesting."

He held out his hand, unfolding his fingers. A five-inch marble chunk rested on his palm, the shard from a bust or statue—a partial face, with a broken nose, cheek, and one eye, one *painted* eye. Theseus flicked a match. The iris shone bright blue, the protuberant eye lined in black paint beneath a black eyebrow.

"*God in Heaven*, Theo, do you see? How wonderful!" She peered up at him, thrilled to her bones.

He brushed a calloused finger across her cheek. "Somehow, it made its way to the surface beneath many feet of dirt and stone for me to find. I am convinced it was meant for you, and I showed Xanthe. She insisted I gift it to you." He laughed. "Though she made me trade for it, of course."

Claire laughed, giddy with the painted fragment. "Oh, dear, what did you trade?"

"She wanted my spyglass, and as I always carry two, I gladly gave her one."

Claire shouldn't say it. They were in such accord, and it might prompt an argument. And yet she could not help herself. She held the painted stone aloft. "Well?"

Instead of anger, she got laughter.

"Theo?"

He took her free hand and held it. "Apologies. Profuse ones, though the irony does not escape me. I am fully convinced! You were correct, and here is incontrovertible proof that the antiquarians were wrong."

"Would that this shard convinced them."

"Oh, m'lady, your task is a Sisyphean one. Dion, my antiquities dealer friend, believes in colored marbles, or polychromy, as you call it. Sadly, he is convinced that no matter the proof, those in high places will not relinquish their perceptions of the ancient Greeks or their concept of white purity of form. Their ignorance of polychromy is willful."

"An unfortunate fact. Nonetheless, I shall continue onward." Claire tucked the shard into the pocket of her hooded cape.

"As well you should," he said, a fierce look on his face. "Someday, someone in authority will read your thesis and have a eureka moment. They will believe."

She smiled. "The truth is the truth, no matter how people try to bend or break it."

"The shard..." His body stiffened, hands thrust in pockets, looking anywhere but at her. "I am poor with words other than academic ones. This shard, I... I wished it to show how much you mean to me."

She cupped his cheeks, turning his face to hers, his words speeding her heart faster. "You mean much to me as well."

She stood on tiptoe and brushed her lips across his. Parting, he rested his hands on her shoulders, and they stared at one another as if for the first time, as if they were new and special.

Emotion overwhelmed her, for Theo was strong and bold and kind, and he promised companionship and laughter and safety.

Claire breathed in the night air, the bones of Delphi calling, a soft resonance vibrating beneath her feet. Theseus would say her feelings were folderol. Or perhaps he sensed it, too. "I feel things here, Theo. Things I cannot explain."

"It is the spirit of the land." His arm slid around her waist, and he drew her closer. "Some discover it. Others do not. The Greeks have a word for it, though I cannot recall which one." He laughed. "Or perhaps I was meant to forget the word. You know, magic and all. I have always felt a resonance at certain sites. A comforting feeling, no?"

"It is, though a strange one."

He took both her hands in his. "Marry me, Claire."

The sounds of the wind, the forest creatures, and the townspeople's voices faded as she stared at those green eyes full of hope. No getting down on one knee for Theo. For he stood tall and strong, his hands gripping hers, his eyes imploring.

Claire was momentarily mute until her scrambled brain blurted out, "Oh, my!"

He drew back, though he did not release her. "I wish to wed you for myriad reasons, lovely Claire. Your passion. Your determination. Your intelligence. Your kind nature. *You*. All that you are, I admire."

She admired Theseus, too, but what of love? Did he love her? Did she love him? Though she would not swear to the latter, her affection had grown...large. What did her feelings mean?

Claire wanted more kisses. She liked those, nay, she liked *his* exceedingly well. In fact, she often wished to touch him, much as Lottie had said she adored touching Patrick. More interesting—she wished he would touch her...all the time.

But his was far more than a physical pull. They held the same passion for antiquities, each loved journeying to faraway lands, too, and Claire could picture them exploring antiquated worlds. Theseus was bold, and she liked that, as she did his wit. Even his love of falconry intrigued her, a pastime she would like to learn.

"My pretty woman," Theseus said. "You know, I forget your beauty at times because you blaze a path with your dazzling mind. When your eyes go soft, like melted amber, you warm me. We would suit, Claire, would we not?"

Oh, the man was perfectly fine with words. Claire had *never* imagined herself a wife, for what husband would put up with her never-ending research? Theseus would. She imagined a *partner* in her research, a man who listened, who took her thoughts and words into account, and gave them consideration. A bright feeling. Love might follow, might it not?

"Yes, Theo. I say yes." Claire stretched up for a kiss, sealing their agreement. When they parted, his teeth glinted in the moonlight from his smile. "Good."

He drew her close again, his arms banding about her, and feathered kisses on her neck, her cheeks, her eyelids, and finally, her lips. Passion swept Claire into its maelstrom, a surreal feeling, as if in some fever dream. She gripped his biceps. "Is this real? Are we truly to marry?"

His laughter boomed, his joy dazzling. How ironic to once have thought him taciturn and unapproachable.

His eyes roved over her, his face solemn. "*Σε λατρεύω, to αστέρι μου.*"

She was almost afraid to ask what the phrase meant. But of course, she must. "What did you say?"

He winked, the devil. "Penelope may know. Certainly, most in the village do. Think of it as a wee quest."

"You are a beast of a man," she said amidst laughter and affection.

"I confess I am." He grinned, and never had he looked more like a pirate aimed at plunder.

## CHAPTER
# TWENTY-THREE

The remainder of Claire's evening passed in a blur. Was she really to marry Theo? Become a wife? A chattel?

No, not that. Yes, her mother's marriage to Fielding was appalling, but both Lottie's and Rose's unions were harmonious, each a joyful pairing.

Yet she would explore the world with this man, her passions understood and shared. A thrill coursed through her.

Her feelings fountained, bubbling and restless, Theo's pull unrelenting. He was the most interesting and intriguing man of her acquaintance. She leaned closer to his warmth as they walked toward the village hand-in-hand. She ran her fingers down his arm, unable to resist. He smiled at her. Never had she wished to caress another, not the way she did Theseus.

How would those muscled shoulders feel beneath her fingers? Would running her hands down his chest tickle? The textures must be divine. Yet her chest tightened at the prospect of marriage.

Easy to picture their future adventures, but living day-to-day with another...a man. That gave her pause. She suspected he was an early riser, as was she…mostly. Was he grouchy in the morning, as she was, or chipper? He disliked opera, though he enjoyed plays and poetry, and loved to ride. Claire did, too.

She shook her head. Cataloguing Theseus' likes and dislikes was an exercise in futility. What mattered was how they got on with each other. One thing she knew—Theseus was no Fielding, thank all the stars.

The wedding wasn't tomorrow. Nor for many days, for that matter, as they would marry in England before her family and his. A deep breath eased the pressure. Plenty of time to think of all her decision entailed.

Full dark had fallen when Theseus left her at the cottage, their parting full of kisses and smiles. Claire was eager to tell Penny of Theo's proposal. What would she say?

Entering, Claire found chaos. Dresses flung across beds, the medicine kit open, and the woman herself, hair askew and face flushed, racing around the room.

"Pens! What's wrong?"

Penny whirled, eyes wide, as if shocked to see Claire.

"What has got you in a dither?" Claire said.

"The Ferguson rifle is gone."

"Gone?" Claire said.

"I kept it in its case beneath the bed. It is nowhere to be found." Penny slumped. "I still have my Baker. Spyros kindly offered to clean it for me, so he has it."

Claire had a suspicion, particularly after finding the stolen bust. "Someone in Lord Garland's party stole it."

"Do you think so?"

"I do, though I cannot be sure who. Those with us during the attack must have chattered about your skills and the strange rifle." Claire told Penny of the stolen, broken bust. "One of the Garlands' party stole Homer as a "souvenir," and I doubt not someone in their party took your valuable rifle as well."

Penny flung herself across the bed. "It is a terrible loss. I loved that gun, and it cost our steward a pretty penny, too. I shall have to replace it."

Claire lay beside her friend and took her hand. "I am so sorry."

"The Baker is not the same." Penny lurched from the bed and began throwing clothes into her trunk, then closed the medicine kit and replaced it in its niche by the bed.

"The Pythia wishes to see you," Penny said. "We should go."

"Xanthe is older," Claire said. "Will she not be asleep?"

"I suspect she is waiting for you. For us. Come."

"But…" Claire wanted to tell Penny of Theseus' proposal.

"We must!" Penny took her hand and dragged her outside.

Penny hustled her up the hill toward Xanthe's home, the words of her engagement near spilling out, not to mention the translation of the Greek phrase Theseus had spoken. Penny was chatting with Spyros, and she must wait.

When they knocked on the Pythia's door, a young woman opened it with a smile. "We have been expecting you."

Spyros remained outside, his indignation at the theft causing him to set a man guarding their cottage.

Closing the barn door after the horse, she feared.

The large room looked welcoming and calm, with the Pythia seated in her padded rocking chair and several handmaidens scattered about the room.

"Sit, my friends." Xanthe waved her hands. "Sit."

They took a pair of fat cushions, and Claire breathed deep of the soothing spices and herbs scenting the air, candles giving the space a warm glow. A young woman offered retsina, whilst another held a tray of *baklava*. Impossible to resist.

"Where are Nomiki and Glauca?" Penny said.

"Off on a familial errand," Xanthe said. Turning to Claire, the Pythia's sharp eyes danced with humor. "I see big changes are in store, Lady Claire."

Claire's blush rose.

"What is Xanthe talking about?" Penny said.

"Nothing that need concern you at the moment, my curious friend," the Pythia said. "Lady Claire and I have business to conduct."

Business? Claire could not imagine what.

The Pythia glanced at a young woman, who scampered from the room.

"It seems a mystery, Claire," Penny said. "What could it be?"

Claire opened her mouth, but nothing came out.

The woman reappeared holding a large, square box, unwieldy as she set it on the floor before Claire.

"I am excited!" a young attendant said, with an accompanying giggle from the girl seated beside her.

Claire smiled at the girl's animation.

"Thank you, my friend." The Pythia grinned as she moved her attention to Claire. "We all know of your quest, Claire Pheland. And I have thought long and hard on this. Thus, I have two gifts, loans in truth, that may aid your pursuit. You are to keep these until you prove to the world your hypothesis." She nodded again, and Nomiki removed the box's lid, though in the low light, Claire could see little.

The girl withdrew a large *krater* from the box by its double handles and set it on the floor.

The large red and black jar was ancient and exquisite.

Facing her was Herakles' protectress, Athena, seated in conversation with one of the Dioskouroi, whether Castor or Pollux, she wasn't sure. Hermes, his son Pan, and Eros were also depicted.

"What a splendid *krater*," Claire said. "It is in near-perfect condition."

"That it is." Xanthe nodded again to the attendant, who rotated the jar to its other side.

"*Heavens!*" Claire goosebumped. She'd viewed numerous ancient pots over the years, but this *krater* left her breathless, for it depicted an artist *painting* the lion skin on a statue of Herakles. "I am over-whelmed."

"This particular vessel was used for mixing wine and water," the Pythia said. "It was crafted in 360 BC or thereabouts."

Claire wished to say something profound, but all that came out was, "Incredible." The jar *proved* her thesis.

Xanthe winked, eyes dancing. "A long ago Oracle discovered it in the cave we now use for our rites and rituals."

"The one you visited, Penny?" Claire said.

Penny grinned wide. "Yes. I knew of this and have been so *excited*. It was near impossible not to give away the surprise!"

"The vessel is for you, Lady Claire," the girl said.

Claire looked at the Pythia. "Truly?"

"Oh, yes. Until the world accepts your hypothesis. Then you shall return them to the Oracle."

"Them?" Claire said.

The girl again reached within the box and lifted a tiny statue about the size of Nomiki's Glauca, a mere eight inches tall. Claire gasped at the miniature archer. "Oh, my."

"This maquette is a scale model of a much larger statue," Xanthe said. "He represents the Trojan warrior Paris, though the sculpture itself gives no indication. We believe the life-size statue was from the temple of Aegina, and the maquette bears the sculpture's true colors. I have written all this and tucked my notes into the *krater*."

So astonished, Claire could only marvel at the tiny statue.

The Pythia nodded. "An Oracle received it as a gift around five hundred BC."

"You mean Pythias have possessed it for all these centuries?" Claire said.

"We have."

"Has the full-sized statue been found?"

"Word reached us that it was taken to Germany, of all places." Xanthe smirked. "By a man named Schliemann. But one day it shall again rest on Greek soil."

The girl raised the maquette for Claire's inspection.

The archer was near perfect, with but a chip on one foot and on his helmet. His lips were red, his eyes brown, and he wore diamond-patterned pantaloons and sleeves, his tunic a bright golden-yellow with griffins and lions dotting the garment. Barefoot, he crouched on a knee, arrow knocked, bow at the ready.

Claire touched a finger lightly to his hair—long, reddish, and curled. Not marble, but bronze, the locks dangling from holes drilled in the archer's skull. Claire could picture them swaying in the breeze.

"He is near pristine," she said with awe.

The girl smiled as she handed the maquette to Claire. Her hands shook, and she took it with great care and rested the archer on her lap.

"I believe," the girl said, "this was painted using the encaustic method, which is why its colors remain vibrant. That is what Nomiki told me."

"The Egyptians used that method as well," Penny said.

The girl nodded. "Encaustic is more painstaking, according to Nomiki. With easier methods more often employed. But encaustic endures far longer."

Deeply moved, Claire didn't know how to thank the Pythia for her astonishing gifts. "You humble me, my lady," Claire finally said. "These artifacts represent all I have researched. They bear the truth of my hypothesis. But...what if my hypothesis, my proof, fails to convince those in power? I fear, as does Theseus, that no matter the proof, they will not believe. Shall I return them then?"

Xanthe peered into the distance for long moments. Was she prognosticating? Would the Pythia foretell for Claire? Did she even believe that the Pythia could prophesize? Claire almost laughed aloud at her speculation.

After clearing her throat, Xanthe looked at the girl. "The tea is about to boil. Would you remove it from the stove, please?"

The Pythia squeezed Claire's hand. "These are yours until the world accepts the truth."

"What in return may I do for you or your people?"

"Support Penelope's decision to remain in Greece," the Pythia said. "She will come home safe to England, I assure you. Have no fear, for I shall protect her."

Claire imagined all that could happen to her friend. Theseus had agreed, but it disturbed him. She disliked seeing Theo upset, but she trusted Xanthe's words. If Claire were that determined, she would want Penny's advocacy. "I will support you, Pens, though I shall worry."

The Pythia raised a brow. "Penelope is blossoming as a weaver. She will learn and grow and remain unharmed. Do help that brother of hers understand, for she loves him deeply."

"As he loves her," Claire said.

An immense cat strolled into the room, long and lean, its semi-long coat a tricolor pattern, with white predominant.

Penny reached to pet it, and it hopped onto her lap and began to purr.

"I wondered when Mefitis would appear!" Xanthe said.

"Is not Mefitis the god of deadly gases?" Claire said.

Which was when the cat let out a silent, odiferous fart.

"Now, do you understand?" The girl chuckled.

Unfortunately, Claire did.

As they said their farewells to Xanthe and her attendants, the Pythia closed her eyes and held up a calloused finger. "One more thing of note, Lady Claire. Do take the easternmost route to Itea."

"I shall tell Theseus." Perhaps he would listen.

The Pythia snorted, a most startling sound. "I wish you good luck with that one."


The night was warm and fragrant as they walked to their room, Spyros carrying the box holding both the *krater* and maquette.

Theseus hailed them from the porch of his cottage. Claire had yet to tell Penny of his proposal. *Damn.*

"Brother!" Penny said. "Come! We have a surprise!"

His gaze slid to Claire's as he met them. "My lady."

"Theo," was all she managed to say, wild excitement turning her mute.

The four of them squeezed into the cottage, the two large men shrinking its size to minuscule.

"On the bed, Spyros, please," Penny said. "Come look, Theo!"

Claire stepped back, feeling oddly out of place and out of sorts. She should have told Penny her news about the engagement.

Ooohs and ahhs from Theseus and Spyros as the krater and maquette were lifted from the box.

"The Pythia gave these to Claire."

"I have never seen their like, particularly the maquette," Theseus said. "We will crate them up."

"I do not want them in the hold," Claire said. "But in my cabin on the return journey."

Theseus' brow raised. "They will be perfectly safe in the hold, Claire."

"I know, but I want them with me."

He nodded. "All right."

She relaxed a fraction.

"Did Claire tell you our news?" Theseus said to Penny and Spyros.

Penny turned to Claire. "What news?"

Claire's mouth flapped until she finally spat out, "We are to marry."

Spyros laughed, slapping Theseus on the back.

"Why?" Penny looked shocked.

"Because we will suit," Theseus said.

"You will...suit?" Penny said in a flat voice.

Claire slipped a hand through Theseus' arm. "Yes, Penelope. A fine reason to wed."

Penny snorted. "So they say."

Their sunrise departure saw the wagon loaded with their trunks and gear, along with the crate holding Claire's precious artifacts, the villagers surrounding them. Gifts were handed to them—soaps, olive oil, cheese, and *kompoloi,* or worry beads. One man offered a live chicken, and they thanked him profusely but declined.

Two sailors carrying rifles mounted the donkeys, a third man seated in the wagon's bed, for Theseus would drive, with Claire beside him. After hugs, back slaps, cheek kisses, and Andreas insisting they return soon, the townspeople dispersed.

Only Spyros and Penny remained, the atmosphere turning awkward. Theseus disapproved of his sister remaining, and Penny seemed to find no joy in her and Theo's upcoming nuptials.

Theseus drew Spyros aside, while Penny strode to Claire, hands clasped before her.

"What is troubling you?" Claire said, resting her hand on Cullen's head.

"Do you love my brother?" Penny said in a hostile tone.

"I..." Claire was nonplussed. "I do not know."

"How could you not?" Frustration flavored Penny's words.

"I never expected to marry and have never been in love. I do not know how it should feel." Claire checked the knife at her waist, discomfited by having to clarify her feelings. "My affection for Theseus runs deep."

Penny sighed. "That is good, certainly. But I wish you and he were in love. Yes, that is the opposite of the conventional view and rather outlandish. But on the inside, my brother is softhearted, and I would not see him hurt. He is precious to me."

"He is to me as well, Penelope." Theo's sister meant well, but Claire's irritation rose. The choice was Claire and Theo's, and it was a fine one. The right one. "I would *never* betray Theseus, never deliberately hurt him. Our affection for one another is keen, and I believe those feelings will deepen over time. We shall rub along well."

Penny shrugged.

"What about our marriage displeases you?"

Penny shook her head, then bussed Claire's cheek. "I wish... You are my dear friend. He, my beloved brother." Tears welled, but she shook her head and strode off, Spyros following.

"Stay safe, Pens!" she hollered. "You, too, Spyros! Come home soon!"

Penny raised a hand but did not turn around.

# TWENTY-FOUR

Arriving in Itea was like a homecoming, the headman Kostas greeting them with enthusiasm. Theseus had acquiesced to Claire's insistence, and they'd taken the eastern path, though he'd whinged about the early August heat and Xanthe's "absurd" request.

Yet upon their arrival, Kostas asked after the route they had taken down the mountain.

"Thank the gods," Kostas said. "The middle path is swiftest, and I feared you would take that, for a bridge has washed out and is impassable."

Claire tried not to smirk, she really did, while Theseus' brows beetled. Her giggle turned to laughter, which was when he told Kostas of Xanthe's suggestion. Kostas was all ears regarding the stolen marbles, saying no wagons had come through Itea.

Getting a word in edgewise, Claire asked after her aunt.

Kostas nodded, hands on hips. "Not only has she adopted Milo, but she is inquiring about the children, and wouldn't a few love to visit England with her!"

Claire grinned. "She is funning you, of course, though I suspect Auntie intends to bring Milo home."

"A force of nature, that one. Her splint will be off soon." Kostas blinked, eyes wide. "I find that idea…"

"Terrifying?"

He boomed a laugh. "No! We have enjoyed her stay immensely."

With that, Claire bustled off to see Auntie, who was her usual bright self. At her appearance, Milo hopped from her lap to bump his nose with Cullen's, the tiny pup facing the immense Cullen, always comical.

She packed up her aunt with the aid of Elina, who chattered with Auntie the entire time, seemingly fast friends. They spent the night on land, and Claire missed Penny, hoping all was as she wished in Kastri. Auntie joined them at the taverna, and over glasses of ouzo, Kostas informed them of Pantelis' disappearance. His face dour, he explained Pantalis had set the bandits on them.

Claire knew Theseus had called the man a friend. "I cannot believe this."

"Sadly, it is true," Kostas said.

"Why, in God's name?" Theseus said.

Kostas shook his head, but another chimed in. "He lost his wife and child, perhaps a year ago, the unfortunate result of a misguided raid. Pantelis's anger grew, and—"

"He began to drown his grief in retsina and ouzo," another said. "He became unhinged."

The headman leaned close. "It is true, I fear. I cannot imagine what the Ottomans offered him, but his family's deaths triggered his collusion. The Turks did not want the sculptures restored to Hellas, hence the bandit attack."

Kostas took a healthy swig of retsina and continued. "Pantelis has vanished. Perhaps the bandits killed him? We do not know."

"I hope he lives, though how he could deceive us so…" Theseus rubbed a hand across his forehead.

Claire leaned close. "I am sorry, Theo."

"No more than I."

The next day, the sun lustrous across the azure waters, they set sail. Agnes was made comfortable, and though her spirit was eager, she rested onboard, only waking to bid farewell to her new friends as she cuddled Milo close.

Claire's gifts from the Pythia and the shard from Theo were safely stowed in a well-padded crate, as was her microscope. Both were tied down in her cabin, where she could see to their safety.

The crossing was smoother than the outbound voyage, and she reveled in her and Theseus' time together. Claire was sketching on deck when he approached wearing a smile. It was a beautiful smile and far more frequent than on the outbound voyage.

Leaning against the rail, he faced her as she drew. "You have not brought up our nuptials."

Her hand stilled, and she set her charcoal in its box and her pad in her knapsack. "I have not. You see, I am rather terrified."

"May I ask of what?" He clasped her waist and drew her close, his face solemn.

The idea itself panicked her. When they would marry was some vague point in the future, distant and obscure. The idea of going through the trumpery that attended a peer's wedding...the vast preparations, the lavish expenditures, the tedious fittings, the immense crowds...too much. Claire preferred the background, yet by the event's nature, she would be the center of attention.

She stopped her racing mind. What mattered was the marriage itself, not the panoply surrounding it. The result would be the same. And she *did* want to marry Theo, could picture their many adventures together, though she shied away from their bedroom proceedings.

Yet...she yearned to touch him...everywhere.

Why women of her station were so uninformed about all things intimate, she did not know. The act was a natural one creatures performed daily. Francis Bacon had said knowledge was power, and she agreed. Lottie certainly knew more...now. As did Mama. Why had they never discussed relations with her?

Claire's hands slid to his shoulders, her fingers smoothing his coat. "I wish I knew, for marriage is an unexplored land, and while I am usually most excited about mysterious places, I fear that is not the case with our upcoming event."

"Is it the wedding itself? Or the marriage?"

"Do you not see? I like to think of myself as...well...competent. I know nothing about the marriage bed, not even a little."

"Society expects you to be uninformed." He brushed a stray curl that had escaped her chignon. "And though I find that outlook antediluvian, it remains fixed. You need not know a thing, for your response shall be instinctual, as will mine. We shall explore love-making together. There will be no fear. No control issues. I would not hurt you for the world, *to asteri mu*."

She tried to smile. "I believe you, but..."

"We shall go as slow or as swift as you wish. There is no pressure, for making love shall be a beautiful, shared experience."

Her lips quirked. "No pressure?"

"Only from yourself."

"That is plenty!" She laughed. "I confess the idea of the festivities gives me hives, too. You are an earl, an important man, a member of the House of Lords. But when I picture our immense wedding with throngs of—"

"Good God, woman!" He brushed a hand across her shoulder. "Do you know me so little? I would be happy with just the pair of us at the ceremony."

"Truly?"

He nodded.

"I should like my family there, too."

"Naturally. And Devonshire as well, for he is a good friend of mine and your family's."

"Most often I forget he is *not* of the family, for he joins us in all celebrations."

"Where?" Theseus said.

Claire blinked. "Where what?"

"Where would you like the ceremony held?"

She leaned in and kissed his cheek, uncaring of the sailors bustling around them. "You are being quite amiable, I must say."

His soft chuckle warmed her heart and lower, much lower. A strange reaction that had been happening more often of late. "Take what you can, love. I doubt it will last."

It was her turn to laugh. "At Wolf Court, I think, or perhaps Halafair? Whichever is easiest."

He nodded. "I shall procure a special license, and we shall set it for a week after we land. Late August or early September at the latest. A fine time."

"A week?" Panic fluttered her chest. "What about the banns?"

"Would you prefer three weeks?" he said. "See how amenable I can be?"

She looked at Theo, admiring his imposing form and handsome face, but of all, she cherished the inner man. So soon, though? She recalled her promise to Penny to wait for her return. Another worry.

Those thoughts were for another day, for today she rode the waves beneath a blue sky with a man for whom she had much affection. She would ask Lottie about the marriage bed as soon as they arrived at Woodbine, their first stop on their way to Wolf Court.

Theo leaned forward, his breath warm on her ear. "Take down your hair for me."

"With this wind, it will become a tangled mess." But his eyes burned, so she lifted her hands, removing the pins slowly, one at a time, as his eyes heated, until her waist-length hair flew around her like a banner.

Theo's strong, blunt fingers wove through her hair, examining it with wonder. "You are Daphnaie, the laurel, a dryad incomparable."

"Theo," she wrapped her arms around his waist, resting against him, the soft linen cool against her cheek. "When you say such things, my heart beats fast, like Cullen's when hunting a rabbit."

His chest bounced with laughter. "My love, only you would compare your heart to Cullen's chase. At all times you make my heart beat faster."

He had called her "my love." Claire held on tight, content, and reveled in the moment. How this man made her heart sing.

On a bright August morning, they docked at Plymouth, Theseus planning to sell the frigate. At his request, Claire and Agnes remained aboard ship while he attended to business. When he returned, a lady's maid accompanied him, a girl named Jane, to assist Claire and Agnes.

Soon, they were off, their trunks stowed in the traveling chariot, a bright vehicle with four large windows. Accompanying them were two postillions, two outriders, and a saddled horse for Theseus if he chose to ride. They would make Woodbine in a mere five or six hours, depending on the roads and weather.

The boxed *krater*, maquette, and shard were secured on the floor beside Claire's feet, Theseus seated beside her, with Agnes and Jane across from them. Cullen lay on the floor between them, taking up a great deal of space, the petite Milo snuggled on Auntie's lap. She'd brought a bowl for Cullen, and as expected, he soon cast up his accounts. Once cleaned up, they bumped and thumped along, their new maid opening her tapestry portmanteau to produce a green something. She began to knit, but every so often, Jane would glance at Cullen, then return to her work.

"He will not hurt you, Jane," Claire said. "Cullen is a sweet boy."

"He is a *cù mòr*," Jane said.

"A big dog," Theseus said. "That he is."

Today, her fiancé was full of restless energy, peering out the window often. Claire could stand it no longer. "You wish to ride, do you not?"

He dipped his chin, his smile chagrined. "It appears I am quite transparent, my lady.

"If only that were true, my lord, but in this instance, yes." Claire rapped the ceiling of their carriage, which soon came to a halt. Theseus bussed her cheek. "Thank you, love."

Claire thought she would doze along with Agnes and Milo, yet sleep eluded her. For several moments, she watched Jane ply her needles.

"What are you knitting?" Claire said in a quiet voice so as not to awaken Agnes.

"A jumper for my nephew," the girl said, her Scottish brogue thick. She held up her knitting, a tiny, intricate thing.

Claire leaned forward. "Your stitches are exquisite."

"Thank you, my lady." Jane ducked her head and resumed her work.

"Might I ask a somewhat personal question?" Claire said.

The girl looked at her askance but nodded.

"Is Jane your true name?"

Pink stained the girl's freckled cheeks. She shook her head.

"Might I ask what it is?"

"Eilidh," she said, staring at her stitches.

"It sounds like EH-lee. How do you spell it?"

"E i l i d h," she said.

"Scots Gaelic, I would guess."

"It is, my lady. It means 'from the island,' for Shetland is my home."

"I was there once and found it austere and beautiful, a mysterious yet welcoming place."

Eilidh's small smile appeared. "Tis a land I love."

"No more of this Jane business. Eilidh, it is."

The girl resumed her knitting but seemed to glow with pleasure.

They rode on and on, and Claire dozed until the carriage jerked to a halt. The sounds of rifles and pistols clicking, preparing to fire, boomed in her ears. A highwayman attack, just like the bandits' assault on Parnassus. Twilight had descended, and she peered out the carriage window, seeing little.

Theseus' horse neared the carriage, and he bent close. "Are you wearing your knives?"

"I most certainly am."

"Unidentified riders approach. Six of them."

*Blast and damn!* Claire slipped her hand through her left pocket to wrap her fingers around the hilt of the knife strapped to her thigh. Both the *krater*, the maquette, and the shard rested safely at her feet. She could not lose her precious artifacts. She simply could not.

Eilidh opened her carpetbag to stow her knitting, her hand returning with a long leather sheath. She withdrew a knife over a foot long. "May I?"

"Absolutely," Claire said. "Is that a Scottish dirk?"

Eilidh's hint of a smile accompanied her nod.

Claire saw the knife, long and lethal, and was back on Parnassus, guns blazing and bullets zinging. She bit her lip hard for control. This situation was *not* the same. She had survived the bandits. She would survive this, too, with calm and control.

Agnes stirred, and Claire awakened her with a whisper. "Auntie?"

"Mummm?"

"Unknown riders approach."

Her aunt's eyes flew open, though Milo slept on. She scrabbled for her reticule, from which she withdrew a pocket pistol. "I am prepared."

Claire peered out a window. Theseus had rejoined the outriders, the trio flanking the pair of horses pulling the carriage. Sweat dampened her hands and brow, and she glanced at the girl, who could be no more than twenty-one years of age. Her face was calm, the knife resting in her right hand.

"We shall be fine," Claire said to Eilidh.

"A course we shall, m'lady." Eilidh clutched her knife. "Old Betty here is my good friend."

Which begged the question—how had Eilidh wielded "old Betty" in the past? Best not to ask.

Thundering hooves...shouts, cries, and...

*Laughter?* Cullen yipped.

The coach halted, and Agnes raised a kerchief to her nose. "Can you see anything?"

"Not yet, Auntie." Gripping Cullen's collar, Claire peered outside. Nothing, though one of the mounted outriders now stood alongside the carriage.

"Claire!" Theseus called in his booming voice.

The outrider hopped to the ground, opened her door, and lowered the steps.

"Auntie, you and Eilidh should stay here for now. Please."

Her aunt harrumphed but nodded.

With not a small dose of apprehension, Claire descended the steps, knife in hand, Cullen by her side, and walked to the front of the carriage. She spotted Theseus mounted beside a group of riders.

Relief made her dizzy. With a smile, she sheathed her knife and ran, unladylike or not.

"Welcome home!"

"Hail the traveler!"

"Well met!"

Atop their horses sat Rhys, Rose, Patrick, and Thomasina.

Cullen bounced with excitement as all dismounted, except Patrick, greeting each arrival with yips and licks.

Rose raced over, arms wide, and Claire was enfolded in a fierce hug. "I am so glad you are safe."

"As am I!" Claire said. "I thought you were highwaymen!"

Rose stepped back with a laugh. "We would make a good crew, would we not?"

"Absolutely! How fares Gareth?"

"Busy as a bee! The little man is crawling everywhere, and he adores the horses and stables! I am so pleased."

"My sister?"

"Back at Woodbine. Charlotte's stomach was bothering her," Rose said. "She stayed with Susannah, Henry, and Banby, though

Henry was frothing to come. The lieutenant insisted he complete his morning lessons with Akiko, much to his disgruntlement."

"But are all well?" Claire said.

"All are well. Where is your aunt?"

"In the carriage with Eilidh, the new maid Theseus hired. And Milo, of course."

"And whom, might I ask, is Milo? Your aunt's swain?"

Claire's laughter pealed. "Our ship's captain was most enamored of Auntie, but Milo is a four-footed swain of diminutive proportions who won Auntie's heart in Itea. He is now her boon companion."

Though the rest had dismounted, she walked to Patrick, still seated on Diablo. Paralyzed from the thighs down by an accident at sea, her brother-in-law had relearned how to ride using special gear and determination. Undoing his rig took time, so he remained in the saddle.

"How are you?" she said.

Patrick peered down at her. "Much better now that you all are returned."

"Rose said Lottie is unwell."

He shook his head. "Nothing to trouble you, Claire. A passing megrim, is all."

Claire thought Rose had said a stomachache. She would know soon. Aunt Agnes emerged, and hugs were exchanged along with backslaps for Theseus from Rhys, with Thomasina giving Theo an exuberant hug.

Soon, they rode on to Woodbine, Rose joining them in the carriage. Claire couldn't wait for their arrival, particularly to see Lottie, for worry gnawed at her. Her sister was game for anything, always hale and hearty, even after her kidnapping. What could be wrong?

No, Charlotte was fine. Of course she was, and Claire couldn't wait to see her.

CHAPTER
# TWENTY-FIVE

That last day in August, Woodbine sparkled as they rounded the bend. The Tudor manor felt warm and welcoming, complete with pups bouncing at their feet. Cullen and Milo joined the melee, chaos ensuing as people greeted them, including Lottie and even Devonshire.

It was so good to hold her sister once again, and Claire squeezed her tight...except her sister felt...odd. She clasped Lottie's shoulders, her sister wearing a blush and a secret smile.

"You are different," Claire said. "Well, you feel different."

"Do I? Given your three-month sojourn, things have... progressed."

"Progressed?"

Lottie trilled a laugh. "Perhaps because you are hugging two people, rather than one?"

*Two people...?* "No!" Claire said.

Lottie's hand flew to her belly, her face wreathed in a smile, her blue eyes sapphires of joy. "Yes! In about six months, we shall greet Baby Lansdowne! For now, I call him or her Bubby."

"Oh, Lottie." More hugs with tears thrown in. Claire swiped at her damp cheeks and leaned back. "I shall be an auntie!"

"You shall," Lottie said.

"Things have progressed with me as well."

But before she could explain, Theseus approached and slid an arm around her waist.

Everyone stilled, the silence profound.

Claire dipped her chin.

"What is *this*?" Devonshire said, waving a hand at the pair of them.

Leave it to the duke to say what everyone was thinking.

"Claire and I are to marry," Theseus said.

More silence.

Rose cleared her throat. "That is wonderful, exciting news!" She ran to Claire and kissed both her cheeks.

Everyone chimed in, but it was obvious all were stunned. All except for Auntie, who looked smug in the extreme.

Hearing Theo's words aloud had shocked Claire, too. The idea felt surreal, especially now they were back in England.

The butler opened the doors, and they entered the family salon en masse. Patrick, now seated in that amazing chair he had constructed, wheeled beside Lottie, her hand resting on his shoulder. How lovely. She and Theseus seldom held hands, though she recalled their walk the night he asked to wed her. That night, her assent had felt right. Now, doubts assailed her.

Soon, tea and a stand of sweet and savory treats were set before them. Baby Gareth appeared, held by his nursemaid. He'd grown so big! Rose took the smiling child, kissed his cheeks, and set him on the floor. He giggled and began crawling toward Cullen, who met him halfway. The babe reached up to touch Cullen's nose, and the dog slurped his tongue up Gareth's hand. The baby toppled, and they all laughed, including Gareth. Rhys scooped up his son, and the boy laughed harder.

Claire made a plate for her aunt, popping a seedcake into her mouth as she surveyed her family, pausing to stare at the handsome man to whom she had said yes.

Was she really going to marry Theseus and move through life as a couple?

Rather, could she imagine Theo *not* by her side? Impossible.

The next morning, Claire lifted her arms and stretched, luxuriating in the comfortable bed. She'd had a good sleep, her best in memory, eager to take on the world. Time to compile her notes from Greece. She scrunched the pillows and sat up, then reached for the glass of water on the bedside table. A letter with her name lay beside the lamp.

Claire took the missive and broke the seal.

*Pardon my absence. I am off to sell* Nemesis *and acquire our special license. Back in six days.*

*Your intended,*

*Theseus*

Claire read and reread the note.

Six days. And then...marriage.

Claire whooshed out a long breath, laid the letter aside, and went to retrieve her journal.

As the day waned, Theseus clopped through the streets of Portsmouth, having traveled to London to acquire the special license, now secure in his breast pocket. He'd been gone from Claire for seven days and was eager to return. He'd often switched horses, yet he hadn't ridden this hard in months. He ached, his bones weary.

He'd stopped in Portsmouth to learn of inquiries about purchasing the frigate. Nothing, and it would take time. He could afford that.

Eager to reach Claire, he spurred on his mount, planning to change horses in Ivybridge for the final leg to Rhys' estate.

The night sounds increased as he left town—the cry of a hawk, the rustle of a fox, the skitter of a squirrel—a symphony he found soothing.

As he neared Ivybridge at a canter, his horse began to flag, for he had pushed the gelding hard. He brought him down to a trot.

Up ahead, a rider melted out of the trees, pistol pointed at him. "Stand and deliver." He rode closer.

Theseus was well armed—a pistol at his waist, one in his boot, with several knives about his person. He slowed the gelding to a walk.

A click from behind, then a bang, something slamming into his shoulder, propelling him forward. *Bloody hell!* He'd been shot. Bugger it, that hurt.

Theseus' thoughts sharpened. He had done this dance on the Peninsula and deliberately slumped in the saddle. With subtle leg movements, he steered his horse toward the side of the road. He toppled by the tree line, landing in a bed of leaves, deliberately crooking his left leg. *Bollocks!* A rock poked his back. He had bigger problems.

Theseus flopped to his belly and froze, listening for the clip-clop of the riders' approach.

This was no robbery but an assault.

With care, he slid his right arm toward the pistol at his waist, snugging his hand around its grip and drawing it from the holster. Slow and easy, his left hand reached into his boot to withdraw his smaller pistol. He cocked both pistols and waited.

To his right, the thump of a rider dismounting.

"He dead?" the rider on his left said.

"Cain't tell."

A man moved closer, but not close enough. Not yet.

"I dunna see him breathing," came a third voice. Bollocks, three of them! Theseus reorganized his plan.

"I'm gonna tell the man," said that third rider again.

"Stay. Until we know he's dead. Move close and kick him."

"You ain't my boss."

The sounds of a horse trotting off.

"Bloody prick, leavin' like that," said the man on the horse.

"Thinks he's better 'en us." The one on the ground stepped near.

The warm blood soaking Theseus' shirt had reached his waist, the pain in his shoulder a vicious throb. He had to end this soon, or they would succeed in their mission.

The horse on the left stepped near to see a hoof, as did the man on his right. Now.

Theseus flipped to his back and fired both pistols, dropping them and drawing his knife.

As the mounted attacker fell from his horse, he got off a shot. Missed. The second villain lay on the ground, eyes open, face bloody.

Theseus stumbled to his feet, knife in hand, and staggered to the second bandit, who lay supine, bloody breath bubbling from his lips.

"Who sent you?" He thrust the point of the knife beneath the man's chin.

The bandit grinned. "Wouldn't ya like ta know." Then he wheezed out a long breath. Gone.

Theseus' horse had trotted off, and he swiped the reins of the bandit's horse, now idly nibbling grass. He fell to his knees, pressing a hand to the horse's flank, panting. He closed his eyes to rest against the horse, just for a moment or two. Or three. He forced himself to push to a stand. More panting.

Mounting the beast seemed impossible, yet if he did not, he would die out here from blood loss. His shoulder and side screamed, and he was weakening by the second. Fisting the reins, he placed a hand on the cantle and lifted his left leg. It took three tries until he managed to secure his foot in the stirrup. One... two... With a mighty heave, he mounted the horse, swinging his right leg across its back to slide his foot into the stirrup.

Theseus leaned over the horse's withers and rested. Sweat coated his face, the night throbbing, the stars winking in and out like a fantastical dream. He squeezed the horse's flanks, urging it forward, though he couldn't seem to push himself to an upright position. A kick, and the horse broke into a trot, then a canter.

The night sounds dimmed, the breeze chilling, until all Theseus could hear was the thrum of the horse's hooves.

And then he heard nothing.

After a restless night of waking and dozing, dawn finally broke, its gray light filtering into Claire's bedroom. Her mind cleared to crystal. Today was the eighth day. Theseus had assured her he would be back in six from London. She hadn't worried on the seventh day, not much, but today her concern spiked.

The room was warm, a maid having lit her fire, and she shucked her bedclothes and donned a serviceable morning gown that buttoned in front. She dashed from her room and opened the door across the hall, his room. It was pristine, the bed untouched.

A sleepy-eyed footman approached. "May I be of service, my lady?"

"Has Lord Ashworth returned?"

"I am afraid I do not know."

"Is anyone else awake?"

"Lord Ravenscroft is in the breakfast room, I believe."

"Thank you." She raced to find Rhys in the breakfast room.

"Has Theseus returned?" Claire entered knowing she must look dreadful.

Rhys shook his head, spreading jam on his toast. "I checked when I arose."

She slumped into a chair. "Something has happened to Theseus. Something terrible."

Rhys leaned forward and took one of her hands. "I have sent several search parties out."

Claire closed her eyes in an effort to dam her tears.

Theseus swam to consciousness through a fog of pain, the sounds of chickens clucking and a cow's moo reaching his ears. He blinked, opening his eyes to a pair of rheumy ones staring back. His fingers worked, and his toes. If he had to defend himself, at least his body was mobile. The eyes disappeared.

"Yer awake," an old man's voice said.

He scanned the room. He lay on a pallet in a one-room cabin that held a stove, a chair, clothes hanging from pegs, and a Baker rifle standing against a corner wall. An older man, thin, of middling height, leaned against a counter wearing a farmer's smock, braces holding up gray army trousers, dilapidated field boots on his feet. Long gray curls framed his face, along with a pepper-and-salt beard and bushy brows.

"Last night," the old man said. "On me way back from the pub, I found you bloody and unconscious on yer horse."

*Not my horse.*

"You look to be shot, young fella."

Theseus' mouth felt drier than the Gobi. "Water?"

The old man dipped a mug into a bucket, then limped over.

Theseus drank, sipping slowly. His hands trembled, *goddammit.* He was weak as a kitten. His hand roved to where he'd been shot, a large bandage now covering his shoulder. "Thank you. I doubt I would have survived without your help."

"Oh, you'd a been dead all right. You were bleedin' all over everything."

*Claire.* She must be worried. The rest of them would be in a dither as well. He sucked in a large breath and swung his legs to the floor. *Bollocks*, that hurt.

He sat up. "My name is Theseus. Yours?"

"Andrew, but they call me Old Andy since I've been around these parts since William the Conqueror."

A smile twitched Theseus' lips. "And where exactly am I, Andy?"

"Totnes."

He had no idea of the location. "How far to Torquay?"

"Under ten miles. So you're headed to Torquay, are ya?"

In his state, it would take three to four hours to reach Woodbine on horseback. He peered out the small window above the bed. The sun rode high in the sky, already noon or thereabouts. He'd best get on the road. He heaved to his feet, a burst of pain making him clutch the windowsill. *Damn*, he must leave, though he was unsure if he could manage.

"Is my horse still saddled?" he said.

Andy shook his head, his curls bobbing back and forth. "I took care a him, fed him, and all."

*Did he have the strength to saddle his horse?*

He could stay and recover, but if his wound grew infected, he would die. *Bugger this.*

"I got some soup," Andy said. "You want some?"

"Yes, thank you." Theseus thumped back on the bed, resting his pounding head in his hands.

While Andy warmed the soup, Theseus' thoughts turned to last night's attack. Those men were no thieves, that was clear, with him as the intended target. They would have killed him had he not ended them first. But the who and the why remained a mystery. No clue or hint indicated those behind the attack.

They ate in silence, and when finished, Andy took the two bowls and placed them on the counter. "You know they found two dead fellas up the way a bit. You have anything to do with that?"

"Does anyone know them?"

Andy shrugged. "Haven't heard."

"I am going to saddle my horse." Theseus stood again, pressing his hand to the wall so he wouldn't collapse.

"This should be entertaining," Andy said with a grin.

That was one way to put it.

"You might wanna wear your boots iffen you're gonna ride."

His Hessians stood by the door, his coat on a peg. His guns...

First, the boots.

Once donned, along with his jacket, he checked the special license. Still there. He patted his small pouch of coins, though his saddlebags were long gone. He hoped someone had found his damned rented horse. "My pouch?" He'd worn it slung across his shoulder, and it contained ammunition, two knives, and other sundries.

Andy pointed to it resting on the counter.

Bracing himself on the wall, he turned to the old man. "My guns?"

The old man opened the closet door and reached inside, producing a bundle wrapped in tattered cloth. His chin jutted out. "I ain't no thief. Two guns, three knives."

Theseus retrieved his pouch, then distributed the weapons around his person, the effort making him sweat. A chill wound up his spine, making him shiver. The ride would be hellish. "I never thought you were a thief, Andy, but rather a Good Samaritan."

"You gotta help a body. Tis only right."

Theseus pointed to the Baker propped in the corner. "You served, did you not?"

Andy nodded. "In the Rifles, 95th Regiment of Foot, on the Peninsula. I was at the Battle of Copenhagen and Corunna, too."

A sharpshooter. "I was at Corunna as well, and Talavera, too."

Theseus stared at Andy, recalling the many soldiers Rhys had helped after the wars, the army doing little to aid their veterans. From the look of things, Andy was a prime candidate for assistance. "Why do you live here, alone in the forest?"

The man's face darkened. "After they mustered me out, what use was I? I'd been in uniform since I was fifteen. Don't know anything else. The years after Napoleon's defeat ate me up." He shrugged. "Life here ain't so bad."

Nor was it very good. "Ride with me?"

Andy jerked back in surprise.

Theseus held out a gold sovereign. "This is my thank you, whether you accompany me or not."

Andy looked offended. "I helped you 'cause I wanted to, not because I expected payment."

"I am aware of that. But you could have taken my money, my weapons and left me for dead."

"I could'a. You want me to ride with you so you make it home in one piece, huh?"

"That is the idea."

"So how am I supposed to get back home?"

"The horse will be yours, as well as his tack."

"I gotta think on it." The old man walked outdoors and soon began to speak. Unable to catch his words, Theseus peered out the window to see Andy talking to the cow.

The man looked up, sharp-eyed, patted the cow once, and strolled back inside the cabin, closing the door.

"We got us a problem." Andy limped to the front window and unlatched the sash, lifting it inward to latch it on a ceiling beam, then did the same for the window on the side.

"Outside, we got three, maybe four shooters. Best prepare."

Theseus loaded his two pistols, then lugged a stool over to the window, taking a seat and resting the pistols on the sill.

"You set?" Andy said.

"I am."

Andy rested the barrel of his Baker on the sill, aimed, and fired.

A cry from the woods.

Bullets flew toward the cabin, and they took cover. After a minute or so, quiet again descended.

Theseus crouched to where Andy stood against the wall. His head pounded, and he shivered. He rose, peeking out the window. "Bollocks!"

The poor cow and chickens were dead, though the shed with the horse seemed undisturbed.

*Those knaves.* "Do you see?"

Andy's face was stern, his eyes afire. "They killed me Ella and me chicks."

"I am sorry, Andy."

His eyes narrowed. "Not as sorry as they're gonna be."

Claire had disappeared to the stables, and now she curried the huge Friesian named Odysseus, Odi for short, an old fellow long retired. The brushstrokes soothed, and Claire found a rhythm, repeating them over and over and over. Odi nickered. Claire scratched his ears and moved to his other side. When done to her satisfaction, she hauled a small crate to the Friesian and stood atop it to curry his back.

Her heart pounded, her chest bound in an iron fist. *Where was he? Where was Theo?* Claire's breath sped until she could not catch it. She growled, throwing the brush against the wall.

Odysseus continued to chew his hay. She laid her head down on his immense back and squeezed her fists. The scents of barn, horse, and hay usually comforted her. *Where was he?*

"Claire?"

She sighed, raising her head. "In here!"

Charlotte opened the stall door. "Was that your growl?"

"Unfortunately, yes. I am amazed the stable boys did not come running."

"Oh, they did!" Lottie tightened the shawl around her shoulders. "I waved them back."

"I see."

"Are you going to descend from your perch and talk to me?"

"I have to finish currying Odi," Claire said as she petted his back.

"With your hand?" Lottie said. "You have gotten this old boy shinier than a mirror. Come down."

Claire stepped off the crate, smoothing her hand across Odysseus' side, telling him he was a good boy. She retrieved the curry brush, setting it in its bucket, then removed her gloves. Finally, she withdrew the apple in her pocket and gave it to him.

"What do you wish to talk about, Lottie?"

"Oh, nothing but the elephant in the room."

"That phrase always amuses me," Claire said.

"It comes from a Russian fable, 'The Inquisitive Man.' I find it terribly clever."

"Indeed."

Lottie snugged an arm around her waist. "They will find your Theseus."

"Will they?" She had felt fear like this before, when Lottie had been kidnapped. It was hard to speak, hard to think.

"Come." Lottie clasped her hand and walked her from the stall. "Let us go have some tea. Possibly with brandy."

Perhaps that would help.

# TWENTY-SIX

A burning torch flew toward the cabin, falling short.

Andy gave him a feral smile. "Thinking ta burn us out."

"So it seems." In a crouch, Theseus made it back to the side window and again sat, resting both pistols on the sill. Another torch flew, this one near the back of the cabin. It landed close.

Andy growled. "I'll go out there and—"

"Too risky," Theseus said.

Andy's eyes widened. "The way you walk, them clothes, yer voice —you were an officer."

"I was."

Another torch flew to blaze beside the cabin, close enough to set it alight.

"Well, Captain, what do you suggest?" Andy said.

He'd been a major but didn't correct the man as he scanned the woods for movement. Their enemies' plan was to set the cabin alight to get them outside. Not a bad plan. *There.* Movement. He fired both guns. A scream.

"That makes two," Theseus said. Wounded or dead, they had

reduced the odds. "Is there any exit other than the front door?" He would bet a hundred pounds the old soldier had crafted an escape route.

The man gave him teeth. "A course."

"I suggest we depart, circle around, and pick them off."

Andy's eyes narrowed. "They'll know we left the cabin since we won't be returning fire. We got ta be fast."

Theseus grinned. "I can do fast."

Andy pushed a tall chest aside. "I'll go first and circle left." He opened a door no taller than five feet, bent at the waist, and scooted outside. Theseus followed, closing the door behind him, and stepped into the woods. He paused, listening, and moved to the right as silently as he'd once done on the Peninsula. The war crashed back—the scents of smoke, the sounds of pain, the smells of death. Long ago. Or was it yesterday?

He shook himself, recalling Claire and her beautiful spirit and how very much he wished to return to her. He proceeded at a cautious pace.

A movement at about fifteen yards. Theseus hunkered down, listening, watching. Once he fired, the enemy would know his position. His shot must count.

A boom in the distance. A flutter of leaves up ahead. Theseus aimed and fired. A cry, the shot finding its target, from his gun or Andy's, he was unsure.

More shots, his adrenaline spiking. Hoofbeats sounded.

A ruse, or was it over?

Bent near in half, he walked to the foot poking up in the grass. The body lay prone beneath an ancient apple tree. Dead. Theseus rifled his pockets, finding a leather drawstring pouch, empty but for a few shillings.

He squeezed his eyes tight, groggy, the adrenaline receding. Wary, he slipped back to the cabin, a spike of pain as dizziness assailed him. He braced himself against the wall. Passing out was unacceptable.

"All clear," Andy called.

"All clear," he said, though it sounded more a croak, his entire focus on remaining upright.

Andy reappeared wearing a grin. "Got 'em." He gave Theseus the once-over, then tucked his shoulder beneath his arm. "You best go lie down inside."

He *must* get back to Claire, and he shook his head. "Home."

Andy rolled his eyes. "Poor idea."

"I must...get...home."

"Come on, then. I'll get you there."

A bloody man tottered out of the woods, raised his pistol, and fired. Andy pushed him aside, but Theseus pulled the trigger, shooting the villain between his eyes. Theseus swayed.

Andy wrapped an arm around Theseus, taking most of his weight. "Nice shooting. Now we get you home."


Claire sat at her secretary, surrounded by papers, books, and multiple quills, compiling the notes from her journal. Except the words swam before her, her concentration nil. She picked up the painted shard from Theseus by its pointed ends, careful to not disturb the paint. Her heart seized.

Other men might give her flowers or jewels or candy. Not Theo. But this gift represented all that he meant to her, a talisman.

Somewhere along the way, she had fallen in love with him. Desperately, madly, completely.

Perhaps it had begun when he tried to trick her with that fake Renaissance bust. Or when he handed her that gun during the bandit attack, showing he believed she wouldn't panic. Or perhaps any of the hundreds of moments they'd spent together these past months.

Analytical by nature, Claire wished to dissect her feelings, much as she would an ancient marble. Impossible. Her emotions defied scrutiny yet consumed her with both euphoria and fear.

She gritted her teeth. Theseus was *not* dead, he was *not* lost. He was on his way back to her, *dammit*. He must be.

The clock read ten at night, and Claire rubbed her eyes, her heart heavy. She swung the window wide, the early autumn breeze bracing and crisp. Nine days. Too long. Much too long. She lowered her hand to Cullen. "Where is he?"

She rang for Eilidh to help her undress, and soon she was tucked in bed, eager for rest. She doused the bedside lamp and tried to find relief from her busy mind and tumultuous emotions.

Hours later, sleepless still, a cacophony of voices and barked commands drew her attention. Claire flung off the covers, shrugged on her dressing gown, and ran from the room.

In the entryway, she saw Theseus held upright by an older man and a footman. He was bruised and bloody, so bloody. A tremor slid down her spine, her vision blackening. She rushed to him.

He was warm and smelled awful, but he was alive. Claire's hand fluttered, for she wasn't sure where to touch, though she wanted to wrap him in her arms. She cupped his cheek.

"Sorry to be late, love," he said with slurred words. His eyes rolled up, and he slumped, unconscious.

"Christ!" Rhys said. "Send for Crawford."

"The old physician died, I am afraid," Rose said, turning to address a hovering footman. "Fetch Hannah Broker."

"We must carry him to his room," Claire said, her eyes burning.

Two footmen took his torso as Rhys lifted his legs. "The salon is closer."

"No," Claire said. "When he regains consciousness, he shall wish to be private."

Rhys raised a brow, but nonetheless the men carried him down the long hall and into his room, Rose running ahead of them and drawing the covers back. They lay Theseus on the bed with care, yet he groaned.

"I shall see if Mrs. Broker has arrived," Rhys said and disappeared.

Rose vanished as well, and Claire and the man began to divest Theseus of his clothes and boots.

"Who are you, sir?" Claire said.

The old man's filmy eyes took her in. "Me name's Andy." He nodded to Theseus. "Found him by the road."

By the time Theseus was down to his buckskin breeches, Rose had returned wearing an apron and carrying a bowl of hot water, dressing, honey, and a vial labeled turpentine. She set them on the bedside table, then poured water into Theseus' washbowl and cleaned her hands, looking at Claire. "Mrs. Broker insists."

A makeshift bandage marred his chest, bronzed from the Greek sun. Her love, brought low by curs. Claire would cheerfully kill them all.

Andy said the bullet had passed through his shoulder, thank the heavens, so they wouldn't have to dig it out. Claire observed, unable to turn away, as Rose removed the old bandage and proceeded to clean the wound. She applied the turpentine, much to Theseus' displeased groans, and then the honey, finally wrapping it all in a fresh, thick bandage.

On shaky legs, Claire helped Rose remove the refuse and straighten the room, giving Theo's scattered clothing to a maid to burn. "Please bring a fresh pitcher of warmed water."

A middle-aged woman stormed into the room, cloak billowing, a leather bag in hand. She set the bag on a table, opening it to reveal numerous medicinals, tubes, and other mysterious items.

Rose leaned close to Claire. "Mrs. Broker was the surgeon's assistant. She is better than him by half."

"Dressing looks good, Lady Ravenscroft," Mrs. Broker said.

"It should," Rose said. "You taught me how to do it."

Mrs. Broker smirked. "A 'course I did. We must watch for infection—the real enemy."

A maid entered with a fresh bowl of steaming water and soap, and Mrs. Broker washed her hands.

"Rose did that, too," Claire said. "She said you insisted upon it."

The healer, sorting her vials, raised her head. "Call me Hannah. I dunna know why, but I learnt from my mam that ifin we wash our hands, the patient has a better outcome. *Her* mam taught her that." She shrugged. "So I do it, too. Seems to work a trick."

Hannah took Theseus' pulse, then bent to press a wooden "hearing tube" above his heart. She straightened, smiling. "A good, strong beat."

Claire exhaled.

"You got plenty of that willow bark tea, Lady Ravenscroft?" Hannah said. "Feverfew?"

"Willow bark, yes," Rose said. "But I could use more feverfew."

Hannah handed Rose a vial of powder from her kit. "Do not be stingy with it. Feverfew will ease his pain, and, more importantly, it brings down a fever."

They thanked Mrs. Broker, and she repacked her case, then stepped back to stare at her patient. "He is a fine figure of a man."

That he was, Claire thought. The finest.

"We shall see how he does." Hannah left in a swirl of her cloak.

Which left Andy hovering over Theseus like a mother hen.

"Time for Lord Ashworth to rest," Rose said, bustling him out.

"Wait just a moment, Rose," Claire said. "I shall stay, but I want to fetch some books in case Theseus awakens and I can read to him."

She flew to the library, returning swiftly with four books.

Rose helped Claire pull a wing chair beside the bed, kissed her cheek, and hooked an arm through Andy's. Once they'd gone, she lifted a book, the recently published *Ivanhoe*, and began to read.

He lay so still, this man who always bristled with energy. Only his eyes moved, darting beneath closed lids. She hoped he wasn't having a nightmare.

Restless after but an hour of reading, Claire slipped a bookmark onto her page and began to straighten the sheet atop Theseus.

"Do not fuss," came the grumbly voice.

She gasped, then fireworks of joy blasted through her. "I would not think of fussing." She filled a glass of water, eased onto the edge of the bed, and lifted Theo's head to help him drink. "This is not fussing."

He winked. And she was so relieved to see his humor emerge, tears welled. She'd been so worried, so frightened, and it all avalanched onto her. With care, she laid the glass aside and sat back in the wing chair. If she touched him, took his hand as she wanted, her floodgates would open. Tears would upset Theseus, so she sat with hands clenched, trying to remain serene. "Is there anything you need, anything you would like me to fetch?"

He shook his head, then his brow scrunched. "I have an anvil pounding my head. Do you have any of that cure-all you gave me in Greece?"

Claire bounced up, thrilled with a task, and offered a smile. "I shall be right back!"

As she fled to retrieve the *Chuan Xiong*, the floodgates opened.


Though the man named Andy Trelows looked half-starved, Rose admired the way he chewed deliberately and how he savored his tea. Rhys was pacing in circles, his usual mode when in thought, having sent messages to Devonshire and Patrick about Theseus' arrival.

"Might I pour you more tea, Mr. Trelows?" Rose said.

"Call me Andy," he said. "Mr. Trelows was my papa. Yes, ma'am, I'd like more tea. Best I've had in a long while."

Rose refilled his cup. The man must be fifty at least.

Rhys took a seat opposite Andy and peppered him with questions.

"It appears we have a mystery," Rhys said. "For Andy here has no idea what prompted the attack, other than Lord Ashworth being the target. We must wait for Ashworth's awakening to learn more."

"He don't know nothin', either," Andy said. "We talked about the trouble where I found him beside the road. He said it were a mystery to him, too."

"From your description," Rose said, "the two attacks were not random."

Andy nodded. "Even that first time after he were shot, he felled his two attackers. Impressed me. Ya gotta have a strong will to stay calm after taking a bullet, then turn the tables on the blokes who tried to kill ya."

"That second attack," Rose said. "Four men assaulted you at your home, yes?"

"Yup," Andy said. "We got 'em, though. Shot up my cabin pretty good, killed my poor cow and my chickens for no damned reason."

"I am so sorry, Andy. You look worn out." Rose rang for the butler, directing him to escort Andy to the prepared guest room. Once they'd departed, she turned to Rhys, who wore his stoic mask. Oh, dear—his memories of the wars had flared.

Rose's hand slid atop his. "Your thoughts, darling?"

He blinked rapidly and whooshed out a breath. "Theseus is an academician and an antiquarian. I cannot help but believe these attacks are related to his recent travels in Greece."

Rose slid onto Rhys' lap, resting her head on his shoulder. He wrapped his arms around her. "I am afraid I agree, and yet I do not see how they could relate."

"Nor can I," he said. "Worry not, for we will find out."

Days later, Theseus was on the mend. He had risen from bed, his arm in a sling, but tired easily, becoming cranky and restless.

Claire staggered to Theo's suite carrying another armful of books, nearly toppling them when she spotted Cullen and Milo in bed beside Theo. Both man and beasts watched her with intent.

"Auntie!" Claire said.

Her aunt stilled, setting down her ubiquitous needlework, then waved a hand. "Milo insisted we check on the patient, and he could not have Cullen cuddling without receiving some cuddles himself."

"Of course." Claire laid the books on the floor and gave each pup a scritch under their chin.

Auntie stood, holding out her arms, and Milo bounded off the bed into them. "He is such a clever boy, isn't he? I shall see you at dinner, Claire." She bussed Theo's cheek, lifted her needlework bag, and swanned from the room.

"Your aunt is a delight," Theseus said. "Not to mention her dog."

"Agreed." Claire grinned. "I thought to read something new. You get to pick. When did Cullen arrive?"

"He has become one of my nursemaids," Theseus said with a glance at the pup. "He appears daily and oft leaps atop the bed and sticks his nose in my face, I assume to assure himself I am breathing."

"You do not mind?" Claire flopped into the bedside chair.

Theseus stroked Cullen, who sighed in contentment. "Not in the least."

"Here are your choices." Claire read the title she was sure he would choose, a treatise on the different column styles in ancient Greece. "It is newly published."

"The second?" Theseus said, his restless legs shifting beneath the covers.

"*The Well-Managed Estate.* Everyone seems to be agog over it. I thought you might find it informative. The third is a compilation of Byron's works, including 'The Dream' and 'Manfred.'"

"Um hum."

"Finally, I brought a novel, *Sense and Sensibility.* Though it says 'By A Lady,' we now know the author to be Jane Austen, revealed after her sad passing." Claire assumed he would not give three pence for it, but she adored the work and could not resist.

THESEUS STARED into those amber eyes. They were so hopeful, so intent on helping him. But he didn't miss the fear lurking as well. Fear for him.

With the exception of Penelope, he couldn't think of another who worried about his safety, not the way his Claire did. She was like a golden cup of honey, all bright and warm.

He moved, grimacing from the shot of pain. Claire, thankfully, did not fuss. Though she presented a calm and amenable face, she'd clasped both hands in a white-knuckled fist.

The pain receded, and Theseus reached for a glass of water.

"I have dosed it with feverfew," Claire said.

He nodded as he drank, feeling as if his every bone ached. After he laid down the glass, he placed his right hand on her fisted ones. "Love, this will pass, and I shall be well. Where is Andy?"

Claire rolled her eyes. "He and Susannah have become fast friends, bonding over guns of all things. I believe they have gone to the north field to practice."

He grinned. "Andy was in the Rifles during the war."

"So I have learned."

"Would you find Ravenscroft?" he said. "I need to discuss some business with him. Afterward, I would very much like you to read to me."

The tension pouring off Claire eased. "I shall hunt him up." Rising, she tossed him a saucy smile. "Have you chosen the book?"

"I have."

Cullen leapt off the bed to stand by her side. "And...?"

Theseus smiled. "Why, *Sense and Sensibility*, of course. I do love a good romance."

CHAPTER

# TWENTY-SEVEN

The next morning, Claire peeked out her door, curious as to the strange sounds coming from the hall. Two footmen were hauling a table toward the front entry. She spotted two more footmen lugging an immense vase from one of the rooms. She slipped on her dressing gown, let Cullen outside to do his business, and went in search of Rose, finding her in the breakfast room.

"Is all well?" Claire said as she breezed in, the scents of pastries and hot chocolate making her mouth water. "The hall was abustle with footmen carrying all sorts of things."

"Oh," Rose said. "I am so sorry to have disturbed you. This is for the preparations."

Rose spoke as if Claire knew to what she referred. "What are you preparing for?"

Rose's gaze was surprised. "Your wedding."

Claire's legs wobbled, and she sank into a chair. "My wedding?"

"Why yes," Rose said. "Theseus spoke to Rhys yesterday about all that was necessary. You are to be wed two days hence."

Shock sizzled from Claire's head to her toes. "Theo has said nothing."

"That seems to be habitual with our family," Rose said. "Our men are high-handed, with surprises, special licenses, and swift weddings."

"Charlotte's was all that, certainly," Claire said. "Come to think, yours was too."

"Indeed, it was. Rhys arranged it all."

"Well, it is good to know that I am following in step, though I do not know why Theseus said nothing." Highhanded was an understatement, yet her spurt of anger failed to manifest. Claire was so glad the obstreperous man was alive.

Rose paused in buttering her toast. "I should be surprised, but I am not. Men fail to realize we ladies like to prepare for these events, perhaps the most consequential in our lives."

Claire nibbled a honey cake, then poured herself a cup of hot chocolate. She remained incredulous that Theseus had arranged this without consulting her. And yet, she could, for Rose was right. Men did not think.

She had nothing to wear, nothing special at least, all her finery at Halafair. Claire wanted to be beautiful for Theo on their wedding day.

As he became more restless, he'd been ordered to stay put for several days. Would their wedding be at his bedside? Not that she would object, but...

"Two days," Claire said. "Was a time mentioned?"

"I believe ten in the morning, with the wedding breakfast to follow. Your mama shall arrive today, as will the Hawthorne contingent. I do not doubt Henry's pup, Stella, will accompany them as well."

Picturing the boy and Stella, Claire couldn't help but grin. "Henry and that dog of his. They are inseparable. I am sure Bram and Isla will join in, too, not to mention Cullen and Milo. Let us all hope Percy does not."

Of all things, she did not want the parrot at her wedding. A vain hope, she suspected. She smoothed her linen across her lap. Was she truly prepared to wed Theseus? Forever. Marriage was forever. Was love? Her feelings for Theseus overwhelmed her at times. Did Theo feel the same?

"I fear asking, but," Rose said. "Do you have a suitable dress?"

"I have not," Claire said, with a sniff. Given that she traveled to Woodbine from the frigate, all she had were the clothes she'd brought to Greece, none of which were appropriate wedding attire.

"Worry not," Rose said. "I will happily loan you one of mine if necessary, but I suspect your mama will bring something suitable."

Claire's laugh was semi-hysterical. "If not, I can always wear one of my field dresses and a research apron. Elegant, no?"

Rose reached out and clasped Claire's hand. "We will have beautiful flowers from the hothouse, and I shall make you a bouquet and a wreath for your hair. You are so lovely, Claire. No one will notice what you are wearing."

"Thank you, dear Rose." Claire shook her head. "I should not be surprised about all this. Theseus had hoped to marry soon after we arrived home from Greece, and when the man gets a bee in his bonnet, he gallops full-bore. I do not know, but... I fear he sees our wedding as a business transaction."

"Absurd!" Rose shook her head. "Have you not noticed the way he observes you? How he beams you warm smiles, ones I have never seen him wear before this?"

"Um, perhaps?"

Rose tossed her a mischievous smile. "He burns for you, sister. I suspect business is the farthest thing from his mind."

Her chest warmed. Were his emotions as engaged as hers?

Rhys and Theseus breezed through the door, accompanied by Cullen. Theo's left arm bore a sling, his hair windblown, his cheeks flushed. They halted when they spotted the women and offered them bows. Rhys turned to Rose, kissing her on the lips. Theseus bent to do the same, but Claire turned her face, instead bussing her cheek. He straightened, his eyes uneasy.

"What is wrong?" he said in that husky voice that always sent pleasurable trills through her.

She held up a hand. "You were not to do anything strenuous for three more days, yet you have ridden out with Rhys." She huffed. "Not to mention how you failed to *mention* our impending nuptials. What, exactly, am I to wear?"

Theseus clasped her hand and leaned close. "I have a gown for you."

"Pardon?"

"A surprise," he said. "One I have given to the maids to press."

"But..."

"I know. I know, *to asteri mu*. I have taken this out of your hands, too. But whilst in Greece, I acquired a special garment I believe you will find much to your liking. It is a pale green, which shall look fetching on you."

"You bought me a *gown*?" The warmth in his eyes nearly upended her. Oh, she did love this man. So much.

He slipped into the chair beside hers. "I do not care for ceremony. You know this. Once you said yes, I pictured you in a particular ensemble." He shrugged. "If it is not to your taste, you can always wear your research clothes."

She caught Rose's eyes, and their laughter pealed, confounding both Rhys and Theo.

Just the way Claire liked it.

Returning to her room, Claire found Eilidh and Agnes standing beside her bed, two large swaths of green fabric lying across it, one piece spring green, the second made of a heavier fabric in a darker hunter. She touched the lighter one. Silk, its hem embroidered with gold birds and acanthus leaves. The darker cloth was a very light wool. Resting beside them was a belt woven of gold thread.

Eilidh wore a broad smile, eyes alight, while Agnes looked smug.

"His lordship brought these on the ship from Greece," Agnes said. "Telling me it was a surprise. Here you have the finest chiton, an exquisite belt, and a himation, all made by the women of Kastri. For you."

Made by the women... What an incredible gift. "The work and fabrics are exquisite."

"Do you wish to try them on?" Agnes said, setting Milo on the bed.

Claire stood before the long mirror holding the gown's shoulders, turning this way and that, the fabric's movement like a cloud drifting across the sky. The gold belt rested above her waist, the silk cascading to the floor.

Eilidh lifted a pair of gold brooches from her apron pocket, each shaped like an acanthus leaf and set with yellow stones. They pinned the chiton's shoulders, leaving her arms bare.

"The pins are also from Ashworth," Agnes said. "The gems are topaz."

Eilidh set the himation around her shoulders.

"You look splendid!" Eilidh said.

Agnes nodded. "Like you stepped from an ancient myth."

The ensemble made Claire feel magical, as did the man she was about to marry.

The next day, Claire retrieved her and Theseus' daily mail. They'd delayed their trip to Wolf Court, directing their correspondence to Woodbine instead. They would remain until they discovered why Theseus had been attacked and the perpetrators apprehended.

The thought made her anxious, for she was on constant high alert, fearing Theseus' enemies would target Woodbine and kill him. Absurd, of course. The horse breeding estate was served by well-armed, ex-military men, not to mention Rhys and Theseus themselves, both of whom had fought Napoleon. They were well protected. But anxiety nibbled at the joy of her imminent marriage, a constant gnaw, not to mention how jangled she was about their marriage itself.

Walking the wide carpeted hall to her suite, Claire passed the portraits of past Lansdownes—dour ones, cheery ones, pretty ones, and not-so-pretty ones—as she sifted through the mail. They peered down at her, those strong, dignified men and women. They might not be Ashworths, but nonetheless she whispered, "Protect him."

She paused at the thick packet from Penny for her, whilst Theo's from his sister was quite thin. Unusual. She left his letters on the secretary in his suite, then set hers atop her sitting room table, taking Penny's as she sat in the bergère chair.

Pages and pages of foolscap flew by as Claire skimmed the contents relating Penelope's travels in Greece. As she wrote, she boarded the ship for home. No. Claire had misread that. *They* boarded the ship.

Claire reread the last line, then the one that followed.

Penelope and Spyros were *married*, and the letter included a PS.

*If you would refrain from telling Theseus, I would appreciate it. I wish to do so myself.*

Claire was in a state. How could she not tell Theo about Penny's marriage? He was to be her husband, her partner.

A fluster rose, as in childhood, to near panic levels. Claire did not wish to keep the secret from him. Feeling light-headed, she placed a hand on Cullen, and he leaned against her knees. Claire took a deep breath, then another, until her heart calmed. Better. Manageable.

Theseus was on his morning ride, and she suspected later today he and Rhys would stop at the pub for a comfortable round...or ten. Tomorrow was their wedding, after all.

Claire found Rose in the stables, to be precise, stable three, the mares' barn. Rose sat on a hay bale, her pup Bram beside her as she petted a late-season newborn foal. She didn't know the mare's breed, her coat a golden blonde, as was the colt's. Though under-sized, he thrived.

Cullen braced his front paws on the stall door, peered over the top, and yipped.

Rose laughed. "Come in! See the foal! Bram will be pleased Cullen is here."

"Are you sure her ladyship will not object?" Claire said, gesturing to the mare.

"Star is a gentle girl who would never think of harming you or Cullen."

Claire unlatched the half door, closing it behind her, and took a seat on the hay bale beside Rose. For a few moments, they lavished pats and praise on the mare and colt, the foal snuffling at Cullen.

"Something troubles you, Claire. The wedding?"

"Well, no...yes." She sighed. "I am all at sixes and sevens about that. One day until... It still feels unreal. But no, I have sought you out for a different conundrum. As you have been a wife for quite some time, I thought, perhaps, you might advise me."

"Advise you...?"

Claire summarized Penny's letter, emphasizing her almost-sister's request to keep a secret.

"Ah!" Rose stood, brushing hay off her skirts. The foal left its mother's teat to stand before her on wobbly legs. She gave the mare a treat and the colt another scritch. "Come. A discussion like this needs tea."

Rose entered her study as if on a mission. The handsome hunter-green room was filled with books on horses and their breeding, along with numerous horse embellishments—paintings, a sculpture, and, in pride of place above the hearth, a gorgeous Stubbs depiction of a woman atop a white horse.

They sat before the embers of a fire, the day warm enough to not need a blaze. Moments passed as they waited for the refreshments, and by the time they finally arrived, Claire was jumping out of her skin. The tea poured, Claire explained Penny's letter in detail, though she didn't reveal Penny's secret, concluding only with the post-script's request not to tell Theseus.

Aunt Agnes waltzed into the study carrying Milo.

Claire went still.

"Aunt Agnes, do join us," Rose said.

Agnes waved a hand. "You need not silence yourselves. I heard my darling Claire's entire recitation." She took the chair beside the settee, settled Milo on her lap, and took Claire's hand. "You are in a pickle, m'dear!"

"That is an understatement, Auntie," Claire said. She glanced at Rose, then continued. "I wish to have a truthful and honest relationship with Theo. I hate secrets, at least ones of this sort. They always produce problems. If I do not tell Theseus and wait for Penny's arrival, and she tells him... What shall I do when he turns to me and says, 'Did you know of this?' What do I say, Auntie? Rose?"

Agnes sipped her tea, her eyes distant, then laid her cup on its saucer. She plucked a sweet from the tier and popped it into her mouth, while Rose munched a finger sandwich.

Claire thought she might explode.

"I would tell him," Rose said. "If it were Rhys."

"So Claire would betray a dear friend's request?" Agnes said.

"My husband and I keep nothing from one another," Rose said.

"Secrets are like boomerangs," Claire said. "You know, those Australian weapons that return to the sender. I fear my marriage will be damaged if I do not."

"I confess I fear the same." Rose reached down to pet Bram and Cullen, both asleep at their feet.

"This is solvable," Agnes said. "Before you tell him Lady Penelope's secret, ask him to not reveal it to anyone, including his sister."

Claire shook her head. "Auntie, I do not like making Theo promise. It is unfair until he knows what the promise is about."

"If his sister discovers you told," Rose said. "I suspect she will understand."

Milo stretched over Agnes' lap to see the other dogs, and she set him down, where he curled up beside them.

"I do not think Ashworth will understand if you keep the secret," Agnes said.

"Telling his sister's secret feels like a betrayal of her." Claire shook her head.

"That may be true, but you must choose," Rose said. "You said it was important, her secret."

"I would lay bets." Agnes swooped Milo onto her lap. "This is about Spyros."

Claire held her gasp, barely.

She smiled at her aunt, who stood. "I must run, as I am meeting Susannah at the archery range. Until later."

"Have you decided what to do?" Rose said after her aunt left.

"I must think on it more. I, um, I do have another question."

"You look so serious, Claire," Rose said, leaning forward.

"What does a woman do in the marriage bed?"

Rose's eyes became saucers. "You and Theseus have not..." She cleared her throat. "Experimented?"

"You mean kisses?"

Rose scrubbed her face. "I had this talk once before, with Lottie. I cannot say it went well."

"You mean the horse thing?"

"Well, yes, I did use horses as a sort of metaphor for people."

Claire grinned. "Oh, Lottie told me all about that. I prefer not to hear about horses, Rose, but people."

"I cannot explain it using humans." Rose flushed and raised her teacup for a sip. "Making love is such an intimate experience. Let me just say it is very pleasant. Blissful, even."

"That is encouraging." Claire nodded, somewhat assuaged. "When Lottie arrives, I shall ask her. You are acquitted."

Rose gave her a somewhat shaky laugh. "Thank you, sister. But tell me, do you enjoy Lord Ashworth's kisses?"

"Indeed, I do. Excessively."

Rose rested a hand on hers. "Then all will be well."

Claire sighed inwardly. Easy for Rose to say, she'd been married for ages.

# CHAPTER
# TWENTY-EIGHT

Somehow, the day advanced to night, and Claire hadn't managed to tell Theo of Penny's marriage.

The following day dawned—her wedding day.

Neither had voiced their feelings, and Claire admitted she was a coward. But what if she said she loved him, and Theo did not say the same? That would crush her. Best forget the words...and hope he felt as she did.

They held the ceremony in the larger formal salon, and Claire felt like a goddess in her silken Greek dress. She'd taken Rhys' arm as he walked her down the aisle, Cullen hugging her other side. All the family and pups were in attendance, all except for Penelope, whom she dearly missed.

Theseus stole her breath—tall, broad, and magnificent in his formal wear. He stood beneath an arch of sweetpeas, honeysuckle, and climbing roses, Devonshire beside him. As Claire walked the pale carpet toward Theseus, the distance looked infinite, yet soon she stood across from him. She handed her bouquet to Charlotte, beautiful in her striking blue gown, whilst Patrick's eyes glowed with love for his wife.

Of all things strange and yet somehow inevitable, Percy the parrot clung to Thomasina's shoulder, Sina beaming beside Rose. All the family smiled while tears ran down her mother's cheeks.

Henry looked like a miniature Patrick, her extended family resplendent, with exquisite flowers filling the room with heady, soothing scents.

Claire's eyes locked on Theo's, and the world vanished, his gaze ardent as they stood beneath the arch.

The ceremony began, and when Devonshire handed Theseus the ring, she held out a trembling hand, gasping as he slipped it on her finger. The warm antique gold held an almond-shaped carnelian intaglio bearing the helmeted head of Athena. Just as it appeared on an ancient *diobol,* or coin, from the Classical era. Theo's eyes smiled, though his face remained impassive. He knew this ancient ring would thrill her.

Their wedding breakfast was chaotic with laughter, raucous jokes, and the dogs milling about, all heightened by Percy's avian antics. Though their meal included both English and Greek dishes, Claire tasted little and ate less until Theo led her from the dining hall to their new suite.

She was a wife. That sounded very odd.

They talked of their next trip to Greece, their wedding trip, which they would defer until the stolen marbles and Theseus' attack were settled.

One entered their suite by the salon, flanked by a bedroom and dressing room at each end. Claire was eager to give Theo his wedding gift, one found in Delphi's soil. Most of her unearthed frag-ments remained in Kastri, but one excelled—a small bronze horse head, perhaps five inches high and exquisitely rendered. When she'd shown it to Xanthe, the Pythia insisted Claire gift it to Theo. For a trade, naturally. Now, the Pythia sported Claire's lapis hair comb with great pride.

She handed him the box bound with a silver ribbon.

"I found this whilst digging and traded with the Pythia for you." Claire smiled. "To celebrate our marriage."

He pulled the ribbon and lifted the lid, raising the bronze high. "Stunning." He turned the small piece this way and that. "The detail is astonishing, its expression fierce."

"Just like you!" Claire was thrilled at his pleasure.

He opened the secretary and lifted a square blue velvet box, moving behind her chair to fasten a necklace. She pressed her hands to it as she walked to the mirror.

The piece rested against her breastbone, a quarter moon of solid gold hung from a woven chain, the upper portion carved in the Greek key motif, the lower holding five amber cabochons. Claire couldn't stop touching it as tears raced down her cheeks.

"You are beautiful," he said. "Like an ancient Greek goddess."

"I am a watering pot." Claire sniffled. "This necklace... I have never seen its like."

"One of Dion's contemporary artisans made it for me. It is after a Hellenistic one, and I knew it would be perfection on you. It is. The stones match your eyes." He offered his pirate grin. "I want to see you wearing it naked, *wife*."

She flushed, knowing she was bright red, and swiped her tears away with a giggle. "You are too much, *husband*."

"I fervently hope not." Theo's arms wrapped around her, his chin resting atop her head. He kissed her.

Her husband. Her *husband*. When they surfaced for breath, an outrageous idea popped into her head.

Oh, she could not.

But what if she did?

Sparks flew through her, and she stepped back wearing a smile as she began to unpin the left shoulder brooch. Once done, she removed the right, and she let the bodice fall to her waist, baring her chemise.

Claire set both pins on the nearby table and began untying the belt.

Theo's eyes had grown wide, then wider still, while he stood and watched, seemingly frozen in place.

Her blush in full form, Claire chose not to care as she undid the knot and dropped the belt to the floor. The remainder of her dress went with it, and she stood in her short-stay corset, chemise, stockings, and shoes.

Theseus reached for her, but she shook her head. She untied her corset and flung it away. Her grin widened at Theo's expression, reminding her of Cullen just before dinner.

This husband of hers, so eager to touch her, to hold her. She could barely wait, too, but she was determined to realize his fantasy. She slipped one, then the other chemise strap from her shoulders. Claire held his eyes as she let the garment drop to the ground.

She stood naked but for her stockings, shoes, and the necklace. She also must look like a boiled lobster from embarrassment, but she straightened her spine, her smile falling away, expecting him to seize her.

He did not. Nor did he say a word, and Claire's anxiety grew. Perhaps he did not find her pleasing? Maybe her body was a disappointment, her stripping offensive to his sensibilities? Oh, what had she done?

He cleared his throat. "Claire... I am... You are Aphrodite come to life."

She bit her lip, not knowing what to say.

"Are you real?" he said. "Or a fever dream?"

"Theo, I am most uncomfortable with being naked and you wearing all your clothes."

He tugged at his cravat with abandon, the rest of his clothing vanishing within seconds. My gods! Her hands shook enough so she clasped them tight so they wouldn't tremble. True, she had seen him at the pond, but he was so close, so big, and that...that member of his jutted out like Priapus!

Her imagination raced down terrifying paths. Then his arms reached out, his hands smoothing across her shoulders. "My dearest Claire, I have never seen such a profound look of fear on your face, not even when gunfire blazed."

"Fear? I am not afraid!" She was, but Theo was warm and so near, his touch sending shivers through her, and she wished to touch him, too, and so she did.

Hard. He was hard everywhere, the light fur on his chest tickling her fingers. She did not look down, could not, and she gasped when his lips brushed hers, light as thistledown.

He began to speak.

*"To feel for ever its soft fall and swell,*

*Awake for ever in a sweet unrest,*

*Still, still to hear her tender-taken breath,*

*And so live ever—or else swoon to death."*

"How beautiful," she said. "I have never heard the like."

"It is by a friend, John Keats. A poem of his called 'Bright Star.' You are my *το αστέρι μου, Σε λατρεύω.*"

"Am I your star?"

"You know you are."

"I never did learn the meaning of *Σε λατρεύω.*"

His eyes softened. "'I adore you.'"

He took her in his arms and laid her on the bed, touching her, loving her, and she responded in kind until the only sun in her world was Theseus, her love.

When he entered her, slowly and with caution, she urged him on. The pinch that followed, with its attendant pain, soon transformed to an ache of want, though what that was, Claire did not know.

Then on and on, moving in and out, him touching her, whispering lovers' words, kissing her cheeks, her lips, her chin, her jaw. One arm slid down between them further and further until he touched a spot that in moments shot her into a sunburst of pleasure. She cried out as the sensations went on and on until he arched, groaned, and stilled atop her, both of them breathing as if they'd won a race.

Sounds intruded. Someone padding down the hall, a bird trilling from a branch, laughter. Except the latter was hers, and she squeezed him tight so he would not leave her. "I feel as if I have seen heaven."

He kissed her neck, then rolled to his side, resting his head on his hand. "Is that so?"

She cupped his cheek. "That may well be the most marvelous experience of my life."

There was that pirate grin. "Mine, too."

"But you have done it before, have you not?"

"Not like this. Not with you, love. It was as if it were my first time. Our pleasure will only increase, you know."

Her brow scrunched. "I do not see how that is possible."

"You will."

They cuddled, and she felt woozy with joy and completion, surprised at how intimate the aftermath with someone she adored.

They lay on their sides, face-to-face, stroking one another.

"Come, I shall plait your hair," Theo said.

His comment surprised her. "Would you truly enjoy that?"

"I find your tresses move me to near poetry, if I ever wrote poetry, that is." He threaded her long hair through his fingers. "Our vigorous lovemaking has turned it wild, and while I love it free, I fear it has become a massive tangle. You braid it before bed, do you not?"

"I do."

She sat with her legs crossed on the bed, her back fixed against his chest, his legs stretched out, surrounding her. So personal. So wonderful in a way she had never experienced.

While he wove her hair, they discussed what prompted the Greeks to move from the stiffer archaic style of carving to the more relaxed classical style. All of which, as she pictured the statues, made her think of penises. Theo was quite lengthy and thick, much to her surprise, for his was the only phallus she had seen in the flesh. She was dying to ask him a question, even knowing it would make her blush.

"Theo?"

"Yes, love?" he said, his hands soothing as he wove her plait.

"Um, now that I have seen you...fully, I have a rather odd question."

"Do you?" he said, a smile in his voice. "Fire away."

"Well, you see, I find you rather...large...down there, even when you are not..."

"...erect?"

She nodded, which pulled against his hands, her face aflame.

"I have really never compared." He chuckled. "What prompted this line of inquiry, my sweet girl?"

She cleared her throat, mortified, yet she soldiered on, all in the name of research. "Now that I have seen you, I am rather perplexed by the numerous statues I have viewed."

"Perplexed by what, exactly?"

"Their phalluses are, well, they are so small! All of them. Yours is much more, um...lengthy and substantial."

Again, he laughed softly. "By the time I reached sixteen, I wondered the same thing. I, too, found it peculiar in the extreme. So I asked my father."

"Did you, really?" she said. "How very brave."

"Yes, well, if you knew my stickler of a father, you would see how true that statement is. He had little time for boys and their questions."

"He does not sound like a terribly kind man," she said.

"He was not. But he did answer my query. Gods, emperors, and other elite men from ancient Greece are all depicted with small phalluses, as large penises were not a desirable thing."

"Why ever not?" Claire said.

"The Greeks believed small genitalia symbolized someone who made up for his lack of length down below with an expansive and potent intelligence up top."

"No! In all my research, I have never read such a thing."

"Statues wear only small genitalia because the sculptors wished to make clear that these men were rational intellectuals with their urges under control. Aristophanes, in his play, *The Clouds*, noted a male's ideal traits. 'A gleaming chest, bright skin, broad shoulders, tiny tongue, strong buttocks, and a little prick.' So you see, my love, a diminutive penis equaled the Greek ideal of male beauty, Priapus being the singular exception."

Claire huffed. "I have seen two renditions of Priapus, a statue and a krater. Both phalluses were terrifying, though given he is the god of fertility, it makes sense."

He reached for her ribbon curled on the bedside table, then kissed her shoulder. "It is an interesting subject, for simultaneously the ancients depicted lustful, depraved, and villainous men endowed with large, erect phalluses."

"To symbolize a lack of brainpower?"

"Yes, as well as recklessness and dissolute behavior. Damn. I have dropped the ribbon. Hand it to me, would you?"

Distracted, she did so, mulling over this new and surprising information. Claire worked on accepting the rationale, yet connecting the brain to the phallus seemed so very odd. "No matter which way I turn this, their reasoning sounds nonsensical. Why, you are the most intelligent man I know, and yet..."

He boomed a laugh as he tied off her braid. "Thank you, my dear, for that heady compliment." He bent close, his warm breath a caress, and kissed her neck, then wrapped his arms around her. "Depraved creatures were oft depicted as part-man, part-animal, and totally lacking in restraint—a quality despised by Greek society. Large phalluses were seen as vulgar and sported by barbarians."

He bussed her neck again, and she reached back to brush her hands over his shoulders.

"Though I have just completed your plait," he said. "I fear this discussion has gotten me rather—"

"Randy?" she said. "You are not alone in that sensation, good sir."

Claire turned in his arms and kissed him, and words became irrelevant.

The following day was bright and clear with a soft breeze. Claire and Theseus had awakened late, Claire pleasantly achy in interesting places. They indulged in breakfast, not in the suite's salon, but in bed! Shocking and great fun.

But the determination to tell Theo of Penny's marriage hovered, a malignant cloud. Today. Claire must do so today...at the proper time.

That morning, Rose proposed an exciting day of horse races, the family chiming in with enthusiasm. They set up in the far pasture, an immense fenced-in expanse, and were soon at it.

Claire found the races vastly entertaining, especially hers against Lottie, which her sister won. A remarkable feat, given Charlotte had a long-standing fear of horses, which she had conquered. Even Mama and Henry raced against each other of all things. They winnowed down the contestants to a final race—Thomasina opposing Patrick. It was a close-run thing, but Patrick squeezed an extra ounce from Diablo to win the prize—a magnificent syllabub.

The rest of the day was spent in quieter pastimes, and she and Theseus explored one another once again, much to their mutual joy.

All seemed weary after dinner that evening, convening in the family salon. Claire tucked her hand into Theo's arm—time had run out. Standing on tiptoe, she whispered, "I must speak to you about an important matter."

He wore a faint smile as he watched Bram and Isla wrestle on the carpet, Cullen observing with interest. "What might that be, sweetheart?"

"I cannot..." Claire said with a whisper. "Not here. Shall we return to our suite?

"Now?"

Claire screwed up her courage. "Yes."

As they left, Rhys waylaid them. "I meant to mention at dinner... I have been gifted some very fine cigars," Rhys said. "A friend from the Peninsula. Patrick and Devonshire are most eager to sample them. Care to join us in my study?"

Theo began to speak.

"I am certain Theseus would enjoy that," Claire said.

Theo raised a brow. "Are you sure?"

"My news will wait."

He smiled. "I would be delighted, Ravenscroft."

The men left, much to Claire's relief. Shame on her. Nonetheless, she now had bought a bit more time regarding Penny's marriage.

CHAPTER

# TWENTY-NINE

Once the cigars were distributed, Theseus, Devonshire, and Ravenscroft lit them while Patrick stared at his.

"I have never tried one," Patrick said, "though I have smoked cheroots aplenty."

"Cigars are different," Ravenscroft said, approaching his brother with a pair of scissors and taking up Patrick's cigar. "First, you cut, not too far. See?"

Ravenscroft cut his own near its head, then lit it. "Light it gingerly. Too much contact will turn the thing into a pile of char." Ravenscroft handed the cigar back to Patrick, who took several puffs.

"No, brother!" Ravenscroft said. "These hail from Sevilla, the finest in the world. Savor the puff. Enjoy the rich, woodsy flavor.

Patrick chuckled on a cough, waving his prize. "Indubitably!" He took another puff, leaning back in his wheeled chair, whilst Devonshire and Theseus sat facing the hearth. Ravenscroft leaned against the mantle of the room he proclaimed his favorite.

"This is superb," Theseus said. "Brings back memories, good and bad."

"I echo that sentiment," Ravenscroft said.

"Indeed," Patrick said, tapping his cigar's end on a nearby ashtray.

"While the cigars are a pleasant ruse," Ravenscroft said. "I thought we might toss around ideas about who might want you dead, Ashworth. And, more importantly, why?"

"Theseus," Devonshire said, waving his lit cigar. "I can see no reason for anyone to attack you. To be blunt, you are a bit of a misanthrope, avoiding society, traveling often, and hiding away at Wolf Court. I simply cannot fathom it."

Ravenscroft flung the window wide, his hand wafting the whirls of smoke out the window. "Rosie dislikes the smell."

"I find it a mystery as well, Ashworth," Patrick said. "You have been back in the country for, what, a few weeks?"

"Barely," Theseus said.

Ravenscroft waved his hand, leaving a trail of smoke. "We must conclude the attack has to do with your journey to Greece."

"I cannot disagree." Theseus leaned forward. "This can go no further, but while we were still in Kastri, seven of the sculptures were stolen. Whoever did so killed the man guarding them."

"Murdered!" Ravenscroft said.

"We believe he may have colluded with the thieves to effect their theft. Whether true or not, Georgios was undeserving of that fate. As we buried the sculptures—"

"You buried them?" Devonshire said. "Whatever for?"

Ashworth explained the delay in collecting the sculptures and how they had interred the marbles to keep them safe.

"Seven," Patrick said. "How would that translate to pounds sterling?"

"Easily a thousand pounds," Theseus said. "Given their desirability, perhaps more."

"Why those pieces?" Ravenscroft said.

Theseus shook his head. "Though the theft was highly calculated, the marbles taken seem random. They vary greatly in worth, and all were busts, I assume because of size."

"This cannot possibly be laid at Byron's door," Devonshire said. "He sees himself as too noble and principled to thieve."

They had been given a recounting of Byron's and the Garlands' arrival.

Devonshire tamped out his cigar. "Garland is the obvious suspect, though I always thought him a bit of a fool."

"He is rather dull-witted," Theseus said. "He was much the same at Harrow. But there is a canniness to him as well."

"I propose we should invite the ladies to join our discussion." Ravenscroft waved a hand. "Though we discuss dangerous subjects, I have learned not to exclude Rosie."

"Indeed?" Devonshire said.

"Rose often offers compelling insights."

"A good suggestion," Patrick said. "With her artist's eyes, Lottie often sees things I miss."

"I shall go wrangle them up," Ravenscroft said.

The men dispersed in search of their ladies, but it seemed the women had retired to bed.


Days later, scribbling away in their suite's salon, Claire had yet to tell Theseus of Penny's marriage, the situation an imposing mountain impossible to scale. Auntie and Milo had left for home, but Agnes assured them all she would return soon.

Claire busied herself with collating her journal's notes to prepare a new paper for The Society of Antiquarians, her pen scratches satisfying. She pulled a fresh piece of foolscap from the secretary, sharpened her quill, and continued.

As Claire reviewed her notes, she found herself a bit dazed by the volume of work before her. Which, for no reason, made her think of her husband. Then again, he popped into her thoughts with increasing frequency. He was all she admired, a man deeply respected by the Antiquarian Society, having been honored by them many times. Whereas she was a nobody.

In truth, she preferred it that way. Nonetheless, she must prove a suitable wife to this esteemed man. A weighty thought.

Cullen nudged her, and she gave him a scratch, then returned to her journal. Minutes or hours later, Theseus strolled in to peer over her shoulder, the thrill at his presence a deep pleasure.

"Hello, love." He kissed her shoulder.

Theseus was shocked, not by Claire's work, but rather by the setting. Admittedly, this was not the first time his Claire had surprised him, yet words eluded him.

Ink blotches dotted the foolscap, and her journals, papers, and books were strewn about—on the floor, on a chair, and in her lap. A sea of paper coupled with a half-eaten apple, her tea, several broken quills, and other detritus.

"I am surprised, love," he said.

"Hummmm?"

He kissed her neck because she was irresistible.

Claire sighed, and it was the good kind.

"You are utterly disorganized," he said.

"I am," she said in a fake-contrite voice.

"In Greece, you were impeccably neat."

"Of course! We had limited space, and there was simply no place to sprawl. I find this much more comfortable."

He chuckled. "I see your childhood habits persist."

She cocked her head. "I do not understand."

"You once said you would spread your father's mythology books about you on the floor."

Claire recalled their discussion aboard the *Nemesis*. "You are quite correct."

"I always find you full of surprises, my lady. Fascinating ones."

Cullen yipped, tail wagging, as if he were the one being complimented. Theseus ruffled the pup's fur. "What are your plans once you have compiled your entries?"

A pause. Claire cleared her throat. "I plan to present my findings to the Antiquarian Society."

*Bollocks.* While he fully supported her theory, he imagined her hurt yet again by men's cruel words and actions. Hating the idea, Theseus began removing her hairpins. "I worry for you, *to asteri mu.*"

"You fear I will be again jeered at," she said.

"I do."

"No matter." She shrugged. "No matter if they mock or throw vegetables or laugh, I *will* speak. My findings must be released into the world, whether I am believed or not."

"My darling Claire..."

CLAIRE SAID NOTHING. She knew, as well as Theo, that it was unlikely anyone could wrangle her another presentation, considering the Fellows now knew she was female. Yet Theo feared her being humiliated. As she was now his wife, did he fear the same for himself?

"I will do my best not to mortify you, Theo."

"Mortify me?" He reared back. "Love, I do not give a fig, as you could never embarrass me. I simply do not want your feelings injured again."

He had surprised her. Then again, Theo often did so. "The world must know that the Greeks polychromed their statues. But I have grown stronger. I was in a gunfight, after all. Having dealt with that, I can withstand the antiquarians' taunts."

"Trust me?" He gently squeezed her shoulders. "I shall find a venue for you that will inform the world yet will not subject you to derision."

She turned away to lift one of the thick books scattered about the floor. "I do not see how that is possible."

"Sweet Claire, believe what I say," he said, his voice husky. He leaned close, his breath on her ear sending trills of want through her.

"I do, Theo, but..."

Theseus kissed her cheek, removed a final hairpin, and lifted her from the seat. He wrapped her in his arms, her long tresses a honeyed cascade down her back. "I have another project that needs attending."

"Do you, indeed?" she said, her tone arch.

"Oh, yes, my dear. One I believe you will find quite illuminating."

Since announcing the where and when of their marriage in *The Times*, invitations to country weekends and parties besieged them. Given the threat to Theseus and the stolen marble, they considered sending all their regrets. But Lottie had pointed out that weekends such as these might very well include the Garlands or one of their associates.

Thus, the following day, early fall returning to near summer's warmth had them doffing their outerwear in the carriage. They traveled to Taunton in Somerset to attend the Sampsons' country weekend and ball. Everyone would be there, and Claire hoped that "everyone" included the Garlands.

Their horse threw a shoe, and they arrived late, the ball already in progress. Patrick and Charlotte, Rose and Rhys, and Mama, along with herself and Theo, entered the glittering room where the host had provided a ramp for Patrick's chair. Claire was impressed. To scope out the attendees, the couples and her mother scattered, Mama, beautiful as always, in a cerise gown and fine form.

Claire's unconventional husband had first refused to wear knee breeches and stockings, and their discussion was lively, to say the least.

"You will stand out if you do not," she had said. "You loathe that."

"A cogent point." He gave her teeth but relented.

The vast ballroom shone with hundreds of beeswax candles, the floor chalked with florals mimicking the flowers blooming throughout the room. After being announced by the Master of Ceremonies, they descended into the milling crowd, sweet tunes playing by musicians seated on a small balcony above the dancers.

Theo despised these events, Claire disliking them as well, for this was but yet another sparkling affair with sparkling people wearing sparkling dresses, the conversations grinding away on the weather, the king, and gossip. None of which interested her or Theo.

A crush always exacerbated her misery in crowds, and she clutched Theseus' arm as if it were a life raft.

Footmen circulated offering drinks and ices, with a table across the hall, a punchbowl filled with ratafia, likely containing enough brandy to lay her low. Then again, not a bad idea.

Claire wondered how long it would take Theseus to move on to the card or billiard room.

All of which made her want to visit the retiring room, a breather she could use. She dared not, for their purpose was to gather information, not retreat. The awful Lord Elgin was in attendance, and as he approached, she released Theo's arm to glide toward their host, holding forth amidst a small group. As she neared Mr. Sampson, she caught sight of Lady Garland hovering before a handsome man, hands clasped, lips pursed, blinking rapidly. Claire did an about-face and headed for her mother.

Over her shoulder, Elgin was bearing down on Theseus. No exit to her right. If she turned, she must confront Lady Garland. It was too soon, yet Claire had no escape.

Theseus hated this trumpery, the room filled with vacuous people, their sole aim to increase their stature with the *ton*. He meandered through the billiards room, Patrick in his chair rolling beside him, to enter the card room. A dozen tables were set up with men and a few women playing whist, piquet, and vingt-et-un. They moved to the sideboard with its row of illicit scotch, brandy, and cordials, including exotics such as *kirschwasser*, vermouth, and the decadent absinthe. He poured them each two fingers of the single malt scotch and handed one to Patrick. Two chairs sat in a corner, and he notched his head in that direction.

Once Theseus was seated, Patrick to his right, he surveyed the room with purpose. An attendee had raved about the wondrous Greek bust the Sampsons had recently acquired. Theseus spotted it diagonally across from them, perched on an ebony plinth. Theseus didn't need to move closer to recognize his namesake, a bust Theseus' father had unearthed in Crete years earlier. One he had brought to Kastri intended for repatriation. Yet here it rested in Sampson's card room.

Lady Ablethorp, a hideous gossip, sat beside it in an over-stuffed wing chair. He'd bet she knew how Sampson had acquired it.

"A refresh?" he said to Patrick.

Patrick shook his head.

"I will be right back." Theseus approached the sideboard to refill his glass, then strolled to the bust, feigning admiration when he wanted to take it and run.

He stared at the white marble, the slight chip on its nose yet another verification the bust was, indeed, his father's Theseus.

"Pretty, is it not?" Lady Ablethorp said, jowls wiggling.

"A stunning example of the Classical era in Greek sculpture," he replied.

The woman's reptilian eyes anticipated any scandalous remark he might inadvertently drop. "I must congratulate you on your recent nuptials."

Theseus nodded. "Thank you."

She waved a hand at the bust. "Have you seen its like before, Lord Ashworth?"

"I have."

"Where, might I ask?"

"My father owned one quite similar, though it is long gone."

"Long gone?"

"Yes." He gave her teeth, the emulation of a smile. "Returned to its home in Greece."

"Greece? Those people. Why, they are but Philistines, an impov-erished nation ruled for centuries by the Ottomans. What could they possibly do with such exquisite art?" She sniffed into her handkerchief.

If Theseus spoke, he would call her an "idiot." That would make a scene and thus destroy any chance of discovering how Sampson had acquired this particular piece. "Do excuse me, but I must return to Lord Hawthorne."

"Poor Lord Hawthorne. His lordship does not get on very well these days, does he? His infirmity and all."

Theseus' blood sizzled, but he kept his tone measured and light. "I must disagree, my lady. Hawthorne remains a bruising rider and an altogether accomplished athlete and human being. I would say he gets on exceptionally well. Do excuse me."

His bow was curt, and he sipped his scotch as he returned to Patrick in hopes of cooling his fury. The woman was a barnacle on the ass of humanity.

CHAPTER

# THIRTY

People clustered around Claire, who sat beside Charlotte, somewhat obscured by a large palm. No foliage could help her, for the attendees foamed around her like a rogue wave. She'd smiled so much, her teeth ached.

"Lady Claire!" Lord Garland had worked his way through the mob to stand before her.

"Good evening, my lord."

He raised a brow, his smile wide. "Am I not correct that I should now call you Lady Ashworth?"

She nodded. "Indeed, you should."

"Congratulations!" The orchestra began the strains of a waltz, and Garland held out a hand. "Would you do me the honor of a dance?"

Though she was sick of smiling, dancing with Garland prickled her flesh. "I would be honored."

He led her to the throng of swirling dancers, and they began. Frances had said her husband was elegant, and she found his dancing to be accomplished. Garland was but an inch or two taller than Claire, and as they danced around and around, the noise, laughter, and crush of the room, suffocating.

"You look a bit strained, my lady," Garland said. "Shall we take a breather on the terrace?"

They soon waltzed through the French doors and onto the terrace blazing with torches. Others were scattered about the large area, none of them nearby. Claire could finally breathe.

Garland paused by a balustrade, extensive gardens and a maze rolling out before them, all lit by torches. The full moon turned the world a shadowy gray while stars spangled the blackness, a few wispy clouds rushing by on their way to nowhere.

"Better?" he said.

She closed her eyes and nodded. "Infinitely."

"Would you care to dance beneath the stars?"

"How delightful."

They whirled, lit by the moon and torches, the strains of the distant music soothing.

It was time. "I confess, I miss Lord Ashworth's exquisite sculptures. Do you as well, my lord?"

Garland's face darkened. "They were worth thousands of pounds. How could he just leave them like that?"

"I believe Lord Ashworth's reasoning was to return them to their home."

"Their home? Perhaps thousands of years ago. But now? Those people are not the Greeks of old but ill-educated peasants who know nothing."

"They are most certainly not as you describe, and those sculptures are their heritage."

"We are England. We are empire. We take what we want, showing our might."

What a prig. "Do you not feel for them?"

Garland's excessive hyperbole nearly made her laugh. Theseus despised empire building, and she had come to agree with his point of view. Why destroy others to elevate their nation's worth? Why acquire and then acquire more? Garland, Elgin, the Earl of Moira, and their ilk perceived the world far differently from her and Theo, as if nations were a bonbon for their devouring. Distasteful in the extreme.

"Do I feel for them?" Garland said. "Why, no, for they are but a conquered people."

Not for long, she believed. Or rather, she hoped. Though a challenge to imagine the Greeks defeating the Ottomans, if the stars aligned...

"Any new finds, my lady?" Garland said.

Her laughter pealed. "Finds? Since our return to England, I have had no time."

"Sadly, neither have I." He sighed dramatically. "My lady wife is sick of my antiquarian bent. She cares for fashion, gossip, and little else. Her fears guide her every move, and she is afraid of *everything*."

Claire said nothing, finding his wife's disparagement offensive.

"You look lovely this evening," he said.

"Thank you, my lord."

"Would that I had married someone like you, someone with an antiquarian passion to match my own."

"Lady Garland seemed quite compelled by some antiquarian subjects."

He shook his head. "She is vapid in the extreme."

The music ceased, and Claire was most thankful. She tried to step back, but Garland's arms remained about her waist.

"Lord Garland, the music has ended."

"It has. Yet holding you, knowing of your passion, makes me wish for more."

What was the ridiculous man about? "Do excuse me." Claire again attempted to move away, and yet his hands remained clamped. He raised his left hand to her shoulder and tugged her closer.

She stood stiffly, leaning back. "Release me now."

He did so, yet grasped her right hand, squeezing it tight. "I am married, as are you. Yet I cannot believe you are satisfied. Ashworth is a brute. He must be so in the bedroom."

Shock rippled through Claire, along with revulsion, though she kept her face impassive. "I find your conversation uncomfortable in the extreme."

"I, on the other hand..." Garland plowed on. "I am an artist, an impresario, if you will, when it comes to a woman's wants and needs. I would love to bring you to the heights of pleasure."

*God in heaven.* How could he both frighten her and make her want to giggle at the same time? Claire's lips twitched, and she bit her cheek to stop her anxious laughter. She executed a brief curtsy, awkward considering his hand remained fastened on hers. "I take my marriage vows seriously, my lord. Good evening." She turned toward the ballroom.

He yanked her back. "Do not dismiss my suggestion, dear Claire. Imagine the two of us, beneath the moon and stars, touching, feeling, and loving one another." He dragged her forward toward the maze.

Fear spiked, and Claire pulled in the opposite direction to little effect. "I am newly wed. Release me *now.*"

He lifted her hand and kissed her palm, his eyes sparking with innuendo. "I understand you must protest to protect your dignity, but no one shall see us. Think of how we are in harmony."

Her stomach squeezed tight. "Rather discord, sir."

He resumed dragging her, giggling, his behavior both absurd and bizarre.

What would he do to her? He wouldn't rape her, surely not. Yet that glint in his eyes... Claire was done, and she dug in her heels, her heart beating triple time. Their progress halted, she would give him one more chance. "Release me immediately."

He tugged onward. Or tried to.

Inwardly, Claire sighed. Rather than stepping away, she moved close. Could she do this? She must.

Her open-handed strike to his throat, a soft, vulnerable area, enabled her to break free.

She jerked her hand away, whilst Garland stumbled backward, catching himself on a bush. "What in bloody hell was that?"

She withdrew several steps further. "The martial art of *Kalari*. I had a good teacher."

His eyes widened. "You are *demented*."

She continued to back away. "Not nearly as much as you, my lord, to think you could match Lord Ashworth in any realm."

Her eyes glued to his until she felt distant enough to turn and run toward the ballroom. At the entry, Theseus marched toward her as if a bugle had sounded, people parting before him. When he stood before her—tall and broad and beautiful—he snugged her close. Claire rested in his embrace, welcome and reassuring, to banish Garland's manhandling.

"I have been searching for you," Theo said in a grumbly voice.

"I was on the terrace." Breathless, adrenaline receding, she laid her cheek on his chest, hoping to ease her frantic heart. If not for her *kalari* move, Garland would have pulled her into the maze and... Best not to think on that.

Theseus peered down. "You appear flustered, *to asteri mu*. What happened?"

Claire made light of Garland's actions, for she wished to avoid Theo's fury. Nonetheless, his face turned thunderous.

"Mr. Sampson is bearing down on us." His eyes were alight as if on a mission.

"We shall discuss Garland's behavior later." He clamped his jaw.

Mr. Sampson posed before them, his monocle to his eye. "Lord and Lady Ashworth! I have been searching for you."

She smiled, for her husband still looked furious. "Have you really, Mr. Sampson? I must thank you for this delightful fête. It is truly marvelous."

His smile was quick and sincere. "I thank you, my lady. Her ladyship and I do try. Do allow me to show you my newest acquisition. You will be astonished."

"Do lead on," Theseus said. "We will be right behind you."

They followed Sampson into the smoke-filled card room, where Claire spotted a bust. A familiar one. At Wolf Court, she had examined that very marble—the hero Theseus. Shocked would be an understatement.

ANGER COILED WITHIN THESEUS, throbbing for release. He contained it, as he always did, suspecting Sampson had no culpability in the theft and sale.

"It is a bust of Heracles," Sampson said. "Found in the agora in Athens, I believe."

"Magnificent." Claire inwardly fumed. Indeed, it was not Heracles but depicted the ancient hero Theseus.

"Quite," was all Theseus said, obviously repressing his anger. "From whom did you acquire this exquisite antiquity?"

Sampson's teeth gleamed in a ferocious grin. "At Ashley's Auction Room, I proved victorious in a bidding war. Always a circus at Ashley's."

Theseus knew the auction house, though most of his experience had been with Ashley senior, when the man would drag him to sales in Pell Mell. Years ago. Now, he believed the son ran the place.

Lady Garland slipped in beside them, aglow with enthusiasm. "Is this not pretty? I am quite captivated by it, Mr. Sampson." She tittered. "Why, it looks quite like Lord Ashworth, do you not think?"

Claire rolled her eyes. Yet Frances' words had held a disingenuous note, a troubling one.

"The bust is of Heracles," Sampson said.

"La! You are built much like Heracles." Lady Garland laid a delicate hand on Theseus' arm, prompting a spike of jealousy. First Garland, now his wife? They were playing games, though Claire had no idea to what purpose. What was she about? The irony did not escape her, given the bust was of her husband's namesake.

Theo bellowed a laugh, tossing Lady Garland a wink. "I am afraid we must depart, Sampson."

"We cannot thank you enough for this delightful evening," Claire said. "Good evening."

Theseus nodded to both, placed Claire's hand on his arm, and marched from the room.

The following day, Claire sat beside Theseus as their carriage jounced on the awful road from Torquay to London, on their way to Ashley's Auction Room.

"How much do you know about the house?" Claire said.

"Not as much as I would like, for I have never met Alfred the younger. They say his greatest expertise lies in ancient Greek and Italian sculpture and vases."

"I find it curious that he misidentified the bust of Theseus," she said.

"Most curious, given his alleged knowledge. It may have been deliberate, Ashley trying to obfuscate the source. Before the French Revolution, Ashley's was a more modest auction house, but their prominence rose during the conflict. It was Alfred the Elder who transformed auctioneering into an art form, treating his public sales as a performance. He was rewarded with great success."

"I have never been," Claire said. "Is it fabulous?"

"Both a marvel and sad," Theo said. "All the auction houses fed off the artworks of French aristocratic refugees forced to liquidate their collections. After du Barry lost her head in 1793, Ashley's acquired the jewels of King Louis XV's former mistress, selling them for a fortune."

The thought gave Claire shivers, and she snuggled closer to Theo, resting her head on his shoulder. He smoothed a hand over her hair.

Since they had wed, Theo's moments of affection had increased, much to her delight. Claire now knew he lusted after her, but feelings such as caring, warmth, and interest produced affection, and she reveled in it.

They would stay at an inn for the night, the trip taking nearly twenty hours, and be in London on the morrow.

Claire normally reveled in any journey, but they had arrived home from the weekend near dawn, thus barely managing three hours of rest before they were on the road. Though the carriage's sway made her eyes heavy, her curiosity kept her awake.

"How will you approach Ashley?" she said.

"With the potential of a lucrative sale. I shall propose just that while demanding only to deal with Alfred Ashley."

Claire trilled a laugh. "I take it you shall wear your Earlish, pompous demeanor."

"I am never pompous," he said, eyes alight.

She snugged tighter to Theo. "Of course you are, but in the loveliest of ways."

He chuckled. "You are bamming me, love, though I suppose I can be stiff-necked on occasion."

A massive understatement, but Claire kept her amusement to herself.

They entered the fabled auction house after checking into their hotel. Claire explored the entryway's objets d'art while scribbling notes in a new journal, Theseus speaking to a clerk about Alfred Ashley.

Done, he stalked back to her, frustration leaking from his pores. He took her arm and led her outside. "Ashley will not return until this afternoon. Come." He signaled a hack.

"Where is our carriage?" she said as they entered.

"I sent it back to the hotel. Given the thing is crested and identifiable, I prefer to travel in town using a hack."

A grim thought.

They alighted at Berkeley Square, and Claire removed her

scented linen from her nose, the hack redolent of body odor and other unpleasantries.

"I have a treat in store."

"Oh!" She clapped her hands. They'd arrived at Gunter's Tea Shop. Theseus chose a Parmesan ice shaped like a cow, of all things. Being of a tamer bent, Claire ordered a cinnamon ice and Gunter's tea blend. They spent an enjoyable hour, then were off to the Clarendon.

The lobby was a beehive, their suite opulent, the rooms an explosion of trinkets and baubles, busy in its beauty. Claire nestled on the sofa, itching for Greece's simpler charms—the severity of the land, the pellucid azure waters, and the spare grace of her cottage in Kastri.

Theo rotated his shoulder as if it ached, his injury bothering him. It disturbed her, too, but for a different reason, his safety a constant concern. She was tired, yet images of Theseus' bloody, unconscious form haunted her until sleep stole her away.

Kisses awakened her, and she smiled up at her husband. "We are to meet Mr. Ashley?"

"In less than an hour," Theseus said. "You have been sleeping as if dead."

Claire pushed herself up, noting her aches from their days of travel. "I shall take care of my ablutions and be right with you."

Thirty minutes later, they entered the auction house's lobby once again, the same clerk speeding over to greet them, all smiles and deference. He bowed. "My lord, my lady, do follow me."

They traveled down several halls until the clerk stopped. He knocked twice, then swung open a door. They entered the most chaotic office Claire had ever seen, much worse than her own messes. A man hunched over his desk, peering through a magnifying glass at a pottery shard, a lock of his neatly pomaded hair falling across his forehead. Without looking up, he raised an index finger while jotting notes with the other hand.

The clerk gestured to a pair of chairs, pressed a finger to his lips, and backed out of the room, closing the door behind him.

They sat, and after long minutes, Alfred Ashley massaged his eyes and rose. He set his hair to rights, then came around the desk and bowed. "Greetings, Lord Ashworth, Lady Ashworth. Forgive the delay, but I had to get that information down on paper." His smile was too eager, his deference obsequious.

Claire surveyed the room with awe, for there was much of interest. Pottery shards. Two *kraters*. A bust of Hera and a Renaissance painting of the Pythia seated on her tripod, steam rising from the floor. The man genuflecting was Philip II of Macedon, while beside him stood an immense horse.

The work reflected the tale of Philip asking the Oracle whether he would conquer the world, to which the seer replied that anyone who could master the horse Bucephalus would triumph across all nations. Not Phillip but his son, Alexander the Great.

Claire had never seen the painting's like, and she wondered what Ashley would make of the modern Pythia.

"It is good to meet you, Lord Ashworth," Ashley said, bowing. "How are you?"

Her husband donned his fierce face, the one he'd worn when fighting the bandits, his eyes flashing. "Not as well as I would like, Mr. Ashley."

Ashley fussed with his cravat. "I am sorry to hear that, my lord. My clerk said you had something of interest to discuss with me. A possible acquisition?"

Theseus leaned forward. "I am afraid not. I am more interested in your recent sales."

"Which ones?" Ashley said.

"I recently viewed a bust, allegedly of Heracles and allegedly from the Archaic era, though it was neither of those, its origin Classical."

Ashley's Adam's apple bobbed, his agitation obvious as he shuffled papers around his desk. "We sell many busts, particularly Greek ones. I do not recall the Heracles, unfortunately. Might I excuse myself to look it up?"

"Of course," Theseus said in a deferential tone. "I shall be delighted to accompany you."

The man's eyes bulged. "That is not necessary, my lord."

"Oh, but indeed it is." He turned to Claire. "We shall return shortly."

Ashley looked from Claire to Theseus, conflicted. "Would you care to accompany us, my lady?"

She shook her head. "I prefer to rest here, Mr. Ashley, but thank you."

He couldn't haul her from the room, though he looked as if he wished to, and led Theseus from the room.

Claire began to explore. No matter how much she wished to examine the room's marvelous objects, she turned her sights to Ashley's desk. Perhaps some register or log might indicate how Ashley had acquired the bust. If he had unethically purchased the sculpture, he might hide such documentation here rather than in the more public ledgers.

The papers atop the desk were of little interest, so she tried the drawers, which were locked. Claire smiled as she removed a pin from her hat and got to work.

# THIRTY-ONE

Theseus accompanied Ashley as they walked the circuitous halls of the massive building. He suspected their meandering was to give Ashley time to devise a way out of the mess he'd made. They marched past rooms filled with elegant objects desired by the *ton* or anyone who could pay for them. Renaissance paintings. Jewels galore. Acres of furniture jumbled into vast rooms.

Finally, they arrived. Ashley unlocked the door, revealing a smallish room filled with stacks of leather-bound journals. Ashley pulled over a stool and stood upon it, then ran his finger across a series of shelved ledgers. He pulled one out and stepped down, opening it with a moistened finger.

Ashley began flipping pages. "Ah!"

"You have found the transaction?" Theseus said.

"I have." Ashley handed the open ledger to Theseus, pointing to a line mid-page with a scrawled signature.

"Unfortunately," Theseus said in a dry tone, "I find chicken scratch difficult to read."

"Apologies." Ashley retrieved the journal. "The purchase of nineteen Grecian marbles from..." He peered up at the Theseus. "Deciphering the name is a challenge. I cannot." He chuckled. "Some of our clerks have simply abominable script."

Clerks normally had impeccable script, which was one reason they were hired. "Come," Theseus said. "I grow rather tired of your dissembling, Ashley. Let us bring this to Lady Ashworth. She is an expert at deciphering handwriting."

Back they went, Theseus' temper bottled, arriving to find Claire sitting demurely as she perused a marble shard. She looked up at him, her eyes smiling.

"My lady," Ashley said. "His lordship suggested you might be able to decipher this entry. I shall fetch my head clerk, for he too may untangle this poor penmanship."

Ashley handed her the open ledger and fled, Medusa seemingly on his heels.

"He appears quite terrified," Claire said, slapping the book closed and standing. "I cannot read this scribble, but I suspect it is an intentional obfuscation meant to defy interpretation." A smile wreathed her face, and she dropped her voice to a whisper. "But I have found a paper in Ashley's desk that makes this faked entry moot."

"And what is that, wife of mine?" He walked to his wife and slid an arm around her waist.

Claire set the ledger on the desk, then fished in her reticule to withdraw a slip of paper, handing it to him. "This is the copy I made."

The paper listed the seven stolen marbles with most of the titles crossed out, new ones scrawled beside them. The bust of Theseus now read Heracles.

The document was unsigned, but at the very bottom lay a sigil.

"This is the true signature," he said.

"I agree," she said. "I have seen many sigils, but I do not recognize this one."

"Nor do I," Theseus said, scratching his cheek. "Though... It could be Mycenaean... No, it is not, yet I have seen something similar before. If we learn the meaning behind the image, we shall discover our thief." They would also find the person behind the attempt to kill him. He said nothing as thoughts of his near-death disturbed Claire.

"Let us leave before Ashley returns."

"I am of a like mind." Claire slipped the paper into her reticule, took Theseus' arm, and sauntered out as if the world were their oyster.

The sun blazed, and Claire whooshed in relief. "I am glad to be quit of that place. I should have loved it, and yet it made me uneasy. I suspect they deal in many stolen objects."

"Sadly, they do, love," Theo said.

Pell Mall bustled with people heading to their clubs, shopping, or simply sauntering to be seen.

"Shall we go to the British Museum?" she said. "Their extensive library may contain an image of the sigil."

Theseus shook his head. "They will allow us in, of course, but our visit will be noted, something I wish to avoid. Instead, we shall visit the Temple of the Muses."

Claire raised a brow. "How intriguing."

"I have a subscription," he said. "They claim more than one million volumes, and I suspect they have several on sigils. Come, let us find a hack."

The corner bustled with people, and Theseus raised his arm.

But Claire had seen a glint, just as she had when fighting the bandits, and she shoved Theo.

Boom!

*"God's teeth!"* Pain radiated from her shoulder down her left arm as she slammed into Theo. He grabbed her, whirling her around and into the shadow of an awning.

"Claire!"

That beautiful face was now filled with concern. The pain persisted, making her dizzy, her eyes having trouble focusing. "I fear..."

Theseus removed one hand from her waist, shiny and coated with red. Not madder red nor cinnabar, but a vivid crimson. How strange. "Is it not odd, Theo?"

"What, love?"

His arm supported her, and Claire grew drowsy, the pain a fire to her senses, her mouth emitting a slur of words. "Color, my love. Color."

Claire knew no more.


Theseus stared down at his wife. She lay on her belly, her face turned outward, her left shoulder sporting a bulky bandage. So still and pale. They were in the surgery rooms of his good friend, Richard Cartwell, Lord Haven, a recent viscount, an eminent doctor, and a former battlefield surgeon. He had considered taking Claire to a hospital but chose Cartwell instead.

The man had traveled the world, much as Theseus had, but in the pursuit of medical knowledge, having earned degrees from Leiden University and the London Hospital Medical College. They'd met at Harrow, Cartwell two years younger than he. Early on in the wars, before he had been deployed to the Peninsula, Theseus had traveled to the Cartwell stud farm, where Richard and his father raised the famed horses intended for Britain's cavalry.

Richard entered with his typical jaunty smile and slung an arm over Theseus' shoulder. "Your lady is doing well. Her sleep is restful, not fractious. Come, I think you could use a scotch, a gift from my cousin."

Theseus scrubbed his face. No one ever told him how it would feel if someone he loved took a bullet in front of him. He'd never felt such a cauldron of emotion—fear, fury, her safety, and even more fear. He still reeled from it, didn't want to leave her, not even for a minute. Logic told him her wound, while not superficial, was not life-threatening, particularly in Richard's care. The man had actually snuck into France during the wars to study their medical procedures, methods allegedly far beyond British expertise.

Theseus braced himself on either side of Claire and lightly kissed her cheek. "Whiskey sounds just the thing." He drew up Claire's blanket—she could catch a chill—then stared at the maid, whose eyes dropped. "Take good care of her. We shall return shortly."

Seated in a fine leather chair in Cartwell's library, Theseus sipped an exceptional scotch, Claire being shot sinking into him like an anchor tossed in the sea. He began to shake.

"Your lady will be well," Richard said, leaning forward and pressing a hand to his knee.

"Of course she will," he replied, assured of no such thing. He regained his control with effort.

His friend leaned back to peer down at his scotch, swirling it around. Richard was an imposing soul, with the swarthy complexion and dark curly hair of his Spanish mother. An intense man, though far more playful than Theseus' more reserved nature.

He'd been that way at Harrow and on the Peninsula and had grown in stature as the years passed, his fierce integrity powered his strong will.

Richard sipped. "In all the years, I have never seen you so… discomposed."

"My wife has been *shot*," Theseus barked.

"You, as well as I, know that her injury is not grave, my methods for controlling infection ample. She protected you?"

Theseus blinked, again hearing the shot. "I deduce she saw the barrel's glint, and she pushed me away, which put *her* in the bullet's trajectory."

"Are you certain the bullet was not intended for her ladyship?"

"Nothing gives me a reason to believe so. No, it was meant for me."

"She must love you very much." Richard's voice was pensive.

Did she? They had not spoken the words. Never hinted at them, though they called each other "sweetheart" and "love." He hoped Claire loved him, hoped rather emphatically, if truth be told.

Richard waved his drink. "I suspect you love her as well."

*Of course he loved her.* Indeed, he did, though *why* he had never voiced the words made him think. He ruminated, the scotch going down easy, warmth filling him. He was afraid, damn him. For the words would leave him vulnerable. His inaction, in truth, was cowardly. He downed the glass.

"So why is someone using you for target practice?" Richard said.

"The 'why' is simple." Theseus explained all that had happened in Greece and back home. "The who is more problematic and the reason we are in London."

"You suspect Garland."

"Most definitely."

"I remember him from school." Richard lifted the decanter and offered Theseus more scotch. Once his own glass was refilled, he continued. "A boy who had not an ounce of steel in him."

"He has found a bit of mettle since Harrow, but not much, and his temperament remains fickle, his intelligence slender." Theseus took a sip of his scotch. "That is the problem. Oh, he could have hired an assassin, but I struggle to see him acting with that level of viciousness and determination. As I noted, Byron was in Kastri as well, but he would neither steal the sculptures nor ambush us."

"What of your Greek friend, Dionysius?"

"He is wealthy with a thriving business, not to mention his fine character." Theseus shook his head.

Cartwell nodded. "Then you have a mystery on your hands, one I do not doubt you will untangle. You are dogged with all things holding your interest."

Theseus chuckled.

A knock, and the door opened on the maid, who curtsied. "Her ladyship is asking for you, my lord."

Theseus' chest tightened. For a moment he could not breathe. He strode to her side.

CLAIRE KNEW she was being cranky, but she couldn't help it after days of inactivity and Theo's hovering.

"My shoulder itches," Claire said on a plaintive note from the sofa in their suite at the Clarendon. Theseus wished to hasten to Woodbine once Lord Haven deemed her fit for travel. Claire would have none of it, for she was incensed. They must discover who was taking potshots at them. Here. In London.

Whereas Theseus remained overset by her injury, his mood as sour as hers.

"You cannot scratch," he said, pacing the room. "You know that."

She tossed him a saucy smile in hopes of improving his spirits. "Of course I do. We still have that visit... What was the name? The Temple of Muses or somesuch?"

"I have been," he said, his tone grumpy. "Knowing you as well as I do."

"And what is that supposed to mean?" she said, pushing herself higher on the sofa, though she could not help her wince.

"I expected your refusal to return to Woodbine. The last thing I want is you out and about."

That annoyed her further. "What about you out and about? They were not aiming for me, but you!"

"Sshh," he said in soothing tones. "Do not work yourself up. It cannot be healthy for your wound."

"I do not see how getting upset will affect my wound in the least."

Theseus raked his hands through his hair, making it extraordinarily rumpled. Poor man. He could not seem to get past her wound. "Did you find anything?"

He sighed as if at his tether's end. "Three books on sigils, and while we are both eager to examine them, you must not exhaust yourself."

Claire did not roll her eyes, but, oh, the urge was strong. "My dearest husband, perusing pages in a book will not tire me."

He opened his mouth to speak.

She held up a finger. "And if I do get weary, I shall take my rest."

"I have seen you at work, m'dear. You become obsessive."

"Please, Theo." She patted the sofa. "Sit, my love."

He froze, whooshed out a breath, and sat with great care beside her. She pressed a hand to his cheek. "I promise I will not overdo."

With an immense sigh, he rose and left the room, returning with three thick tomes, one stacked upon the other. He set them on the table before the sofa.

"You take one," she said. "And I shall take another." She slipped the top book onto her lap, and they began.


Two days later, they were still examining the books, a process both tedious and fascinating. They had written the family, giving assurances of their well-being while extending their stay. They omitted any mention of her injury.

Today, Claire felt more the thing, her energy increased with a near sense of normalcy. Certainly, if she banged her shoulder, it hurt like mad. But the constant pain had receded, ever present but manageable.

"This!" Theseus exclaimed.

"Show me!" She scootched closer and peered at the book.

# THIRTY-TWO

"I have never seen its like. Where is it from?" Claire looked for the description. "This is no help. It depicts the sigil with nothing to identify it but the words 'used as a seal.' That is no help whatsoever!"

"I cannot identify the image yet..." Theo bit out angry words. "I would swear I have seen it before. *Bollocks!* I cannot remember where."

"Let us hope it comes to you. A seal. Humm. What does this bird-woman-bull represent? It is rather indecent."

His finger ran along the tiny print. "The ancients used seals to lock things, effectively leaving a signature—do not touch. Seals were oft worn as necklaces by the nobility, and they were traded as well."

"Interesting. I am sure what it signifies matters."

"Agreed. *Damn*, it is frustratingly familiar."

"Which means we are making progress!"

"That we are." He scratched his stubbled chin. "Though... Is there truly a meaning behind the thing, or is it merely something obscure they used to impress?"

"I see your point." Claire said. "But why bother with it? I think it *must* have meaning for the thieves. Papa oft quoted Bacon, saying knowledge meant power, which was why he insisted Mama educate us beyond manners, piano, and embroidery. If we gather more information on the seal, the closer we shall come to finding the perpetrators."

He nodded, and they both went back to work.

After two more days, Theseus' gruff responses said much. Normally, he was an active man, riding for an hour or more each day, flying his birds of prey, or some other physical pastime.

Claire oft found him in Woodbine's woodshop working on some project or tramping the estate with Rhys. She'd even watched him spar with Patrick, both seated. This prolonged period of physical inactivity wore on him. On Claire as well, for though they walked the environs of the hotel, always together, swarms of people stopped them, insisting on vapid conversation. Her arm in its sling, in particular, drew a great deal of interest and was much fodder for gossip.

A knock, and Theseus went to answer it.

Out the Clarendon's doors, the city bustled, and Claire swore she felt that energy all the way to their suite of rooms. She had never seen herself as a country girl, yet she far preferred rural Greece or England to Londontown.

When not retrieving books, Theseus had glued himself to her side. Claire felt confined and restricted, neither of which was his fault. If they understood the sigil, they might identify the user. Long odds, true, but they had little else to go on. Theseus had also hired two Bow Street runners to investigate his attack. Another long shot, but a smart one.

Footsteps, then Dr. Cartwell entered the salon, followed by Theseus. The doctor nodded. "My lady, how do you fare today?"

She marked the page she'd been examining and closed the book. "Other than my eyes, which are blurry from staring at sigils, symbols, and seals, I feel quite well. At times my shoulder aches, but that seems normal to the healing process."

"Good to hear." He smiled, a handsome and kind man with an

innately warm demeanor, his mysterious eyes near black as coal. "Shall we repair to the bedroom so I might examine your wound properly?"

Theseus' lips thinned.

"Of course." Claire rose.

"Sigils, eh?" Cartwell said as they entered the bedroom. "Whatever for, Ashworth?"

Theseus showed him the seal. "We wish to learn what this means."

"What an odd depiction," Cartwell said.

"It certainly is that," Theseus said. "At least to our modern eyes."

Claire moved to stand beside Theo.

Cartwell rested his medical bag on the table. "I am afraid... Although, wait..."

"Yes?" Claire said.

"At Oxford, I found myself forced to study Apollodorus, much to my dismay."

"Dismay!" Theseus said. "He was an eminent scholar and historian, a student of Diogenes."

The doctor cast him a baleful glance. "Nonetheless...the seal reminds me of the Minotaur. You are familiar with the myth?"

"Indeed."

"I am not," Claire said.

"The Minotaur was a half-human creature with the head of a bull on the isle of Crete," Cartwell said. "He dwelt at the center of the Labyrinth, in a maze designed by Daedalus."

Excitement welled in Claire. "Theo, we must pursue this!"

"The bull's head is quite clear on the bird-woman," Theseus said.

"Do you think the seal Cretan?" Claire said.

"Perhaps. Though not the Greece I am familiar with." Theseus slashed a look at Cartwell. "Is my wife fit to travel? The last thing we need is for her to reopen her wound."

"Do excuse us," Cartwell said, "and I shall have an answer for you shortly."

Thirty minutes later, they began to pack.

WHEN THEY STAGGERED into Woodbine after the trip from London, Claire was wrung out. But she marshaled her energy as the questions regarding her arm bounced around the entryway. Cullen's exuberance nearly toppled her, but she was equally thrilled to see her pup, and after a few moments, Theo took charge. He excused them to usher her to their suite, promising to return and reveal all in a few minutes.

Claire lay down, Cullen sitting beside the bed with a pitiful stare. She patted the surface, and he launched onto the bed, curling in circles until he nestled beside her.

"Rest," Theseus said. "The journey was hard on you. The last thing we need is you becoming ill." Though his voice had been gruff, those emerald eyes darkened with concern.

"I want to be there when you discuss the seal," she said, raising her hand. "I am fine, love."

He pressed her hand to his cheek. Theseus looked tired, with dark bruises beneath his eyes and black bristles covering his jaw.

"You are done in," he said in a calm voice.

She closed her eyes, petting her pup and searching for patience. In truth, she was bone-weary. "Do tell the family about our adventures. But if I rest, you will wait to talk about the seal until I can be present? I want to watch their reactions firsthand, you see. Promise?"

Palpable relief crossed his face. "As you wish, love."

Eilidh moved forward to assist in undressing her, but Theseus dismissed her. "My task today, Eilidh." He made sure a full water pitcher and a glass rested on the bedside table, removed her shoes, unbuttoned her dress, and loosened her corset.

"Do you wish to don your dressing gown?"

Claire shook her head.

He drew the coverlet over her. "Comfortable?"

"I am," she said. "Though I would be more comfortable were you beside me in bed."

He tossed her his pirate's smile. "Were that the case, I fear no rest would occur."

"You are the naughtiest of all husbands." Claire tried for a coquettish smile.

"And *you* are to rest." He ruffled Cullen's fur. "Take care of your mistress while I am gone."

"I shall dream of what I prefer you doing in this bed," she said.

His pirate grin flashed again before he left the room.


What felt like minutes turned out to be hours once Claire looked at the mantel clock. Near four. As she went to rise, every muscle shrieked its objection. Nonetheless...

Claire shucked her clothes and, with effort, donned a morning dress, one pleasantly loose. Cullen hugged her side as she walked down the hall, her muscles loosening, the pain lessening, her injured shoulder merely an annoying ache. A footman swung wide the salon doors, revealing all enjoying pre-dinner drinks.

Claire surveyed the room—all the Ravenscrofts were there, plus Mama and... Auntie had returned!

*Oh, my!* She'd brought Arthur, her capuchin monkey. Perched on her shoulder, he wore a tiny tailcoat above a white shirt, with tailored buff breeches fastened with buttons. She'd never seen the like. The Hawthorne contingent had arrived as well. All looked at her as Cullen went to play with the pups thronging the room.

Theseus hurried over. "Why are you out of bed, *to asteri mu?*"

She chuckled. "I am just a little sore. Nothing else."

He set her free hand on his arm. "I waited to show the family, as requested."

They gathered around the table between the two sofas, and Theseus set the image before them.

"A seal, eh?" Rhys said, putting a finger on the corner of the copy.

"We discovered this receipt in Mr. Ashley's office," Claire said.

Rose tossed her a wink. "Did you use my method to acquire it, Claire?"

Rhys turned to his wife. "Whatever did you teach her, Rosie?"

"Never you mind, husband." Rose's serene smile made her husband bark a laugh.

"Indeed, I did." Claire beamed. "My hairpin worked a charm on the locks."

"This differs markedly from the receipt Ashley showed me in the records room," Theseus said. "Note how the proper names are replaced with newly invented ones. The original identifiers exactly match the stolen marbles."

"Ashley must have known they were stolen," Patrick said with a frown.

"I believe this paper proves that," Theseus said. "As you can see, the seller used his mark as a signature. We are trying to find the meaning behind this particular seal." Theseus pointed.

"It might be Greek," Claire said. "Dr. Cartwell thought the bull evoked the myth of the Minotaur."

"It is awfully...odd," Patrick said.

"Rather shocking, really." Mama pursed her lips.

"I agree," Claire said. "We spent hours looking through tomes containing seals and sigils."

"Given the depiction," Rhys said, tapping a finger to his lips. "I question that any man would use a symbol such as this."

Claire gave him a sharp look.

"Because of the enlarged breasts and..." Rhys cleared his throat. "Open legs."

The men glanced at one another, all discomfited.

"Ravenscroft has a point," Theseus said.

"The thing makes me deuced ill at ease," Patrick said.

Lottie took his arm. "Much as I see what you are all implying, it fails to prove the perpetrator was a woman."

Auntie lifted the page to peer through her spectacles. Arthur did the same, minus the glasses. "What harm if, for a moment, we consider the thief or thieves as women?"

"I see no reason not to," said Rose, her eyes scanning the room. "Who might this woman be?"

"In addition to Penelope and Claire," Theseus said. "Lady Garland and her maid joined our trek."

"Helene," Claire said, her thoughts arrowing to Lady Garland as well. Though Frances presented as a mouse, she wondered if that were an act. "Theo, I am finding it a challenge to picture Lady Garland or Helene in the role of the thief, but if so, it only solidifies my belief Garland must be involved, too."

"I agree," Theseus said. "Yet I sense malevolence behind the theft, the motivation beyond pounds sterling or stolen statuary."

"Do you?" Claire asked.

Theseus clasped his hands behind his back, head bent, and was silent for moments. "This feels...*personal.* As if the theft, the deaths, the sale—as if they were aimed specifically at me, though I can see no reason why."

"Whether that is true or no," Rhys said. "Now what? How do we find these people and draw them out?"

"Easy enough to find the Garlands," Rose said.

"Easy or no, we need a lure." Lottie rubbed circles over her increasing belly. "Something that will tease the culprits out of hiding."

"Lady Garland has little passion for artifacts, from what you have noted," Patrick said.

"You spent more time with these women than I, Claire," Theseus said.

"Passion?" Claire said. "No. I would say both Lady Garland and Helene were intrigued. In particular, expressing great interest in Aspasia, if you recall, Theo."

He nodded.

"This may be about more than money," Rose said. "But it must be a part, as they sold them to Ashley. Are the Garlands in need?"

"No idea," Theseus said. "I will put out feelers."

"As will I," Agnes said. "I may have a few resources you do not, Lord Ashworth."

"Perhaps the Garlands do need funds," Rose said. "Or mayhap, simple greed drives them. Or, as you say, Ashworth, their purpose may be more opaque."

"Helene made me anxious," Claire said. "Though why, I cannot say. About Garland—he did not go to Trinity with you, did he, Theo?" Cullen rested his head on her lap, peering up at her with a plea.

"No, Harrow. I shall look into his university days, though I question whether his buffoonery is an act."

"I must take Cullen out for his constitutional." Claire stood.

Theseus cast her a doleful look. "Let a footman—"

"I promise not to exert myself." She brushed a hand down his cheek.

"See that you do not," he said, his voice gruff, to place his hand over hers, eyes imploring.

She bussed his cheek, and out they went.

Cullen took off like a shot, the air crisp. She could taste fall on her tongue.

"Cullen! Do your business!"

He trotted to the edge of the wood, where he could find privacy. Funny boy.

Could it all have been a ruse—Lady Garland's fragility, Garland's antics? She had little trouble seeing Helene as the perpetrator, mostly because of her unflagging severity.

Georgios was *murdered*. Had the Garlands arranged that cold-blooded killing?

After returning with Cullen, Claire went to change for dinner, still conflicted. When Theseus breezed in, Eilidh was arranging a lock of her hair that had come loose, and the maid left with a curtsy. Now was the perfect time to tell him about Penny and Spyros' marriage. *God above,* she dreaded it, yet it hovered at the back of her mind like a fat black spider.

Eilidh left with a curtsy.

"No matter which way I turn," Claire said. "The idea of Lady Garland as the thief... I strain to see it."

Theseus nodded. "I struggle as well, but I suggest her deference and timidity were a performance...for us."

"That would make her an exceptional actress, though I certainly saw another side of her and Helene that day at the pond."

"The pond?" he said.

A flush sped from her neck upward, surely making her resemble a tomato. "Um, I may not have mentioned..."

He crossed his arms. "Pray continue."

Forcing herself to look into his eyes, she recounted the day she had seen him bathing in the pool. Oh, my, his face reddened. The man was trying not to laugh.

"Hrrumph!" Claire squeezed her eyes tight from embarrassment but was glad he found the incident humorous. "They were outside of enough in their comments."

"Her ladyship and her maid may be working as a team," he said.

"For a lady's maid, Helene was unusually assertive," Claire said.

"Combine that with the seal, it seems possible they might be the culprits."

"If those two *are* the perpetrators," Theseus said. "Garland must be culpable as well. I can see it no other way, though our suspect list is dismally short. Have we missed something?"

"Not that I can see." Claire rearranged a hairpin that was poking her skull, essentially buying time, for she would tell Theo about Penny's marriage. Now was the perfect time...

She gave him a bright smile. "We shall find a way to ferret them out."

He leaned down and kissed her. As always, she was transported to a warm, safe, and welcoming place with endless possibilities. She rested her hands on his shoulders and sighed. All of her warmed as his arms encased her, and she fizzed from the tips of her toes upward, her emotions surging. Theseus had become *everything* to her.

When they parted, with swollen lips and heated eyes, Claire took his hand, leading him into their suite's salon. She could not put it off any longer. He deserved to know.

"You look rather serious, *αστέρι μου*," he said. "Should I worry?"

She sat on the settee, tugging him down beside her, and held his hand tight.

"Love, given your death grip." His eyes darkened. "I suspect something is amiss."

She peered up at him. "Penny has married Spyros."

# THIRTY-THREE

Theseus blinked rapidly. "Perhaps I misheard you?"

"You did not. I received a letter from Penny detailing their marriage. She wrote just before they set sail for England."

His entire body seized, muscles taut, perhaps even his brain had frozen because he sat statue-still as if her words were incomprehensible.

"It is true, Theo."

"Did Penelope happen to mention *why* she married Spyros?"

"She did not say."

"Damn!" He raked a hand through his hair.

"Do you fear Spyros compromised her, forcing the marriage?"

"No." He shook his head. "Spyros is a man of honor. He would not do so."

"Think about this, Theo." Claire said. "Penny is uncompromising and forceful. Spyros has always taken great care with her. There really is only one conclusion to make."

"You believe they are in love, do you?" he said, his voice cut with steel.

Ouch. He was trying to keep his anger in check, though he was furious. But she also saw pain and confusion as well. She brushed her fingers across his cheek. "I believe it is possible."

He walked to the sideboard and poured a three-fingered dose of brandy, which he downed in one gulp, then poured another.

"Theo, he is a good man," she said from the settee. "Your dear friend." He looked wrecked, bewildered, and unhappy.

He rounded on her, setting his glass down with care. "I know that."

She had never seen him as overset. "Do you object that he is not of Penelope's station?"

"I do not give a bugger for his station, as you should know. It seems Penelope does not, either. Fine with me." He refilled his glass yet again and slumped into the chair across from her to stare at the amber liquid as he swirled his glass.

"Then what has you so troubled?" she said.

"My sister has become a mystery. Why not tell me of this? What makes her fear me so?"

Claire recalled his similar words when the bandits attacked, and Penny had used the Ferguson. He was hurt. Deeply so. "We all have corners of ourselves that we do not share. Pieces that we keep hidden for whatever reason." She shrugged. "You know your sister, as do I. But Penelope has had many experiences in Greece we—"

"That she has," He knocked back the whiskey and stood, aiming for the sideboard.

"She adores you, but she is a woman grown. She spent much time alone while you and your father traveled. That has made her exceedingly independent."

"This I have learned."

"Sweetheart, what will you do?"

"*Do?* Why, nothing. She has made her choice, and I shall support it."

"Will you?"

His eyes were cool, but she saw the fire banked beneath, those flames more about his wounded heart than anything else. He would sort it, but he needed time to settle.

"We must arrange a family celebration," she said. "I suspect they will journey to Woodbine, as they knew that was our first destination."

His shrug was nonchalant. "I leave it in your capable hands. I am going for a ride."

She repaired to their rooms. Theseus wasn't angry with his sister but wounded. Claire *hated* seeing him in pain, most especially when there was no way for her to fix things.

She lowered the secretary's leaf, took out a sheet of foolscap, and proceeded to write Penny a scathing letter.

An hour later, Claire balled up her fifth attempt as a cacophony of barking arose. She tossed her useless note in the bin, set her quill aside, and went to see about the commotion.

At the landing, shock took her words. The family was effusively greeting Penelope and Spyros, who stood in the foyer looking bewildered.

A throng surrounded them—Rhys and Rose, Susannah and Thomasina, Auntie, and the Hawthornes.

Claire hurried down the steps. "Penny! Spyros!"

Her friend's smile was wobbly as she hurried to Claire and enveloped her in a hug.

"How did you arrive so swiftly?" Claire said. "Congratulations are in order!"

Penny offered a shy smile. "Congratulations to you as well, dear sister, though you were to wait for me before you wed!"

"Ha!" Claire snorted. "You did not even *tell* me of your serious interest in Spyros, though I sussed it out myself."

Penny's eyes twinkled. "I cannot fathom it! We are both now married ladies, as evidenced by that stunning ring on your finger."

Claire blushed, for her mind went to those nightly activities she found so satisfying.

Penny held out a hand for Spyros, who clasped it greedily,

flashing Claire a fierce smile. "Greetings, sister!" He kissed Claire's cheek with a loud smack and laughed. "Where is the rogue? I do not see him and pray he makes my death painless."

"We shall see." Claire grinned.

They all decamped to the salon, where the excitement and chatter continued, Cullen in transports at the newlyweds' arrival, while Isla and Bram bounced around like hoppy toys, Arthur appearing to chitter away. Tea was soon served while a footman went in search of Theseus.

"We expected your arrival," Rhys said, offering Spyros a splash of brandy in his tea. "But did not anticipate it for several more weeks."

Spyros set his cup down, his face somber. He glanced at Penny, expression grim.

"You left, and we reconsidered, and..." Penny bit her lip, then looked to Spyros. "We returned the swiftest way possible." She blew into her handkerchief, her sneezes and coughs emerging with her arrival on English soil.

"There is more," Spyros said.

Penelope's eyes filled with tears. "Nomiki and Glauca had familial obligations the night you were given your gifts, remember? The following morning, Xanthe went silent. She *knew*. We could not leave until we found Nomiki." Penny shook her head.

"Andreas discovered Nomiki's body in a ditch." Spyros cleared his throat. "It was covered in leaves and detritus, her throat slit, Glauca standing guard beside her."

A sharp, hard pain pierced Claire's heart. Not Nomiki—shy, intelligent, and kind. Why would anyone kill that sweet, innocent girl?

"Did you know her well?" Susannah asked.

"Well enough," Claire said. "We cared a great deal for her. A lovely girl about to reach womanhood."

The air filled with shock and grief as Spyros continued. "She must have witnessed something to do with the theft, hence her elimination."

"Yet the Garlands had already left," Claire said.

"We found evidence of several minions," Spyros said. "None were from Kastri, but ruffians we believe the Garlands left behind to clean up loose ends. The fools discarded a list in the fire, only partially burned, that contained the stolen sculptures. We missed them by minutes, their fire still smoking. Though we followed, we failed to capture them."

Penny sniffled into her kerchief. "I did not write you of this, as I wanted to tell you in person."

Claire blinked rapidly to stop her tears, which proved useless. "What a loss. Xanthe must be crushed. She loved Nomiki dearly, like a daughter."

"Nomiki was prized by the whole village, and all are shattered." Penny shook her head. "Xanthe took Glauca into her care, and they journeyed to the cave. We stayed until they reappeared two days later and settled."

Theseus strode in, took in the gathering, and stormed to Claire. "Why are you crying?"

Conversation trailed off.

Spyros eyed his old friend as he stood. "Let us talk in private for a moment."

"Private?" Theseus snapped. "Whatever for?"

Claire cleared her throat. "Nomiki is dead."

Theseus froze, then looked to Spyros, who summarized the tale.

Theo's hands curled into fists. "These murderers and thieves deserve to be drawn and quartered."

"The pleasure will be all mine," Spyros said.

"And mine," Theseus said.

The atmosphere thickened. Theseus thumped into a chair beside the settee, where Claire, Penny, and Spyros sat.

Thomasina and Susannah stood, Sina offering Theseus a plate of treats, and he took one and thanked her.

She stared at him, tilting her head left, then right. "You appear much like one of my stallions about to bite me, Lord Ashworth."

Theseus' eyes softened, and he offered Thomasina a smile. "I promise I shall not."

She wagged a finger. "You had best not bite *anyone*."

His glance slid to Spyros. "That, Thomasina, I cannot promise."

"Perhaps this will comfort your nerves." Susannah handed him a cup of tea, which Rhys had liberally doused with brandy.

He thanked her as well, his eyes moving from his sister to his new brother, his jaw bunching yet again.

Claire hoped her poor husband didn't break a tooth. How to stave off the coming storm? "Do tell us about your wedding."

Penny laughed, rolling her eyes, and whispered, "You are fueling the fire!"

"Better to let the flames free than have them build further."

"I suspect the explosion to be spectacular," Penny whispered.

Claire fervently hoped it was not.

Spyros charged into the conversation. "We were married in Kastri. A beautiful ceremony, though a simple one, but filled with hope and joy."

Theseus snorted.

"It was lovely, brother," Penny said. "I wore the most beautiful Greek wedding dress, with Spyros donning native apparel as well. Xanthe officiated."

"Are you even *legally* married?" Theseus ground out, his sarcasm in full force.

"Of course." Spyros turned to Penelope, warmth in his eyes. "Before our departure for England, an Anglican minister at the embassy wed us as well."

"*Πώς θα μπορούσατε να το κάνετε αυτό χωρίς την άδειά μου?*" Theseus said.

"*Η Πηνελόπη είναι ενήλικη!*" Spyros said. "*Δεν χρειαζόμασταν άδεια!*"

"*Έπρεπε να ρωτήσεις!*" Theseus barked back.

Penny leaned close. "I most certainly did *not* need Theseus' permission to marry!"

"That is not the cause of his upset." Claire whispered.

"Do excuse us." Patrick wheeled forward, taking Lottie's hand. "We must complete packing for our departure on the morrow."

With them, a flood of humans and dogs escaped, leaving the four of them. Cullen remained at her feet, eyeing the treat tray as the air thickened again once the doors snapped closed.

Theseus strode to the tall windows, hands clasped behind him, to peer at the garden beyond, where a gust of wind sent a flurry of dandelion seeds floating into the air.

"Theo feels excluded from your plans," Claire said. "From your emotions, really. He is hurt. I believe his anger masks his wounded feelings."

"Oh!" Penny said with surprise. "We did not mean to hurt him, not intentionally. I know he loves me, but I do not pique his interest, not as his digs do."

"That is untrue, Pens," Claire said, though she quickly amended her words. "It may seem that way, but Theo now realizes..." Claire waved a hand. "Ask him."

"Ashworth," Spyros barked, rising to his full height.

Theo turned but said nothing.

"I love your sister," Spyros said.

Striding to where they sat, Theseus lifted his teacup and took a sip. He peered over the rim. "Do you indeed?"

Penelope straightened. "He does, and I love him as well."

Theo deflated, closing his eyes. "I am pleased for you both." With particular care, he set down his cup and walked from the room.

# THIRTY-FOUR

That hot, late-summer afternoon, Theseus pounded nails in the cooperage shed, the man having gone off to the village for supplies. He needed physical activity, knowing well he was behaving like an ass. Were he at Wolf Court, he would fly Ares and lose all sense of time and place whilst doing so.

He pounded another nail, hard, almost hitting his thumb. Damn. Theseus paused, squeezing his eyes tight, trying to find his celebrated control, which seemed to have abandoned him upon hearing of Penelope's marriage.

He whacked another nail.

Humidity clotted the air, and though he'd doffed his cravat, jacket, and waistcoat, he was still sweating like a dock worker. He scrubbed his kerchief across his face and tossed it aside.

When he looked up, a shadow darkened the doorway. Penelope. "Come!" he barked, sounding quite like a martinet. He hadn't meant to. "Do come in, Penny."

She walked across the room to stand before him, hands clasped. "Might we talk?"

He hammered in another nail, noting the bloom in her cheeks, far healthier than he'd observed in years. "Not much to say, is there? Your marriage is a *fait accompli*."

"Well, yes." She laid a hand on his arm.

He thumped another nail.

"I understand my marriage was swift," she said. "Nor is elopement approved by society. Neither is the difference in our stations."

He grunted.

"Spyros and I did not ask for permission, and I am sorry. That would have been courteous. But I did not really need it, as I have reached my majority."

More pounding, for words eluded him. Odd, how he could talk to Claire on any subject, and yet with his sister, emotion silenced him. He did not know what to say nor how to explain his feelings.

"You are my brother," Penny said. "My beloved brother. You have cared for me all our lives, certainly giving me far more attention than our father ever did, even if you did treat me as if I were wrapped in cotton batting. Do you not realize how much love and protection you afforded me as I grew? Without you, I would never be the woman I am today." She wrapped her arms around his waist.

He shook it off. "I am all sweaty, Penelope."

She stood on tiptoe and kissed his cheek. "I do not care."

His hand rose to the spot she had kissed. Why did she look at him that way when he'd failed her miserably?

Again he raised the hammer, then tossed it on the bench and whooshed out a breath. "I feel I do not know you. I feel guilty for missing so much, for not being attentive enough, for not showing more interest in you and your pursuits. It was wrong of me, and though my apology is late in coming, I do sincerely offer one."

Penny startled. "I thought you did not find me interesting."

"Of course I find you interesting." He'd nearly roared.

"You do?"

"How could I not?" He shook his head. "You are clever and bright. But I knew nothing of your shooting prowess. Had no idea that you had grown so independent. Had little understanding of your passion for tapestry weaving. Worse, I had no concept of your interest in Spyros, a man you have known for ten or more years. Why did you not tell me of these things?"

She studied her hands. "Because I thought you would forbid me to pursue them. Well, the shooting and Spyros, not the weaving."

Theseus' impulse was to deny her assertions, but he could not. He would have forbidden her any activities he saw as dangerous, including her relationship with Spyros. "You are correct. I was a tyrant."

"Oh, Theo, you were not. Just overprotective. It was not your responsibility to stay home and guide me, but rather our father's. When you were at Wolf Court, it was you who made sure of my comfort. You, who talked to me when I was troubled. You, who ensured the staff would accede to my requests and support me while you and Father were gone. *He* remained blissfully unaware. There were times when I was unsure Father knew of my existence.

"You were my stability, my reassurance, my bulwark. It was you who gave me the confidence to seek my own path."

Words again failed him, and he blinked, the burning in his eyes bothersome as he sorted through her words. Sweaty or not, he clasped Penelope in a tight hug, emotion bringing him low.

When he released her, she took his hand and said, "Come."

They walked to the rose garden, the blooms fading with fall, to a wooden bench.

"I wish to tell you about Spyros in the sunshine rather than in that gloomy shed. He is a good man."

"This I know."

"I first detected his fondness for me as our journey from Itea progressed." She peeked at him. "I always had an interest in him, for I found him kind and attentive, yet not overbearing. And very amusing, too. He never tried to sway me from my path, whether it was shooting or attending the Pythia. I still hope to retrieve the Ferguson, I might add. But he also made sure I came to no harm, and a few of my more unusual ideas he tossed figuratively into the refuse bin. He always asked cogent questions about my ideas and perceptions that made me pause and ponder. I liked that very much."

"Spyros is bright, sometimes too much so." He laughed. "He was also a mischief-maker at university, frequently engaging in hijinks."

"I am sure you joined in!"

"Naturally," Theseus said with great solemnity. "I also thought them up!"

Penny's smile was mysterious.

"He did not ask me to court you."

"He did not, at my behest," she said.

"Why in God's name?"

"Because you would have fussed, thought of a thousand reasons why marriage was a bad idea, my health being paramount. I fear you continue to see me as a child, though I am a woman grown."

"I do not—"

"You certainly act as such," Penny said. "But that is neither here nor there. He is lovely, Theo. Simply lovely. In Greece, I found my heart warming to him."

Claire popped into his thoughts, and he pictured her and her independent spirit, which never waned. He admired Claire's tenacity. His wife was no fainting flower, thank the heavens. It seemed Penelope was not either.

"You love him," he said.

"Yes." A smile trembled across Penny's lips. "Do you love Claire?"

Theseus jerked back, oddly shocked, for of course he loved her. "I do."

"Then you must know how much I love Spyros, for he is the most wonderful of men." Her eyes took on a dreamy look. "I picture our future, our children." She giggled. "I even picture those children playing with yours!"

*Christ in heaven, children?* That hadn't even occurred to him, yet the way he and Claire relished making love... Children would be the product of such activity.

"He has money," Penny continued. "We have my dowry. We shall be comfortable."

"Comfortable." He chuffed. "What does *that* mean?"

"We may not live in high style, but we shall buy a home in England, and Spyros owns one in Greece."

The revolution and its dangers came to mind. "The country is unstable. Soon, it will become more so. You cannot possibly be safe in Greece."

"We plan to stay in England..." she said. "For a time at least, and then choose between returning to Greece or remaining here."

"How can you even—"

"No matter what we decide," she said. "It will be made with fore-thought and care."

He looked at his sister—a grown woman, a married woman, wed to a man he both liked and respected. Easy enough to bluster, to intimidate her enough to stay in England until the revolution was done.

Trust—a discussion he had with Claire more than once. It was hard enough trusting Claire to manage her many proposals and plans. Now, he must learn to trust his sister and her decisions, as well as Spyros. At least the man had a solid dose of wisdom and common sense.

He must trust. But it was so damned hard.

"Come," he said. "I wish to show you something." He winged his arm, earning a smile from his sister. They entered Rhys' study, where he had left the paper with the seal's image.

"Do you recognize this?" He handed her the paper. "Perhaps know its meaning?"

"I believe..." Penny leaned close, narrowing her eyes. "Is that not the head of a bull?"

"Yes," he said.

"The Minotaur?" she said.

"We suspect so, as the bull was an icon of the Minoans."

Penny pressed her hands to her cheeks. "When I had the vision in the cave in Kastri, a voice said, 'Beware the Minotaur's seal.'"

A bit too mystical for Theseus' taste. "And…?"

"This has meaning. It represents the Minotaur. Well, his head. I have seen its like before." She nodded. "Around Helene's neck, as a soapstone focal point."

"Are you positive?"

Penelope pressed her lips together. "I think so, for I found it quite singular. When I admired its uniqueness, Helene said it was a gift from her mother. I believe this image is the same, though I cannot be positive."

"Good enough for me."

THESEUS WENT in search of his wife. Instead he found Spyros, who was looking for him.

"Spyros." Theseus nodded.

"My friend, greetings." Spyros held up a sheaf of papers. "I have worked up some settlement agreements."

"Before we discuss that, take a look at this." He showed Spyros the seal.

Spyros raised his brow, shaking his head. "I am unfamiliar with it."

Theseus was about to speak when Spyros continued.

"The settlements are amendable, but I wish to reassure you of my ability to care for Penelope."

He read the papers. Spyros' contributions were generous, extremely so—ample pin money for Penelope, her request for a cottage in Kastri, and monies that could not be touched, which included half of her substantial dowry and ample settlements for any children.

Penny had said they intended to purchase a home in England, and several of his unentailed properties came to mind.

"My grandfather loved to fish," Theseus said. "As do I, you, and

Penelope. But Father never cared for it, so our property in Lifton, including miles of the Tamar River, is uninhabited other than for its caretakers. The cottage from the seventeenth century is large and well-maintained. Along with the fishing, pheasant and partridge abound, the property itself covering forty acres."

Spyros scratched his cheek. "We cannot—"

"If it would suit," Theseus said. "I shall include Lifton with Penelope's dowry."

"I have ample funds, Theo," Spyros said.

"I do not doubt it." Theseus huffed. "But it would please me to gift it to you and my sister."

"I shall discuss it with Penelope." Spyros laid a hand on his shoulder. "A generous offer, Theo. Thank you."

Claire ran Theseus down in the orangery, seated on a bench amidst the fragrant trees. His eyes were distant, as if he were seeing other places or other times, his solemn expression near painful.

She sat beside him and took his hand in hers, though he didn't react to her presence.

Remaining silent, Claire wondered at his thoughts, hating his turmoil. She wished to reassure him of her affection and support. Yet she could not, as he seemed to need contemplation to resolve whatever churned within.

He squeezed Claire's hand. "Penelope believes Helene wore that seal as a necklace."

"Really?" Claire's brow creased. "I wish I recalled that, but I do not."

Theseus looked into her eyes, as if she were his entire focus. "I love you, Claire Cassandra Pheland Ashworth."

She gasped.

"You are the embodiment of all my hopes and dreams, of all that I wished for." He tore his eyes from her to stare at the ground, his face chagrined. He shook his head. "As you know, lovely Claire, I am not particularly good with words."

Her hands rose to his face, turning it back to her. "How very wrong you are, for those were beautiful words, Theo. You must know I feel the same."

His eyes widened.

"Theo, you are my everything, and I love you madly."

The warmth in his eyes melted her, and she leaned forward to brush her lips across his. "How could I not love you? For you are my dreams made real."

His fierce kiss tossed all thought skyward. And while the bench wasn't particularly wide, it was nonetheless serviceable, and they delighted in each other for a long time, kissing, touching, and making love on that beautifully uncomfortable bench. When they found repletion, Claire lay in Theo's arms, content, her heart full to bursting.

"I wonder if anyone has made love in this orangery before," he said with a smile in his voice.

"I suspect so, for it is a heavenly place."

Theo squeezed her tight, nuzzling her neck. "Heavenly." He held her as he sat up. "Come, love, we have plans to make and schemes to orchestrate now that we believe the seal to be Helene's."

"You said Penny was not entirely certain."

"No. But the necklace caught her eye, and she has a keen one. Add that to other indications and hints, and we can speculate the Garland party being the villains, the source of the theft and the deaths. I have an idea that may catch those who have wronged Kastri and us."

Claire scrambled off his lap to stand before him, fluffing her skirts as he began to button her bodice. "Tell me more."

"It has to do with Aspasia, but I must roll it around in my mind first."

"Can I not be your sounding board?" she said.

He kissed her cheek. "In all things, but let my ideas solidify a bit before we exchange thoughts."

Days later, Theseus sat at the secretary in their suite, dreading the tower of correspondence that had accumulated, though the two busts he'd had shipped from home to Woodbine had arrived.

At Claire's request, Rose had added a table to their sitting room large enough for Claire's sprawl as she wrote her presentation, which she hoped to give three weeks hence.

Now, as he slid open the first letter's seal, his wife was bustling around the room, collecting...whatever it was she collected.

All the infernal woman wore was her blasted dressing gown, and his mind veered to what was beneath that bit of cloth. Smooth skin, full breasts, and...

"*Christ!*"

"Wʜᴀᴛ ɪs ɪᴛ?" Claire wafted over and kissed his cheek. "Delicious."

"Stop that!" He swatted her away. "*Damn!* I cannot work, cannot think." He combed his hands through his hair.

"What is wrong, darling?" She laid her hand on his shoulders.

He paused for a long, long while, trying to settle. "Carnal thoughts."

"Pardon?"

"Ever since we first made love. No, before that. Maybe always. Damn, I do not know, but no matter. Whenever we are in proximity, carnal thoughts burst into my mind. You have scrambled my brains!"

He would swear she was laughing, but when he looked over his shoulder, her face had that come-hither look he adored—a small smile, a brow raised, a heat kindling those amber eyes. "Dearest Theo, you are not the only one. I have them, too. Often! What do you expect? We took no honeymoon, which is where carnal activities are supposed to occur. Hence, our continuing agitation."

As he rose, the stack of letters toppled. He paid them no mind, for his mission had little to do with correspondence.

# THIRTY-FIVE

Their plans for the Garlands were coming to fruition, and Claire prayed they were successful. She sat back in the chair. It creaked. She'd worked like a woman possessed preparing her presentation. She, Theo, and the family had discussed his plan to capture the Garlands. All the while, thoughts of Nomiki brought her low. She swiped at her eyes, leaned forward, and continued her revision.

An hour later, Theseus blew into the room.

"Theseus?" she said.

"All is ready. Come." He held out his hand, and she accompanied him down the hall to the salon where the family awaited.

Her family crowded beside each other on the sofas and chairs, Theo standing before them.

"Thank you for coming so swiftly." He unfolded a piece of foolscap he'd taken from his pocket. "We shall return to the Society of Antiquaries, where Claire shall give an exclusive presentation to highlight her findings."

Rhys' brow furrowed. "The hecklers—"

"Claire will not be jeered, not this time," he said in a deceptively soft voice. "Our invitations shall invite specific Fellow antiquarians and the elite, along with Devonshire and you. We intend to draw the perpetrators out of hiding. Our lure—a marble bust."

The thought of standing before those mocking men made Claire shudder. But she would expound before them, naked if necessary, to reveal Nomiki's killer.

"You mentioned a bust?" Rhys said.

Theseus chuckled. "Aspasia. I keep her in trust for a Greek family."

"How will Aspasia suss out the miscreants?" Susannah said.

"We suspect the Garlands, do we not?" Rose said.

"Yes," Claire said.

Theo flashed a grin. "Both Lady Garland and her maid expressed a unique interest in Aspasia."

Claire nodded. "They were rhapsodic in their admiration when they first saw her. Unusual, as no other sculpture seemed to interest them."

"Why, I wonder," Rose said.

"On our return, I deepened my research on Aspasia," Claire said. "She lived around 500 BC and was a woman of many parts. A courtesan, the great Pericles' lover, then wife, and the mother of his illegitimate child. She was powerfully intelligent, yet without an Athenian woman's restraints, for she was not a citizen.

"Renowned for her wit, charm, and intellect, she held gatherings for the Athenian elite, including Xenophon, Socrates, and many others. Plutarch notes her 'rare political wisdom.' Aspasia commanded respect and admiration, not to mention her great beauty."

"Interesting," Rose said. "Perhaps this Lady Garland sees herself as a similar shining light?"

"Perhaps," Claire said. "Or she believes herself Aspasia returned to life. I do not joke. No matter, for Frances and Helene were fixated on that bust."

"I possess two Aspasias." Theo flashed a grin. "The Roman copy was a gift, the original Greek herm on loan, as I mentioned. As Claire presents her paper, she will display the original Greek by the podium. Backstage afterward, we shall facilitate the theft of the Roman copy. If we catch them in the act, we shall have them. If not, we shall put our follow-up plan in motion."

The scheme set, Theo had addressed the Society of Antiquaries' Council, explaining the purpose behind Claire's presentation. They acquiesced, and the family decamped to Ravenscroft's London townhouse.

The invitations were mailed and included the pieces Claire would discuss—the archer maquette, the Heracles krater, and the Greek herm of Aspasia.

Theseus would accompany Lord Elgin's invitation with a note, a surprise for Claire, a distraction for the audience, and a way to buy needed time. His request must hold allure. The man was rich but greedy and arrogant, believing his opinions correct in all things. Money wasn't enough.

A bet. That would do. He challenged Elgin to wager one hundred pounds that Claire would find paint on whichever object Elgin chose to submit.

Theo grinned as he sealed the letter. Elgin would be unable to resist.

Days later, as Theseus plowed through his correspondence, his spirits rose. Elgin had accepted.

He swiveled on his seat. "Claire, love, be sure to bring your kit, including those dishes for paint samples."

"Why?" She straightened from examining the Aspasia bust.

"I have a surprise," Theseus said.

"Theo," she said with asperity. "I am as nervous as a cat without having to examine a strange sculpture."

He rose, taking her hands in his, and kissed her knuckles. "You shall enjoy the challenge, love, for your investigation shall not be left wanting. Trust me."

"I am not so sure."

He couldn't help but smile. "I am."

On the day of the presentation, Claire's nerves had reached unprecedented heights. Theo had hired men to be stationed around the hall, including his two Bow Street Runners, in hopes of trapping the perpetrators and quashing hecklers.

Claire imagined all that might go wrong as she stood beside Penny and Spyros offstage. As the audience filled the hall, people kept coming and coming. Her body tightened, her throat closing.

With relief, she spotted her family and Devonshire—friendly faces all. Sadly, the usual unpleasant suspects were there, too—Mr. Planta, Sir Joseph, Lord Elgin, the Earl of Egremont, and Lord Liverpool.

Tremors snaked through Claire, and Penny reached for her hand and squeezed.

"I am uncertain about this," she said with a whisper.

"Echoes of your earlier presentation, is all. Wholly understandable."

"Yes! I am terrified, Pens."

"Are you really?" she said, her voice droll. "Claire Ashworth, you have fended off kidnappers and fought off bandits. Think on *that*."

Claire inhaled deeply. On those occasions, she had neither wept nor fallen to pieces. Claire clenched the shard Theo had given her months ago. Her good luck charm. Penny was right, she was no wilting flower. "That worked a trick."

Her nerves settled until she saw something so astonishing, she froze. "Was that..." She raised a hand to her brow, then narrowed her eyes. "I fear I have lost my mind."

"Why is it?" Penny said.

"Look to the left, toward the back," Claire said.

Penny peered at the audience.

"I would swear..." Claire paused. "Is that not Theo's friend, Dionysius? You know, from Kastri."

"The antiques dealer?" Penny said.

"It is Dion," Spyros said, his tone dry.

Penny gasped. "Now I am for Bedlam, for I see Xanthe."

"Where?" Claire scanned the crowd.

Spyros gestured. "It *is* she, standing between Andreas and Dion."

"How are they *here*?" Claire noted all wore modern British clothing, the Pythia resembling a turbaned Englishwoman of indeterminate age. "*Why* are they here?"

Spyros slid his hands into his pockets. "Revenge."

"To observe the Garlands' capture?" Claire said.

Spyros remained silent.

Penny poked Claire. "Look, there are the Garlands and Helene. See? The maid just dropped her reticule, the man retrieving it, Garland."

"They shall pay." Spyros said through bared teeth.


Claire's talk was going well. The archer's bright colors had impressed the crowd, as did the krater, both accompanied by "oohs!" and "aahs!"

Aspasia was next, though the climax would be Theseus' surprise. Claire admitted to excitement along with a good dose of fear, though Theo was certain she would be successful. The surprise examination would buy them time offstage to switch busts.

Theseus neared, carrying the Greek Aspasia, and Claire launched into brief details, including Aspasia's history and Phidias' renowned work, the bust and herm likely a grave marker.

Claire had marked the marble with a light pencil, denoting color, and she lifted her pointer, noting spots of color—dark brown tucked in her forehead curls, black on her eyes, and a deep red for her lips. Her *himation*, or head covering, hid blue. "This is either lapis lazuli or Egyptian blue frit, which I also found on her *chiton*."

Chatter rose, making Claire pause. Aspasia's bust surprised the audience, for she'd never been seen in public.

Rhys and Theseus approached, her brother-in-law taking Aspasia offstage.

"Your surprise?" Claire said to Theo.

His pirate smile bloomed, eyes glittering with anticipation. He turned to the audience. "We have a surprise this evening for both you and for Lady Ashworth. Through the generosity of Lord Elgin and the British Museum, we present Lady Ashworth with a fragment of the Parthenon marbles for examination."

Nothing could have shocked Claire more. She had wanted to inspect the Parthenon marbles forever. Now she would do so...in front of several hundred men and women, including caricaturists and reporters. Heaven help her.

It took two men to carry a large sculpture across the stage, and they strained with effort. The marble was of a woman's torso, one thigh outthrust, both legs broken off at the knees, as well as missing her arms and head. A base of dark marble supported the piece, which they set atop the velvet laid across the table.

Theo, looking pleased as punch, kissed both cheeks and whispered. "You will find color. *I* did so before I made the bet."

Time passed, and murmurs arose as she tried to focus on her task. But with each passing minute and no resulting color, her nerves began to prickle her arms and shoulders. Theo had found color. Claire would too.

When she came to a crevice beneath the woman's breasts, she bent closer.

"Oh!" Claire smiled. She knew that precise color, faded though it was, and straightened to face the audience. "I have found Egyptian blue."

The crowd hushed.

With a smile, Claire took in the audience before she lifted her magnifier. The Garlands and Helene were gone.

Backstage, reassured that all was in place, Theseus hid, their plan to catch the Garlands in the act. If they failed, they would execute the second plan, for Lady Garland wanted the *Greek* Aspasia, not a Roman reproduction. The original depicted a bold, brave, and brilliant woman. Ironic—her ladyship echoed Aspasia not one bit.

"Purple!" Claire exulted, staring into the audience. "Egyptian blue and purple. These two colors will suffice to demonstrate that the Parthenon marbles were painted, as were many other Greek sculptures, friezes, and busts.

"In closing..." she said, to the audience's faint applause. The crowd streamed to the exits. How rude.

Xanthe, Andreas, and Dionysus remained, as did but a smattering of attendees. The crowd's silence evinced their disapproval, her hypothesis unconvincing. *Damn!*

"Thank you for your consideration," she concluded to the smattering of attendees. Claire traveled a rocky path, she reminded herself. She would persevere.

She walked down the stage steps toward Theseus, noting their Greek friends had gone.

"You were marvelous, as always," Theseus said. "You made a compelling case."

She snorted, tipping up her lips. "Thank you, but we both know the audience failed to be captured. Most of them, at least. Did you speak to our Greek friends?"

His expression was shocked. "I suspect your eyes were playing tricks on you, love."

"Spyros and Penny saw them as well."

As they exited the hall, Theseus grew contemplative. Perhaps he imagined they'd inhaled mist from the Pythian cave. Theseus helped her into their carriage, and she sat across from Spyros and Penny. "What happened backstage?"

Theseus huffed. "I was awaiting the thieves when a fire erupted near the side exit door. I called 'Fire!' then ran for the buckets of sand near the wings. A Runner and porter assisted in putting it out. We discovered a pile of refuse had been lit in a bin. When all was settled, the Roman Aspasia had vanished, presumably out the rear exit."

"No!"

"We expected something, and they delivered." He smiled. "I suspect the Roman copy will make them most unhappy. Let us proceed with Plan B."

It took two carriages piled high with luggage to carry them, their servants, and one large, unhappy dog to Wolf Court from Woodbine.

Poor Cullen. With the rocking and confinement, he whined until he heaved up his supper into the bowl Claire had set on the floor. Once complete, he returned to his cheerful self, thank heavens.

After two days, Theseus' estate appeared on the horizon, which was also hers. What a strange and wondrous thought.

The estate was beautiful, one of Devon's oldest, Ashworths having inhabited it from 1250 onward. Named for Woolacombe, which meant Wolves Valley, she'd loved its gardens, paths, and vistas, along with the house itself. It was said the vanished wolves of Woolacombe protected the family.

Theo told her the expansive manor had once been a humble cob with a thatched roof, Theseus' grandfather adding the library wing. Along with Theseus, Penny, and their staff, a dozen tenant farms worked the land.

Claire pictured her tomorrows with Theo, working side-by-side, having babies, projects, and adventures to share—a thrilling idea.

They pulled up before the pillared courtyard, travel-stained and weary, the servants having lined up, greeting them with warmth. As the manor's new mistress, she had much to learn, and she relished the challenge.

Spyros and Penny would remain until their trap was sprung. Though Penny sniffled occasionally, it seemed not as often as before their Greek trip. They had accepted Theo's offer of the Lifton house, but a four- to six-hour carriage ride away. Such a pleasing thought.

After dinner, they dismissed the servants to talk freely about trapping the Garlands.

"We shall hold an intimate soirée," Theseus said.

Claire laughed. "At least intimate by the *ton's* standards."

Late September, London would be abuzz with social activities, theaters reopening, and the political meetings that preceded Parliament's reopening.

"Given the time of year," Penny said. "I hope they come!"

"They will," Theo said. "We shall host thirty-five people or so, including some luminaries."

Spyros scratched his chin. "You believe the Greek bust will flush them out?"

"Yes," Theseus said. "Aspasia means something important to Lady Garland and to Helene as well. I suspect both are furious that they took the wrong bust."

"If I had stolen the bust, I would have made certain it was the right one," Penny said.

Claire shook her head. "In the hullabaloo, I doubt they had time to note the difference between the two, though I bet in the aftermath, they did." She turned to Spyros. "Did you speak with Xanthe and the others after my talk?"

He exchanged a glance with Penny, the kind couples make in silence that is an entire discussion.

"They will come to the soirée," Spyros said.

"I had hoped they returned to Greece," Claire said.

Spyros' oft-sunny demeanor darkened. "As I noted, they are here for revenge."

"*Christ*, Spyros," Theseus said. "They intend to kill the Garlands?"

"I suspect so." With care, Spyros laid down his knife and fork. "They have not included me in their plans."

"Murdering a peer and his wife on English soil," Claire said. "Disastrous."

Spyros shrugged, forking up a mouthful of beef and chewing with deliberation. His eyes shot to Theseus. "Perhaps."

"That is all you will say?" Theseus said. "*Perhaps*?"

The two men switched to Greek, their rapid-fire exchanges too swift for Claire, though Spyros had become red-faced, whilst Theseus grew grimmer. Both stood, shouting epithets at each other.

Claire slapped her hands on the table. "Both of you, stop this. We have much to do, and you both are acting like children."

They startled, but after exchanging nasty glances, they sat once again.

Claire made two dessert plates at the sideboard—syllabub, cheese, and raspberry soufflé, the scents delectable. She handed one to Theo as she returned to her seat. Yet anger and frustration remained thick in the air. Claire could not eat her soufflé fast enough.

"Shall we retire to the salon, Penny?" She stood and held out her hand. "Let us leave them to their...discussion."

Penny took her hand, and they swanned from the room. At least Penny would translate what the two had been arguing about.

# THIRTY-SIX

Penny settled into a comfortable salon chair, Claire pouring each a glass of port, then following suit.

"What were those two arguing about?" Claire said.

"Theseus was insisting they not allow the Greeks into the soirée."

Claire sipped her port. "How can we deny them entrance, particularly Xanthe?"

"It matters not how we feel about this," Penny said. "Our men will duke it out, verbally, I hope. If they come to blows, we will be left to clean up the mess."

Cullen rested his chin on Claire's thigh, that beggar. Those big golden eyes stared up at her, hope eternal. She had brought several chunks of beef wrapped in linen and offered Cullen a piece, which vanished instantly. She was amazed at the gentleness of those jaws —the wolfhound could easily bite off her hand. He was always tender with her, and she scratched his forehead in appreciation.

"No matter what Theseus says," Penny continued. "We must facilitate their entry."

Claire did not agree, nor would she deceive Theseus. "I agree with my husband and will not go against him."

Penny tilted her head. "But this is *Xanthe*."

Claire raised her palms. "Even so. Theo and I are honest with one another, and I would tell him of your plan."

Penny crossed her arms, huffed, then sighed. "I am honest with Spyros, too. But are there not times one must act at one's own discretion?"

"Of course." Claire slipped Cullen another treat. "This is not one of them, at least not for me."

Penny gave her a too-quick smile. "You are correct, and I will let it lie."

Claire didn't believe her for a minute.


Two weeks later, the event that evening, Claire put the finishing touches on her lecture. The setting would be Wolf Court's chestnut-paneled reception room with its triple-windowed walls and glass doors that opened onto the terrace. After her event and dinner, dancing would be held in the grand ballroom.

Mrs. Perkins, the housekeeper, seemed entirely competent, though this soiree was a first since Theseus had come into the title. Though her husband had led a private life, it was obvious the staff was up to the challenges. The manor bustled with energy.

In but a few hours, Claire's event would begin. Her head spun.

Eildih was helping her dress when Theseus appeared. He kissed her shoulder.

"I have never seen you this fraught, love."

"I have never put on a soirée and given a lecture to catch a killer," she said. "In truth, I have never organized anything at all. Now, family and important people arrive in two hours. I cannot seem to settle."

He cupped her face, his large hands warm and reassuring. "Having observed you in many a fraught situation, I know you are up to the task."

"I am so very glad one of us is."

The family arrived early, all looking weary yet excited, especially Henry and little Gareth. Holding Mama, hugging Lottie, and embracing Rose and the rest of them settled her nerves. She led them to the bright yellow salon, where tea was served. Much joy ensued, as if they had been apart for months rather than weeks.

How Claire loved them all. She knew some families were fractious or disgruntled. And while they argued on occasion, even engaging in fisticuffs, they dearly loved and supported each other, no matter the cause.

A blessing. One she would always cherish, particularly after the horrific years spent with Lord Fielding.

In what felt like minutes, guests poured in, a glittering array of peers, academics, antiquarians, and three Bow Street Runners disguised as attendees.

She and Theo stood on the portico greeting them, and when the Garlands' crested carriage appeared, fuzzy caterpillars raced up and down her spine. Claire looked to Theo, a solid presence beside her, a contained man, all thought and feeling wrapped tight within.

"We are ready for this," she said.

"More than ready, I would say. Your hands are cold."

She had dabbed lemongrass on her kerchief and lifted it to her nose, inhaling deep. Theo was here, and that was enough.

"Oh, my dear, have you a cold?" Lady Garland said as she ascended the steps, followed by his lordship and Helene.

The Garlands were dressed to the nines, excepting Helene in her black garb. Few women had brought their personal maids, yet Claire had been certain Helene would attend. There was something about the woman... An attitude? More. Rather a feeling she was deceiving them in some way. She turned again to the Garlands, but they were lost in the crowd.

Claire hastened to the formal drawing room, where beverages

and sundries were being served. She scanned the throng but saw no sign of the Greeks. Her chest eased.

Penny was speaking with Lady Ablethorp, having insisted upon inviting the noxious gossip. After exchanging greetings, Claire asked Lady Ablethorp to excuse Penny for a moment. The woman's eyes lit, sniffing for blood. Claire simply smiled and left with Penny in tow.

"I have not seen the Greeks," Claire said. "Have you?"

"Nor have I." Penny shook her head. "They will not give up."

"I know, *dammit!*" Claire said. "Look at Garland. He looks bored in the extreme."

Theo spoke with Lord Liverpool. He'd invited aristocrats and luminaries, feeling they would add gravitas, an additional lure for the Garlands.

Claire worried more about the Greeks. They were friends. If she could speak with them, explain their plan to bring the Garlands to justice, perhaps they would hold off on revenge. Much as she wished that were possible, Claire had her doubts.

Her mind turned to their plan, her prayers for its success intense. The Greek bust of Aspasia sat in an anteroom, off the reception room where she would give her talk. Before her presentation was the perfect opportunity to steal it, for it appeared unguarded.

Her watch read a mere fifteen minutes until her lecture. She rubbed a thumb across her gloved palm.

All thirty-five guests had been contained in the formal drawing room, and anyone leaving, whether for the retiring room or outside for a smoke, was shadowed by one of their people. Few had exited, including the Garlands.

Penny took her hand. "I am nervous as a cat."

"My palms are sweaty," Claire said.

"I prefer bandits, with their straightforward attack, rather than this game of cat-and-mouse."

Thoughts of the bandits and her actions that day stiffened Claire's spine. The waiting shredded her nerves. She looked at Theo talking to Rhys and nodded, slipping her hand into her pocket for her good-luck shard.

"*Fustian!*" she said.

"What?" Penny said.

"The shard Theo gave me is gone." She'd placed it on a shelf when she'd been hunting for lavender in the butler's pantry. She'd best hurry. "I must fetch it, for we begin soon."

"Now?"

"It is my good luck, Pens. I must have it."

IT SEEMINGLY TOOK FOREVER to make it to the pantry, as numerous guests halted her progress for small talk. She made it to the bustling kitchen and rounded a corner to unlock the butler's pantry.

Cursing the lack of light, Claire considered fetching a lantern as her hand groped along a shelf for the shard.

Footsteps, but there. Was that a white edge overhanging the shelf? Her fingers felt for the marble. Got it.

Movement over her shoulder. The butler.

Her fingers gripped the shard, and she slipped it into her pocket. Relief. Claire turned to hasten to the reception room.

A large shadow, hunchbacked, stepped into the light.

Pain blinded her.

CLAIRE'S HEAD pulsed in time with a rhythmic sway, insisting she awaken. She lay on her belly, the surface greasy and rank. She moved her right hand, except her hands were tied. Bollocks!

She was in a moving vehicle, a carriage most likely. Not good. She knew who had taken her, but why they had done so eluded her. How stupid.

Claire fluttered her lids, but before she opened them, she assessed, the dull pain making her thinking muzzy. She'd been hunting for Theo's shard, seen a hunched figure, then agony. Someone had coshed her on the head! No wonder it hurt like blazes.

Claire slit open her eyes. A black bombazine skirt pooled in front of her. Helene. She'd bet the Garlands sat across from the maid, facing Claire's back.

How had staff not seen her abduction? Not that it mattered, that hammer in her brain unrelenting.

On the seat beside Helene sat Aspasia, an arm wrapped around the herm.

Claire inhaled deep, furious and frustrated. Perhaps there was something about the Phelands that shouted "kidnap!" Her sister had been a prisoner of a madman for several weeks. This trio must be equally loopy to take her.

Unlike Lottie's case, where the kidnapper wanted *her*, Claire's abduction felt opportunistic. Easy enough to have murdered her in the butler's pantry. Most likely, she was insurance of some kind. Delightful.

The atmosphere was tense. Given the proprietary way Helene held the bust, it could be she, not the Garlands, who steered this monstrous ship.

A shiver coursed through her, and she reached for her knife, the one always strapped to her thigh. Easy enough to acquire it via the opening in her dress pocket...if her hands were not tied. They *had* bound them in front. Stupid.

She might access her knife with both hands if only her head didn't pound like an anvil. Again, Claire found herself fading to black.

Theseus might be frantic, but no one would know, for he strode through Wolf Court barking orders to mount Claire's rescue party.

*Christ*, he wished... Wishes did nothing.

Cullen appeared and placed a paw on his thigh. He yipped—out of character for the wolfhound. He was as alarmed as Theseus.

Out the window, horses stood at the ready, Hawthorne mounted and strapped in. He stared into Cullen's black eyes. "Can you find her, boy?"

The dog looked back.

"Come." He whooshed out a breath. "Let us find your mistress."

Claire awakened again, fully aware. She pushed up on her elbows before she vomited on herself. Once done, she swiped her bound arms across her mouth, then scooched away from the mess. "What are you people *doing*?"

A snort from Helene. "Is it not obvious?"

Ignoring Helene, she spoke to the Garlands. "Might I have some water?"

Garland produced a silver flask and put it to her lips. She spat out the first sip, but the second tasted heavenly, a third setting her to rights.

"Thank you." She swiveled to glare at Helene. "No, it is not obvious why you have taken me, considering a posse thunders behind us."

Helene's face turned hard, and she lifted her chin. "I shall take note." She slid a hand behind her back and withdrew a large, shiny knife, aiming it at Claire. "There really is no point in keeping you alive."

Frances gasped. "Do not be absurd, Helene. Her capture will ensure we remain free."

"Will it?" Helene smiled. "Poor Ashworth would be crushed by the death of his bride. What a pleasant thought. Her neck is almost as tender as that Greek girl's was." She ran a finger down Claire's neck.

Claire turned her head and bit the finger, hard, which resulted in a fist to her temple, making her reel, her stomach again heaving. The carriage lurched over a bump, jostling Claire further.

"Why in God's name you rented a hack, Garland, I will never know." Helene crossed her arms. "Couldn't you have acquired something more unobtrusive?"

Garland waved a hand. "I say, what is more unobtrusive than a hack?"

"True," Helene said with disgust. "Were we in *London*."

Claire went to rise, seeking a more comfortable and less odiferous position.

Helene's booted foot punched her back down.

"You are awful human beings," Claire said. "All three of you."

The Garlands looked away, but Helene just shrugged. "Tossing such unkind words at your sister...so sad."

"You are no more my sister than Garland is."

Helene waggled a finger, wearing a smile, the first Claire could recall from the woman. It transformed her sour face to beautiful, resembling... Helene leaned forward, a necklace dangling, its focal point the seal hidden amongst the ruching. Penny's recollection had been right.

"Do you not see the resemblance?" Helene continued. "The proper term is half-sister, for I am the get of the dead Lord Ashworth and a Greek village woman."

Claire sucked in a breath. Helene had truly shocked her. Theseus' sister? Yet... "Who? What village, exactly?"

A sly smile rose on Helene's lips. "Though I was born in Dimitsana, in the mountainous Peloponnese region, Mama is descended from a long line of Cretan nobles."

"Is that so?" Claire said, weaving disbelief into her words.

Helen set the knife beside her, lifted her necklace, and leaned forward. "See this?"

Claire said nothing.

"It is a Cretan seal, passed down through generations to me. On my mother's side, I am as noble as any Ashworth."

"How fascinating," Claire said.

"I belong at Wolf Court."

"Why not tell Lord Ashworth of this?" Claire said. "He could make things right or better, at least."

Helene sneered. "When my mother presented us at my father's

estate—I was but six—that arsehole turned us away. With all our funds gone, we were forced to remain in England. I never forgot, can still see that cruel man who rejected us."

"The current Lord Ashworth would have welcomed you." Claire tried to imagine her impoverished life and failed. A hard one, she was sure.

"Ashworth?" Lady Garland said. "He most certainly would *not* have,"

"You cannot be sure of that," Garland said.

"He is an earl, Garland."

They knew Theseus not at all, for he would have helped his sister. But Helene was blinded by her birth, her difficult childhood, and Ashworth Elder's rebuff.

"It was you who spearheaded the theft and murders," Claire said. "Was it not, Helene?"

"What do you think?" Helene said with sarcasm, looking proud of her "accomplishments."

"And Aspasia?" As Claire held their attention, she moved both hands to her pocket in hopes of reaching her knife.

"We have a buyer," Helene said. "He is paying a king's ransom for the authentic Greek bust. *Not* the Roman copy."

She had been wrong, at least partially, about the trio's motivation. The Garlands wanted money, but Helene wanted more—revenge. The tips of Claire's fingers touched the leather handle, and a thrill went through her. Sliding her hands lower, she wrapped both around the handle and began withdrawing it from its sheath.

"Lift her onto the seat, Garland," Helene said in a commanding voice.

"Why in heaven's name?" Garland's voice was thready, his foot tapping a staccato rhythm on the floor.

"God may forgive your sins," Claire said to him. "I will not."

CHAPTER
# THIRTY-SEVEN

"We kill her, of course," Helene said. "Given their obvious affection, her death will crush Ashworth. Lift her!"

Garland did as requested, hefting Claire onto the seat beside Helene.

"You stink," Helene said.

Claire grinned. "The better to annoy you."

Locks of hair had fallen from Claire's coiffure, and Helene gripped them in one hand, forcing her head back, neck exposed.

Helene lifted the gleaming knife.

*God above*, the woman was going to slit her throat. Claire stuttered in a stuttered breath, groping for something clever to stay her execution. Theo would be devastated. So would Mama and Lottie... Others, too, and poor Cullen. Was this really happening?

She'd had to release her knife when Garland lifted her. No time to retrieve it. She must do *something*.

"No," Garland said in a firm voice.

Helene's eyes burned when she looked at him—madness, loathing...lust. She released Claire's hair to pat the seat, giving him a coquettish look. "Then come sit beside me."

Helene slid the bust to the floor beneath her skirts. Garland gave his wife a glance, her mouth open in shock.

"What an odd request." Frances took Garland's arm. "Really."

"Is it?" Helene said, her fiery gaze fixed on the viscount.

Frances looked between the two. "What exactly is this?"

Garland huffed, drew away from Frances to switch seats, squeezing between Helene and the side of the coach.

"You two are lovers," Claire blurted out.

Garland paled, but Helene smirked. "We are."

Frances' shock turned to anger. "How dare you both! Garland, how could you?"

His expression sheepish, he shrugged. "She offered me something you cannot, Frances."

Frances slapped her husband, then turned to smack Helene, who caught her wrist.

"I suggest not, Frances." Helene squeezed, and Frances jerked her wrist away.

Claire had stepped into a melodrama. Her bound hands rested on her lap, and she moved them across her skirt to the pocket.

"We proceed as planned," Helene said.

"No, we will not!" Frances said.

Helene pointed her knife at Frances. "Shut up, or Garland might use his gun."

"Alfred?"

The man nodded, cheeks flushed, one foot tapping the floor.

Helene wrapped Claire's hair in an iron grip, again pulling her close. Claire shook her head, moved her body, kicked.

Helene punched her temple. "Stop that. Hold her down, Garland. She's squirming too much for me to get a good cut."

She spit, hitting Helene's face, a burst of satisfaction just as Garland pressed her down on the bench.

"Bitch!" Helene drew back her knife.

*Boom!*

The coach lurched, Claire tumbling from the seat. When she

lifted her face, Helene slumped against the Garland, dark eyes wide, staring at nothing. Blood streamed down her face from the hole in her forehead.

Claire's stomach lurched, and she swallowed hard.

Frances screamed.

Garland shoved Helene to the floor, his pistol aimed here, there, and everywhere.

Outside, Dionysius atop a horse, Xanthe riding pillion behind him, smoke wreathing his gun.

Relief burst through Claire, making her giddy, when the door flew open to reveal Andreas, his pistol pointed at Garland. Frances fainted.

"Care to try, my lord?" Dionysus leaned down from his horse, his gun also aimed at Garland. "I would love the opportunity to end you here. Set your pistol on the floor with care."

Garland looked to Frances, now blinking to consciousness. When Garland did nothing, she hissed, "Do what he says."

Once he complied, Dionysius swung his right leg over the horse's neck and slid to the ground, his pistol barrel never leaving the viscount. He helped the Pythia to the ground, then approached the coach.

"My Lady Ashworth." He nodded to Claire. "Please come here."

She rose to her feet, staggered a bit, and moved toward the door. Dion's gun never leaving Garland, he wrapped one arm around Claire's waist and lifted her from the carriage. She swayed, and Andreas took point while Dionysus held her upright.

She held out her hands, and he cut her bindings. Pins and needles rushed to her hands, and she gritted her teeth until the prickles subsided. To her surprise, Xanthe now sat inside the coach pointing a huge pistol at the Garlands.

"Theseus will be here soon." Claire's voice sounded reedy and small. "He will."

Dion tossed her a jaunty grin. "We are quite aware, my lady."

Andreas climbed to the driver's bench and took up the reins.

"The coachman?" she said, peering up at him.

"We left him back there." Andreas waved a hand. "Somewhere. He is fine."

Claire would not die today. She was saved, and she became wobbly all over again.

Garland's hand shot out as if to knock the Pythia's pistol away.

Xanthe shot him, her expression serene.

Garland screamed, and his hand flew to the injury.

"Our Pythia is also a warrior," Dionysius said with a smirk. "You have been but winged. Nothing serious, old man."

"Nothing serious!" Garland said. "The woman shot me, and I am bleeding!"

"As you, sir, intended to harm her."

"I just meant to take her pistol."

Claire snorted.

Dion gave his horse's reins to Claire and walked to the carriage.

She tried. She really did, but her legs crumpled, and she flopped to the ground. At least she still held the reins.

Dion lifted Aspasia's bust from within and set it beside Claire on the ground, then slammed the coach door closed.

He crouched beside her. "Water." Then he mounted the driver's bench beside Andreas.

"Wait," Claire said. "What are you doing? Where are you going?"

"Theseus will arrive soon," Dionysus said. "He is not far behind."

"Forgive us for leaving!" Andreas flicked the reins, and the coach moved forward.

"Come back!" Claire scrambled to her feet.

"Tell our old friend we shall see him soon!" Dion hollered, wearing a grin. "*Ελευθερία ή θάνατος!*"

*Freedom or death.* The coach's plume of dust grew faint, then disappeared.

She leaned against the horse, thankfully a calm one, and made a rude gesture at the vanished coach. She'd learned it in Kastri, and she liked it.

A chill breeze tickled her neck. The horse munched grass. Birds twittered, and small rustlings came from the trees. Her fingers dug into the leather saddle, head pounding, nerves fractious. Tears welled. She wanted to go home.

*Where was Theo? Why wasn't he here?*

How stupid. Whining helped nothing. How to get home. Claire leaned against the horse, clutched the saddle, and lifted her left foot. Damn, but the beast was tall, her foot failing to reach the stirrup. She would try again. Her right hand gripped the cantle while her left raised her leg higher, and she slid her foot into the stirrup. More panting as she rested for a moment.

Reins tight in her left hand, Claire grasped the saddle's skirt, gave a huge hop, and swung her right leg over the horse.

Except her leg fell back to the ground, the left foot dangling from the stirrup, nearly upending her. Unable to mount the horse on her own, she pulled her foot from the stirrup to look for a rock or log she might stand on. The grass was smooth, the trees spindly. Nothing in sight.

She collapsed onto the grass beside the sculpture. At least she still held the horse's reins.

In her haste to escape, she had forgotten about Aspasia!

She patted Aspasia. Claire couldn't leave the precious object in the open. The heavy-boned bay continued to chew grass.

She must try again. Perhaps if she attached Aspasia to the horse's saddle...if only she had some rope.

"Bollocks!" Her eyes burned. She could not secure Aspasia or achieve the bay's back. Tears erupted, and she told herself to stop it. *Just stop it.*

A yip!

Cullen and Theseus thundered from the wood at a gallop.

Her heart beat triple time. She was *home*. Claire pulled herself to a stand using the stirrup, determined to present a composed woman.

Theseus spotted her, and his expression transformed from feral to profound relief. Cullen reached her first, and she braced herself on the horse as Cullen leapt, slapping his paws on her shoulders, his tongue lapping her face.

"Down, Cullen!" Theseus said.

Her pup obeyed.

Theo flung himself from the saddle and wrapped her in a fierce hold.

ARRIVING HOME, the uproar was expected, yet someone unexpected took her hand. Thomasina.

Sina's blue eyes spoke of peace and safety, which calmed her further.

"Give her some air, *dammit!*" Theseus said.

They jumped back, except for Sina, who offered her a drink, the water, with its soothing chamomile and peppermint, perfect. She must tell Theo about Helene, yet she hadn't quite the energy.

"More?" Susannah said in that gentle voice of hers.

Claire nodded, and in barreled Lottie, enveloping her in another hug.

"You look about to pop, dear sister." She patted Lottie's medicine-ball belly.

Lottie laughed. "Not for a while yet."

Before anyone could ask what happened, the women whisked her to their suite. There, they tended her wounds, the head pounding lessening, bested by profound exhaustion.

"I think I must lie down."

They exchanged her dress for her nightrail, drew back the covers, and eased her onto the bed. Mama drew the covers up to her chin. "I never wish to experience that fear again, my dear Claire."

She dug up a smile. "Nor do I, Mama."

Someone set a steaming mug by the bed, and she sipped. Strawberries and mint. Claire soon warmed from inside out, and she took in her gathered beloveds—Penny, Mama, and Lottie, Susannah and Thomasina, and Rose.

These were mighty women, a smile formed recalling their victorious battle against Lottie's kidnapper. These sweet, loving women were fierce as hell. And so was she.

CHAPTER

# THIRTY-EIGHT

Theseus sat in the sculpture room, now empty but for a few busts, a stele, and a *kouros,* his thoughts dark and disturbing. He was not a man who feared easily, having grown up in a world where guns or knives might appear at any moment, held by men who wished to steal what they had unearthed from the Greek soil. The Peninsula had hardened him further until even the bandits atop Parnassus failed to ruffle his presence of mind.

Claire's disappearance proved an altogether different matter, the horror at discovering her in murderous hands yet to recede. He spoke with her often, followed her around until she objected to his hovering, and held her through the night, only releasing her when he got the shakes.

Somehow, his heart and body failed to comprehend what his mind understood—Claire was home and safe.

Theseus wished to please her, to delight her, to assure her she would always be safe.

Yet had he not done so before? That had proved to be a lie.

She was his *to asteri mu.* Would that he could gift her a firmament of stars to show how much her love meant. Baubles, jewels, even sculptures were well enough, but they would signify little. No, he must find something meaningful.

A thought. Yes, he liked that very well and went in search of Susannah, finding her in an oft-occupied nook, writing.

"Lady Susannah." He bowed. "Do not rise, please."

"Might I help you with something, Lord Ashworth?" she said.

"You are a writer, correct?"

Her smile was shy. "I try."

"I wish you to compose a piece for the newspapers."

"My work is fiction. I am no journalist."

"I understand," he said. "Think of it as, say, a part of your novel or some such."

She tilted her head. "You have speechmakers galore here—Patrick, Rhys, Devonshire. I do not—"

"I want this kept between you and myself. I think you shall enjoy the composition."

Susannah grinned. "I shall do my best."

That evening, Theo sat beside her bed reading aloud *Cecilia* by Frances Burney when Claire laid her hand on the open book.

Everything hurt, as if she'd tumbled from her horse, but she must tell Theo Helene's truth. How would he react? Would he be crushed? Angry? Disinterested? No, not that.

"I have news that I have held back," she said. "Rather shocking news, actually."

Eyes questioning, he closed the book. "What might that be, love? I would say we have had shocks aplenty."

"I am afraid this one will set you back." Claire told him of his half-sister and his father's perfidy.

"A pox on my father!" He lunged across the room, fists clenched, to stand motionless by the balcony doors. "That cad is still causing havoc years after his death. How could he turn away his child, my half-sister?"

Theseus met the usual setbacks with a moment's ire, swiftly

overtaken by a calm logic that sought a solution. But when emotion overcame him, his silence turned profound. She'd seen the latter only once, in Greece, after she nearly slipped off a precipice.

"Theo?"

His chest billowed, fists unclenching and clenching.

"Theseus, do come back."

He clasped his hands behind him and returned, eyes empty of emotion.

"Your father behaved monstrously." Claire ran a hand down his arm.

"That does not excuse Helene's evil." He scrubbed his face. "Funny, I saw hints of the familiar with Helene twice, though they failed to focus. Perhaps a mannerism of Penny's or an expression of my own? I know not, but a spark in me saw a resonance in her. At the time, I failed to understand its meaning."

"I never saw it," Claire said. "Nor, had you seen the connection, would it have made a difference. Helene was fixed on her course of revenge long before you met." She tugged him down to the chair.

He bent forward, elbows on knees. "I feel ill. How different things would be had my father acknowledged her."

"Perhaps or perhaps not," Claire said. "Theo, look at me."

He did, and she saw a mix of sorrow and fury in his eyes.

"From all you have said, your father never would have."

"No, but *I* would."

Claire leaned over the edge of the bed to brush her lips across his. "I told Helene so, but she did not believe me."

THE FOLLOWING days saw the Bow Street Runners and a good dozen additional men on the hunt for the Greeks and the Garlands. So far, they were out of luck.

That afternoon, Claire descended the stairs almost herself, her aches fading along with her fear. Impossible to be afraid when Theo held her through the night.

Theseus stood tall and strong at the foot of the staircase, his eyes warm and welcoming. Claire's heart trilled. She was the luckiest of women.

"I have word." Theo held out a hand, led her to his study, and closed the door. Spyros and Penny sat in comfortable chairs before the crackling fire, holding hands. Theo walked her to the settee, and they sat, a paper resting on the table before them. He leaned back, crossed his arms, and told his sister and her new husband of Helene's parentage and his father's execrable behavior.

"How could Father do that?" Penny said. "To our sister, his daughter." She wiped at her tears.

"A messenger arrived this morning," Theseus said. "No name is attached to the missive, but we know it to be from our Greek friends."

He handed Claire the paper. "The Garlands are dead, buried at sea along with Helene's remains."

"They simply tossed them overboard?" Penny said.

"I believe so," Claire said. "I quote, 'Given to Poseidon.'"

"Their ship was Greek," Spyros said. "No one aboard would interfere."

Penny shivered. "All murderers, true, but their deaths chill my bones."

"As it does mine," Claire said. "The Greeks gave them no quarter."

"Nor should they have," Spyros said. "They addressed the murder of two villagers. It could end no other way."

"The Greeks learned much," Theseus said. "They have shared their information with us."

Claire's hand slipped into Theo's.

"Bow Street has submitted a report regarding Helene," Theseus said. "An industrious higher-up at Phillips & Son, an auction house known for contemporary art sales, thought Phillips should enter the antiquities business. Helene was a catalogue writer and occasional appraiser at Phillips."

"Not at Ashley's?" Spyros said.

"No," Claire said. "We assume Helene left her employment and chose Ashley's as she was unknown to them."

"Interesting." Penny nodded. "Given her sad beginnings, Helene rose far above her station and did well for herself at Phillips. What precipitated her actions now?"

"The house official promised a hefty finder's fee for any antiquities deemed worthy." Claire looked at Theseus. "She hated the Ashworths enough to risk her good standing."

"Who is this person at Phillips?" Spyros said, thunder in his voice.

"The man has left for parts unknown." Theo paused. "I would lay odds the Greeks suggested he disappear."

"Given her interest in all that was Ashworth," Claire said. "Helene discovered Theseus' journey and its purpose. The Garlands would frequent Phillips, which is where we believe they became known to one another. Lord Garland's disastrous gaming pursuits were out of control, and they needed money, but it was Helene who orchestrated the scheme and found Aspasia's buyer."

"The deaths they caused," Penny said, cheeks flushed. "Nomiki's. So needless."

Claire's heart sighed, pained by Nomiki's and Georgios' deaths. She knew too well how money or the lack thereof could drive a person.

"I am saddened by it all," Claire said.

"I suspect Garland was along for the ride," Theseus said.

"Perhaps," Claire said. "His and Helene's affair remains perplexing."

Penny's gaze grew distant. "I wonder if she planned to do away with Lady Garland and assume her position."

"Helene was ruthless." Spyros gave her a wan smile. "I suspect that was her intention."

Theseus rose. "Come, let us join the family."

When they arrived at the salon, Claire rocked back on her heels.

Each family member sat or stood reading a newspaper. How very odd.

"Why are you all reading newspapers?" Claire strode into the room.

Beside her, Theo remained solemn. "An important bit of news."

Rose looked up, a twinkle in her eye. "I think you shall like the article, Claire."

"I find it quite satisfying," Agnes said. "Do you not, Milo, Arthur?"

A fat stack of newspapers sat on the sideboard, and Claire retrieved one.

*Lady Ashworth Kidnapped!* shrieked the headline. "This is dreadful, Theo."

His pirate grin flashed. "Read on, *αστέρι μου*."

Claire tilted her head but did as asked.

*When kidnapped, Lady Ashworth was presenting a symposium on the nature of Greek statues, detailing how the Greeks painted them with color. Though many at the event were skeptical, including Lord Liverpool and other luminaries, Lady Ashworth's sterling presentation stunned the guests and convinced them all.*

The article continued, and while it did address her kidnapping—though naming no perpetrators—it also inserted information on her research and thesis.

Theo flung himself into a chair, seemingly both discomfited and pleased. "This has appeared in *The Times, The Morning Chronicle, The Morning Post, The Observer,* and *The Courier,*"

Auntie peeked above her paper. "I expect many others will carry the story as well."

Thoughts swirled amidst a giddy euphoria, Claire realizing the meaning behind the article. People would be attracted by its salacious headline, but they would learn of her research, which was now out in the world.

"*You* sent the article to the London papers," Claire said.

Theo nodded, color flushing his cheeks.

She sat beside him and kissed his cheek. "Thank you."

"Susannah composed the piece," he said, with a glance to Rhys' sister. "I am not much good at writing this sort of thing."

"Theo, *everyone* will know of my thesis, including those antiquarian skeptics at the Society."

"I suspect so." His grin was sheepish.

She slid onto his lap and leaned against him. "You beloved man, doing this for me. Whether anyone believes the truth or no, my research is out in the world."

"For all to see and, perhaps, for some to believe." He bussed her cheek.

Joy bubbled inside her, and Claire spoke with certainty. "Whether they now believe or not, I shall pass down my notes, the paint samples, the maquette, and the *krater* to our children. There will come a time when the world sees the truth of the matter."

"I love you, my star," Theseus said.

She tossed him a saucy look. "I love you more."

His lips thinned. "No, you do not."

"Yes, I do."

"Indeed, you do not love me more than I love you." Though his face tightened to stern lines, his eyes danced with laughter.

Lottie started to giggle, Thomasina chiming in, and then all of them were laughing, Arthur chittering, whilst Cullen and Milo yipped for all they were worth.

Theseus cupped her cheeks, his face intense. "There shall be no more talk of who loves whom more, though it is obviously me."

He took her lips in a fierce kiss, and the world fell away.

# EPILOGUE

The weather was glorious when they landed at the island of Santorini, one of the Cyclades islands, the sculptural white buildings with bright blue doors and roofs stealing Claire's breath.

The following morning at the charming inn Claire had booked, they took breakfast in the *taverna*, a meal that replicated many eaten in Kastri.

Theo held out her chair. "This surprise of yours is quite daring, love."

"You have given me so much, Theo." She bit her lip. "I knew it was a risk, but you mentioned never having traveled here. I wished to surprise you with something worthy, a gift of the heart."

He froze, like a hare caught in the open, his stoic face masking a powerful emotion.

A vase depicting a squid caught Claire's attention, and she walked to get a closer look.

Its narrow stem stood on a small round base, widening to a large bowl with handles on each side. She reached to touch it, then fisted her hand, knowing she should not.

"Theseus, is this not remarkable?"

He'd followed to stand beside her, wrapping an arm around her waist. "Quite unusual."

"I wonder what treasures we shall find here."

He chuckled. "I have already found mine. Come, let us eat our breakfast and be on our way."

With Spyros' help, Claire had arranged for them to fly a pair of kestrels, and though she had done a bit of hawking since their return to Wolf Court, today felt different. Magical. After several hours, they said their farewells, both light of heart and sweaty.

Claire peered at the map she'd received from Spyros, who'd helped her arrange the trip. "We go this way."

The sun blazed as they climbed a hill, their eyes scanning the terrain for anything unusual—a shard, an odd shape, a color protruding from the stones.

"I have a surprise," Claire said, reaching the top of the hill. "If you are willing to leave off our exploration for a few hours."

"Mysterious." Theo offered his pirate's grin and held out his hand.

Claire led him on a seemingly endless trek, climbing hill after hill, to traipse down a goat path, thankful for her sturdy boots. Hills rose on their right, while a drop to the sea plummeted to their left. Another glance at her map, and they wound them down and up and down again, Claire gripping Theseus' hand tight until they came to level ground.

Before them, the translucent sea lapped the sand beneath a lazuline sky. Theo carried a small knapsack that included her pastels and sketchpad. Later she would capture the setting, now they would swim.

To their right arched a cave with shafts of light pouring through to the sea from holes dotting its roof.

"I thought we might have a swim." She began unbuttoning her bodice.

"But..." Theo stared at her wide-eyed. "I am truly shocked, my lady."

She trilled a laugh. "The cove is hidden, with no one about. We can see anyone coming, either from the sea or land. At least, that is what Spyros said."

He raised a brow, a smile in his eyes. "And you trust him?"

"Implicitly!"

Theseus loved swimming nude, as she had learned from their journeys to the hidden pond at Wolf Court. The sea was even better.

Claire removed her straw bonnet.

"Here, give me that," Theo said. "I will place it out of the wind."

She handed it to Theo and slipped off her bodice, skirt, stockings, and boots, placing them on a rock. Turning back, all breath vanished. Theseus stood naked before her, imposing and glorious in his strength and beauty, smiling at her with half-lidded eyes.

Claire could barely wait to touch him.

Her chemise fell away, and the breeze sang across her flesh. Theo strode to her with purpose.

She held out a hand. "Shall we, my handsome husband?"

"Indeed, love." He leaned forward to brush his lips with hers. "You, Claire Cassandra Pheland Ashworth, are my greatest find of all."

She pressed a hand to his cheek. "As you are mine."

They stared into each other's eyes, turned to the sea, and jumped.

# POSTSCRIPT

PRESENT DAY

Time to go.

Cassie hated flying from California all the way to Germany, a seemingly endless journey. But it was a must-do for her mission. On the floor, beneath the seat in front, sat a heavy-duty pet carrier, silent, given it held no animal. But precious, nonetheless.

Rain accompanied her afternoon arrival in Munich, an imposing city, and she shouldered the heavy carrier, rolling her overnight bag. Cassie found a taxi, and headed to the offices of Ulrike Koch-Brinkmann and Vinzenz Brinkmann, researchers who had made their study of the polychromy on ancient marbles their life's work, their exhibition, "Gods in Color," touring the world. Cassie had only seen the exquisite images online.

That the Greeks painted their ancient marbles was now the norm, but those in power during Lady Ashworth's day had mocked the possibility.

Cassie had an appointment, and when she pulled open the door to the large building, she closed her eyes and took a deep breath. At last she would fulfill Claire Ashworth's final request.

Inside the Department of Antiquities and Asia at the Liebieghaus

Skulpturensammlung, Cassie read the gold-lettered sign for the office suites. The Brinkmanns were on the second floor, and she soon stood before the mahogany door and raised her fist. Cassie hesitated, biting her lip, then knocked.

A silver-haired woman opened the door—Ulrike. They'd corresponded, and she'd seen her photo online.

Mrs. Koch-Brinkmann welcomed her inside, a middle-aged woman with gloriously curly hair and a kind smile. "Vinzenz will return in fifteen minutes or so. We have both been eager to meet you. We are intrigued."

Her accented English was thick but easily understood. Paint samples, a few sculptures, and many drawings occupied the large main room. Ulrike indicated a table.

Cassie set down the pet carrier. "Do you mind, if we wait for Herr Brinkmann before I open the carrier?"

Mrs. Koch-Brinkmann nodded. "Do call me Ulrike. Waiting is only proper." She smiled. "I have both tea and coffee, as well as scones, an addiction I developed while visiting England."

"Coffee would be wonderful," Cassie said, feeling rather shy. "And I love scones, too."

As Cassie bit down on her second cinnamon scone, Vinzenz breezed in, a handsome middle-aged man full of energy.

She rose, and greetings were exchanged, first names requested. The Brinkmanns cleared of all but her precious carrier. When ready, Cassie unzipped the lid. Aromas from dozens of old leather-bound journals and loosely bound paper wafted up. Claire reached inside, a few tired paper flecks falling to the table as she set the stacks on its surface.

"As I said in my email," Cassie said. "They are my ancestor's notes, but before you read them, I'd like to show you some images." She pulled out her phone and found the pictures.

"These pieces have been passed down in the family. I have the maquette, while my brother has the *krater*." She also had Claire's prized shard, a gift from her husband, Theseus. Cassie's good luck charm, as it had been Claire's. That, she kept private. "My brother and I shall soon return them to Greece, the world now knowing the truth of polychromy."

She handed her phone to Ulrike, who gasped and then showed her husband.

His eyes widened. "How did your ancestor come to possess these? I have seen a similar krater, one was discovered early in the twentieth century."

Cassie detailed Lady Claire's first visit to Kastri, though she had taken many more with Theseus after the revolution, and meeting Xanthe, the Delphic Oracle.

"Incredible," Ulrike said.

"Particularly the maquette," Vinzenz said. "The life-sized Trojan archer was found on Aegina in the Temple of Aphaia. We have re-created him in color." He laughed. "He is said to be Paris, the Trojan who stole Helen away."

"Your ancestor was not alone," Ulrike said. "At first, we were met with much skepticism. How splendid are these!"

"Her ladyship made copious notes, as you can see," Cassie said. "These journals and papers include her research, her chip samples, and her thesis that the Greeks painted their work. Her ladyship often mentions her husband, who supported her endeavors. He was a unique man of his time."

"I know of Theseus Ashworth, a noted antiquarian," Vinzenz said. "Though I've read several of his papers, ones that mention polychromy, I have never come across anything on his wife's archeological studies."

"She was ignored, laughed at, and placated," Cassie said. "By most. Some, a very few, believed."

Herr Brinkmann opened a journal, sending its chocolate, smoke, and earth scents to her nose. He read while Ulrike took another journal. Cassie had read them many times.

"Her ladyship was prescient." Vinzenz glanced up.

"She was," Cassie said, eager to hear more. She waited...and waited.

"*Ach du meine Güte!*" Vinzenz said. "This is a treasure trove!"

"That it is." Ulrike waved a page. "Why did you not bring this to a museum?"

Cassie shrugged. "The British Museum and the London Society of Antiquaries were particularly unkind to Lady Ashworth. It is you who have brought polychromy to the forefront. You deserve these documents."

"We are both humbled and thankful," Vinzenz said.

Ulrike slipped a hand over hers. "Thank you, Cassandra. And many thanks to your ancestor, as well."

Cassie breathed deep as she left, rolling her carry-on, her eyes burning with the completion of her task. Tomorrow, she would lunch with the Brinkmanns and take a personal tour of the painted marbles in-house.

*Ah, my dear Claire and Theo, I wish you were here to see this.* Who knows, perhaps they were looking down from on high.

Cassie laughed and waved down a taxi.

# Acknowledgments

My readers are so special, and I thank you all for your support, enthusiasm, and daily inspiration! You're the best!

I appreciate those who shepherded *THE SEER* to the finish line. Mmy matchless editor, Aria Jones, again worked her wizardry. No matter the genre, Aria is superb at what she does!

To the extraordinary Camille Cotton—this book wouldn't exist without you. To the amazing Rosemary Hill, whose friendship, aid, and insights are both invaluable and inspirational. To Monica Enderle Pierce—for your fabulous aid.

To my much-loved Betas: Ro, Camille, Joanie, Wayne, and Vivi and to Lorelai—who brings me joy through the sweat and tears.

To Eleanor Brindle, whose attention to detail is unparalleled, as is her friendship.

To my exceptional cover artist, Blake Ricciardi, aided by Mike Le, Juan Diaz, and Jorge Alvarez—my dream cover was turned into reality by you. Thank you!

To Parris Afton Bonds, who hugs my soul, and my Yoga and Trivia pals— you keep me sane and laughing.

To Andrea , Suzanne , Pat , Donna , CJ , and Linda—love you. To Betsy , Georgi , Alison , and Karen for your love and friendship. To Cynthia , for your friendship and giving Cranberry love.

To Peter, Kathleen, Summer and George—your love and support make my world turn. Love you! Finally, to my beloved boys, Blake and Ben—for all that you are, for all that you have gifted me, and for all your abiding love. I'm the luckiest mom in the world.

Any errors or screw-ups are mine alone.

# THANK YOU! AND NEWSLETTER

***Thank you*** for reading *The Seer*! **Reviews** mean everything—they're an author's lifeblood as readers find us through your reviews. If you enjoyed Claire and Theseus tale, leaving an honest review would be a kindness.

**Would you like a free book?** Do sign up for Vicki's newsletter (Sanna doesn't have one ) and receive her bonus novel, *Body Parts*. Her monthly newsletter contains info on The Secret Tales, The Made Ones Saga, the Afterworld Chronicles, life in L.A., and lots more yummy stuff.

*Come visit with me...* VickiStiefel.net & SannaBrand.com
**Facebook • Instagram • Twitter • BookBub**

# THE UNSEEN
## BOOK 4, THE SECRET TALES


### Chapter 1

1821

Lady Amalie Northbrooke was in a dither. Admittedly, a small dither, but nonetheless it felt like a stone in her shoe or a splinter beneath her nail, unpleasant enough to trouble her nerves, thus raising her anger.

Uncle John was leaving for London, according to the note beneath her door that morning. Another meeting of the Linnean Society, which seemed to meet every other day instead of every two weeks.

She dressed quickly in her front-button day dress, not bothering to call Edna, her domineering lady's maid. Cleo lumbered after her, per usual virtually attached by a yard of string.

Amalie scurried downstairs, Cleo at her heels. She was relieved to find her uncle in the breakfast room, reading a monograph while finishing up his typical enormous meal.

Amalie waved a hand, and Cleo sat. She added toast, jam, and a poached egg to her plate, then seated herself and lifted the teapot.

"More?" she asked.

Uncle John shook his head, shoving in another forkful of bacon.

Amalie took a small bite of toast and bolstered her courage. "Uncle John, I wish to purchase a new dress for the assembly in the village next month."

He kept on eating and reading. "Hum? Another dress? Why, you own many fine dresses."

Amalie forced herself not to sigh. The man was perpetually distracted by his pastime of birds. Everything was about birds. If she had feathers, he would pay much more attention. Sadly, she did not.

A new dress was a pittance given her inheritance, and she failed to understand why her uncle, Sir John Northbrooke, was so tight-fisted.

"The assembly is a special one for the Christmas holidays." She dived into her poached egg. "My newest gown is three years old and quite out of fashion."

"Fashion?" he rumbled. "What needs we for fashion here in the middle of the forests and fens?"

She squeezed her eyes tight. Words stuck in her throat until she was able to voice them. "Fustian! I read the magazines and the papers. I may not be worldly, but I am aware of the world. Why do you do this, Uncle? Why force me to struggle for any purchase I wish to make? I have ample funds. You need not touch yours. Yet you do this tug-of-war each time I wish to buy anything."

He turned a page in the monograph. "Hum." Another page turn.

"Uncle?"

He peered up at her, eyes glazed beneath spectacles. "Is that not what a guardian should do?" His distracted tone was echoed in the darting of his gaze back to the monograph, which she saw detailed the defense of berry-bearing trees by the Mistle Thrush.

"I do not know, for you are the only guardian I have ever had." She tossed down her napkin and rose, Cleo following suit.

"Clarence and I leave for London within the hour. I have a special meeting with some colleagues from the society."

Her uncle spent more time in Town than at Mere Manor, as did his son, her cousin Clarence. Much more time this past year, and though she had asked her uncle why the change, his excuses dealt with taxidermy and a watercolorist for his own monograph and were thin, not to mention mysterious. Amalie suspected all the secrecy related to his alleged sighting of the lost white-tailed eagle, or as Uncle called it, *Haliaeetus albicilla*, to appear in Devon. The bird hadn't been seen since 1780! But there was no point arguing.

"Enjoy Town," she said. "I shall be busy with the hounds. Gracie is about to present me with a new litter." And she must set about altering her three-year-old gown for it to be presentable.

He swiped a hand across his thinning hair. "Their baying disturbs the birds."

"Does it?" She had only heard that phrase a million times...or more. "We raise the best scent hounds in Britain, and they are eagerly sought." Not to mention she loved each and every one.

He licked his index finger and turned another page. "Why my brother insisted on breeding those dogs I will never know."

*Because Father took pleasure from it,* she thought, though she would never voice those words. Uncle John's pleasures were all about birds.

"As I said," Amalie repeated. "Enjoy Town."

Amalie was upset enough about the dress to hesitate a few moments before entering the barn, unwilling for her beloved animals to sense her distress. When she stepped into the aisle, the bassets howled, the horses nickering. She gathered their treats—carrots, apples, and biscuits she'd made for the bassets—Cleo now bouncing around like a hoppy toy.

A thousand cuts. Wasn't that a Chinese torture she'd read about in one of Father's books? No, she hadn't been literally cut, but again and again she'd been refused, denied, and insulted, particularly by Edna, who had assumed more and more oversight over the years as her uncle grew more and more distant. All of which she noted in the journal she carried. She wrote about much, particularly the past—her mother, father, and Charles—for her memories of them were fading like a too-oft laundered gown.

At twenty-two years, Amalie was a woman grown. Why her father had insisted she turn twenty-five before she came into her trust and was freed from Uncle John's guardianship, she did not know.

She wanted clarity. Needed it. Amalie wished to see her father's will, to read those words in black and white, something she had never done. Things Uncle John found too unimportant or distracting. In truth, most things in their world failed to hold his interest, including Amalie and his son, other than his beloved ornithology.

Her uncle's distance, the hovering Edna, and Clarence's...she did not know what, for her cousin affected an intensely languid air in all things. An oxymoron if ever there was one.

Yet Amalie felt constrained in every way. She was not permitted to go to London, as Uncle John said it was far too dangerous for such a country-bred lady. Nor might she visit the seaside, an allegedly dangerous place with many swindlers and pickpockets. Riding and driving were also lethal, according to her uncle, and she'd learned to ride a horse and drive a trap in secret. She was proscribed at every turn, the man wrapping her in cotton batting until she turned twenty-five. She could not bear it.

Beaworthy village and its environs were the scope and breadth of her life. She hadn't had a governess since she had turned thirteen, her uncle firing the beloved woman when he'd become disgruntled with her teaching of theology. Or perhaps for some other reason. She never knew. All she *did* know was her uncle had never hired a replacement. Nor a dancing master. Nor a companion or considered a finishing school for Amalie.

Amalie would have become an ignorant twit but for her father's extensive library—he'd been a curious soul—and she'd read his and her mother's many books again and again. It boggled the mind that Uncle John didn't know who the Mongols or the Goths were! Or any

Russian or Sanskrit! Or the difference between a roe deer and a red deer, or a grass snake and a viper!

If only her brother, Charles, would return to Mere Manor. Eleven years on, that hope had become a mere wisp. After their parents' deaths and Uncle John assuming the guardianship when she had been ten and Charles fifteen, life had turned dark and sour.

Charles could not bear Uncle John's distance, nor his constraints, and fled a year after their parents' deaths for parts unknown. He was now the Earl of Westlake, after all. Everyone was horrified that her brother had vanished. Though Charles promised to return for her, after eleven years, six since his last letter, her brother had gone silent.

"What is this commotion, Lady Amalie?" said Bruno, the stable master, friend, and sometimes confidant. "Sounds like a riot!"

She returned to herself, realizing that the hounds were baying and the horses neighing. "I am sorry, Bruno. I was woolgathering and forgot to hand out the treats. I shall do so immediately."

"Well, thank all the angels in heaven." He laughed. "They get rowdy when they are denied."

Amalie began passing out treats, and as was typical, Wind's nippy mouth made an appearance. Amalie's finger bopped her on the nose, and she returned to the good girl she truly was. She checked on Gracie, who appeared still a few days from whelping. After the treats were gone, she crouched down and handed Cleo hers. Cleo had learned patience. And though she had a disabled leg, she was a smart girl, a boon companion, and the sweetest pup in the world.

"Bruno?" she said, walking toward the stablemaster, who was checking the horses' water buckets. "Would you tack up the trap after my uncle leaves, please? I plan to go to the village as soon as I change."

"Will do, m'lady."

"I shall be back in a trice." Now all she had to do was escape Edna's protective clutches.

Uncle John and Clarence might be long gone, but her maid had stationed herself at the side door wearing a frown. Much like an anticipatory crow. Edna was far too large and muscular for Amalie's comfort, as she often appeared about to pounce, literally, upon her. That would end poorly, for Amalie was small, with miniature breasts and little flesh on her bones, though her form was pleasant enough.

Edna huffed as Amalie doffed her work boots and donned her slippers on her way to change into a suitable outfit for her village jaunt.

"What in all the saints are you wearing?" Edna's Gaelic accent grew more pronounced the more upset she became. She trailed Amalie much as Cleo was. Cleo was cuter.

"My day dress," Amalie said. "I was intending to garden but got sidetracked by the bassets."

Edna crossed her arms and harrumphed. "Those dogs."

Amalie ascended the steps, ignoring her. Uncle had conveyed his dislike of the bassets to Edna, who was equally disdainful.

"Which gown do you wish to wear, m'lady?" Edna said, hovering far too close. "I shall set it out for you."

"None right now, Edna. I plan to take a small rest."

The woman was on point this morning, and Amalie must find a way to elude her for her trip to Beaworthy after she'd written her letter.

Cannot do this. Cannot do that. Gurrrr.

She'd wear her barn hat, coat, and workboots, thus few villagers would take notice.

After washing up and replaiting her hair in a simple braid, which she pinned to her head, Amalie sat at her secretary to write her solicitors.

Dolly was a good girl and loved any outing, the roads dusty from a dearth of rain as they trotted into town. But given the hovering black clouds, a downpour was soon to come. Amalie snapped the reins, eager to mail her letter and return home before she was missed.

No one took notice when she tied Dolly to the hitching post. The wind had picked up, lashing at her skirts as if in anger. Smelling the scents of town, particularly certain delectable ones, and feeling a bit mischievous, she entered the bakery and purchased a sugar biscuit, nibbling as she walked toward the post office, her missive safely tucked in her reticule.

*Oh, but wasn't that the prettiest ribbon she'd ever seen?*

Though winter approached, Amalie couldn't resist the spring green temptation dangling in the window. It would look well in her auburn hair, and she must have it.

Soon, she tucked her purchase into her reticule, quite pleased with herself, as she walked the few remaining steps to the post office.

To her surprise, the lobby was busy, with two tall, rather handsome gentlemen in riding clothes, one with auburn hair and the other with curly dark brown. Mrs. Trent stood bickering with the postal officer, as was her wont, and the cooper's apprentice was shuffling with impatience, the two ahead of her in line. Amalie peeked to see the two gentlemen observing her. She lifted her lips in a tentative smile.

Amalie had seen gentlemen before, of course, ones who visited her uncle or Clarence. Yet she had never seen men like these—extremely fit, one quite tanned and burly, while the other was almost as large and imposing. Both sported understated but well-made clothing, unlike Clarence's friends, who sported about in garish colors that blinded one.

Mrs. Trent finally finished up and exited, shaking her head, a common occurrence, just as two more men entered. They wore ill-fitting top hats they removed to reveal Beau Brummel hairstyles.

The man before her was swift, and soon she was handing over her precious letter to the postmaster.

A small sense of accomplishment wove through her. Her world could change, *would* change, and this letter was the first step.

Dr. Richard Cartwell, Lord Haven, stood beside his close friend, Lord Theseus Ashworth. Both were magistrates, he here in Beaworthy and Highampton, and Theseus in Woolacombe. He had gotten word from a Bow Street Runner, a longtime acquaintance, saying a robbery two days hence at the Beaworthy Post Office might take place. The county sheriff was off...someplace...and the Runner hadn't received word back from him. Thus, he'd asked Richard to go to the post office on the off-chance the tip was valid. Theseus had been visiting Highampton to purchase a mare and a gelding, and he'd invited him along.

Though Richard had not officially been active during the Napoleonic wars, other than as a field surgeon, unofficially he had seen flurries of action during the months he'd spent in France studying medicine in secret. He was a decent shot and felt confident in a crisis. Theseus, having seen action as well, made a good companion.

Now they stood in the small lobby. He had posted a letter to himself, but now they hovered while trying to appear casual. Which wasn't easy.

A boy lounged near a wall, kicking his heels back. An older woman was about to post a package. Behind her stood a young woman who had entered a few minutes earlier, dressed rather strangely. What struck him was not merely her elfin beauty and her air of innocence, but how she fairly bristled with excitement, her freckled face lit from within.

She approached the counter as two men entered. They were well dressed, though not in high style, but their clothes looked ill-fitting, their eyes darting around the lobby.

Richard looked to Theseus, who nodded, and they placed their hands where they could easily reach their weapons.


Amalie stepped away from the counter so the next person could take care of business when she was hauled around the waist and snugged against someone smelling distinctly of onions.

"Let go of me, sir!" she said

Something sharp pricked her throat, and she froze. For a moment, her vision went blurry, and she swayed. But she got herself under control because this would not do. Would not do one bit.

The man's companion currently pointed a gun at the people in the lobby, whilst aiming another at the postmaster, his left hand striking her as odd. *No time for folderol*, she told herself.

"Hand over James Marshall's mail sack," the man holding the guns said. "Or we kill her first, then each time you hesitate, we kill another."

The postmaster was whiter than a bath linen, the apprentice's eyes saucer-wide. Her eyes slid to the handsome gentlemen she'd first noticed, sensing they might be of aid. Both appeared oddly relaxed, too relaxed, which made her reason they were about to do something. She hoped. The curly-haired gentleman gave her a subtle nod, which she acknowledged with a slow blink, as much as she could do with a knife to her throat.

*Would the man with the knife really kill her?* She closed her eyes for a moment and whispered to herself—*be strong. Be strong.* When she opened them, the postmaster had unlocked the office door and was dragging a heavy sack into the lobby.

Would the man slit her throat before they left? Would he run that sharp blade across her neck and...

She again looked at the gentlemen who seemed a sea of calm whilst the thieves barked orders. The curly-haired man who had nodded closed his eyes and made a dip with his body, a subtle one.

*What did that mean?*

Then, she saw a hand at his waist, which was missing an index finger.

Amalie *thought* she understood, but if she were wrong, she would die. An inadvertent shiver ripped through her body.

"Stand still," her captor barked.

The curly-haired gentleman kept those three fingers pointing from his waist. Once again, she did a slow blink. Once again, he gave his subtle nod.

"I do not feel so well," she said.

"Too bad." Her captor laughed.

"Dizzy," she said, slurring the word as she watched the gentleman's fingers. One folded in. Then the second.

On the third, she allowed the muscles in her body to go limp as if she were fainting.

Her captor released her, and she thumped onto the floor, a sharp neck pain making her wince.

Gunshots rang, and suddenly her captor lay beside her, blood flowing from his temple and from the back of his head.

Shouts, screams, footsteps. Amalie lay there, unwilling to move, eyes closed.

Silence.

She still didn't open her eyes or move until two gentle hands squeezed her shoulders and lifted. "Are you well, miss?"

He was very tall, and when she peered up at him, he gasped.

"You are hurt," he said.

The man had the blackest eyes she'd ever seen. She could get lost in those eyes fringed by ridiculous lashes. Was that a double row of them?

She opened her mouth to speak, but nothing came out, so she nodded.

He removed his coat and folded it to use as a pillow, then removed his handkerchief and wound it around her throat. "Too tight?"

"Fine," she croaked, mesmerized by his ministrations.

He began to lift her into his arms.

"I can stand."

He nodded and eased her feet to the floor. Momentarily dizzy, she clutched his waistcoat.

"Take your time," he said.

Amalie tried to avoid looking at her captor, dead on the floor, blood leaking from his wound. Except... She gasped, blinked repeatedly, then settled. She would not let that horrible man's death overset her. The second robber had escaped, and she heard shouts and people hollering in the distance.

She had to get home. Edna must have noticed her absence by now and jotted it in her report for Uncle John. Amalie didn't want to make matters any worse than they already were.

"If you would walk me to my trap," she said. "I would appreciate it."

The man wrapped an arm around her waist, holding her steady, and they proceeded to the door, his friend reappearing at the entrance.

"I have sent a rider for the sheriff," said the auburn-haired man.

"Good," said the man helping her.

His friend took a look at her with thunderous eyes. "Will she be all right?"

"Fortunately, the cut was relatively superficial."

It didn't feel superficial but hurt like the dickens.

"I shall escort her home."

"You need not bother," Amalie said. "I can drive—"

"You shall not fare well."

She conceded the point, given she felt a wee bit drunk, something she'd experienced once when Uncle John had gone to Town and she'd been curious about what he called his "happy juice." The experience had not ended well for her.

Amalie nodded, pointing out her trap and Dolly, and the curly-haired man lifted her onto the passenger seat while the second gentleman tied a saddled horse to the trap's rear.

"You will see to things here?" her rescuer said.

His friend nodded, and the man climbed into the trap, took up the reins, then turned to her. "I am Dr. Richard Cartwell from Highampton. My friend is Lord Theseus Ashworth from Woolacombe."

Her mouth felt stuffed with taffy, but she managed to get out, "I am Amalie. Amalie Northbrooke."

Lord Ashworth bowed, and Dr. Cartwell nodded. "We are off. Which way are we headed?"

She pointed toward the road home, and as Dolly walked off, she found herself leaning against the doctor.

"I will fix you up once we arrive at your home," the doctor said.

"No need," she mumbled. "No need."

"Where are we going?" Dr. Cartwell said.

"To Mere Manor. On this road." Then darkness with stars, pretty stars, sparked before her eyes. "There will be a sign."

Amalie drifted off into the pretty stars.

... To Be Continued

# A NOTE ON TRUTH VS FICTION

In *The Seer*, much regarding the land of Greece and certain famed historical luminaries is true, including Sir Joseph Banks and his sister, Sarah Sophia Banks. The legendary Byron lived, and in fact, he died in Greece. Lord Liverpool was prime minister, Planta was Head Librarian, and many others who walk *The Seer*'s pages existed as well.

Though much that I've stated in the book is factual, I amended history a bit in service of my novel. For example, Itea was not actually founded until 1830. Though I nudged that one a bit, I have tried to stay true to the era and its denizens.

# ABOUT THE BRINKMANNS AND "GODS IN COLOR"

The Brinkmanns' exhibition, *Gods in Color*, inspired Claire's quest in *The Seer*, which takes place in 1820. My protagonist was not the first. Antiquarians (archaeologists) before Claire had noted color on ancient Greek and Roman statues, friezes, and other marbles. Yet they were ignored—all in authority clung to the belief that the Greeks valued purity of form—aka whiteness—above all.

Today, Vinzenz Brinkmann and Ulrike Koch-Brinkmann use Spectroscopy, UV, VIL imaging, and other modern methods to reveal both the colors and patterns on ancient marbles. With the mounting of their first exhibit—*Gods in Color*—audiences gasped. For the formerly white marbles were now painted in their *original*, true-colored forms.

Seeing the polychromed statues completely alters our perceptions of ancient Greece and Rome, splashing their streets, their temples, and their homes with bright, vivid color.

*Gods in Color* traveled the world, from the Glyptothek museum in Munich to the Vatican Museums to the Louvre to the Metropolitan Museum of Art and many more. Their newest version, *Golden Edition,*

*Gods in Color*, can be found here: https://buntegoetter.liebieghaus.de/en/

You will be astonished.

I cannot thank the Brinkmanns enough for their inspiration and their permission to depict one of their reconstructions—Archer from the Temple of Aphaia, ca. 480 BC—as a maquette on *The Seer*'s cover.

# IMAGES FROM THE SEER

I thought you might enjoy some images referenced in *The Seer*.

~

KASTRI/DELPHI

The village of Kastri on Mt. Parnassus visited by Claire and Theseus is no more. Now, much of Delphi has been unearthed and we can view a bit of her former splendor. Here is what Kastri looked like when the book takes place.

Taken 31 December 1893 by the French Archaeological School

Model of Ancient Delphi, Staatliche Antikensammlungen, Munich; Carole Raddato, FRANKFURT, Germany

Delphi today, taken by Daniel Enchev

## THE ARCHER

Though the cover pictures a maquette of him and is referenced in the novel, I created the maquette. The full-sized painted Archer is very real, and some say he's a depiction of the Trojan Paris, who stole away Helen and began the Trojan War.

The Archer (from the cover)—The existing marble Archer stands beside a replica of the original painted one, which is how he would have looked when first created around 400 BCE.

From *Gods in Color*: Archer from the west pediment of the
Temple of Aphaia, ca. 480 BC | Experimental color
reconstruction of an archer, the so-called Paris, in the costume
of the horsemen of the neighbouring peoples to the north and
east. Along with a number of other figures, the archer once
stood many meters above the ground on the west pediment of
the Temple of Aphaia on the island of Aegina. In antiquity,
painting was used as a means of making individual figures
easily visible from a distance, thanks to their vibrant colors.
Their colorfulness made the individual figures appear alive.
*Courtesy of Vinzenz Brinkmann and Ulrike Koch-Brinkmann*

## ASPASIA

What I wrote about Aspasia in the novel is true. To put it simply, at
the height of the ancient Grecian civilization, Aspasia had a mighty
infulence.

Unlike in *The Seer*, Aspasia's original herm (her grave marker)
has never been found. We do have the Roman copy, which resides in
the Vatican Museums.

The herm of Aspasia, after the Greek Hellenistic original carved in 500 BC. The Vatican Museums

A closeup of Aspasia's herm.

## THE CHITON

Theseus gives Claire a chiton, an ancient Greek form of dress worn by all strata of society, from the poort to the wealthy. Men wore shorter chitons, while women's were to the ground.

Statue of Artemis. Chiton, péplos, himation. About 100 BC,
National Archaeological Museum of Athens

## THE KRATER

The ancient Greeks used *kraters* as large vessels to mix wine with
water during symposia and other social gatherings.

The ancient Greeks usually diluted their wine with water, for they saw drinking it undiluted as barbaric. The *krater* served as the communal bowl where this mixing occurred, much like the modern-day punch bowl.

Some *kraters* were also used for ceremonial or funerary purposes, and they were often painted with meaningful scenes or mythological events. There are several different types of *kraters*.

Very few examples of artists at work exist.

Terracotta column-krater depicting an artist painting a statue of Heracles. Late Classical period, 360–350 BCE. From the Metropolitan Museum of Art. "Representations of artists at work are exceedingly rare. This vase illustrates a craft for which virtually no evidence survives, that of applying pigment to stone sculpture using the technique of encaustic."—Metropolitan Museum of Art

## A CARICATURE

How could I resist this 1812 caricature of the Society of Antiquaries?

Satirical print by George Cruickshank of the Society of
Antiquaries, with Lord Aberdeen in the chair, 1812. The society
still exists today.

## THE PYTHIA

The famed Oracle of Delphi certainly existed in ancient times. I
created my own Pythia for Claire and Penny to meet.

The Oracle imagined and paint by John Collier in 1891

Oracle of Delphi, red-figure kylix, 440-430 BC King Aigeus in
front of the Pythia. Antikensammlung Berlin, Altes Museum

# About the Author
## BY VICKI STIEFEL, AKA SANNA BRAND

Award-winning author Vicki Stiefel's romantic science-fantasy series, The Made Ones Saga, concluded with *Ascendant*. Vicki continues work on her Afterworld Chronicles, a five-book series begun with *Chest of Bone*. Her mystery/thrillers feature homicide counselor Tally Whyte, and Vicki's knitting love produced *Chest of Bone: The Knit Collection* and *10 Secrets of the LaidBack Knitters*.

Having grown up in professional theater, Vicki planned to become an actress. Instead, she slung hamburgers, managed a scuba shop, and taught at Clark U. She's a mom to two wonderful humans and is currently playing with her animal menagerie while pounding the keys on *The Unseen*, the fourth book in The Secret Tales.

*Come visit with me...*
vickistiefel.net

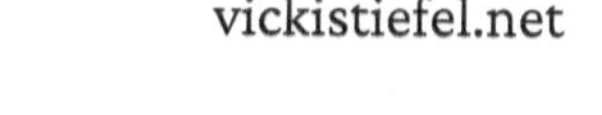

facebook.com/vicki.stiefel.5

x.com/vickistiefel

instagram.com/vickistiefel

pinterest.com/vickistiefel

bookbub.com/profile/vicki-stiefel

# Also by Vicki Stiefel & Sanna Brand

**The Secret Tales**

*The Bond*

*The Deception*

*The Seer*

*The Unseen (coming June 2026)*

**The Made Ones Saga**

*Altered*

*Changed*

*Ascendant*

**The Afterworld Chronicles**

*Chest of Bone*

*Chest of Stone*

*Chest of Time*

*Chest of Fire* (to come)

**Tally Whyte/Homicide Counselor Series**

*Body Parts* • *The Dead Stone* • *The Grief Shop* (Daphne duMaurier Award winner) • *The Bone Man* (Daphne duMaurier Award finalist)

***Nonfiction***

*10 Secrets of the LaidBack Knitters*

*Chest of Bone The Knit Collection*

Visit with Vicki:

**Website • Facebook • Instagram • BookBub**